Jackie Ashenden wri[...]
alpha heroes who've j[...]
only to have it blown [...]
heroines. She lives in [...]
husband, the inimitabl[...]
When she's not torturing alpha males and their gutsy
heroines she can be found drinking chocolate martinis,
reading anything she can lay her hands on, wasting time
on social media or being forced to go mountain biking
with her husband. To keep up to date with Jackie's new
releases and other news, sign up to her newsletter at
jackieashenden.com.

Lifelong romance addict **JC Harroway** lives in
New Zealand. Writing feeds her very real obsession
with happy endings and the endorphin rush they create.
You can follow her at jcharroway.com, Facebook.com/
jcharroway, Instagram.com/jcharroway and Twitter.com/
jcharroway.

If you liked
In the Dark and *Bound to You*
why not try

Have Me by Anne Marsh
Devoured by Cathryn Fox

Also by Jackie Ashenden

The Knights of Ruin

Ruined
Destroyed

Kings of Sydney

King's Price
King's Rule
King's Ransom

The Billionaires Club

The Debt

Billion $ Bastards

Dirty Devil
Sexy Beast
Bad Boss

Also by JC Harroway

The Pleasure Pact

Bad Business
Bad Reputation
Bad Mistake

Billionaire Bachelors

Forbidden to Want
Forbidden to Taste
Forbidden to Touch

Discover more at millsandboon.co.uk

IN THE DARK

JACKIE ASHENDEN

BOUND TO YOU

JC HARROWAY

MILLS & BOON

First Published in Great Britain 2021
by Mills & Boon, an imprint of HarperCollins*Publishers*
1 London Bridge Street, London, SE1 9GF

In the Dark © 2021 Jackie Ashenden

Bound to You © 2021 JC Harroway

ISBN: 978-0-263-29789-8

MIX
Paper from
responsible sources
FSC™ C007454

This book is produced from independently certified FSC™ paper
to ensure responsible forest management.
For more information visit www.harpercollins.co.uk/green.

Printed and bound in Spain
by CPI, Barcelona

IN THE DARK

JACKIE ASHENDEN

MILLS & BOON

To the Ashendens

CHAPTER ONE

Vesta

I STOOD OUTSIDE the St George Hotel, housed in a gracious brownstone on New York's Upper East Side, taking a couple of deep breaths and trying to calm my racing heartbeat. I didn't get nervous often, but I was nervous now, and with good reason.

The instructions my friend Maggie had forwarded to me were quite specific.

I was to go to the desk and ask for the penthouse suite which had been booked specifically for the night. The door would be ajar and there would be no need to knock. I was to go into the living area and sit down in the armchair. A blindfold would be provided on the table next to me. I was to put it on and make sure it was secure. And I was not under any circumstances, no matter what I heard, no matter what happened, to take it off.

Maggie hadn't had this particular client before, but he was apparently renowned for his specific instructions. And for his massive tips. And for his magical ability to give orgasms to every woman he hired from Company of Strangers.

Clients who used Company of Strangers didn't expect sex—it wasn't that kind of agency—but every single woman this client hired always wanted it from this guy. Even though they never, ever saw him.

A mystery man. A faceless stranger.

Perfect for my purposes, in other words.

I wanted someone to help put behind me the man I'd loved since I was sixteen, who consistently refused to have anything to do me. Someone to take the virginity that had hung around my neck like a millstone for the past nine years.

Someone I could imagine as someone else.

Yes, he'd do.

I took another breath and approached the hotel, pushing open the discreet wrought-iron black gate and going up the marble steps. The heavy front door opened soundlessly and I found myself in a flagged marble atrium, very old-world with luxurious leather couches and jewel-toned Persian rugs everywhere.

A huge chandelier hung over the antique oak of the check-in desk, scattering glittering prisms of light over every surface.

The place breathed money and glamor, uncomfortably reminding me of my own privileged upbringing, though that was seven years in the past and almost an entire continent away. A much more West Coast kind of rich. Infinity pools and white stucco, martinis and plastic surgery.

Ugh. Thank God I'd left all of that behind.

Gathering my courage, I put a bit of 'fuck you' confidence I didn't feel in my step as I approached the check-in desk.

Maggie had told me that there was no need to go all out with my clothes or make-up, so I'd decided on discreetly sexy. Blue silk bias-cut shift dress with very narrow straps. Simple, but it left my shoulders basically bare, showing off my ink, and it matched the blue tips of my hair. I'd dressed it up with some black platform sandals with ties winding up my calf, and no underwear, just for kicks. Because what woman pretending to be a high-class escort, filling in with a client for her friend, would go to said meeting with underwear on?

I hadn't checked with Maggie about that. But then, I liked to live dangerously.

I gave Maggie's name to the woman at the desk and she gave me a professional smile and directions to the penthouse suite. Unlocked the private elevator. She didn't give me a key.

I moved over the marble floor towards the elevator, trying very hard not to look as though I was pretending to be someone I wasn't.

Company of Strangers provided high-flying business people of both sexes with 'company' for however long they required it. 'Company' could be just that—a friend to talk to for people who had no time to build friendships and were happy to pay for them.

Or it could involve more, depending on the agreement of both parties.

My best friend Maggie had been working for them for a couple of years, and she'd been very happy with the arrangement, though I'd been unsure when she'd first started. It had initially seemed like a glorified escort agency to me—not that there was anything wrong with that—but I'd realised as time had gone on that it was a little more complicated.

All the clients on Strangers' books had been vetted for the safety of those working for them. Meetings were conducted as 'friendship and company' only, but sex could become part of it if the two parties were willing. All employees had a panic button they could press if things became difficult and security was only a minute or two away at any given time.

It was all very organised and above board. Maggie liked working for them because she viewed herself as providing an essential service—providing human contact to very lonely people.

It helped that Strangers paid staggeringly well.

Which was part of the whole reason I was standing in an enormously overpriced hotel in New York pretending to be Maggie. She'd scheduled this job for herself, but then another request had come through at the same time, and she'd been desperate to take that one because she really liked the client who'd requested her.

She'd tried to find a replacement in amongst her

colleagues, but no one was available, and she'd been upset about it. For whatever reason, she'd particularly wanted to be available for her preferred client, but she couldn't leave this one in the lurch, either—not if she wanted to retain her standing in the company.

So what was a girl to do when her best friend needed help? Offer to fill in, of course. Maggie had refused point-blank. The company absolutely forbade that kind of thing—something to do with agreements, contracts and all kinds of bullshit that I didn't listen to when Maggie had tried to tell me what a terrible idea it was—and she would get into terrible trouble if I was caught. She'd be fired, taken to court, et cetera, et cetera…

I'd just told her I'd make sure I wouldn't get caught. She told me it wasn't that simple. It might have ended at an impasse if she hadn't wanted to be with her preferred client so desperately, but she did. I was concerned about that and told her so, since falling for a client couldn't be a good idea, surely? She'd explained why minding my own business was a better one. And then she'd finally let me do the decent thing and help her out.

Not that it was entirely selfless of me. The money was a big drawcard, especially as I was hoping to get a second tattoo shop up and running. But it was more that my latest attempt to make contact with Eli had resulted in yet more silence and I'd decided that I had to do something to get the bastard out of my head.

Saving one's virginity for a man who would never

see you as anything more than his best friend's little sister would do that to a girl.

Move on—that was what I needed to do. Being a tattooed virgin at twenty-five was just sad, as I'd told Maggie. She'd said she'd thought I didn't care what people thought of me. I'd said that I didn't. I cared what *I* thought of myself. And I thought I was sad.

She'd had no answer to that.

The private elevator was mirrored, and almost silent as I rode it up the building. I didn't look at my reflection, not wanting to see any sign of the nervousness that was gathering in my gut.

I could still pull out, send an apology via the check-in desk, but quitting was for sissies, and I wasn't a sissy. This was my chance to get over Eli once and for all and I was going to take it.

The elevator chimed as it reached the top floor and I took another breath, trying to calm my nerves and resisting the urge to wipe my sweaty palms down my dress.

The doors opened and I stepped out into a small hallway. It was utterly silent, the noise of the city muffled behind layers of brick and steel and sound-proof glass. Not to mention copious amounts of money.

I had no idea what to expect from this. As sex was only something that happened if both parties agreed, there was a chance this client wouldn't want sex with me.

Especially when he'd chosen Maggie. Maggie

was not only beautiful, she was also very warm and very friendly. She knew how to talk to people. How to make them feel at ease. How to make them drop their guard and feel comfortable. She was nurturing while I...wasn't any of those things.

I was sarcastic, spiky and difficult. Challenging, my brother called me, when he bothered to call me anything at all. Selfish, according to my mother. My father, who thought the sun shone out of my brother's rear end, simply ignored me and had done all my life.

Yeah, the client was probably going to get a shock when he got me instead of golden and beautiful Maggie. But, hey, maybe he'd like my tattoos. Maybe he'd like the piercing in my eyebrow and the one in my nose.

Maybe he'd like being the first man to see me naked. The first man to touch me at all. Some guys did. Some guys really liked deflowering virgins, so that was kind of my back-up plan. If he really didn't want me, I'd tell him I was a virgin and he could have me at a discount.

You're always a discount.

Shut up, brain. No one needs you.

Nervousness fluttered in my gut like a frightened bird as the elevator doors closed behind me.

Maggie had said this client was what the company termed a 'black star client.' That apparently meant he treated employees exceptionally well and paid very good tips. He never requested the same woman twice—which was part of the reason Maggie hadn't protested about my filling in quite as much as she would have normally—and another reason I'd said I'd go in her stead. It suggested that he wasn't fussed about which woman he had, he just wanted a woman.

Which hopefully meant he wouldn't mind getting me. I'd simply tell him that Maggie was sick and hadn't been able to make it, and that I was filling in for her. With any luck, he'd simply shrug his shoulders and go with...whatever it was he wanted to do.

The door was ahead of me, slightly ajar, as per the instructions. A streak of light coming from the penthouse illuminated the black marble floor of the hallway.

My black platform sandals made no sound as I went towards it, then I stopped again.

Hell, I was a lot more nervous about this than I thought I'd be.

Maggie had said that some clients were very specific about what they wanted from a meeting, and some weren't. But the company's rules were very strict when it came to sex: anyone forcing one of their employees would be reported to the police, no matter who the client was. And, even if the client was a stand-up individual, they couldn't penalise the employee for refusing sex. The employee would get paid for an entire night regardless. *Sans* tips, of course.

But you're not an employee. Those rules don't apply to you.

Well, no. But hopefully the client wouldn't figure that out. And, besides, his reputation was stellar within the company. Maggie had mentioned that some of her colleagues were desperate to be picked by him for a night because of his ability to give them the most incredible pleasure. Not to mention the fact that a night with him was easy money. You didn't have to talk or make nice, flutter or flirt. All you had to do was sit in a chair, follow his instructions and bring on the orgasms.

That sounded like me. I could just sit there and let someone else do all the work. It'd be a nice change from all my self-administered orgasms over the years.

I moved to the door and stood outside it, my heart-beat speeding up. Nervousness was careening around inside me, sure, but also something else I couldn't identify.

No, I knew what that was. Excitement.

I shivered.

I needed this. Nine years was a long time to want a man, especially a man who had precisely zero interest in returning the favour. A long time to stay celibate. I was sick of that. Sick of pining. Sick of wanting what I was never going to have.

It was time to put the ghost of him down.

I stepped inside, leaving the door slightly open, as instructed.

The suite was quiet, the only sound the gentle, subsonic hum of the air conditioning.

Slowly, I moved down the short hallway to the suite's living area.

Big windows looked out over the street, framed by
long, rich, blue velvet curtains. The room was very
cosy, with comfortable couches in soft-looking dark
brown leather and lots of cushions made of out of
jewel-bright Indian print silk. The floor was carpeted
in the same deep blue as the curtains, thick and soft,
with more Persian rugs over the top. Hand-carved
occasional tables and shelves in dark wood were scattered around the room, everything lit with side lamps
carved of the same wood, with silky shades.

A sumptuous room. Like something out of an
English country manor or a castle.

Well, except for one of the wing-backed armchairs
that had been dragged into the centre of the room.
There were discreet spotlights in the ceiling to give
added light, and the chair had been placed directly
beneath one.

It was kind of like a display pedestal.

Interesting.

Beside the chair was a small table, a black length
of fabric coiled neatly on top of it.

An odd little thrill went through me. All the clients of Strangers had their identities kept confiden-
tial, but this guy was even more mysterious, as no
one even knew what he looked like. He could be an
old guy in his seventies or some young buck in his
twenties. No one was sure. But he'd had all the req-
uisite background checks that the company required,
so he wasn't a psychopath at least.

I didn't care. As long as I could wear that blindfold and pretend he was Eli, that was all that mattered to me.

I moved over to the chair and put my bag down on the floor beside it. I laid my phone down on the table next to the chair and sat down. The leather was as soft as it looked and it warmed quickly.

I reached for the blindfold. The fabric was thick, soft and very silky, and it felt nice against my fingers. I stroked it for a few moments, strangely comforted by the sensation. Then I took a deep breath, lifted it and tied it around my head securely.

The darkness was absolute. I could hear my heartbeat thumping in my head, and the hum of the air-conditioning seemed louder. The leather beneath warmed still further and I was very conscious of the press of the silk of my dress against my skin.

Was this what it was like for my brother? Trajan had been steadily losing his sight for about five years and was completely night blind, much to my parents' distress. He was the golden child, had graduated high school with honours, and was planning a long and illustrious career in the armed services. At least, until he'd started losing his sight.

Not that Traj had let that stop him from being as successful as he could possibly be. Since then, despite his incipient blindness he'd gone on to build a multi-billion-dollar company with his best friend Eli, off the back of a patented material used in making highly specialised armour for the military. He and Eli had subsequently widened their focus to broader commercial applications, such as bullet-proof vests for bodyguards, the police and anyone else who needed body armour.

Yes, he was very successful, was Traj. My parents thought he was a god. They didn't think as much about their daughter, who preferred drawing to doing anything else. Who'd dropped out of high school and who could barely read. And they didn't consider a highly profitable and Instagram-famous tattoo parlour in New York to be a success.

As far as they were concerned, I wasn't pretty as my mother, and I didn't like lunching with her and her friends along Rodeo Drive, and I didn't have degrees for days and a solid career in advertising, which was what my father thought I should be doing.

Tattoos and piercings were for failures, which I guess made me and my extensive client list a failure. I was okay with that. At least I wasn't an asshole like my dad.

I leaned back slightly in the chair.

The instructions hadn't been clear about what I was supposed to do now. Just sit and wait?

I stared at the blackness behind my blindfold. The air was cool on my skin, giving me goose bumps. I would have put the air-con up a couple of notches for comfort's sake, if I'd had a choice. Clearly this guy, whoever he was, preferred a cooler room.

Then I heard a soft click—the front door of the suite closing—and my breath caught. Was that the client? I couldn't hear anything so either it wasn't the client, and the door had shut on its own, or he was here, moving soundlessly.

My breathing got faster. I tried to control it, sending my awareness out to see if I could sense anyone in the room—Traj could do this with uncanny accuracy when he was night blind. He'd told me once it was because he paid attention to the rhythm of people's steps, the sound of their clothing and the way they smelled.

I couldn't hear anyone's steps, couldn't smell anything, either.

And then—I don't know what it was…some movement of the air, or maybe even a sixth sense I didn't know I had—suddenly I was aware that I wasn't alone.

CHAPTER TWO

Elias

SHE WAS SITTING in the chair in the middle of the room, right where I'd instructed her to be. And she had the blindfold tied around her head, as directed.

Except she was not who I'd asked for.

The woman I'd chosen for the night from Company of Strangers' extensive list had rich gold curls, an hourglass figure, deep golden skin and the kind of mouth men dreamed about. A generous smile. Melted honey, warm and sweet, in human form.

This woman was not melted honey. She was all sharp, awkward edges, narrow shoulders, jutting elbows and skinny knees. Her hair was as spiky as the rest of her, short and black and dyed midnight-blue at the tips. I couldn't tell much about her face, as she was wearing a blindfold, but it looked as sharp and angular as the rest of her.

She wore a plain shift dress of dark blue silk, presumably to match her hair, that was cut on the bias and did good things to her slight curves. She'd paired it with a pair of black platform sandals with sexy black velvet ties that wound around her slender calves.

It wasn't all bad. She had lovely skin, smooth and pale as fresh cream, and the kind of wide, generous mouth that would fuel a month's worth of fantasies. She also had more than a few tattoos, to which I wasn't fundamentally opposed, and these ones were pretty. A scattering of stars over her right shoulder disappeared beneath the blue silk of her dress, and what looked like a long-stemmed, thorny rose wound around her left arm and bloomed on her left shoulder, dropping petals that also disappeared beneath her dress. They'd been inked with some skill, the colours vibrant against her skin.

Her head had turned slightly as I'd come in, obviously hearing me enter, and there was something about the movement that was familiar to me.

There was something about her that was familiar to me in general.

But she was still not who I'd asked for.

I'd had plans for the warm and lovely blonde, but now this spiky brunette had turned up, and I was annoyed. I wanted what I wanted when it came to my weekly nights with a woman from Company of Strangers and I did not like having to adjust. Especially when I hadn't received any notification that the woman I'd initially chosen wasn't available.

The company knew my needs and I tipped generously. I was a valued client. I should have been informed about the change.

'Uh…are you there?' the woman asked, clearly forgetting my very-easy-to-follow instructions that she wasn't to speak. Her voice had the slightest huskiness to it which, much to my added irritation, I found sexy.

'You're not who I asked for.' My voice sounded harsh and gravelly in the silence of the room. It was always a shock to hear myself, even now, years after the fire. Smoke inhalation had wreaked havoc on my vocal cords, changing my voice completely.

It didn't bother me most of the time, because in my line of work I dealt with hard-asses every day, and sounding as if you'd been through hell was only an asset. Yet for some reason I was very conscious of the change now.

It was difficult to fantasise about the old days, back when I'd had it all, when I sounded like the Creature from the Black Lagoon.

She'd gone very still the moment I'd spoken, as if my voice had affected her in some way, and not in the way I'd wanted.

Too fucking bad. Part of the reason I used Company of Strangers was to have sex that was uncomplicated and unencumbered by the usual bullshit you had to go through to get it. Flirting, charming, building a friendship, building a relationship… Yeah, I was done with that. I didn't want a relationship. I didn't even want to talk.

Company of Strangers provided exactly what it said on the tin: company for people who wanted it.

But I didn't want company. I only wanted sex. No talk, no questions. A blindfold so they wouldn't get distracted by the way I looked. So I would see neither pity, horror nor anything else that demanded an emotional response from me, and so they wouldn't feel compelled to ask questions that I didn't want to answer.

Absolute and complete control over the entire interaction from start to finish was what I wanted, what I paid exorbitant amounts for, and that was what I got.

It was never the same woman twice. They wore the blindfold, they sat in the chair and I told them exactly what I wanted. If they didn't agree, they were free to walk away at any time. They were paid for the entire night, whether they walked away or not, and I always, always, got them off.

But this wasn't about them. This was entirely about me.

Some nights I wanted to pretend that I was still the same man I'd once been—the golden boy, the star quarterback with a great career ahead of him. The guy who had it all: looks and charm and physical skill. Who could have any woman he wanted, and did, and sometimes more than one. The guy who women worshipped and men wanted to be.

I would never be that guy any more. I'd left him behind in that hospital bed. These days I was charmless and scarred, my body shot all to hell. But you didn't need charm or good looks when you were rich as fuck. Money was the perfect mask and it was a damn sight more reliable than empty concepts such as loyalty and love.

Money bought me back my past, even if it was just for a night, and it certainly bought me pleasure. I didn't have women falling all over themselves to have me any more, but I could pay them. And, even though I couldn't throw a football any longer, light up a room with a smile, I could still make them beg. I'd always been good in bed, and those skills at least hadn't deserted me.

'Yeah, I know, I'm sorry about that,' the woman said, sounding not apologetic at all. 'Maggie was sick. I hope you don't mind me filling in for her.'

I leaned against the door frame, staring at her.

Blue silk, black hair, pale skin, ruby lips…a regular inked-up Snow White. Not what I'd initially wanted for the evening, but not wholly bad. A thorny rose in amongst the soft silks and warm, jewel-toned rugs of the room.

Then again, I'd chosen golden curls and warm, honeyed skin, to remind me of the cheerleaders at Stanford who'd once competed to be in my bed, and this woman was not in any way a cheerleader.

'I do mind,' I said flatly, still annoyed. 'The company is supposed to notify me if my woman of choice isn't available and they didn't.'

Her head cocked and again that sense of familiarity swamped me.

Shit, I knew this woman. I didn't know how or

why, but I knew her. I was sure of it. She wasn't someone who worked for Howard and Hart, the company I'd started with my best friend Trajan eight years earlier, I was certain. And she wasn't a friend, as I didn't have any except for Traj. A client of Howard and Hart, maybe? Or maybe I'd had her as a Strangers hire at some point before. But surely not? I'd have remembered her.

Whatever. If I knew her it was going to present me with a number of different problems.

Firstly, if I did indeed know her, then perhaps she would know me. Although I wasn't ashamed of the fact that I used a high-end escort agency on a regular basis, I didn't necessarily want people all over my private life, either.

Traj's and my company was highly successful, providing body armour to the military and various other organisations—we'd patented a material that was light, easy to wear and better at stopping bullets than anything else on the market, and we were now branching out into commercial applications for the general public. I was also investing money in researching new treatments for burns patients, and it probably wouldn't be a good look for my private bedroom fantasies to come out while that was happening. Questions would be asked, my past dragged up… Yeah, I didn't want that.

Secondly, I was sure that I hadn't seen her profile on the Company of Strangers books, which meant she was a new hire. And, while that normally wouldn't be an issue, it was an issue now because I didn't know what were her list of dos and don'ts, and whether or not she had hard limits.

Thirdly, Strangers had a whole raft of contracts that both employees and clients signed, and I liked to look at the signatures just to be on the safe side. Rules were important in situations like this and, as I played by them, I wanted to make sure the woman I'd chosen for the night also did. And I hadn't checked hers out.

Fourth, she was familiar. Again, a problem.

'How weird,' she said. 'I don't know why you wouldn't have been notified. I'll follow up on it tomorrow.' Her mouth curled into a smile that made the blood rush suddenly hard in my veins. 'Unless of course you want me to leave?'

There was a hint of challenge in that smile and, while I wasn't the football star I'd once been, I hadn't lost my competitive edge. It was still there and it was still strong. It was partly why Howard and Hart had been so successful.

When I played, I played to win.

Suddenly golden curls and golden skin seemed a little less intriguing than they'd seemed a moment ago.

'Not yet,' I said, shifting my shoulder against the door frame and studying her properly this time. As if I'd actually chosen her.

The light of the perfectly positioned spotlight illuminated her. Not beautiful, not like Golden Curls, but…arresting all the same.

That short hair looked spiky but I bet if I put my hands in it, and gripped it, it would feel very soft. And her skin would flush beautifully with arousal. That huskiness in her voice would sound more pronounced too, with any luck, and it was always particularly erotic when they started begging.

And they all begged. Every last one.

I might be scarred all to fuck, but I could make a woman come like nobody's business.

'So…uh…you just going to stand there and look at me or what?'

People always talked when they were nervous and it seemed as though she was no different. Odd. Surely Strangers would have sent her my profile so she'd know what to expect? And presumably she'd agreed to fill in for her friend because she was okay with that profile, in which case she had no reason to be nervous.

And she was nervous. I'd got very good at gauging a woman's mood, and her mood was important, because if she wasn't into it, if she wasn't enjoying herself, then she wouldn't come. And her coming, and coming hard, was the name of the game.

Sometimes they pretended, but I could spot a fake orgasm a mile off, and when they faked I generally called a halt to the proceedings. If it wasn't genuine, it didn't work for me and that was not what I paid for.

'You're nervous,' I said, watching her.

'No,' she flat-out lied. 'Of course I'm not. Just wondering when you're going to get this show on the road.'

'If you'd read my profile, you'd know. And you're also speaking, which I instructed you not to.'

Colour moved under her skin, a pretty flush of rose that got my reluctant dick stirring. One thing was for sure: she'd look beautiful naked and aroused, begging me to make her come.

One of her narrow shoulders rose in a negligent shrug, pulling the material of her dress tight over one small, round breast. Making it plain that she wasn't wearing a bra. 'Hey, I'm a rule-breaker, what can I say?'

'I don't want a rule-breaker. You're supposed to do what I want without argument. That's the whole point. Did you even look at my profile?'

'Oh, who cares about profiles?' White teeth pressed against her plush lower lip as she bit it. 'Come on, ace. Show me what you've got.' Then she shifted, the light catching on the faint silver thread of the necklace she wore.

A five-pointed outline of a star inlaid with tiny diamonds glittered at the hollow of her throat.

It was familiar, that necklace. I'd given it to Vesta Howard-Smith, my best friend's little sister, on her sixteenth birthday, and according to him she never took it off…

Wait.

Every part of me went very, very still as the air caught hard in my lungs.

I stared at her. Stared hard.

At her angular yet very feminine face. At the

black hair cut into a short, spiky pixie cut. At her narrow shoulders and long, slender legs. At the determined tilt of her pointed chin. At that generous, pretty mouth…

It's her. You know it's her.

The last time I'd seen Vesta had been at that awful sixteenth birthday party her mother had organised for her. Her black hair had been long, and her face had still had some of that childish roundness, but not the rest of her. She'd been skinny and awkward and shy, her fingers perpetually stained by the ink she used in her drawings.

She'd smiled at me the way she'd always done, as if I was her hero, because then I still had been. I'd been twenty-two and a football star, destined for million-dollar contracts and millions more in endorsements. The guy with a future all laid out ahead of him.

Until the fire. I hadn't seen her since then, no matter all the emails and texts and phone calls she'd once bombarded me with—attempts at contact that had gradually reduced over the years but had never entirely gone away. That I had mostly ignored.

But I couldn't ignore them now.

Because it was Vesta sitting there in that chair.

Vesta, my best friend's little sister, to whom I'd once been as close as an older brother. Vesta, who I'd cut out of my life entirely.

Vesta, the woman I was down to fuck.

CHAPTER THREE

Vesta

HE WAS BEING very quiet. As if I'd shocked him, which was a strange idea, given he was the one with all the weird blindfold stuff.

My heart was beating faster and, no matter that I didn't want it there, the nervousness I'd felt earlier gathered tight in the pit of my stomach.

Had I not answered one of his questions correctly? He'd said something about profiles, and I know Maggie had mentioned something about them when she and I had been discussing this, but I'd kind of blocked it out. I didn't like spending too much time looking at a computer screen because reading made my brain hurt and looking at words on a screen was even worse.

My own stupid fault, of course. I should have asked Maggie more about profiles and stuff, as she knew about my dyslexia, but even though I'd got better about asking people for help I still didn't like having to. So I'd ignored it. Told myself I'd figure it out when the time came.

But the time was now, and if I didn't want him to know that I wasn't authorised to be here, and that I wasn't a Strangers employee at all, I was going to have to brazen this out.

Luckily, I'd got very good at bullshitting people over the years.

'Just so you know,' I said into the silence, hoping to allay his fears about the fact that I hadn't looked at his profile, 'I'm down for anything you want, okay? Anything at all, I'm game.'

I really didn't want him to send me away. I wouldn't get another situation like this, not so perfectly set up for me and my specific fantasy. Oh, sure, the money I'd get out of this would be good, but it was the fantasy I wanted.

Pleasure at the hands of a faceless stranger whom I could imagine was the man I really wanted.

You couldn't do that with a normal guy. Normal guys wanted it to be about them, and the ones who didn't didn't care about your pleasure, either—at least, according to the various sources I'd asked.

No, it was this—the stranger. The blindfold. The pleasure.

Only this could give me what I wanted, a chance to put Eli behind me once and for all, and I couldn't let that slip through my fingers—not now.

He was still quiet, but he was watching me. I could feel it, the pressure of his attention like a hand pressing down on the top of my head. The back of my neck prickled.

The darkness behind my blindfold was absolute and I pretended it was Eli standing there. Beautiful, golden Eli watching me with his intense green-gold stare.

I imagined him as he'd been the last time I'd seen him—at the terrible party my mother threw me for my sweet sixteenth, when she was still trying to make me popular.

He was the only thing that had made it bearable, turning the party into something almost fun. Giving me a taste of what it was like to be pretty and popular. A taste of what it felt like to be wanted.

He'd worn jeans and a tee, simple clothes that had fitted his tall, muscular figure so perfectly. He'd looked like a movie star who'd come down from the Hollywood hills to mingle with the common folk, not like what he actually was—the son of our house-cleaner.

Not that that had ever made any difference to me.

He'd appeared when I was only five and his mom had come to work for us. He'd instantly made friends with Traj, which was hard to do, because Traj wasn't an easy guy to be friends with. But Eli had managed. And then he'd made friends with me.

He was the only one who ever noticed me, the only one who ever paid any attention to me and, as I was used to being ignored, I found his attention absolutely intoxicating. He was the older brother I'd wished Traj had been, telling me jokes and making me laugh, helping me with my homework and being patient when I couldn't do it, because I could never do it. Showing me the best way to climb a tree and how to kick a ball. Once, when I was ten and he was sixteen, I'd shyly showed him some drawings I'd done and he'd been so kind, telling me they looked fantastic and how I should study art.

I'd worshipped him.

And then I'd grown up and that childish hero-worship had turned into something more complicated and more adult. I'd started to notice his broad shoulders and the hard, carved muscles of his chest and stomach. His lean hips and powerful thighs. The masculine beauty of his face—high cheekbones and straight nose, chiselled jaw and sensual mouth. The sparks of gold and green in his hazel eyes. His shaggy, surfer-blond hair…

And then the day of my party, when he'd smiled at me and given me the little star necklace, I'd fallen head over heels in love with him.

He'd been destined for the top, for greatness, so it had come as a huge shock when, not too long after that, he'd been benched for an entire season and lost his chance with the NFL scouts. Then he disappeared, leaving rumours about where he'd gone and why swirling in his wake.

I'd tried to find out what had happened to him, but no one seemed to know. Traj had said not to worry about him, that he was 'taking some time out.'

When he'd reappeared again, some eighteen months later, I'd tried to get in contact with him. He'd answered the first couple of attempts—an email saying he was okay—but that was it. Then he'd gone dark and wouldn't answer any of my further timid attempts to reconnect.

It was as if I'd ceased to exist.

I still never took that necklace off. Even when I wished that I could.

Maybe tonight, though, I would.

Except then he said, 'You need to leave. Pick up your things and go.'

His voice was rough, harsh and very deep, the sound of it scraping over my nerve-endings and sending weird chills through me. It was familiar too, but I couldn't place it.

Shit, he sounded mad. He'd worked out I wasn't the real deal, hadn't he?

'Seriously?' I tried to remain calm, though my heart was beating even faster. 'Why? Did I do something wrong?'

'Of course you did something wrong. I don't know how you got in here, or why, but I do know that you don't work for Company of Strangers.'

Busted.

I gritted my teeth. I had to be careful here, because if I wasn't and said the wrong thing not only would I be out on my ear, but Maggie would lose her job, and I did *not* want that to happen.

Playing nice had never been my favourite choice,

and being good only got you ignored, but even I could sense that taking a confrontational approach would be a bad move. Brazening it out and lying through my teeth would also be dumb, especially when he could check my credentials with a quick glance at the Strangers website.

No, it would have to be the truth. Maybe if I looked pathetic enough that would endear me to him…

'So, you got me,' I said, making a decision before I could think better of it. 'It's true. I don't work for them. But it wasn't Maggie's fault, so please don't report her, okay? It was my idea. She was very sick and couldn't get a replacement in time and, since I'm a friend of hers, I told her I'd do it for her.' I tried a smile. 'I know I'm not her, but I could be if you'd let me.'

There was a very long silence.

I couldn't hear him, not even his breathing. He didn't make a single damn sound.

'You know this isn't like covering a waitressing shift, right?' The rawness of his voice was a shock. 'Or stepping behind the counter in a store. This is about sex. About getting naked and fucking a total stranger. You get that, don't you?'

I didn't want to blush, but I couldn't stop the tide of heat that washed through me, my face burning in embarrassment.

Patronising asshole. Of course I knew those things. I wasn't stupid, and I loathed being made to feel as if I was, because that was what every damn person in my life, with the exception of Eli Hart, had made me feel.

Stupid and dumb and backward, because I had difficulty reading and found writing hard.

God, this guy wasn't supposed to be this way. He was supposed to tell me what to do, get me off and that would be it. Who knew he'd be so fussy?

Anger glowed inside me, but I couldn't really blame him, even though I wanted to. It was anger at myself and my own failings, because if this little plan failed it was on me. I hadn't done the research I should have and I certainly hadn't thought things through properly.

I'd just been desperate and had snatched at the opportunity Maggie had presented without considering the consequences. But getting angry about it wouldn't help me with my little fantasy and, hell, I was here now. Walking out would be stupid. I just needed to convince him to hire me for the night.

'Yes,' I said, struggling not to let a sharp edge creep into my tone. 'Believe it or not, I do get that.'

'Then you'll also know that Strangers' employees are all vetted, as are their clients, for the safety of all parties involved. All parties are also required to sign NDAs, again for the safety of all involved.' He said everything flatly, as if he was reading from a manual or a rule book. 'Clients sign an agreement that a meeting can be ended at any time, by either party, though payment is always required whether a meeting is ended early or not. This agreement also extends to a clause stating that any force or coercion, again by either party, will be met with legal action.'

My mouth dried. Oh, shit, was this the contract stuff that Maggie had mentioned, that I hadn't listened to?

'You have signed no agreements,' he went on in that strange, harsh voice. 'You are bound by no rules. And that means you're putting both of us at risk. Do you understand?'

The blush in my cheeks burned hotter, as did the anger inside me.

Way to live up to everyone's expectations. You're really blowing his mind.

I gripped my hands together tightly in my lap, trying to think this through, because self-recriminations would do me sweet FA.

'It's not a problem.' I tried to sound as confident as he did. 'I can sign—'

'No, you can't. All the agreements drawn up by Company of Strangers have been looked over and approved by lawyers. They are legal and binding, and if you think I'm going to write something down on a shitty piece of hotel notepaper for you to sign then you're sadly mistaken.'

There was another silence and then he went on, 'I could be anyone. I could be someone who doesn't care you're not affiliated with the company. Someone who might take this opportunity to hurt you and you'd have no back-up to call on.'

Very interested in my safety, wasn't he?

'I'd think of something.' I stared in his direction, suddenly struck by the fact that he hadn't moved. If he didn't like this, why hadn't he simply walked out?

Why are you thinking about him at all? He's not supposed to matter.

Well, if I didn't think of him, nothing else would matter, and I didn't want that to happen.

I opened my mouth to speak, but apparently he hadn't finished.

'And what about my safety?' he went on. 'You haven't signed an NDA. You and I could have a pleasant evening and then you could leave and report me to the police. Or go online and put every second of our encounter on the Internet for everyone to see. You might even blackmail me.'

Okay, so I hadn't thought about it from his point of view, but blackmail?

'Seriously, dude? Why would I do that?'

'You'd be surprised at what people do for money.'

'What?' I snapped before I could stop myself. 'Like turn up as a surprise escort to fill in for their friend?'

There was a pause.

'This is about the money for you?' he asked.

It wasn't, or at least not wholly. But that was part of it. I wanted to set up another tattoo parlour in LA, and to do that I needed some capital, of which I didn't have much. A night with him would help, especially with his apparently very generous tips. He didn't need to know about the fantasy part.

'Of course it's about the money for me. I'm not in the habit of setting myself up to screw complete strangers just for fun.'

Another silence.

Ugh, I'd said too much, hadn't I? I was letting my anger get the better of me and was alienating him. Maggie would have known how to handle him. Maggie always knew how to handle people.

'Okay, confession time,' I said before he could get another word in. 'Yes, I need the money. Specifically, the tips. I…have a business I want to get off the ground and I can't do that without some capital.' I didn't want to give too much away, such as how much the business meant to me and how desperately I wanted it to work. But I figured a little more truth wouldn't hurt. 'So, if you didn't send me away, if you kind of…just pretended I was a Strangers employee, I'd appreciate that.'

'Pretended?' Disdain dripped from each syllable.

I couldn't blame him. It was a lame suggestion, but it was the only one I had, so I ignored him. 'Maggie really couldn't get anyone to fill in and she didn't want to leave you in the lurch. I'm her friend and I offered to do it for her. She didn't want me to, but I talked her into it. So, if you're going to blame anyone, blame me.' I took a little breath. 'And please don't call the company. They'll fire her.'

I didn't want that. Maggie was a good friend and

this wasn't her fault. I'd been the one to talk her into it, to convince her that I wouldn't get caught. I just hadn't realised this asshole would be so quick on the uptake.

You're going to have to fix this.

My muscles had gone very tight, tension coiling through me. I had no idea how I was going to fix it but, yes, I would. I couldn't let my friend get fired because of me.

'Not my problem,' he said.

Shit. Shit. Shit.

'I'll do whatever you want,' I rushed on. 'Anything. Everything. I have no hard limits. And hey, I'm wearing a blindfold, so I don't even know who you are, which makes blackmail a little difficult. Ditto the police. I just want some good tips for my business and I'm prepared to work really hard for them.'

He said nothing.

Clearly it was my turn to demand answers.

'Well?' I asked. 'Does that change your mind?'

'No.'

That voice. It was sexy.

I stared at the blackness in front of my eyes, trying to sense him through it. 'Then why are you still here?'

CHAPTER FOUR

Elias

GOOD FUCKING POINT. Why was I still here? Because I should have walked out the moment I'd recognised her.

Yet I hadn't.

I'd wanted to know exactly what the fuck she thought she was doing, turning up here as a glorified escort, without all the necessary rules and regulations that made the interaction as safe as it was possible to get for both parties. Why she was fully prepared to get naked in front of a stranger and do everything he told her just for some spare cash.

Little idiot.

I'd nearly given myself away, asking her all those questions, but shit, she had to understand what stupid risks she was taking. I could have been anyone, some creepy asshole who got off on pain or fear. Or some bastard who liked humiliation.

Christ, she'd said she'd do anything, no limits. Did she even know what that meant?

I was very tempted to tell her exactly who she was talking to, as it was clear she hadn't recognised my voice, but that would lead to some very awkward questions—including why I'd barely answered all the emails, texts and voicemails I'd received from her over the past few years. Not to mention why I'd cut her from my life the way I'd cut everyone all those years ago—except Traj.

And I did not want to talk to her about that.

I never wanted to talk to anyone about that.

Besides, Traj would have fifty fucking fits if he knew she was here. He used Strangers too, so thank God she hadn't turned up as a replacement for one of his encounters, because that would have been awkward.

God, it was awkward now. What the hell was I supposed to do with her?

That's not the right question. The right question is, why haven't you walked away?

I could have. I should have. I should have walked out without a word and left her sitting here. She would still have been paid, no harm, no foul.

No tip, though. That was for women who stayed. And, if she'd heard about the tips, then she'd probably heard about the other aspect of my reputation, the part where every woman who spent the night with me got off, and got off hard.

Did she know about that? Had she heard?

Why are you even thinking about that? She's little Vee. The kid sister you never had. The only person other than Traj who ever just liked you for you and not for what you could do for her.

Yeah, shit, it was true.

Bright little Vee. Who'd hero-worshipped me, who had no idea what had happened to me, because the only person who did was Traj. I'd kept the fire and its aftermath from everyone else, wanting to put the life I'd had behind me for good, never to think of it again.

I was different now. A different man, with a different life, and it was only these nights once a week where I reconnected with my old self.

Not that I wanted to be him again. He'd been an idiot, a fucking fool who'd let other people define who he was, while I didn't let anyone define me.

I defined myself.

And, right here in this room, I could be whoever the fuck I wanted.

Not if she finds out who you are, you won't be. You'll be him again. Her hero...

My jaw ached as I stared at her, the thought winding through my brain.

She'd always been a bright spot in my previous life. Her parents had no time for her, and Traj was too busy trying to make his old man proud, so she'd been forgotten. It hadn't taken much to make her happy. A smile and a bit of conversation and she'd glowed like a lightbulb being switched on. I'd liked making her glow, because it'd seemed everyone else in my goddamn life required me to do so much more...

Shit, no, I didn't want to think of that.

I wanted to end this, and quickly, before either of us discovered the truth.

'I'm still here, because I want you to promise that you won't pull this stunt with anyone else,' I said, because it was probably something Vee would do.

She'd always been stubborn that way.

'What are you, my brother?' She was derisive. 'What do you care what I do?'

Since when had she become so snarky and sharp? She'd been a shy, sensitive kid, empathetic too, always wearing her heart on her sleeve. I hadn't seen a lot of her after I'd got a football scholarship to Stanford, but the times I'd visited with Traj she'd seemed the same as she always was.

Not quite the same. She had a crush on you, remember?

Oh, yeah, I remembered that. Around sixteen, she'd got all shy, blushing furiously whenever I talked to her. I'd found it cute and, because she was so much younger, she'd been like a sister to me.

She's not a kid now. And you're definitely not her brother.

I didn't know where that thought came from and I didn't want it. But it sat there in my brain, glowing like a neon sign, and I found my gaze dropping to where the star necklace glittered at her throat and her pulse beat fast. Then further down, to the inked stars and petals on her body that disappeared under her dress. The silky fabric had pulled tight over the curve of her right breast, outlining the shape. Small, round and perfect, a hard nipple pressing against the fabric…

Electricity rippled down my spine, my suit pants suddenly feeling a little tight.

Ah, fuck.

I cleared my throat, ignoring the feeling. 'I care because you're a young woman who hasn't thought through the consequence of her actions, and who's put herself at risk, not to mention her friend's job.' I didn't bother to sugar-coat it. 'And if you do it again with someone else, someone who doesn't care either about you or your friend, things might go very differently. So, if I were you, I'd take the money you'll get for the night and leave.'

Her head cocked slightly, the light from the spotlight above her glossing her black hair and making the blue tips of it glow. The colour was almost an exact match with her silky-looking dress.

'No,' she said.

'What do you mean, no?'

'You heard me.' Her pointed chin lifted at a stubborn angle. 'I'm not leaving.'

I remembered that chin. I remembered that stubbornness too. She had dyslexia, which her father had refused to acknowledge, and she'd subsequently tried to overcome it with the sheer force of her will. She used to sit at her desk in her bedroom upstairs, her jaw set, tears running down her face as she'd painstakingly forced herself to write out a report. It had taken her hours, even with my help, and it used to break my heart. I'd tried on and off to convince her father to get her some help, but he wouldn't listen to me. Yet she'd never given up. She'd pushed and pushed and pushed.

Seemed as if she was still pushing.

Once, I'd had patience to deal with that, but I didn't now. That had vanished along with my ability to throw a ball or run or basically do anything that I'd once found so easy.

'Too fucking bad.' I wasn't polite these days and I didn't bother to hide it. 'Promise me you won't pull this stunt again, then get out of here.'

But she didn't seem at all bothered by my tone and she didn't move. Her skin was getting all goose-bumpy and I couldn't help noticing that her nipples had tightened beneath the silk of her dress.

Pretty.

No, shit, I didn't want to think that. I didn't want that goddamned thought anywhere near my brain, but it was there all the same. Because she was. Not beautiful, but definitely pretty. A different kind of prettiness from all the cheerleaders and other women who used to fall into my bed. One that wasn't immediately obvious, that took time to uncover. A mysterious sort of beauty, rewarding to whoever discovered it...

Jesus, why the hell was I thinking about whether she was pretty or not? All I should be thinking of was getting rid of her. I'd cut her out of my life for very good reasons and I didn't want her coming back into it.

Her chin lifted higher. 'If I don't go, will you hurt me?'

'I don't hurt women,' I growled, annoyed that she would even think it, before realising that of course she might very well think it. She had no idea who I was.

'Good to know.' She tilted her head again, this time at a different angle, as if trying to see through her blindfold. 'So what are you trying to protect me from, ace? Something kinky?'

'Kinky is relative. And that's not a question you get to ask me.'

'Why not?'

Yeah, she was pushing it. Perhaps she needed to be told explicitly why this was a very bad idea.

'Do you want to know what I want from the women I hire for the night, little girl?' I asked, ignoring her question.

Her nose wrinkled, reminding me once again—as if I needed it—of the kid sister I'd once thought of her as. 'Not sure I like the "little girl" thing. Not sexy, dude.'

'Then leave.'

She made an irritated sound and very pointedly settled in the chair, smoothing out the blue silk of her dress.

Yeah, all of this would have been fine if she'd just done what she was told.

The past few years fronting the business had made

me hard, and people generally responded to that by doing exactly what I told them to do. Rarely did they challenge me.

But I couldn't deny the way she was pushing back right now, though fucking annoying, was also... erotic. And it was getting me off.

Bad idea.

Oh, it wasn't just a bad idea—it was a fucking terrible idea.

Me getting hot for Vee wasn't going to happen.

'Tell me, then,' she said after a second. 'Tell me what you want from the women you hire for a night.'

'Their complete obedience. Doing everything I say with no argument and no hesitation.'

The blindfold shifted as she frowned. 'That's it? Do everything you say?'

'Yes.'

'And do they do it?'

'Yes.' And they enjoyed every goddamned second of it.

'Wow.' Vesta bit her lip and my attention zeroed in on it. She really had a lovely mouth, plush and so soft-looking. How had I never noticed? 'What do they get out of it, then?'

'Money. And as many orgasms as I choose to give them. Which you'd know if you'd read my profile.'

She coloured. Which was...interesting. Was this pushy, challenging, stubborn woman she'd grown into embarrassed by the word *orgasm*?

Clearly she knew she'd given herself away, because she gave a forced-sounding laugh and said with a fair attempt at bravado, 'Hey, that doesn't sound bad. In fact, it sounds pretty good to me. So what kinds of things do you get them to do?'

The conversation was obviously making her uncomfortable, yet she was trying to pretend that she wasn't. Another sign that she shouldn't be here. Because, if she found an overtly sexual conversation with a stranger discomforting, then she wasn't going to enjoy the actual sex part, was she?

What? Are you actually considering using her for tonight?

No. Fuck, no. All I wanted to do was put her off.

'An example, then,' I said. 'I might order you to take off your clothes. To face the window. To spread your legs. To put your hands on your pussy and make yourself come.' I paused, noting the colour that deepened in her cheeks as I spoke. 'While I watch.'

She was shocked. I could see by the way her mouth opened, then closed very quickly. Strange that, for all her spiky, blue-tipped hair and her tattoos and confronting attitude, she should find this shocking.

Maybe it was because she was still the same little girl inside, shy and awkward, sweet and sensitive.

Which means you shouldn't be talking to her like that.

Yeah, I probably shouldn't. Then again, she wasn't a little girl any more, no matter that I kept calling her one, and if I wanted to frighten her off I needed to be hard-nosed about it.

'Oh…uh… I see.' She turned her head towards the window, white teeth working at the plushness of her soft bottom lip. 'And…um…they do that? When you ask?'

The huskiness in her voice had become pronounced, the way a woman's did when she was starting to get aroused. And I could see it all of a sudden—her naked in that chair with her thighs spread, still wearing those sandals with the sexy ties wrapped around her slender calves. Her skin would be flushed and her hand would be down between…

Holy shit. Where the hell had that thought come from?

My suit pants had got even tighter, my cock deciding it wanted in on that action, and I had to concentrate hard to shove it aside. The whole point of this was to get her to leave, not to start thinking of what would happen if she stayed.

But ignoring my physical discomfort was something I'd had a lot of practice with the past ten years, and if you could ignore agonising pain then ignoring one inappropriate hard-on was a relatively simple matter.

'Yes,' I said. 'They do.'

'And you get off on that?'

'If you want to stay, you're going the wrong way about it.' I tried to make my voice cold. 'You're supposed to do what I tell you, not ask me questions.'

'I could do that, you know,' she said suddenly. 'I could take my clothes off and do…what you want.'

Christ, if she couldn't even say it…

'If you want the money that badly, I'll pay you right now.' I had the cash in my wallet, as the women I hired liked cash, and I had a lot of it. And in fact, now I thought of it, why hadn't I just done that? If money was why she was doing this, then the simplest way to solve the problem was to pay her. I could afford it. I wasn't the poor boy from the projects looking to make good, hoping to drag his family out of poverty. Not any more.

I'd buried that boy. He was dead and gone.

I was the selfish billionaire now, with a thriving business and money to burn, and if I wanted to pay Vee a lot of money so she didn't go offering herself around to any other guy then I would.

Or you could keep her safe by letting her stay.

The thought streaked across my brain like a rocket trailing sparks and lighting up the night, and for a second I couldn't move, transfixed by it.

Then reality asserted itself. Yeah, that wasn't happening. No fucking way.

'What?' She did that head tilt again. 'You mean, not just the rate for the night?'

'No. Tips as well.' I scowled at her, though she couldn't see me. 'In fact, just tell me how much you need for your business and I'll give it to you.'

She'd gone very still except for a slight quiver, like a little cat sensing a bird. 'So you'd pay me all of that for…what? Doing nothing?'

'No,' I growled. 'I'm not paying you to do nothing. Firstly, I'm paying you to get the fuck out of this room, and secondly, so you don't pull this stupid stunt with any other Strangers client. Because no one wants their special evening ruined by some kid turning up out of the blue when they were expecting to have the woman of their choice.'

As soon as the words had left my mouth, I knew I'd said the wrong thing.

I could almost see the outrage swelling in her, because she got more and more still, the quiver becoming pronounced. I'd hit a nerve and, now that I thought about it, of course I'd hit a nerve. She'd basically been rejected all of her life, and now here I was, rejecting her.

Then again, I'd been doing that for years now already, hadn't I? While part of me regretted and felt guilty about it, the rest of me didn't. And, as I'd let the soft, compassionate part of me die in a hospital bed years ago, it was the rest of me that was in control. The rest of me that had hardened, that was as unfeeling as the scar tissue that covered most of my torso and upper thighs. The part that had been through the flames—literally—and had come out the other side, stronger, tempered like a fucking sword. That didn't give a shit about other people and their feelings, and never would.

'A kid?' she demanded, outraged. 'Why would you think that? I'm not a kid. I'm twenty-five.'

'That's still—'

'And what do you mean by expecting to have a

woman of their choice? I am a woman. Are you saying there's something wrong with me?'

She was angry. Good. I wanted her angry. I wanted her enraged enough that she'd get up off that chair and storm out.

But she didn't.

'Right,' she said flatly. 'That's it. I'm not leaving. You're stuck with me now. And I'm going to show you exactly what a ruined evening looks like.'

CHAPTER FIVE

Vesta

ANGER BOILED INSIDE ME, which wasn't great, when I was supposed to be seductive and sexy. Yet I couldn't keep it locked away.

The paying me bit was fine. Tips for nothing—who wouldn't want that? But firstly suggesting that I was a kid, and secondly that my turning up would ruin someone's evening, was a step too far.

Yeah, I was stubborn. It used to be that I used my stubbornness to try to get attention from my parents. Be my pretty mom's mini-me, my dad's good little girl. Until I realised that neither of them really gave a shit about me, that they were never going to be as proud of me as they were of Traj, and so I stopped caring about being good and instead set about being as mulish as possible.

Eli was the only one who'd seen my stubbornness as something good rather than yet another flaw I needed to overcome. He'd told me he admired it, and that sometimes the only difference between success and failure was the degree of tenacity a person had. Coming from him, with the success he'd managed to achieve on the football field despite his poor background, that had meant a lot. I'd felt I'd done so many things wrong, so having at least one thing I was doing right had been like being given a handful of gold.

Whether staying was the right thing to do now, though, was a moot point. I couldn't give up. Not when I had something to prove to this patronising, dismissive asshole, sexy voice or no.

I gripped the arms of the chair in preparation for pushing myself to my feet, but that sandpaper voice of his cut across me, freezing me in place.

'Sit the fuck down.'

My heartbeat thumped, anger surging inside me. But there was something in the words, a note of steely command, that had me obeying him for reasons I couldn't have articulated.

I sat there, all my awareness centred on that hard, male presence I could sense just off to my right.

He was angry too—I could almost taste it—and I guess he had every right to be. I was an unexpected wrench in his plans and he was pissed that he hadn't been notified. But, hell, I didn't understand why he was prepared to pay me all this money just to leave. Why should he care when I was just some kid he didn't know, turning up out of the blue and ruining his evening?

And it wasn't as if he was even protecting me

from anything seriously kinky, just a little voyeurism stuff. So what the hell was his deal? And, if it bothered him so much, why hadn't he just walked out of the room?

He could pay me the money right now and leave.

Yeah, but he hasn't. And you know why.

A burst of sudden insight shot through me, burning bright in my head. There could only be one reason that he hadn't walked out: I'd intrigued him in some way.

My breath caught and I sat very still in my chair, concentrating on him.

He made no sound, yet I could almost feel the anger coming off him, seething in the air between us. Which meant that I was right, surely? Because if there was nothing keeping him here, and he was that angry, he'd just have walked out.

But something was keeping him here and that something could only be me.

Also, his anger was weird too, now I thought about it. Sure, I'd kind of inserted myself into his evening, and it made sense that he would be annoyed about it. But this felt like more than mere annoyance. There had been a protective element to it too, as if what happened to me mattered to him.

Though it was the fact that he hadn't left that gripped me so thoroughly.

Did he…want me?

Heat licked through me at the thought, making my breath catch.

'I might order you to take off your clothes...put your hands on your pussy...make yourself come... while I watch...'

I'd done a bit of stuff with guys, but not a lot, mainly because I had only ever wanted one guy in my life. Only one I'd really wanted to do stuff with, and he was six-three, golden-skinned, golden-haired, built like a god...

I used to go to all his games because I'd loved watching him play. He'd been the epitome of athletic male grace and power as he'd charged down the field, making my heart race and my mouth go dry.

But he'd never seen me as anything more than a kid, and these days he didn't see me as anything much at all. I didn't exist for him and he'd made that very obvious.

It had hurt then and it still did, even though I'd stopped trying to make contact with him a year or so ago. I didn't even ask Traj about him the way I'd used to.

So if this guy, whoever he was, could make me hot, then maybe there was hope for me. Hope that I could get over Eli Hart and put him behind me once and for all.

'Leave, sit the fuck down...' My voice sounded breathless in the quiet. 'Better make up your mind, ace. A girl could get confused.'

'I've got cash in my wallet. A lot of cash. All you need for—'

'Do you want me?'

A silence fell, but in no way a comfortable one.

'Why do you ask?' His voice was even more raspy, scraping over my nerve-endings like fine sandpaper.

'Enquiring minds want to know. It's easier by far for you to walk out, but you haven't. In fact, if you really didn't want anything to do with me, you could have walked out the moment I came into the room, but you didn't.'

Silence.

'Why not, ace?' I stared in his direction, stared hard. 'But you don't need to answer. I already know. You want me, and I think you don't like that and it's pissing you off.'

More silence.

I couldn't sense him now. Was he still here? Or had he walked out? The thought that he might have made an unexpected stab of disappointment go through me.

'If you don't want to do this, then I'll find someone else,' I went on, wanting to goad him, make him respond in some way. 'I'll find some other guy who doesn't mind—'

'No. You won't.'

I nearly gasped.

His voice was very close, near my ear, as if he'd crossed the space between us to come and stand directly behind my chair.

Every muscle in my body tightened, anticipation racing through me.

'I won't?' I asked breathlessly, trying not to give

away my physical reaction to his nearness. 'And who's going to stop me?'

'You don't need to prove yourself, little girl.' His deep, abrasive voice was so close, sending those chills racing all over my skin. 'Still less to me.'

Little girl... I should have called him out again about that, but I'd lied earlier about not finding it sexy. I did find it sexy. It made all this feel just a little bit wrong, a little bit taboo, and part of me liked that very much.

Not that I was concentrating all that hard on what he was saying as every part of me was focused on him, trying to get a sense of him. There was heat at my back. Was that him? I could smell the faintest hint of expensive aftershave, spicy and warm, like cloves or cinnamon. As well as an achingly familiar scent underneath it that I couldn't quite place.

'But what if I want to prove myself?' My voice had become hoarse. 'And what if I want to prove myself to you?'

'Why? You have no idea who I am. Why would it matter?'

'Okay, so maybe not to you, but what if I wanted to prove something to myself?'

'What the fuck would you want to prove?'

I didn't know why I told him the truth, because it wasn't something I'd told anyone before. Maybe it was that haunting sense of familiarity, or maybe I just wanted to shock him, surprise him in some way. Or maybe it was just that confessing things to complete strangers when you were wearing a blind-fold was easier.

Whatever it was, the truth came out whether I'd wanted it to or not.

'There's someone I need to put behind me,' I said shakily. 'Someone who doesn't feel the same way about me as I do about him. I thought this might give me the chance to do that.'

More silence came from behind my chair, and yet I knew he hadn't moved, because I could still catch his scent. God, he smelled so good. It should be illegal for a man to smell that delicious.

'You're too honest.' His voice was quiet. 'You shouldn't share that kind of stuff with people you don't know.'

I took a shaky breath. 'Too late now, isn't it?'

More silence.

'I know you didn't choose me and I know I shouldn't have just taken Maggie's place like that.' My voice had got even huskier. 'But if you want me, I'd appreciate the chance to just…feel like I'm beautiful and maybe special in some way.'

I didn't mention it wasn't some random dude I wanted to be beautiful and special for. Only Eli. Only ever Eli.

Yet more silence.

I had said too much, hadn't I? If I was wrong and he walked away, whilst I might not die from the humiliation it could be a near-run thing. God only knew why I'd bared my soul to a complete stranger

I'd never even seen, but I did know that if I let him walk out he'd be taking my chance to get over Eli right along with him.

'You know what I particularly like?' he asked after a very long time, that haunting voice of his whispering over my skin. 'I like a woman to beg. I like to have her on her knees, reduced to a weeping mess of desire, desperate for my touch. Utterly dependent on me for the most incredible orgasm of her life.'

I felt the words sink into me, the sense of them lighting fires deep inside me, making me ache and burn.

'Can you handle that?' His voice had deepened. 'Can you handle me making you beg for an orgasm?'

He wasn't going to walk out. He was going to give me a night.

Relief swamped me, my breathing getting faster, an ache between my thighs. I was getting turned on, which was strange, as I hadn't even had a chance to picture Eli from behind my blindfold yet. Weird how just this faceless stranger's voice could get me hot.

'Yes,' I said, already composing my favourite fantasy in my head. Eli breathless with desire, desperate to get his hands on me. Kneeling at my feet and running his hands up my calves, kissing my thighs, getting higher and higher…

I swallowed. 'So…do you want me?' I hoped I didn't sound pathetic. I just wanted confirmation, because it wasn't going to be much of an Eli fantasy if this guy wasn't actually interested in me.

There was another long silence, and inexplicably my throat closed, as if the opinion of this nameless guy mattered to me in some way, which it shouldn't.

Then fingers suddenly rested against the back of my neck, the lightest brush against my nape, and this time I couldn't stop the gasp that rushed out of me as heat flickered over my skin. I shuddered like a tree in a high wind.

'Yes.' The word was soft, his touch on the back of my neck even softer. 'I do.'

I bowed my head instinctively, letting him stroke me, wanting him to. There was a slight suggestion of roughness to his fingertips, as if he had calluses on them, the light abrasiveness making every nerve-ending catch fire.

This man knew how to touch a woman. Even I, with my woeful inexperience, could tell that.

'Do you?' My voice sounded scraped raw, which I hated about as much as I hated the needy note that I couldn't quite hide. But I couldn't stop myself from asking the question. 'You might be just telling me what I want to hear.'

'Why would I do that?' A fingertip gently stroked the side of my neck, and I shivered yet again, my breath catching. 'But if you need confirmation…'

The fingertip was gone, leaving my skin achingly sensitised—and not only the back of my neck, but my entire body. Everywhere tingled and I was aware of everything: of the light press of the silk of my dress and the warmth of the leather beneath me. The cool of the air-conditioning whispering over me.

Then I felt his fingers suddenly close around my right wrist, exerting a light pressure. I froze. His skin was warm against mine and it sent threads of electricity and heat spiralling through my veins.

He lifted my hand and I knew he was standing right beside my chair. I could feel the warmth of his body, smell the faint scent of cloves and the inexplicably familiar scent beneath that.

I knew that scent. I *knew* it. But how? Where from? And why did I find it so reassuring?

Then he took my hand and pressed my palm against something very hot and everything went entirely out of my head as my brain struggled to process what he was doing.

Heat. And softness too. And something long and very hard…

A bolt of electricity shot straight through me and I stiffened, my breath freezing in my lungs. He was pressing my palm against the zipper of his pants wasn't he? And that long, thick, hard thing was…

'Oh, my God,' I whispered before I could stop myself. 'You're—'

'Hard?' he interrupted roughly. 'Yes. I am.'

He released my hand before I was ready, the imprint of his arousal branded against my palm.

I was breathing very fast. 'What do you look like?' I asked, even though it really wasn't important, as it wasn't him that I wanted to see. But his touch had been…electric…and had made him real all of a sudden, whereas before he'd been just a disembodied voice. But of course he wasn't. He was a man, warm and alive, and smelling so delicious…

He was silent a long minute and I had the distinct impression that I'd shocked him. 'Does it matter?' His tone was too studied to be natural.

For some reason, telling me what he looked like bothered him.

'No,' I said, because it didn't. 'I just want to be able to imagine you.'

'You can imagine whoever and whatever you like.' There was a sharp edge to his voice now. He really hadn't liked me asking the question. 'You don't need to know what I look like for that.'

'But I—'

'If you want to prove yourself to me, start by not speaking unless I tell you to. Those were my orders, remember?'

Yes, I remembered.

I bit my lip, fighting the urge to keep talking, keep asking more questions. But he wasn't important and I had to remember that. The only important thing was the fantasy in my head and I didn't need to know anything about him for that.

I nodded without speaking.

He said nothing and I couldn't hear any movement. The spicy scent of his aftershave had gone and I couldn't feel his presence next to me any more.

'Have you been with many men?' His voice came from behind me again, directly behind my chair. 'You can answer.'

Right, so we were going to get into the whole virginity thing, were we? Yes, it was my Plan B for added enticement, but given how much he liked asking questions I wasn't sure I wanted to tell him now. Mainly because I didn't want to give him any more of the truth than I already had.

'Yeah,' I said, trying for casual. 'I've been with quite a few.'

'Don't lie, little girl.' His voice was close, right in my ear, and I could feel his warm breath against the side of my neck. It sent another uncontrollable shiver through me. 'Tell me the truth or else I'm walking straight out that door.'

He meant it. I could tell.

My awareness narrowed, centred utterly on him. He wasn't just standing behind me now but bending over the back of my chair. I could feel it. His scent was around me, his breath ghosted across the side of my neck and I was gripped once again by the most intense feeling of familiarity.

I…knew him.

I had sat like this once before, I was sure of it—or not quite like this, but in a similar position—me in a chair while he bent over me, talking to me. It hadn't been sexual, not like this. He'd been…telling me something or showing me how to do something. A boss, maybe? Or a teacher?

But, no, neither of those felt quite right. I'd been my own boss for quite some time and I hadn't been to school since I'd dropped out at seventeen.

I stared straight ahead through the blackness of the blindfold, my heartbeat now racing, my brain sorting through all the possibilities yet coming up with nothing.

It was right there, though. Right on the tip of my tongue…

'Who are you?' I whispered. 'I feel like I know you.'

CHAPTER SIX

Elias

I WAS BENT over her chair. Strands of her glossy black hair tickled the side of my cheek and her breathing was loud in my ear. She smelled of the candy-floss body wash she'd used as a teenager, a warm, sweet smell, and the exposed skin of her neck was as pale as freshly churned cream.

I went very still.

There was no way she could know me. None. Unless she'd cheated with her blindfold, but I didn't think she had. And it had been years since I'd seen her, fucking years. She hadn't heard my voice since I'd recovered, either, so it couldn't possibly have been familiar to her. It had changed beyond all recognition.

Then again, Vee had always been perceptive, even as a little kid. More so than some adults. I still remembered how she'd once said that I should tell my dad my knee was hurting, that I didn't have to pretend it was okay. I'd been eighteen and had thought

I'd hidden the pain so effectively that no one would know. But she had.

I'd told her she was wrong, but she'd only looked at me very patiently, as if I was stupid, and told me that I didn't have to hide it from her.

I would have been annoyed, as I hated being made to feel like a big, dumb jock, but she'd only been nine at the time so it had amused me instead.

It didn't amuse me now.

How the fuck did she know that I wanted her? How could she tell? And as for knowing me... Sure, we'd had a lot of contact years ago, but not now.

I'd been hoping she'd give up trying to make contact, but she hadn't, or at least not until recently. That tenacity again. I couldn't think what kept driving her, what it was about me that kept her emailing, calling and texting, because I wasn't her hero any more.

I was nobody's fucking hero any more.

I was something better, something harder. My own man, not someone else's goddamned meal ticket.

'You don't know me,' I growled in her ear, wanting to take the tender lobe between my teeth and give her a warning nip. 'And I sure as hell don't know you.'

What the fuck are you doing with her? Why haven't you walked away already?

I should have. But I didn't. She'd said she wanted to put someone behind her, to feel wanted, to feel beautiful, and I hadn't thought I gave a shit about other people's feelings, but apparently I still gave a shit about hers.

What guy did she want to put behind her? Had he made her feel bad about herself? Because if so I wanted his fucking name so I could show him the error of his ways. Not that it was my place to do so, but I didn't like what she'd said about herself.

As if she wasn't beautiful. Okay, so maybe I hadn't fully appreciated her when I'd first walked in and seen her, but that was because I hadn't known who she was. And now I did, and it made all the difference.

She'd always been a bright light, had always had so much going for her, yet the Howard-Smith family had never seen her potential, crushing her down so much it was a wonder her light hadn't gone out.

But it hadn't gone out. I could see it in the flashes of challenge she kept throwing at me and in that streak of stubbornness. In the tattoos she'd covered herself with and in the blue tips of her hair too. Her judgmental mother and her neglectful father might have done their damnedest to make her feel ignored and unimportant, but she was still fighting. Still strong.

It's not about how you feel sorry for her. Come on. You just want to fuck her.

I stared down at the soft, pale skin of her exposed neck and found myself wondering what she would do if I bit her there very gently...

Heat spread through me, closing long fingers

around me and squeezing tight. I could still feel the pressure of her palm against my zipper as I'd held it there, proving to her that I wasn't just saying the words. That I did actually want her.

I hadn't thought I would, and yet…

Shit. I couldn't walk away from her, so what the hell else was I supposed to do? She'd already told me she'd just go out and do this with some other asshole who'd potentially treat her badly, or who wouldn't give a shit for her pleasure, and I couldn't stand the thought of that.

She just wanted to feel wanted and if there was one thing I could do for women these days it was make them feel wanted. Sure, these nights were totally about me, but all my partners got something from them too.

I could have the evening of escape that I wanted and she could get a little bit of validation as well. What was wrong with that? Yes, there was the added complication of who she was—and if Traj ever found out he'd lay me out flat—but she had no idea of my identity and, shit, it had to stay that way.

'Are you sure?' She was very still, her head turned slightly, her attention on me. 'You're so familiar.'

Okay, I needed to distract her, that was obvious.

'The truth,' I said, ignoring her. 'Let's have it.'

She blew out an annoyed-sounding breath. 'My sexual experience? Yeah, I'm thinking that's none of your business, *ace*.'

I didn't miss the emphasis on the last word.

Pissed, wasn't she? So, she didn't like being asked that question, and I had my suspicions as to why. She'd either had way too much in the way of experience, and was ashamed of it, or she'd had very little and the same applied.

Which was it with Vee?

Stupid question. Given the way she blushed, and how her whole body had gone taut when I'd held her hand down on my cock, I was thinking it was the latter.

Probably better that you walk away then, asshole.

Yeah, probably. But I wasn't going to, not now. She'd been treated like shit by her family for a very long time, so if she needed this to make her feel better about herself then I'd give it to her.

That was what I'd been doing before I'd got burned, after all.

'Ace?' I straightened up, allowing some amusement to colour my voice as I moved around the side of the chair, coming to stand in front of it. Standing behind the chair was always a good way to put a partner off-balance, keeping them unsure of where I was, which heightened their anticipation, but I wanted to get a good look at her.

Her head moved with me, tracking me, staring straight at me from behind her blindfold. It was uncanny, reminding me of Traj, who never looked like a man who was losing his sight.

Could Vee see through that thing? Had she left a gap? When I'd been standing behind her I'd checked the ties, and they seemed secure, but maybe she'd cheated.

But even as the question occurred to me I knew the answer. She'd changed in the years since I'd last seen her, it was clear, but Vee had always done the right thing and played by the rules. Despite the whole bad-girl vibe she had going on, she wouldn't cheat.

Traj and I had once played a joke on her in a game of hide and seek, where we'd made a rule that no one was to move from their hiding place if they weren't found. They had to stay in place until they were. We'd laid bets on how long she'd stay there, and I'd bet five dollars she'd last fifteen minutes—she was a sparky kid, never sitting still for long—while Traj had bet ten she'd stay there until she was found. We'd gone to play computer games after that and had forgotten about her until I'd suddenly become aware that she wasn't bugging us quite as much as usual. Then we'd both remembered and had gone to find her. She'd been huddled beneath her bed, big blue eyes huge in her face.

'I stayed,' she'd said. 'I was good.'

She'd been there for two hours. She'd been six.

So, no, Vee wouldn't have cheated.

She faced me and I could finally get a good look at her as half of her wasn't obscured by the sides of the chair. The deep blue silk of her dress outlined her delicate curves to perfection, especially those lovely little breasts with their hard nipples. It highlighted the graceful indent of her waist and broader span of her hips. Rounded thighs. Okay, so she was curvier than I'd initially thought. The dress ended mid-thigh, giving me a good view of pretty, slender legs and, fuck, those sandals… Sexy as hell.

I could go down on my knees in front of her, run my hands up the backs of her calves, touch her smooth skin. Ease the hem of her dress up to her hips and uncover her. Then I'd touch her, stroke her, make her shake with my hands and mouth, make her desperate, make her beg for what she wanted, for what only I could give her…

But, no, not yet. I needed to build her anticipation first.

With an effort I pulled my gaze back to her face and found myself wishing the blindfold wasn't there, that I could see her sharp features and the dark blue of her eyes. Such pretty, expressive eyes. She had a little blue stud in her nose. It was cute.

Christ, what had led her here? Was it the same thing that had made her dye the tips of her hair? That had propelled her into a tattoo parlour? What had happened to her in the years since I'd left? Something had changed her from that sweet, shy, caring little girl into this tattooed, sexy woman. The changes in her weren't bad. No, they had me fucking fascinated. But I wanted to know where they'd come from. What had made her end up in a hotel room preparing to have sex with a guy she thought was a complete stranger to her?

'I'd appreciate the chance to just...feel like I'm beautiful and maybe special...'

My chest tightened in a way that had nothing to do with my scars or the burns that had caused them. Or the pedestal I'd fallen from all those years ago.

It was her parents' fault, wasn't it? Yeah, and Traj's too. The way they'd treated her... Fuck, it made me so angry. Because how could she think she wasn't beautiful?

'Yeah, you got a problem with "ace"?' Her chin came up, stubborn as hell. 'If you get to call me little girl, I get to call you ace.'

'I don't have a problem with that. But what I do have a problem with is your sexual history not being any of my business. Especially given that this whole encounter is sexual.'

She lifted a shoulder. 'So?'

Fuck. Still stubborn. But I liked it...not going to lie.

I had a job that involved meeting a lot of people, being the public face of Howard and Hart. I hustled my way around the offices of our company and the R&D labs, in the corridors of power of various world governments, in the boardrooms of multinationals. People did what I told them to do because I was a hard-ass and they didn't want to mess with me. And the ones that did, I convinced otherwise.

I was good at convincing people, but not because I was particularly charming—Traj was the charming one these days, not me. I'd left my charming days behind. Now I was blunt and straight to the point. Honest. Told it as I saw it. I was the iron fist inside Traj's velvet glove and it worked well.

'So?' I echoed, making no effort to be anything less than the harsh asshole I truly was. 'You're not a Strangers employee, which means you don't have a profile. And, since you don't have a profile, you don't have a list of hard limits. You also don't know mine. And that's fucking important because it helps prevent any misunderstandings. You don't know me, and I don't know you, which means the potential for misunderstandings is fairly high.'

Colour had risen again. She'd always hated screwing up.

'I see,' she said, giving a very good impression of a glossy little blackbird that had had its feathers all ruffled. 'So what makes you choose a particular woman based on their history, then?'

I thrust my hands into the pockets of my suit pants. 'I chose women who don't have any hard limits since they're less likely to be bothered by what I get them to do.'

'Like what? Playing with themselves while you watch? Or…maybe ordering them to get naked and bend them over the arm of a chair so you can fuck them in the ass?'

I couldn't see her eyebrows, but I was betting that she'd just raised one of them. Saucy little minx.

I couldn't help a grin. 'Have you been practising saying that in your head so you don't stutter?'

She gave another little shrug, dismissing it. 'Whatever. So, if I did have hard limits, would you have chosen me?'

I could hear the fearful hope in her voice. Yeah, she really did want to be wanted, didn't she? But I couldn't tell her the truth. Of course I wouldn't have chosen her. She was still Traj's little sister, after all.

'I don't know,' I said flatly, lying through my teeth, even though it went against my nature. 'It depends on what your hard limits are.'

'What if it was…that?'

She was still blushing. She might be able to say the words, but she still found it uncomfortable. Christ, just what sexual experience had she had? I'd thought not much, but how 'not much' were we talking?

'If you can't even say it a second time, then I'm thinking that's one of your hard limits.'

Her lovely mouth firmed. She put her hands on the arms of the chair, fingers resting there lightly, little chin lifted high. 'Tell me your history first.'

'My history is…extensive.' No need to tell her about the years I'd spent sleeping my way around college, knee-deep in pussy. They'd all loved me. They'd all wanted a piece of me. And I'd been happy to oblige. I was always happy to oblige. 'But my hard limit is touch. You only get to touch what I permit you to touch.'

'So…you can touch me but I can't touch you?'

'Yes.'

'You can touch me…everywhere?'

'Yes.'

I couldn't tell what her expression was, but she was chewing on her lip again, obviously thinking about it.

'If you don't like it, you know where the door is,' I added.

'I didn't say that.'

'The offer stands. At any time.' I found my gaze drawn to the base of her throat where her pulse was beating fast. The little star necklace I'd given her glittered in the light, in time with her heartbeat. She'd kept that. And she still wore it…

'Your turn,' I said roughly.

She shifted slightly in the chair. 'That's it? That's your only hard limit? Tough bastard, huh?'

I shrugged, even though she couldn't see it. 'It's only sex. It doesn't mean anything.'

'If it doesn't mean anything then why don't you want women touching you?'

Yeah, I wasn't having that. 'If you keep trying to distract me, I'll start thinking you've got something to hide.'

She screwed up her face in annoyance.

I ignored it, my gaze dropping lower to the scattering of stars inked into the skin of her right shoulder, and then the petals on her left, both of them disappearing beneath her dress. Did they go all the way down over her breasts? Perhaps I could trace the shapes of them with my tongue…

'Okay.' She leaned forward slightly. 'So my experience is probably not…as extensive as yours.'

'Define "not extensive".'

'Uh… I suppose I'm what you'd call a beginner when it comes to this sort of thing.'

'This sort of thing being…?'

'Well, filling in for Maggie, obviously.' She shifted again, clearly uncomfortable but making no move to leave.

I admired her tenacity. I always had and I admired it now. This was obviously way out of her comfort zone, but she was still pushing for what she wanted. She hadn't given up.

You could learn from her.

What the hell kind of thought was that? If you wanted to see fucking tenacity, try months of surgeries and skin grafts. Try weaning yourself off strong pain meds. Try agonising physio appointments where just lifting your arm to your shoulder was an achievement.

Yeah, I had nothing to learn about tenacity. I'd written the fucking book.

'Obviously,' I echoed, keeping my tone dry as dust.

'So, yeah, beginner here.'

'How "beginner" are we talking about?'

'Very beginner. Like…total newb.'

I frowned. 'Be specific.'

Vee let out a breath. 'I haven't done this before.'

'Haven't done what before?'

She chewed on her bottom lip. 'Any of it. I haven't done anything before.'

I blinked, staring at her. 'Anything?'

'No.' She was still looking towards me through her blindfold. 'I'm a virgin.'

CHAPTER SEVEN

Vesta

HE DIDN'T LIKE THAT. I could tell right away. Good thing I hadn't used that as Plan B. I hadn't wanted to tell him but he'd demanded honesty, and anyway he'd have figured it out, especially if his experience was as extensive as he'd said. And most especially because I wasn't much of an actress.

He'd gone totally silent, but I could feel his presence in front of my chair. I concentrated on him, trying to get a sense of the shape of him. He seemed a man with a definite presence who occupied a space and occupied it fully. Or, rather, as if he claimed the space, took it as his due.

I stared hard into the blackness in front of my eyes, that strange sense of familiarity gripping me once again. I'd had it before and he'd sounded pissed with me when I'd mentioned that I felt that I knew him.

Why? It was clear he didn't want me to know who he was, but did he like to remain anonymous to his partners generally? Or was it something to do with me in particular? And why didn't he want anyone to see him?

Was it the whole 'paying for sex' thing? Was he famous and didn't want anyone to know? Or was it more about his proclivities? Or both, maybe? Was he a fine, upstanding family man with a secret life?

And then he said flatly, 'Get your purse. Time for you to leave.'

I gripped the arms of the chair hard. 'Why? Because I'm a virgin?'

'I don't do fucking virgins.'

'Why not? What have you got against virgins?'

The rustle of clothing came and I felt his warmth. He'd taken a step towards my chair and was possibly looming over me. Sadly for him, looming wasn't going to work.

I tipped my head back, approximating just how tall he was and where his face was likely to be. Hoping I'd ended up staring at him full on.

I wouldn't let myself be intimidated into leaving— not by him, not by anyone.

'I haven't got anything against them,' he said harshly. 'But I'm not into coaxing or being patient. I'm not into kind, and I'm definitely not into gentle, either.'

'I don't need to be coaxed,' I snapped, angry with him for changing his mind yet again. 'And I don't need patience, either. Though, really, is that just an excuse for you not to act like a decent human being?'

'I don't hire women for my pleasure for a night

because I'm a decent human being. I hire women so I don't have to be. So I can be as selfish as I want, understand? Inexperience means complications, and the whole point of hiring from Strangers is so I don't have to deal with fucking complications.'

He sounded angry now. I wasn't what he'd wanted in the first place, and now I suppose I'd become even less of a drawcard.

But that's you all over, right?

Yeah, it was. Since my dad had been all about my brother, my mom had tried to make me into her perfect little girl. But I didn't have her looks and I was awkward and shy. I hated being dragged out on shopping expeditions and lunches at fancy places. I hated going out for spa days and 'girl time.' I just wanted to stay at home and draw in my sketch pad.

But I tried, even though I knew I was a disappointment to her. I tried with my dad too, shyly showing him pictures I'd drawn, but he wasn't interested. He was only interested in my rapidly falling grades and why I didn't do something about them.

I was ten at the time, and had only just managed not to repeat the year. But only because Eli had helped me and I'd refused to give up, determined not to be even more of a disappointment than I already was.

I didn't have Eli to help me now, but I was still determined. And I don't know when this guy had become a stand-in for all the people who'd pushed me around over the years, but he had. I knew I shouldn't

care what people thought of me, and I'd put a lot of
time into showing how much I didn't care.

But right now, right here, for some reason I
wanted to prove him wrong. Prove that I wasn't a
fucking complication. That I wasn't the stupid, plain
dyslexic girl who could barely read, the skinny little
nobody whom no one noticed.

I wanted to be a beautiful, powerful, sexy woman.
I wanted to be like Maggie, whom everyone adored
and everyone wanted.

Do you really need this guy to prove that to you?

No, it had nothing to do with this guy. Or any guy,
in fact. I only wanted to be beautiful and powerful
and sexy to Eli.

Eli, whose rejection had hurt the most.

So, no, I wasn't leaving. And, if he really hadn't
wanted anything to do with my virginal self, he
would have turned round and walked out. But he
hadn't. He was still there, standing in front of me.

Which meant the ball was in my court.

I suddenly pushed myself up from the chair so
that I was in front of him.

His breath caught. I heard it in the sudden, deep
silence.

So I had his attention, did I? Good.

'I'm not a fucking complication,' I said.

And, before I could think better of it, I pushed the
straps of my dress off my shoulders and let it slide
down my body to pool down around my feet. Then
I stepped out of it and kicked it away.

He made no sound whatsoever.

The cool air of the room moved over my bare skin, raising goose bumps, though it wasn't only the cool air causing them. I'd never been naked in front of a guy before, still less when I was blindfolded and couldn't see him.

It was probably a dumb move—it wasn't as if I'd been blessed with a lot of curves or sexiness—but stubborn anger was burning like a little fire inside me, making me brave.

He wanted me, I knew he did, so let him look. Let him see that I was determined, that I didn't need coaxing, patience, gentleness or anything else.

I'd be what he wanted me to be, and I'd be so good he wouldn't even think of what he could have had with Maggie. I'd be so good, he'd wish he could have me every goddamned night.

'Shall I get on my knees?' I demanded into the silence, pleased that my voice sounded steady as a rock. 'Would you like me to beg now?'

He was very quiet. I couldn't even hear his breathing. But I felt the prickle of his attention flickering over my skin like sparks of white lightning.

I wasn't nervous. I was angry and shivering with a kind of heated excitement. I had his attention. His complete and utter attention.

'Well? I can suck your dick or—'

'Be still.' The words were even harsher and more gravelly than before. 'Don't say a goddamn word.'

Tension seethed in the air and I fell silent, satisfaction filling me. I'd surprised him, hadn't I? And it was about time.

My breathing was audible, the rush of it filling the space around us, though it was a little difficult to hear through the hammering of my heartbeat in my head.

Then I felt something brush against my shoulder, making my breath catch sharply and everything in me go still. A touch, very gentle and light, almost insubstantial, drifted over my shoulder and down the front of my chest like warm rain on my skin.

I trembled, the air vanishing from my lungs, my pulse going into overdrive.

He was touching me. He was touching me and I couldn't breathe.

His fingers moved over the curve of my right breast and then down between, but not touching anything too sensitive, merely following the line of the falling stars where they lay scattered across my stomach to my right hip. Touching each one. And then the petals of the rose on my left shoulder.

Roses and stars. Pretty and bright. Thorns and sharp edges. The things that made me.

He was Midas, yet instead of turning me to insensitive metal it felt as if he was waking me up. Everywhere he touched was coming alive, awake and aware.

'You like stars.'

His voice had dropped into a sexy, gravelly purr, and for a second, mesmerised by the sound of it and the lightness of his touch, all I could do was stand there, my thoughts flailing.

'And flowers.'

Then I processed what he'd said and I could feel myself blush yet again.

Eli and his deep, warm voice, giving me comfort after Dad had yelled at me for my grades yet again. The same day my mom had got frustrated with my lack of enthusiasm over a planned haircut. It had been Traj's graduation, so she'd wanted me to look nice, while the success of my brother had obviously made my dad more aware of his daughter's lack of it.

Such little things. Small, really. But no one liked to be called lazy or have accusations of not trying thrown at them. Especially when they'd been trying so hard.

Eli had told me not to pay any attention to either Mom or Dad. That I wasn't lazy. That one day I'd show them all. That I was a star who'd one day show the world my brightness, and that I was also a rose who'd stun everyone with my petals…

'Yes,' I said, my voice husky, caught off-guard by the observation. 'Someone I knew…' I stopped. I'd told no one about the reason for my tattoos. That was private.

His hand fell away and for a second there was nothing but silence and the air moving over my sensitive skin. Then came the briefest of touches at my throat where the star necklace Eli had given me sat. I never took it off.

'Did he give you this?' The rough edge in his voice scraped over me, a note I couldn't interpret lurking beneath it.

I frowned behind the blindfold, that familiar note setting off echoes inside me, making me try to catch them. But they slipped from my grasp, flickering away.

Why did he want to know about my necklace? And what…? Wait a second. *He…?*

'I didn't say that someone was a he,' I said.

There was a thick, seething pause.

'A boyfriend, I assumed.' His voice sounded even rougher than it had before. 'No one else would give you a necklace like this.'

It sounded good. Almost convincing. But it didn't convince me. He knew who'd given me that necklace, which meant he knew me.

I forgot I was standing there naked in front of him. Forgot that I was supposed to do whatever he said. That I was going to give him the best damn night he'd ever had.

I forgot everything but him, every ounce of awareness I had concentrating on him. On his presence in front of me, on the warm, light touch of his hand. On the sexy, spicy scent of his aftershave that reminded me of someone I knew. On the rough scrape of his voice and, yet again, that note of familiarity.

Yes, I knew him. He was someone I'd been close to. Someone I liked, very, very much…

It was right there. Right…*there*…

The knowledge came slowly, like the sun rising.

An intimation at first, then getting stronger, more certain. I didn't know how, why or when, but I was certain of one thing: there was only one person in the entire world this man could be.

Eli. He was Eli.

It felt as if I'd put the last piece of a jigsaw in place and I could finally see the whole picture. And it sent the most intense wave of reaction through me, a complex current of emotion I had no hope of untangling.

Shock. Joy. Anger. Curiosity. Desire. Hunger.

Relief. Sheer, bone-melting relief.

Somehow, this man wasn't a stranger to me and, more, he was someone I loved.

I loved Eli Hart. And after nine years of silence he was standing right here in front of me.

Tears flooded my eyes and I nearly ripped the blindfold off my face, desperate to see him.

But something held me back.

He hadn't told me who he was, even though he must recognise me. Why was that? And why was he here? What was he doing buying a night with a woman from an escort agency? Why had he been silent for so many years? Why had he basically ignored me for so long?

No. I had so many questions, but the only one that mattered right now was why didn't he want me to know who he was? He'd told me that I didn't know him and he'd been most emphatic. He hadn't wanted me to tell him that he was familiar. Hadn't wanted to tell me what he looked like.

Yeah, he really did *not* want me to know.

'You're shaking.' His voice moved through me again but this time I heard it differently, remembering the rich, deep tones of it from years ago. They were still there, buried like gold beneath a layer of gravel and sand. But…what had happened to his voice?

'Nervous, I guess,' I said hoarsely.

I couldn't tell him I knew. That was obvious. Because there was no telling what he would do. He might leave and, if I hadn't wanted him to before, I was now desperate for him not to.

Eli Hart had always been my greatest fantasy and I'd never thought I'd have him. I'd literally *saved* myself for him. Yet for him I'd always been Traj's little sister…

Until now. *Now* it was different.

I tried not to shake, but it was next to impossible. And not because I was scared, but because the reality of the moment was tumbling in on me and I could hardly believe it was actually happening.

My fantasy had come to life and was real. So very real.

I stared through my blindfold, fighting to control my breathing, imagining him as I'd last seen him. Six-three with wide shoulders and a broad chest. Shaggy, surfer-blond hair. Mesmerising hazel eyes, caught on the cusp between golden-brown and emerald-green. A smile that could light up a room and render every person in it his slave…

'Tell me what you want me to do,' I said.

CHAPTER EIGHT

Elias

MY HEART WAS beating like a fucking drum, my cock pressing hard against the zipper of my pants.

Vesta Howard-Smith, the girl I'd always thought of as a kid sister, was standing naked right in front of me and it was very, very obvious that she was not a girl any longer.

And she was asking me what I wanted her to do…

Jesus Christ.

'Just stand there,' I managed to force out. 'Let me look at you.'

Because I wanted to. She was so fucking beautiful. I'd had no idea. And, because I'd been so damn mesmerised, I'd almost given myself away about the necklace.

Stupid. Luckily she hadn't seemed to make any connections due to my slip-up, which was just as well. What the hell would she think if she knew who was standing there, looking at her naked?

She'd be angry. Very, very angry. And not only

because I'd cut her out of my life so very definitely over the years, but also because now keeping who I was a secret from her was a shitty thing to do. There would be questions and recriminations. Complications. I would have to explain myself, tell her why I hadn't answered any of her emails, texts and calls. I would have to show her my scars, tell her who I was now.

I would have to tell her that the man she'd once looked up to was dead.

I suppose I really should have tried harder to get her to leave, or have been firmer with myself and walked out.

And, now I'd seen her naked, walking out was going to be…impossible.

She was my past standing before me. I'd once been fast, powerful and handsome as sin, with a bright and glittering future stretching before me. With a father who'd been proud of me and what I'd achieved and a mother who'd worshipped the ground I walked on.

Back when Vee thought I was a god.

Oh, I wanted those feelings again, just for a night. And she could give it to me.

Of course, she might turn it into a complication, making me long for the past instead of putting it behind me the way I'd always done before. But that was too bad.

How can you do this to her? How can you pretend to be someone else? You know you meant something to her. She wouldn't have those stars and petals all over her body, or that necklace around her neck, if you didn't.

My chest felt tight, doubt gripping me, but I ignored it.

If I walked out now without explanation, it would only hurt her. Telling her who I was would do the same thing. And, yes, staying here and taking her anyway was selfish, but I didn't care. I'd earned the right to be a little bit fucking selfish.

So I pushed the doubt away and concentrated on her instead. Staring at her short, spiky black hair and the blue tips of it. At her pale, creamy skin and the fall of stars and petals scattered down her chest, a couple sprinkled over those perfect little round breasts and hard, pink nipples, falling down over her stomach to her left hip.

'You're a star, Vee,' I'd told her, pulling the trite, crap saying out of somewhere, because I'd been full of trite sayings back then, thinking I knew everything there was to know about everything. 'And you're a gorgeous rose. Don't let them crush your chance to shine and to bloom.'

And she'd taken that bullshit to heart, hadn't she? She'd tattooed that onto her skin.

She cocked her head slightly, as if listening. 'Are you done? Or did I kill the mood?'

Her voice sounded shaky, though, and she was still trembling. Was she afraid?

'No.' I wasn't sounding so steady myself, arousal pumping hard in my veins. 'Are you still nervous?'

'A bit.'

'Tell me if it's too much, okay?'

She didn't speak, only nodded.

Good. I needed to pull myself the fuck together and stop thinking about those stars and petals. Get my head back in the game. Treat her the way I treated all the rest. I didn't want to do anything that might prompt her to ask any more questions about me.

'Sit down,' I ordered.

She stayed where she was for a second, then slowly backed up to the chair and sat down on it. Her head tipped back as she looked up at me, her pulse racing in the hollow of her throat, that star glittering in her throat. And I could picture her midnight eyes behind that blindfold, pupils dilated…

'You sure you want this?' I asked to be certain. 'It won't work if you don't want it.'

'I want it.' There was no hesitation in her voice, none at all. 'I want you.'

I felt that ripple through me, so fucking sweet. It was always sweet when they wanted me but somehow, right now with her, it was even sweeter.

She'd been too young for me back then and way too innocent. I'd been far more interested in the beautiful girls who'd flung themselves at me half-naked and pouting, with big hair and lots of make-up, than in shy, gangly teenagers with stars in their eyes.

Shit, she was too young and innocent for me

now, despite her tattoos and punk rock hair. But she wanted me…

It's not you.

Oh, I knew that. But that didn't matter. I'd take what I could get.

I reached down and laid a finger across that sweet pouty mouth, just because I could. Because I wanted to.

Her breath caught.

'Don't talk,' I said. 'No questions, no arguments. No protests. You do what I say when I say it. Nod if you agree.'

She nodded.

I took my finger away and then, bending my head, I covered her mouth with mine.

The rush of her indrawn breath was loud and she went utterly still. Her mouth was soft and warm. I'd intended the merest brush of my lips against hers, but the heat of her swept through me like light through a dark room. And, before I knew what I was doing, I'd thrust my fingers in her hair, gripping onto the short, silky strands, easing her head back as I coaxed her to open for me with my tongue.

For a second she remained rigid in my hold, as if she hadn't yet made up her mind whether she wanted to or not. Then a little moan escaped her, her mouth opened under mine and all her heat rushed into me.

I didn't have a lot of feeling in my torso, not with all the scar tissue, so I used my mouth instead, and I liked to spend a lot of time kissing. Not for the intimacy of it, but for the sensation. For the heat and the taste. For the softness.

And she was all of those things. All of those things and more. Hot. Sweet. Rich. Like a chocolate fudge sundae. She might be spiky on the outside, and challenging and tart, but inside she was all melted sugar and warm honey.

I pushed my tongue deeper into her mouth, tilting her head back so I had better access, exploring her and taking my time about it, my free hand gripping her jaw, holding her still as I ravaged her mouth, tasting her as deeply as I could, then nipping at the full curve of her bottom lip.

She tried to kiss me back, a moan vibrating in her throat, and I let her, loving how her tongue made shy forays into my mouth, tasting me as I was tasting her.

God, if I'd known she'd taste this good, I wouldn't have let myself get distracted by cheerleaders, that was for fucking sure.

I wanted to keep going, but I needed to be careful. She already thought I was familiar to her in some way, and I couldn't risk lingering too close when that was already an issue.

I pulled back, keeping a hold on her as she tried to follow me.

Her cheeks were deeply flushed, her mouth red and glossy. The tips of her breasts were very hard and rosy, and I could smell the scent of feminine musk beneath the sweet smell of her candy-floss body wash.

Were those big, blue eyes of hers wide behind that blindfold? Were her pupils dilated? If I were to pull it away, would she be shocked to see that it was me all along who'd been kissing her? Would she get angry? Or would she pull me down for another kiss?

No, I couldn't let myself think that. I couldn't let her see who I was. The thought excited me, though, which was fucked up in the extreme considering the whole wrongness of it.

I straightened, trying to get my own breathing under control. 'Sit back in the chair.'

She eased herself back obediently.

I reached down, cupping the back of her sleek left calf, then lifted it up and out, gently hooking her leg over the arm of the chair.

She stiffened and gave a gasp, her hands pushing down on the seat beneath her as if she wanted to get up.

But I didn't stop, reaching for her other leg and doing the same to that one so they were both hooked over the arms of the chair, spreading her thighs wide apart, leaving every part of her exposed and open to my gaze.

Her breathing was audible, a panting sound, and she was still sitting there stiffly. She didn't move.

I straightened, the ache behind my zipper getting even worse as I looked at her.

She was so pretty with that little nest of black curls exposed, her flesh pink and slick and all for me.

Tension had gathered in her. I could see it in the

way her arms were pressing down on the seat cushions and in the slight hunch of her shoulders. Her thighs trembled slightly.

'Uncomfortable?' I asked, allowing myself a long, leisurely survey of her beautiful body.

'No.' She'd relaxed back against the chair, her breasts rising and falling, fast and hard. 'I'm just fine.'

'You're not fine.' I studied how soft and vulnerable her mouth had become, and how down between her slender thighs she was all wet. 'You're turned on. I think you like being looked at, don't you?'

'Yes. I like you looking at me very much.' Her hands lifted to her thighs, stroking down them in a caressing motion. 'Would you like me to do… something for you?'

A thrill arrowed down my spine at how eager and responsive she was. God, I'd barely had to do anything and already she was ready to please.

Why is that, do you think? When she was so uncomfortable before?

But that was something I didn't want to think about too hard, so I didn't. She wasn't uncomfortable now, that was the main thing. She was flushed everywhere, and that pretty little pussy was wet. Her nipples were hard.

She was aroused, and obviously so.

'All right,' I murmured. 'Remember that example I talked about? Where you were supposed to get naked and touch yourself?'

'Oh...yes...'

'Then I think you know what to do.'

I didn't know what I expected. Maybe for her to distract me again with another question, or somehow derail things. I'd told her earlier what I'd wanted. Would she remember? And, more importantly, would she do it?

But that determined chin told its own story. Of course she would.

I remembered Vesta as a kid, when I'd helped her with her homework, and recalled her determination not to let her dyslexia put her at a disadvantage. Pushing and pushing and pushing. Crying at how tiring it was for her to work out even a simple sentence, and yet not stopping. Even then she'd been such a stubborn thing.

She leaned her head against the back of the chair and her mouth curled. 'Then prepare to have your mind blown, ace.'

CHAPTER NINE

Vesta

MY HEART WAS beating so hard I thought it might come out of my chest. Shivers chased themselves all over my skin, and I was intensely aware of the smooth leather of the chair beneath me, now warm from my body. Warm at my back too. Aware, also, of the stretch of my inner thighs, the arms of the chair holding them wide.

I ached, burned. The dragging, heavy pressure between my thighs, deep in my sex, was getting worse by the second.

But most of all I was aware of him, standing in front of my chair. *Him.* The man I'd been helplessly in love with for half my life.

The tangled mess of feelings in my chest hadn't untangled themselves yet, but right now the main emotion I'd chosen to go with was joy. Utter joy in the moment. That he was here with me. And that he'd kissed me. And it was as amazing as I'd always fantasised it would be.

I could still feel his mouth on mine. Still feel the imprint of his lips, warm, firm and effortlessly masterful. Could still taste him, mint and dark chocolate, so delicious. Like I'd imagined but better, so much better.

Gorgeous Eli, whom I'd never forgotten, no matter how many times I'd tried.

And I'd figured out why he'd sounded angry earlier, why he'd wanted to send me away. He was trying to protect me because he'd always been protective like that, making sure I was okay, so seeing me here must have been a huge shock.

But he hadn't told me who he was, not when he'd arrived in the room and not as we'd talked. And he hadn't told me when I'd argued about leaving or when I'd taken my clothes off. He'd stayed silent. Even when he'd held my hand down on his zipper...

Which could only mean one thing: Eli Hart wanted me.

A full body shiver coursed through me, my thoughts tumbling around in my head.

Finally, after so many years, Eli Hart wanted me. *Me.* Not a cheerleader or a football groupie. Not someone beautiful or curvaceous. Not one of those bright, glittering women he'd always seemed to prefer. Not much of anything at all.

Just me. Shy and awkward and plain Vesta the virgin.

I could barely breathe, intense excitement filling me, my most treasured fantasy happening right here in this room. It was not some faceless man helping me put down Eli's ghost, blindfolded so I could impose Eli's face over his, but Eli himself. The actual man.

Eli, wanting me. Eli, desperate to have me.

Me. After so many years of me wanting him.

I focused on him standing in front of my chair, focused on him to the exclusion of everything else. He was so clear in my memory, the Eli I'd completely fallen for. Broad shoulders, wide chest and lean hips. Blond hair and the perfect, masculine beauty of his face. High cheekbones and forehead, straight nose, a beautiful mouth that curled at the corners in his flat-out beautiful, easy smile. Then his eyes, golden-brown and emerald-green, fringed with dark gold lashes. Warm and full of amusement.

He was breath-taking and no wonder his future in the NFL had always seemed so certain. He played like a god and his face was pure endorsement material. He was on his way to being king. At least, that was how everyone else saw him.

But I saw the only person who'd ever noticed me. Who'd ever thought I was something special. Who'd told me that I wasn't stupid, that I was a star. A rose. That I was smart and talented, and that I could be whoever I wanted to be.

My chest was tight with emotion, a thousand questions in my head. But it wasn't the time for questions, and the demands of my body were getting to be too much to ignore. He was there, right there, and

I could feel the pressure of his gaze. It was as intent as a predator watching prey, and now I was his prey. He was so hungry for me...

I'd never done this before in front of someone, much less him. There might have been a few fantasies or two back when I'd been younger—him accidentally walking into my bedroom while I was touching myself—but I'd never thought those fantasies would become reality. Never imagined it actually happening.

Now it was. And, really, I thought I'd be much more nervous, worried about disappointing him. Worried that I wouldn't be enough in some way, not as pretty, as experienced or as sexy as those other girls.

But I wasn't nervous. I had his full attention and I knew he was here for me. And he wanted me. I'd felt the evidence of that want and, besides, he'd told me what to do himself, hadn't he? All I had to do was that.

I ran my hands down my thighs, quivering slightly at the touch of my own fingers on my skin. I imagined they were his hands, his fingers lightly stroking. His perfect features would be set in hard lines of hunger and his eyes would be glittering with desire. He wouldn't be able to tear his gaze away.

I stroked down between my thighs, finding slick flesh, making pleasure curl through me. A soft sound escaped and I shuddered as I found my achingly sensitive clit, teasing it gently. The pleasure increased, becoming sharp as I circled it with the tip of one finger, my thighs trembling.

I imagined it was Eli's hand. Eli going down on his knees in front of my chair, watching as he touched me, the focus of his complete and utter attention.

He was silent. I couldn't even hear his breathing. But I knew he was looking. I could feel him watching. Were his eyes golden with heat? Was he desperate to touch me? Was he still hard and aching? Or was this little show I was putting on for him leaving him cold?

A sliver of doubt wound through me, cutting through the heat. Perhaps this wasn't sexy for him after all. Perhaps this was like reading and maths and I wasn't doing it right. Perhaps I was making a fool of myself after all.

My hand faltered, the wonderful, warm pleasure beginning to slide away.

'Did I say you could stop?' His voice sounded vaguely shocking, rasping and rough. 'You can answer me.'

'No,' I said huskily.

'Then why did you?'

'I…' I didn't want to tell him the truth. I didn't want to reveal myself so completely. Then again, I was naked. How much more revealing could I get? Plus, there was something freeing about him thinking I didn't know who he was. Anonymity without actually being anonymous.

This night wouldn't come again and when it was over we'd leave with him believing I thought he was a stranger and me getting to have him as my ultimate fantasy. He'd go back to his company, doing whatever it was he did, and I'd get on with expanding my tattoo business. And, if there was a time when we met again, we'd never speak of this. We'd both pretend it had never happened.

Really, what would I lose if I told him the truth? Nothing.

'Well?' The word was a whip-crack, making my breath catch.

'I couldn't hear you,' I said hesitantly. 'And I didn't know if you liked what I was doing. I thought you might not find it sexy or I might be…doing it wrong or…' I trailed off, cringing inside at how pathetic it sounded.

He didn't speak, the silence gathering thick and hot.

Then he said, 'It isn't possible for a woman stroking herself to orgasm to *not* be either erotic or sexy, understand me? And I know—I've had a lot of women. And how can you do it wrong? The only way for it to be wrong is if you don't get any pleasure out of it.'

A tight sensation I hadn't realised was there eased in my chest somehow. Stupid to care so much, but there was nothing I could do about it. I'd always cared about what Eli thought of me. Always.

'I…I know,' I said huskily. 'But I…'

'Did you enjoy what you were doing? It certainly seemed as if you were.'

'Yes,' I admitted.

'Then what does it matter if I find you sexy? The important thing is whether or not you got pleasure out of it.'

How could I tell him that it mattered because *he* mattered? I couldn't, of course, not without revealing that I knew who he was.

'I just…want to be beautiful. I want to be sexy. I want…' I stopped, breathing fast, staring into the darkness of the blindfold. 'I want you to be turned on by me. I want you to be desperate for me.'

'Why? You really value the opinion of a complete and utter fucking stranger?'

'You're the only man who's ever made me feel this way.' In this I was able to tell him the complete truth. 'Of course your opinion matters.'

'Me?' His voice had deepened, impossibly so. 'There must have been other—'

'No.' My turn to interrupt now. 'There hasn't.'

'What the fuck makes me so special?' He sounded almost…angry. 'You don't even know me.'

The tension that had been there before, the cold sliver of doubt, was sliding away, though I wasn't sure why. Maybe because of his anger. People were only ever angry about stuff that was important to them, and if he was angry about being special to me then it meant that he cared about it. That, for whatever reason, it mattered to him.

For the first time I wanted to push up my blind-fold and see his face, look into his eyes. Try to understand what was going on here, because something was. I was sure of it.

But I didn't.

'I don't know why you're special,' I lied. But I didn't lie about the next part. The next part was absolute truth. 'I just know I haven't felt this way about any other man before. Not once.'

He was silent, but this time I could feel frustration and anger seething in the air around me. And something else too: hunger.

The silence lengthened, deepened. And once again I became aware of the way I was sitting with my thighs spread, the dragging ache between my legs becoming acute.

'Keep going,' he said at last, roughly. 'And think only of what I told you to do, nothing else. I want that hand on your pussy. I want to see you getting hot and wet. I want to see you desperate to come. And I do not, under any circumstances, want to see you stop. Tell me that you understand.'

It was obvious to me, now I was paying attention to his voice, that there was a thickened heat in it, melted honey coating all that gravel. And that, even more than what he'd said, made the doubt slip away entirely.

He was turned on. He really was.

I moved my hands, gently easing one finger inside me, then another. I was so wet there wasn't any resistance, and I gasped softly at the wave of pleasure that swamped me at the feeling. My hips shifted on the seat, rocking gently as I slid my fingers in and out slowly, before getting a little faster.

'Good girl,' he murmured. 'That's what I like to see.'

God, it felt so good, knowing he was watching. That he was staring at me. It made everything feel amazing.

My eyes squeezed closed even tighter and I increased the pressure, pleasure sweeping through me and moving out, an unstoppable wave. I was slick and hot now and the cool air on my skin only intensified the sensation.

Eli, I whispered in my head. *Oh, my God, Eli...*

My toes were curling in my sandals, the orgasm bearing down on me. I bucked my hips, my fingers pressing harder.

And then suddenly a hot, strong grip clamped around my wrists and my hands were pulled away. 'No,' I gasped, my body trembling, unsatisfied and aching almost to the point of pain.

But he was too strong.

He transferred both of my wrists into one powerful hand, holding them down on the arm of the chair next to my thigh. And I felt the brush of his fingers on my inner thigh.

Oh, my God. He was going to touch me. Eli was going to touch me, and I knew if he did I was going to come apart.

'Oh, yes,' I groaned aloud, unable to help myself. 'Please…'

He didn't speak, his touch light as it stroked down my inner thigh, tracing my slick flesh. There was pressure on my clit, and I thought I would come straight away, but I didn't. He knew how to touch me without sending me over the edge, damn him.

I lifted my hips, pressing against that pressure.

'More,' I murmured. 'More. I need…more.'

'You're thinking of someone, aren't you?' His rough voice was close, his breath on my throat. He must have been leaning over me, watching my face even as one of his hands played between my legs, the other holding my wrists fast. 'Tell me who.'

CHAPTER TEN

Elias

THERE WAS PERSPIRATION on her forehead above the blindfold, tiny strands of black hair plastered to her skin and perspiration on her upper lip and throat too. The most beautiful flush extended from her face, down her throat and ran over her chest, heating up all those stars scattered across her.

The scent of her arousal was heavy in the air, a sweet musk that had my heart pounding and the blood in my veins rushing. I desperately wanted to bury my face between those pretty thighs and taste her, make her jerk and writhe, make her beg in that gorgeous, husky voice.

I'd had no conception of just how sexy I would find her when she'd walked in. Of just how badly I would end up wanting her.

Of how much difference it would make to be with a woman I knew, rather than the blindfolded strangers I preferred to use.

Oh, she didn't know me, but I knew her. And

when she said she wanted me I knew it wasn't an act. She hadn't said it because that was what I wanted to hear or because she was hoping for a tip. That was the problem with profiles and the women I hired. They provided a service and they wanted tips. They could see my profile, they knew what I liked, and they acted accordingly. They never faked their orgasms, of course, and I could tell by their physical reactions that they genuinely enjoyed what I did to them.

But I knew that behind their blindfolds they were thinking of someone else. Fantasising about someone else. It wasn't me that that they wanted, not really. I'd always thought that didn't matter. That as long as they said the words I didn't care. I didn't particularly want them, either, so why would they want me? We were both getting something out of it, but not together, which was the way I wanted it.

No complications. No messy emotions.

Yet it was different with Vee. When she'd stopped touching herself and told me that she wanted me to find her sexy, that my opinion of her mattered and that she wanted me, I hadn't been able to shake the feeling that this time it *was* actually me that she wanted.

No other man had made her feel this way, she'd said, which I'd thought was impossible. She was so sexy and interesting that surely there had to have been at least one? What about the one she'd come here to forget? But she hadn't mentioned him. No, it was me that made her feel that way. Me that had made her take her clothes off and touch herself in front of a stranger.

I couldn't think what I'd done to make her feel that way about me, but the fact remained that I'd done something. And that her little confession had made me even harder than I already was.

She wasn't lying, either, or at least not about getting aroused—not when her pussy was so slick and wet and so hot she just about burned my fingers.

Was it me, though? Or was she thinking of someone else? Was she fantasising about some other guy touching her the way all the rest of the women I bought did?

It shouldn't have mattered. I didn't want to be fucking special. But I couldn't shake the hungry, possessive feeling in my gut. The one that liked being the only man who'd made her feel like this.

I'd never thought of myself as a possessive kind of guy—I didn't let myself feel strongly enough about anything to be possessive—but I was feeling pretty fucking possessive now.

She's always been yours, though. Hasn't she?

I ignored that thought. She was no one's but her own, still less mine.

All the same, she was fantasising about someone, and I wanted to know who it was for reasons I couldn't have explained.

Her lower lip was red and slick from her teeth worrying it, her breath rushing in and out. And her body moved restlessly on the chair, her hips lifting insistently against my hand. But I kept my thumb pressed to her clit, providing her with just enough sensation to keep her on the brink yet without friction to push her over.

I could keep a woman on that fine line for as long as I chose, making sure it remained pleasure and not pain—or at least, not unless she wanted it to become pain—drawing out that pleasure for as long as possible.

'You,' she panted. 'I'm thinking about you.'

No, that couldn't be right. They never thought about me. I was sure of it. Not that I cared. They could think of anyone they fucking wanted as long as they were enjoying it.

Yet the way she'd said it…

'You're lying.' I kept my grip tight around her wrists, holding them down on the arm of the chair as I feathered the fingertips of my free hand down one thigh. Her skin was smooth, very warm and silky. Christ, I'd always loved touching a woman.

She writhed on the chair and it was the sexiest thing I'd ever seen in my entire life. How could she think that she wasn't beautiful? That she would somehow touch herself wrongly? I couldn't understand it.

Then again, Vee hadn't had many people in her life who'd seen what a talented person she was. How gifted she was when it came to art, and how perceptive when it came to other people. She'd only ever had people tell her what she was doing wrong, that she'd never measure up. Either that or they'd ignored her completely.

It made the sympathy that sometimes stirred inside me stir again, creaky and rusty with disuse like an old gate that nobody opened.

'I'm not lying.' Her hips twisted, following my hand. 'I'm thinking of you watching me. Touching me.'

'You can think about any guy doing that.' I had no idea why I was pushing this. What did it matter what guy she thought of? 'It doesn't have to be me.'

'I know that.' Her back arched as I varied the pressure on her clit just the tiniest bit. 'But…it just…is you.'

'You don't even know what I look like.'

'That doesn't matter, though. Isn't that what you said?' She let out a shaken breath, her cheeks bright red now. 'Please, ace… I want…'

'I know what you want, but a "please" isn't going to cut it.' I leaned down, closer now, inhaling her scent, warm and musky and so fucking erotic.

The blindfold was inches away and I could imagine those deep, midnight-blue eyes staring at me from behind it. Christ, if she only knew who had their finger on her clit, who was leaning over her like this, torturing her…

For some reason that made it even more intense, even more arousing. Which was wrong, but right now I didn't care.

'Why me, little girl?' I asked softly. 'What about me has got you so fucking hot?'

She was shivering, her whole body trembling as I held her on the edge. 'Your…your voice is so s-sexy. It's all rough and deep and it's like I can… feel it in my chest.' She took a panting breath. 'And you smell so good. Your aftershave makes me want to press my face against your neck and breathe you in. But it's not just your a-aftershave. There's something more… You smell like someone reassuring and I l-like it.'

My voice? She like my fucking ruined voice? And my aftershave? I'd had that comment before and, yeah, it was expensive, which was why it smelled good. But reassuring? No one else had said that to me. No one.

A strange feeling settled inside me, one I didn't recognise.

'And you're p-protective,' she went on. 'You got angry when I wanted to stay and you tried to send me away. You didn't want me putting myself at risk.'

It was true. But I'd also done it to protect myself.

I didn't know what to say to that. I hadn't had a clear vision of myself since losing everything I'd had. My health, my looks, my family, my entire fucking future. Every second since then I'd been taking it a moment at a time, building each minute on each minute until it become an hour. And the hours became days, the days months, and so on. Until I'd built a new future for myself. A future that was all about me and what I wanted, not one based on other people's expectations.

These days I was no one's meal ticket but my own.

But, in spite of the blindfold, Vee had seen me anyway. The ghost of the man I'd once been. Perceptive woman.

Sadly for her, I wasn't that man any longer.

My cock ached and she was so fucking beautiful. So fucking sexy.

I didn't want to talk about this any more. I'd lost my taste for it. Instead all I wanted was to immerse myself in her scent and her taste and her heat. To be blind to everything else but sensation, the way she was.

So I let her go and pushed myself away from her.

She was still for a second, breathing fast and hard. 'Ace? You're…not going to leave me like this are you?'

I dropped to my knees in front of the chair, the desperate note in her voice like the most pure aphrodisiac. 'No,' I said roughly.

She sat in front of me, legs hooked over the arms of the chair, her thighs spread wide. Her pussy was pink and slick and glistening in the spotlight overhead.

Little Vee was not so little any more. She was all woman and I wanted a taste.

I slid my hands beneath the luscious curves of her ass, lifting her slightly, loving how she shuddered. Then I leaned in, inhaling her scent before breathing out, and making sure she felt it.

Her whole body was trembling, as if she was standing on the edge of a cliff, caught on that fine balance between falling over it and stumbling back.

The most exquisite place to be.

'Put your hands on the arms of the chair,' I ordered, not taking my gaze from that sweet little tangle of black curls. 'And hold on. Do not, under any circumstances, touch me.'

'O-okay,' she stuttered, her voice raw. Her hands reached for the arms and held on, her knuckles white. I didn't move for a second, enjoying the agonising moments of anticipation, her quickened breathing, the fine tremble in her thighs.

I loved this part, where a woman waited for me, not knowing when I would touch her, taste her. Her awareness on nothing but me and what I would do. Because this gave them the most powerful orgasms. The ones they'd remember for months to come, after the night was over. They'd remember the stranger in a hotel room who had made them come harder than any man ever had or ever would.

The stranger who wasn't Elias Hart, scarred and broken but a hugely successful billionaire.

A faceless man. Nameless. A man who could be anyone and no one. A man with no past and no future. With no expectations but the ones he determined for himself.

In this moment, I could be whoever I wanted to be.

And this time, I chose to be the man who made

her come. I lowered my head and covered that pretty little pussy with my mouth.

She arched in the chair as if I'd electrocuted her, her whole body going stiff, a cry of agonised pleasure escaping her. The taste of her orgasm flooded my mouth, honey and salt mixed with a tartness that I hadn't expected.

Fucking delicious.

I kept my mouth there, unmoving as she writhed in my grip, panting and gasping, riding out the climax with her, my own cock straining the front of my pants.

But I was an expert at ignoring my physical reaction so I ignored it now as I knelt there, very still, letting her come to a trembling sort of quiet.

I gave her a minute to get her breath back.

Then I got to work.

CHAPTER ELEVEN

Vesta

THE FEEL OF his mouth on me was almost too much to bear. The aftershocks of the orgasm he'd just given me were still crashing around inside me and the touch of his tongue on my sensitive flesh was like an electric current applied directly to my skin.

He licked at me delicately, tracing the contours of my sex with his tongue, unhurried and slow, making the most intense pleasure spear through me as sharp as a knife.

There were stars behind my eyes, exploding with colour and sparking all over my skin, joining the fire he was building between my legs.

I could feel his hands cradling me, the warmth of his palms against my skin, the hard wood of the chair arms pressing into the undersides of my knees, the leather at my back…

He licked me, nipped me, tasted me, his breath hot on my bare skin.

I writhed, lifting my hips, panting. Ecstasy was

spiralling through me, building and building, layer upon layer. Not fast and hard, but slow and relentless, making a sob collect in my throat.

He knew exactly what he was doing. Knew exactly how to touch and to tantalise, to bring the pleasure to a peak without tipping me over. It was maddening. Exhilarating.

I'd always suspected it would be good with him, but I'd had no idea it would be so much better than good.

I groaned, my knuckles white on the arms of the chair as he effortlessly held me on that edge again, that wicked tongue of his exploring my flesh with a single-minded intensity that had me shivering all over.

He made me beg, sounds spilling out of me that I'd never heard before. Some friends had told me that they could take or leave oral sex; clearly that was because they'd never had Eli Hart work them over the way he was working me.

I'd had dreams about him, but they'd been vague and half formed. Of his touch and his mouth on mine. Wispy teenage thoughts that hadn't been too explicit and yet had been hot just the same. They hadn't been this explicit, this raw. His mouth on my sex, his tongue exploring me, teasing my clit, pushing inside, his teeth against my slick flesh.

Eli kneeling in front of the chair, holding me, worshipping me.

It was so good. Too much.

I screamed as it came to a head, jack-knifing in the chair as the orgasm rolled over me, pleasure echoing throughout my entire body. He gripped me hard, preventing me from moving, nuzzling at me as I rode out the incredible waves of pleasure.

And then he started again.

I felt a little bit broken, my voice hoarse and scraped raw. 'I can't…' I forced out hoarsely as that relentless tongue went back to work on me again. 'I can't.'

'Of course you can.' The abrasive sound of his voice rasped over me, and the heat in it eased all the rough edges. 'You're tenacious, remember?'

The words hit me weirdly. They sounded as if… well…he knew me. As if we knew each other. As if he remembered me being tenacious some time before, which of course he would. But he'd been busy pretending he was a stranger, that we didn't know each other.

It was a slip, and I was pretty sure he hadn't noticed it, as he didn't try to explain it or cover it up. Then again, given the attention he was paying to my clit, he probably wasn't thinking of that.

I wanted to ask him about it, push him, for reasons I couldn't have explained as I was sure him realising I knew who he was would end things.

But then he murmured, 'Good girl.' And then, when I shuddered in his hands yet again, he added, 'That's it. You're doing so well.' His voice had dropped into a low, gravelly purr that was somehow even more sexy, his fingers squeezing my ass. 'Once more for me. Once more.'

For him, I would do anything.

So I tried to hold out, to resist. Because it was clear he got off on me doing so. I almost moaned his name a dozen times, my teeth closing on my lip just to stop myself in time. I bit it bloody.

But I couldn't hold out. He was too good and he was the man I'd wanted for years and years. I couldn't have held out even if I'd done this before. And I hadn't…

He held me there so long that time ceased to have any meaning. I existed in a state of the most intense ecstasy, the build of it a constantly rising wave that never broke. I was lost to it, blind to anything else.

And then he did something with his tongue that made the wave not only break but detonate. I screamed again, rigid in the chair, my toes curling in my shoes, my nails digging into the wood of the chair, smashed into tiny pieces by the weight of the pleasure that crushed me.

Afterwards I floated there for a while, not wanting to move. I could hear my hoarse breathing, my heartbeat crashing around in my ears, and gradually the awareness of the outside world came back. His hands were moving, sliding to grab my hips, pulling me to the edge of the chair, and then suddenly the world lurched as he lifted me into his arms.

I shuddered against his hard chest, feeling the slight prickle of wool against my bare skin, and then the intense heat of his body. I'd had hugs from him before, years ago. I hadn't really got them from my parents, which had made Eli's so special. He'd been big, strong and so reassuring. I'd loved it when he hugged me.

And this was like that, only better. He was like a rock I could lean against all warm from the sun. A rock that wouldn't move, that I could hide behind when I got scared, that would shield me.

I rested my head against his shoulder, inhaling the warm scent of his wonderful aftershave. I could hear his heart beating, strong and steady and intensely reassuring.

Maybe I should have struggled, or protested or something, but I simply didn't have the energy. I just lay there quiet in his arms, happy to be there.

He took a couple of steps and then I felt him sit, still holding me. As I settled in his lap, I could feel the hard press of his cock against my ass, insistent. It made me shiver.

'Don't you want me to…uh…do something about that?' My voice was little more than a croak.

'No.' The word rumbled against my ear, impossibly deep. 'There's plenty of time for that. You need a bit of space to recover.'

Something warm settled around me and I realised he must have pulled a throw or a blanket from somewhere and put it over me.

I was so warm, snuggled in the blanket and resting against his body, and I just let the silence sit there for a time and let myself float.

I was here in a hotel room with Eli Hart. Who'd made me come three times in a row. Was this it? Was this the peak of my life? Was this as good as it got? If so, I really couldn't ask for better.

I was so relaxed I nearly asked him what he'd been doing for the past nine years, only at the last minute remembering I wasn't supposed to know who he was. My lip was a little sore from the way I'd bitten it before, but that didn't stop me from biting it again, making me wince.

And he must have noticed because his arms tightened fractionally. 'You okay?'

'Yeah. Sore lip.'

'Hmm.' That sexy rumble again. And then the gentlest pressure against my mouth, the lightest brush of his. 'You should have just screamed,' he murmured. 'No one would have heard.'

Yeah, that wasn't why I'd been biting my lip.

'Why do you do that?' I asked instead, trying to figure out how I could get the information I wanted out of him without letting on that I knew him. 'Draw out the orgasm, I mean. Is that what you do with women?'

'Anticipation makes it more intense.' His voice was a lazy rumble. 'And more pleasurable.'

'And that's what you like to do? Make it more intense?'

'Yes. Women don't expect to get pleasure from these interactions, but I make sure they do.'

I shifted against him, tilting my head back to look

up at him, even though I couldn't see him. He'd always had his arms full of those glittering women, the beautiful ones drawn by his beauty and his fame, and I'd heard the rumours that he was supposed to be a legend in bed. So why was he now paying for sex? And why the blindfold? Why didn't he want anyone to see him? Especially when all these contracts and NDAs were part of the encounter.

'Is that important to you?' I asked. 'That they get pleasure out of it?'

'Full of questions, aren't you?'

'Just a couple. You don't have to answer if you don't want to.'

There was a silence and then he let out a breath. 'I like making it intense and memorable for a woman. I like to give them something they didn't expect.'

Interesting.

'And the blindfold?'

'Ensures there are no expectations. If you can't see me, you don't know my name and you don't know what I look like. I could be anyone. All there is is the pleasure I give you.'

Even more interesting. There must have been so much pressure on him all those years ago. Everyone had thought he'd make it into the NFL draft, that his career in football was a sure thing. He'd mentioned to me a couple of times that his parents were counting on him to make it big, as they'd been struggling financially. His mom had cleaned our house and she'd always seemed nice. His dad had been a big, hulking figure, a bit grim. He hadn't smiled much.

Eli had always talked about his dad being the reason for his success. How he'd been there at every game, pushing him, making him do better. I'd never got the impression that his father had been encouraging, more one of those tennis dads or stage moms, pushing and pushing their kids to do more and more.

His dad must have had major expectations of him, that was for sure. What had happened after that game that had lost him his future? Did that have anything to do with him wanting no expectations now?

'What's the problem with expectations, then?' I asked, still a bit out of it from the after-effects of the orgasms he'd given me. 'Why don't you want anyone to know who you are?'

'Are you hungry?' He gave no sign that he'd heard my question.

'A little.' Actually, now that he mentioned it, I was starving.

'Wait here.'

He gently deposited me on the couch before moving away to somewhere else in the room. I heard the rattle of a trolley and the sound of plates being shifted around, and then the scent of hot food came drifting over.

He hadn't answered my questions and maybe that was just as well. I shouldn't be asking them. I mean, did I really want him to know that I knew who he was? That would mean having to deal with whatever reaction he had to it, and then his reaction to whatever questions I flung at him about why he'd blanked me for so long.

Did I want to hear the truth? Could I bear it? Or was it easier to stay silent? Certainly, right now it was easier to stay silent. About that, at least.

'Orgasms and food too, huh?' I said, drawing the throw more securely around me. 'No wonder they call you a black-star client.'

'The tips are not the only reason for my reputation.'

He sounded very smug and very male, and I couldn't help smiling. Of course, it wouldn't be just the tips, not with the oral skills he'd just demonstrated. And then there was the whole package that was Eli, which wouldn't just be about oral skills. He was rich nowadays—or so I'd heard. And he was beautiful too, though I guessed that wasn't a thing, because of the blindfold.

I could hear him approach again, and the sound of things being put down on a table close by. Then I felt him sit beside me, his hands settling on me as he drew me into his lap once again. It seemed that he liked holding me, which I was totally okay with.

I was totally okay with everything he was doing.

Except you kind of do want to ask questions. This might be the only night you have a chance to find out the answers.

It was true. I hadn't thought of that.

'Open your mouth,' he ordered quietly.

I blinked behind the blindfold. 'What?'

'Wine.'

A cool glass was pressed against my lips and automatically I opened them, the rich taste of a very good red flooding my mouth. It was delicious, so I swallowed it down obediently.

'You don't have to feed me,' I muttered after a second swallow. 'I can do that myself, believe it or not.'

'This isn't about what you want,' he said patiently. 'This is about what I want, and what I want is to feed you.' Then he went on before I could protest, 'And, before you ask, no, I'm not going to tell you why. I hope you like crackers and cheese.'

It was annoying that he wouldn't explain. Then again, hadn't I already decided that it was for the best if I didn't ask questions? Still, there was that nagging thought that this would be my only chance.

Only if you want to know.

I'd always kept my expectations low, both of myself and other people, mainly because other people were always disappointing. Or rather, I was always disappointing them in some way. I wasn't bright enough for my dad. Not pretty enough for my mom. Not interesting enough for my brother.

Basically the only person I hadn't disappointed in some way was Eli. Actually, now I thought about it, maybe he did have a point with the whole expectations thing. I could see how not knowing who someone was and vice versa meant no expectations could be placed on either of you, and you didn't have to expect anything.

Except I'd kind of cheated. I knew who he was and I'd had my expectations of what he would be like. Yet he'd blown every single one of them out of the water.

I wasn't sure where that left me or whether it changed anything or not, though I couldn't quite leave behind the sense of nagging curiosity.

Deciding simply to live in the moment for the meantime, I relaxed in his arms instead, something warm and yet also slightly bittersweet glowing behind my breastbone.

He fed me cheese and crackers, which I happened to love, along with strawberries and grapes, which I also loved. There was more red wine and then some delicious chocolate truffles, which I devoured.

And then, apparently, it was his turn for questions.

'So what makes a lovely young woman get naked in a hotel room with a stranger?' he asked as he pressed the glass to my mouth for another sip. 'Has to be more than simple validation or money.'

I swallowed the wine and licked my lips. 'There's nothing simple about validation.'

'True,' he conceded. 'So what is it, then?'

'I don't have to answer your questions if you're not going to answer mine.'

'Of course you don't. But I have answered some of yours.'

I wrinkled my nose. 'Is this a "you show me yours if I show you mine" kind of deal?'

'If you want another chocolate it is.'

The glow in my chest spread outward. That was the Eli I remembered, slightly teasing, amused and affectionate, and I could hear both amusement and affection in his voice now, as if he couldn't help himself.

'You said I was tenacious before,' I heard myself say before I could stop it. 'What did you mean by that?'

CHAPTER TWELVE

Elias

THAT WAS ONE question I hadn't expected to be asked. Had I really said that to her?

While you were on your knees eating her out, if you recall...

I did recall. Her soft ass filling my palms, the perfect, salty-sweet taste of her pussy filling my mouth. Her moans and cries. The way she'd shifted, restless, unable to keep still as I kept her at the peak. 'Please,' she'd said. 'Oh, please.' And I swore, if she'd known who I was, she would have said my name because it was me she wanted.

Me. Not whatever fantasy was playing in her head.

I'd forgotten myself. I'd forgotten I wasn't supposed to know who she was. I'd called her tenacious, because Vee always had been.

Fuck. She should have been out of her mind with pleasure, too blissed out even to take in what I'd said. Apparently not. Either I was losing my touch or she was far too sharp for her own good.

Sadly, when it came to Vesta, it was likely to be the latter.

I glanced down at her.

She sat in my lap, her head on my shoulder, relaxed and warm against me. The throw I'd put around her had slipped, baring one pale shoulder and an even paler round breast. She was delectable naked, all those sharp angles resolved into a womanly whole that went straight to my dick like alcohol to the brain on an empty stomach.

I'd have preferred it, obviously, if she'd answered my question about just what the fuck had driven her into this hotel room, but if I didn't answer this it might start to look suspicious. And, since she already thought I was familiar to her in some way, that might be asking for trouble.

So I kept my voice calm and didn't let on that she'd surprised me. 'You know what tenacious means, right?'

'Yeah, but you said "you're tenacious, remember?". Like you knew something about me.'

With an effort, I kept my muscles relaxed. 'I don't know anything about you. I was just telling you to be tenacious. No great mystery.'

It wasn't a great mystery as to what her expression would be behind that blindfold, either. Her forehead would be wrinkled up the way it did when she was concentrating on something, usually a line of text she was struggling to read. But she never gave up. She'd work at it until she understood it and could read it.

I bet she was staring at me like that right now behind the blindfold, trying to read me. Had I convinced her? She was sharp. Too sharp.

The temptation was there to keep talking, keep on justifying, fill the silence, but that would only sound as if I was trying to cover something up, so I stayed quiet.

Eventually she made a little settling motion. 'Well, okay then. You got it right, though—tenacious is my middle name.'

Was that relief? Maybe it was.

'Lucky guess,' I murmured. 'Are you going to answer my question?'

'About why I'm here?'

'Yes.'

'Hmm. Will I get a chocolate?'

She couldn't see me, but I smiled anyway. Because she was adorable. She'd been adorable as a kid, and as a teenager, and now she was an adult she was still adorable. And she fitted so nicely in my arms, as if she belonged there.

How weird to feel that way about her, when I never had before.

You don't even know her.

My gaze followed the angles of her face that weren't hidden by the blindfold—sharp and distinct. Arresting. Those eyes had been her best feature— or at least that was what I'd thought years ago—but they were hidden now, letting me see the rest of her, and I'd changed my mind.

She wasn't just arresting. She was fucking incredible. Pretty pointed chin, silky-smooth skin, elegant neck, slight but gorgeous curves. And that ink on her skin, interesting and purposeful, the design beautifully drawn. Definitely not something she'd got as a dare when she'd been drunk one night.

Pieces of me were on her skin. And then there was the necklace that glittered around her throat. The necklace I'd given her almost ten years ago and that she still wore. Another piece of me.

She still cares about you.

My heart shifted inside my chest, broken and bruised. A lump of fucking coal. She'd had almost ten years of mostly silence from me, yet she still wore that necklace. Had got herself tattooed with symbols of something I'd once said to her.

Why? She should have forgotten me by now, at least she should have. I'd made it pretty damn easy, after all. Yet…she was still carrying those pieces of me, even when I'd treated her like shit.

You asshole.

It was true. But that was who I was now. I didn't want to deal with anyone else's feelings, their desires or expectations. I'd carried all of those things for far too long and where had it got me? A fucking hospital bed, pain and years of recovery. I didn't want anyone to matter to me any more, so they didn't.

Still, for some reason I was responding to her, feeling guilty and also protective of her. Though maybe the latter was simply muscle memory, the protectiveness I'd always felt about her ever since she'd been a kid.

No, scratch that. There was something more to the protectiveness now, a certain curiosity. I knew nothing about what she'd been doing in the years since I'd decided to put my past behind me and reclaim the future that should have been mine. I'd been all about making my bank accounts grow, but what had she been doing? I hadn't asked Traj, and he hadn't told me, but suddenly I wanted to know.

'Yes, you'll get a chocolate,' I said. 'And maybe you'll get more if you answer other questions.'

'What? You want to talk now? I thought the whole point of the orders and blindfold was that you don't have to.'

'I changed my mind.' I reached forward and took a truffle from the plate that sat on the little table near the arm of the sofa. 'Come on. Tell me.'

'Okay, fine.' She shifted again, that rounded ass of hers pressing against my still-hard cock, reminding me that, while I might have ignored it so far, it was still hungry for what it wanted. 'Like I said before, the real reason I'm here is because of a man.'

She'd mentioned before that she was putting someone behind her, and I'd thought it must have been some guy, but I hadn't fully taken it in until now. And instantly I was conscious of a twist of emotion in my gut, as if a part of me didn't like that one bit. Which was ridiculous. What did I care if a man was the reason she was here? I hadn't had anything to do with Vesta Howard-Smith for nine years. I had no claim on her whatsoever and neither did I want one.

'What man?' I asked, as obviously I wasn't listening to my own common sense. 'Why?'

She shifted her head against my shoulder, the blindfold turned towards me as if she was looking right through it. 'A man I had a huge crush on a long time ago.' Her voice had got softer. 'A man I maybe loved. But he was…a lot older than me and he never saw me as anything more than a kid. I knew nothing would ever happen between us…but there's a reason I'm still a virgin and it's not because I never had the opportunity.' She sighed. 'It's more that I never wanted anyone else but him.'

Everything in me slowed and came to a complete stop. I could barely breathe, and she must have been able to feel it, because my muscles were suddenly rock-hard with tension.

A man I maybe loved…who never saw me as anything more than a kid…

No. No, it couldn't have been me she was talking about. It couldn't. There must have been other guys in her life, other men who'd only ever seen her as a kid. Better men.

Who else? You know there's only one guy she saw a lot of as a kid and that's you…

'He sounds like a fucking idiot.' I had to force my voice to work. 'Why would you want him?'

In contrast to my sudden rigidity, she'd relaxed. 'He wasn't a fucking idiot,' she protested gently. 'He was wonderful. I have dyslexia and I used to find schoolwork really hard. He used to help me. And he was so patient. He'd sit there beside me, helping me read, and didn't seem to mind sitting there for an hour while I struggled with a page of text.'

Her fingers fiddled with the edge of the throw. 'My family didn't understand the issues I had. My dad thought I was stupid and, since I wasn't pretty like my mom, she didn't have a use for me, either. My older brother was too busy trying to impress my dad, so he kind of ignored me, but this guy...'

Her mouth, soft and vulnerable, turned up in the most beautiful smile. 'He was the only one who ever saw me as something more than a stupid girl who couldn't even read, or an ugly duckling who'd never grow into a swan. Or an annoying little sister not worth paying attention to. He saw me in a way no one else ever did.' That smile held me captive, full of warmth, slightly wistful. 'But never in the one way I wished he would. He was my older brother's best friend and I guess I was always like a child to him. A kid sister, maybe.'

All this time she'd held on to me, even though I'd done my best to pry her loose, as I had with everyone else from that part of my life. So many years she'd thought of me, saved herself for me, while I'd given her nothing but silence.

The guilt hit me hard, along with regret and a fair amount of shame, and I could feel myself getting angry about it too. Because, shit, I hadn't asked her to carry a torch or save herself for me. I hadn't asked for her to care. I'd genuinely thought she'd get the message. Was it my fault that she hadn't?

Silence is not a message. And you knew the way she felt about you even back then. Come on.

Yeah, but she'd been sixteen at the time, still a kid, while I'd been twenty-two, my bed full of beautiful adult women ready to do whatever I wanted.

I still remembered the day I'd given her that necklace. Her mother had thrown her a special 'sweet sixteen' party that Vesta had told me afterwards she'd never wanted. She didn't have any close friends, and the kind of big, social party her mother had wanted for her had never been going to happen. Linda, her mom, had pleaded with me to be there, because then maybe some of Vesta's high school friends would turn up, and naturally enough they had, once they'd found out I would be attending.

Vesta had known they weren't coming for her. That it was me they'd all wanted to see. And yet she hadn't got resentful about it. She'd hovered at the back of the group when I'd arrived, letting all the people who'd turned up, who weren't her friends and never had been, push to the front to be the first to see me.

I'd been angry about it, starting to chafe at all the expectations that kept getting laid on me. Knowing that it wasn't really me that these kids wanted to see but the football superstar. The kid who'd made good and done his family proud. The vessel for everyone else's dreams but my own.

So I'd ignored all those other teenagers and headed straight for the one I'd gone there to see, making it very clear to everyone that it was her I'd come for. My gift to her was private, and I hadn't wanted them to see it, but I'd given it to her with all the rest looking on anyway, because it might have made her feel better.

Being accepted was everything to a sixteen-year-old, so I'd figured being the sole object of attention from someone like me would give her some cachet. She'd opened my present right there and then, the necklace gleaming against the black velvet. Real diamonds. But I'd known immediately that it wouldn't matter to her whether the diamonds were real or not. It was that I'd thought of her. That I'd seen her.

She was the real star, not me.

Her eyes had been full of something that at the time I hadn't wanted to acknowledge. Hero worship had turned to something older and more adult. But I'd ignored it. She'd been too young and far too innocent for the likes of me. And I'd been on my way to the top. Everything had gone to my head—the fame, gifts from sponsors and the girls—and all while the pressure from my dad had become heavier and heavier.

Then, after the fire, lying helpless and in agony in a hospital bed, the last thing I'd wanted was her sitting at my bedside looking at me with big, midnight-blue eyes—her hero fallen off his pedestal. Not so invincible or famous. No glittering future ahead of him. Poor and sad and scarred. Nothing special about me any more. Even my own father hadn't wanted to look at me after that.

I'd pushed her away. I'd pushed everyone away. And even now all these years later, every time one of her emails turned up in my inbox I hit 'delete' and made it go away.

'Yeah, he still sounds like an asshole,' I said hoarsely. 'You really waited for him after all this time?'

She lifted a shoulder. 'I never met anyone else I liked as much as I liked him. And I guess I'm a one-man woman. I thought, if I met with some stranger I didn't know and couldn't see, at least I could get rid of my stupid virginity. Plus...' Her lip caught in her white teeth again. 'I could pretend you were him.'

The feeling in my chest got worse, that brutal mixture of shame and regret becoming toxic, an acid that burned far deeper than the flames ever had.

You shut her out, you selfish asshole. While all this time she wanted you...

No, fuck that. It wasn't my fault she'd fallen for a guy who didn't exist any more and never would. She'd liked the handsome veneer. The confident facade. The football superstar racing his own future into a touchdown.

She didn't know that under all of that I'd been angry and restless. Starting to crumble under the weight of my father's expectations—that I would get them out of the projects and earn enough money so they could have a big house in Bel Air and a fancy sports car. So they wouldn't have to work so hard ever again.

The pressure had been intense, and I'd started to doubt myself and my ability. Started to hate the game I'd once loved. I'd had thoughts about escaping, leaving it all behind so I didn't have to carry it any more, even though I'd known it was a selfish thing to want. But then that was what I'd been at heart— a selfish man.

And I still was. The difference was that these days I owned it. She might remember the man I'd once been, and she might want him. But I'd had nothing to give her then and I had nothing to give her now except pleasure. And maybe that was what I should be doing now, not talking about times that would never come again.

'Time for your reward,' I murmured. 'Open up.'

Obediently she did and I put the chocolate in her mouth.

'And now it's time for mine,' I added.

Then I ripped the throw from her body.

CHAPTER THIRTEEN

Vesta

I SHIVERED AS he pulled the throw from me in one hard movement. I couldn't see his face, but I didn't need to. I could feel his anger.

As I'd talked his entire body had gone stiff with tension and I'd heard the rasp of a note that sounded like pain in his ruined voice, as if my confession had hurt him in some way.

Part of me was glad. I was tired of being the one who always ended up hurt, who always wanted yet didn't get. Tired of holding on to something that would never materialise.

In fact, I wanted to hurt him, and it looked as if I had.

But another part of me hadn't wanted to upset the moment when he'd cradled me so gently and fed me food and wine. When I'd had his own strong heart beating in my ear, the warmth of his muscled body against me.

Perhaps I shouldn't have confessed everything

to him, but there would never be another time. If I didn't do it now, I never would, and I'd decided I didn't want to keep carrying it around for another nine years, not the way I was already doing. I'd had to get rid of it somehow and now I had.

But the reaction I'd always been afraid of had happened. He knew how I felt and he didn't like it.

There was a burst of agony in my chest, but I ignored it because his hands were on my hips and he was moving me, directing me, so I sat upright in his lap, facing him, my legs spread on either side of his powerful thighs.

The pain disappeared, lost under a sudden rush of feverish desire, anticipation and the tiniest touch of fear. Because was this it? Was I his reward? Would this be the moment, after all these years, that I would finally lose my virginity to him?

I wanted it. God, I wanted it more than I'd wanted anything in my entire life.

'A girl likes a warning,' I murmured shakily.

'Deal with it.' He ran his fingers down my sides lightly, from my shoulders to my hips, as if he was tracing the outline of me. 'I told you not to expect any special treatment because you were a virgin.'

Oh, he certainly had. And, now he was angry with me, I definitely wouldn't be getting any. Not that it bothered me. He could do whatever he wanted with me and I'd enjoy it. I knew that much.

'Fair enough,' I said and then everything went out of my head as I felt his hands cup my breasts, his palms big and hot, his thumbs moving to my nipples, circling them, teasing.

He wasn't gentle, abrading the sensitive tips roughly and then pinching them, sending fire along every nerve-ending.

I gasped, shuddering, and then gasped again as he pinched me a second time, arching into his hands. The slight pain mixed with pleasure was a sensation I'd never experienced before and it was so much sweeter than I'd expected.

But then, when it came to Eli, everything was much sweeter than I'd expected.

I felt him move, leaning forward, his mouth at my throat, a kiss burning there, and then his tongue touching my skin. I groaned as he squeezed my breasts gently, testing them with his hands, and then came the sharp edge of his teeth at my throat, another nip.

I suspected he was punishing me. Unfortunately for him, I was enjoying every second.

I reached for the buttons of his shirt but he growled deep in his throat, 'No touching. Already told you that. Hands down.'

'But I—'

The words were abruptly cut off as the heat of his palm pressed against my sex, the pressure of his fingers on my clit, and lightning joined the fire already building inside me.

He pressed harder and his other hand slid round me, down to the small of my back, stopping me from moving away. I was trapped between his hands—the insistent hand on my clit, the one at my back hold-ing me still. I trembled, panting, as the irresistible pleasure began to uncurl inside me.

He didn't stop, didn't give me any chance to take a breath. He slid one finger down to the entrance of my body and pushed gently. I was already wet and it slid into me with barely any resistance, making me shake.

His hand at the small of my back pressed harder as he pushed his finger in deeper, and I moaned at the feeling. So strange, but so good. I wanted more. More pressure. Deeper. Harder. I wanted movement and friction. I wanted the peak that only he could give me, because it had always been him.

It will *always be him*.

Probably. But I wasn't going to think of that now, not when what he was doing to me was so damn good.

'You like that?' he asked in that rough, sandpaper voice. 'My finger in your pussy?'

'Yes. Oh, my God…yes…'

'You want a warning? Here's one for you. I'm going to put another finger inside you, get you good and wet. And then when you're desperate, when you're begging, I'll put my cock inside you. I'm going to take your virginity, sweetheart, and you're going to love every fucking second of it.'

The words felt hot against my skin, like another rough caress, making me burn.

Because of course I'd love it. It was Eli.

And I loved him. I always had.

He was as good as his word, another finger joining the first, and even though his voice and his words were rough, even though he'd said he wouldn't be gentle, he was. He eased that second finger in slowly, letting me adjust to the feel of him.

I shivered and shook, trying to rock against his hand, but he wasn't having any of that, ordering me roughly to keep still. And I tried. But it was hard when he kept moving his fingers in a slow in-and-out, making me want to move and shift, increase the friction any way I could.

His mouth made a slow journey over my collarbone, lingering in the hollows, brushing gently over my skin. He paused to lick and to nip—and, as I didn't know which I'd get, every bit of my awareness was on him and what he was doing.

He knew how to play a woman, that was for sure.

But I could feel that cock of his beneath my ass, long, thick and hard, pressing through the scratchy wool of what felt like suit pants. And I couldn't resist playing with him like he was playing with me.

Because if anticipation worked on me, then it would also work on him, and I wanted him to be as desperate for me as I was for him. So I shifted my ass on him, arching against the hand at the small of my back, twisting a little, moving a little, giving him the same kind of tease. He didn't move, though, and I thought that perhaps it wasn't going to work, but then he gave a rough curse, the hand between my legs pulling away.

I shuddered, giving a soft moan of protest.

'It's your own fault,' he growled. 'If you'd kept still you'd have what you want, but since you didn't do what you're told you're going to have to wait.'

Satisfaction uncurled inside me as I heard the rustle of clothes, the movement of his hands near the zipper of his pants. Another curse, then the thud of something hitting the floor. The tear of foil and more movement, his roughened breathing coming hard and fast, making me pant too.

Then his hands were on my hips, lifting me, and I felt something hot nudge against my sensitive sex. I took a breath full of trembling anticipation before he pulled me down onto him, the head of his cock pushing into me, stretching me wider than his fingers had. A low moan escaped me but he didn't hesitate, easing deeper and deeper.

I stared into the blackness of my blindfold to where his face would be as he gripped me tighter and pulled me down hard, sheathing himself completely.

There was pain, brief and intense, but it was gone before I could even cry out. And then nothing but him inside me, filling me. Invading me. He was in front of me, under me, inside me. And it felt like more…

It felt as if he'd become part of me and I had become part of him. I'd never really felt I belonged anywhere. Not with my beautiful, talented, successful family. Not at school. And even though the life I had now was what I loved, creating art to ink into people's skin, I still felt out of place somehow. An outsider.

But here, with him, I belonged.

I belonged with him.

There was a sudden, complete silence, but it wasn't empty. It was full of tension and longing. Of relief. Of desire and hunger. Of tenderness and peace.

And I knew he felt the weight of the silence too, that it affected him as much as it was affecting me. But the urge to move was overwhelming and I couldn't stop it, even though I wanted to hold on to this moment of perfect understanding. His hands on my hips were directing me, a slow up-and-down, and soon I got the hang of it, moving with him.

Pleasure built, coiling tighter and tighter.

He didn't speak, all the rough things he'd said before falling away. And I couldn't speak, either. My chest was full of something heavy and profound, and my eyes prickled.

He moved harder, faster, and I knew there'd be no drawing out of anticipation. No teasing. He was on the edge of the cliff already and so was I.

Who'd fall over first? Him or me?

But then his hand was between my legs, touching my clit, pressing down and stroking in time with the movement of his hips, with the slow push-pull of his cock. Intensifying my pleasure as he took his own.

Eli Hart had never been a selfish man and he wasn't now.

Pressure built along with the pleasure, like a hand slowly closing around a delicate glass bauble, causing cracks that spider-webbed out, at first fine and then becoming deeper, wider.

I was shaking hard, my breaths sharp pants, the pressure becoming intolerable.

I was going to crack. I was going to shatter.

And suddenly I wanted to see his face, look into his eyes. This was my treasured fantasy and this was the one and only time I would see him looking at me as I fell apart in his arms, watching him as he came apart in mine.

But, as if he knew and wanted to stop the moment, his hand twisted, his finger creating magic between my legs, even as his cock thrust hard and deep, and suddenly I was coming, the orgasm relentless, rolling over me like thunder.

I meant to moan, but it wasn't a moan that slipped out.

It was his name.

'Eli,' I whispered as the pleasure drowned me.

And then I was shaking and shuddering, feeling his grip tighten as he moved inside me, harder, faster, slamming me down on him as he thrust up in a series of hard, brutal movements.

He stiffened, a low roar breaking from him as he came too, his whole body shuddering under the impact of it.

I waited, still drifting with the aftershocks, until he'd quietened and the silence had returned, broken only by our rough, shaken breaths.

Then I raised my hand and jerked the blindfold off.

CHAPTER FOURTEEN

Elias

I KNEW SHE was going to do it. Call it a sixth sense. In the first moments of that post-orgasmic haze—and it was one fucking amazing haze—I could see her hand reach for the blindfold. I could have stopped her. But I didn't.

In those moments, I wanted her to see me. I wanted her to know exactly who'd made her scream. Who'd made her sob. Who'd made her come so hard she'd forgotten her own name. Who'd taken her virginity.

A fucking caveman thought, but there it was.

I didn't want to be nameless, faceless. I wanted her to know who was her first.

And only.

The thought unwound inside me even as I registered something else. She wasn't surprised to see me. She wasn't shocked, angry or anything else.

Her blue eyes were so dark they looked black, pupils dilated, little strands of black hair plastered to her forehead where the blindfold had been pressing. She blinked quickly against the sudden influx of light, her pupils abruptly narrowing into tiny black points in response.

Beautiful eyes, slightly turned up at the corners like a cat's, her eyebrows serious black slashes. She had a silver ring through one of her eyebrows and it suited her whole edgy look.

I remembered those eyes, though. They'd been solemn when she was a kid, going wide every time they looked at me, as if she'd never seen anything like me in her entire life. And then later, as she'd got older, they'd danced with shy amusement as I'd teased her for being so serious, trying to get a grin out of her. She'd been so serious. I'd counted it a victory when I'd managed to make her laugh.

She looked at me with those same serious, solemn eyes, but she wasn't a kid now. Her body glistened with sweat, her mouth was full and red and I was still deep inside her, the clutch of her pussy around my cock already making me start to get hard again.

She'd known all along. Somehow, she'd known who I was.

And now she knows exactly how big an asshole you are too.

'Eli.' Her gaze roamed all over me and she lifted one small hand to touch my face.

I moved before I was even aware of it, gripping her, lifting her, pulling her from my lap and sitting her down on the couch beside me.

'Eli, wait,' she said huskily, reaching for me again.

But I ignored her, getting up off the couch and striding through to the bedroom, and from there into the en suite bathroom.

I shut the door and locked it, aware that my heart-beat was out of control, my fucking cock still getting itself ready for another round. And that my hands were fucking shaking.

How long had she known who I was? Why hadn't she said anything?

A man I maybe loved...

No. Fuck no. No fucking way.

I dealt with the condom, tidied up my clothes, then went to the mirror above the vanity. It floated there, looking as though it wasn't attached to the white-tiled wall behind it, lights surrounding it as if it was framing some Hollywood movie star.

But there was no fucking star in the glass.

It was only me in my black suit, looking like a fucking undertaker.

What had she seen when she'd pulled off the blindfold? Because I wasn't the same man she'd once known.

The same face, sure—the fire hadn't touched that. The nurses seemed to think I should be grateful for that, but some part of me wasn't. Some part of me wished that my face hadn't escaped, so that it was obvious. So no one would assume that I was still the same person, the same selfish asshole my dad thought I was who'd thrown a game so he wouldn't have to bear the weight of all those expectations. Of all those responsibilities.

My jaw was tight, a muscle leaping in it. In the mirror I could see that the top button of my shirt had come undone, revealing the red lick of scar tissue that lay just beneath it. I lifted a hand to do up the button, to exert some control over myself even in this small detail.

She knows. Do you think that matters now?

No, she didn't know. Not everything. She didn't know about the fire. Didn't know about my injuries. Didn't know that all the medical staff who'd called me a hero had been wrong.

I was no one's fucking hero.

I was a coward.

And she doesn't know why you cut her out of your life and then, years later, fucked her in a hotel room, making sure she had no idea who you were.

So? She didn't need to know. She didn't need to know anything. I could go and tell her coolly that there would be no discussion and that it was time for her to leave.

That's a shitty thing to do.

Of course it was a shitty thing to do. But maybe, if I was sufficiently shitty to her, she'd finally leave me the fuck alone the way everyone else had.

A soft knock came on the door.

Every muscle in my body tightened.

'Eli?' she called quietly. 'Are you okay?'

I'd been the one to deceive her, having her naked

in that chair, making her come over and over again. Taking her virginity on the couch like a goddamned animal. Not even having the decency to let her know who I was. And yet *she* was the one asking *me* if I was okay?

That should have been my line. I should have gathered her close and held her, kissed her. Asked if I'd hurt her and whether she needed anything. But no. I'd shoved her off my lap and escaped into the bathroom like the coward I used to be.

And a hypocrite into the bargain. I wasn't supposed to give one single shit what people thought of me and yet here I was, hiding. Afraid of shattering the pedestal she'd once put me on when she found out the truth.

I hadn't fully realised how much I'd needed that pedestal until now. To still be a hero to someone, even if it was only one person, just one. To her…

Except there was nothing heroic about what lay underneath my suit. Scars and selfishness. Anger and bitterness.

Sure. You treated her like shit and yet here you are in the bathroom, consumed with your own pain.

Of course. Why would I care about anyone else's? That was not who I was any more.

I bared my teeth at my appearance in the mirror. 'Yes,' I said flatly.

Maybe she should know. Maybe she should discover the truth about me. Shatter that pedestal once and for all, so she'd finally put me aside. After all, hadn't she said she'd come here to lay the ghost of me? So she could move on with her life?

Perhaps if she knew the truth then she finally would.

'I'm sorry, Eli.' Her voice again, from the other side of the door. 'I know I should have said something, but I...'

She was apologising to *me*? What the fuck? It should be the other way around, surely?

'You what?' A thick, hot anger shifted inside me. This was exactly what I hadn't wanted for this evening. Discussion. Conversation. Going over the past. Compli-fucking-cations. 'Spit it out, Vee. That you knew all along who I was.'

'Not all along.' A pause. 'Just after I...took off my dress.'

That long. She'd known that long.

I closed my eyes. 'How?'

'Seriously? I'd know your voice anywhere. And you smell the same. And it just...felt like you.'

Holy Christ. Hadn't I told myself to be careful? That she was sharp and perceptive?

That maybe she loves you—don't forget that.

My hands clenched into fists. 'Why didn't you say anything?'

Another pause.

'Why didn't you?'

Ah, fuck. Now we were getting down to it. I needed to put an end to it, and quickly. I needed to tell her the truth.

She'll never look at you the same way again.

No, but I'd got through the past decade without her looking at me in any way at all. I was at the top of my game, successful beyond my wildest morphine-induced dreams.

So what did it matter if she changed her opinion of me? What did her opinion of anything matter? It hadn't then and it didn't now.

Then why are you so afraid?

I snarled at my reflection, reaching for the anger and holding on tight. Anger was the only thing I had now. It had got me through those first dark days as I'd realised the full extent of what I'd done. The lives I'd ruined. The dreams I'd shattered.

It would get me through this.

Distancing her hadn't worked and I should have known it wouldn't. She hadn't given up trying to reach me and she never would because she never gave up on anything.

Unlike you. You gave up on yourself.

I ignored the thought, turning from the mirror and striding to the door. I unlocked it, then grasped the handle and pulled it open.

Vesta stood on the other side, big blue eyes coming to mine immediately, light shining on the ring in her eyebrow. She'd put her dress back on and I had a moment's regret that she'd covered up all that beautiful skin, all those delicious curves. Then I shoved it to the side, where I put every other inconvenient emotion I'd ever had.

'You really want to know why?' I demanded, holding her gaze. 'Then I'll show you.'

I backed up into the middle of the bathroom, all the mirrored surfaces bouncing my reflection back and forth between them, the bright, pitiless white light illuminating every single thing.

There would be no hiding now.

I lifted my hand to the knot of my tie and undid it, pulling it off and discarding it onto the ground.

Then I got rid of the rest of my clothes.

CHAPTER FIFTEEN

Vesta

I WANTED TO ask him what the hell he was doing, except it was perfectly obvious what he was doing.

He was undressing.

I stared, my heartbeat thundering, my mouth dry.

Eli Hart, right in front of me. As tall and as broad as I remembered. His presence filled the bathroom, dominated it.

He was dressed in a black suit that fitted him so perfectly it was probably custom-made, highlighting the powerful width of his shoulders and chest and emphasising his narrow waist. Underneath, he wore a black cotton business shirt with a tie of pewter silk. He should have looked like a funeral director, but somehow he didn't.

He'd…changed. The thick, surfer-blond hair that used to hang over his eyes, which he used to push back with an easy movement, was gone. It was cut ruthlessly short now, highlighting the perfect planes and angles of his face.

So achingly familiar, that face. The square jaw and straight nose. The high, carved cheekbones any supermodel would have killed for. His beautiful, beautiful mouth. It used to curve so readily into the amazing smile I used to believe he kept for me and me alone. But there was no hint of a curve in it now.

I met his gaze, foreboding curling in my gut.

His eyes were the same mix of amber and green, a colour that used to haunt my dreams, because in some lights they were pure gold, and in others bright emerald. They changed with his mood, the long, thick, dark gold of his lashes the perfect frame.

Right now they looked dark as the colour of his suit.

Everything about him looked as dark as his suit.

My heart squeezed.

This wasn't the Eli I remembered. This was someone much darker, with a presence that wasn't so much the sunshine Eli used to radiate as a beam of focused, intense light, like an X-ray or a laser.

Something had happened. Something had changed him.

You should have left the blindfold on.

I swallowed, my throat closing up. No point in going over what I should and shouldn't have done. I'd taken it off because I'd wanted to see him. I'd wanted to look into his eyes in that moment, because he was my ultimate fantasy and always had been. And, yes, part of me had been selfish and had wanted to know whether he'd also felt the pleasure he'd given me.

Part of me had known that, in taking it off, I'd destroy something. That a line would be crossed that I couldn't cross back over again. And it looked like I was right.

The moment of comfort and tenderness when he'd held me and fed me chocolate was gone. I'd destroyed it.

It was never real in the first place.

I forced the thought away.

'What are you doing?' I asked, no matter how obvious it was.

He said nothing, shrugging out of that beautifully tailored jacket and dropping it on the floor. His face was so hard, no give in his expression. He looked like a man who didn't even know what a smile was.

What was it that had changed him? Because something had. There was an edge to him that hadn't been there before, a steely ruthlessness. A sharp anger.

He said nothing, reaching for the buttons of his shirt and undoing them one by one. His gaze was intense and dark, pinning me in place.

It wasn't a slow, sexy strip show he was treating me to, and I knew that the moment he ripped off his tie. He was showing me something.

'Eli,' I began hoarsely.

He pulled off his shirt and threw it on the ground along with his jacket, and all the air in my lungs vanished.

At first I couldn't work out what I was seeing, because it didn't make any sense. His skin wasn't the smooth burnished gold I remembered, all beautifully etched pecs and abs, any woman's complete sexual fantasy of a man. It was…oh, God…it looked like his skin had melted. It was red in some places, and shiny, twisted in others and pulled tight. In other places it was white…

Scars. Massive scars. One licked up almost to his throat.

I blinked, not really taking it in, too shocked to speak.

But he wasn't done.

His hands were at his belt, undoing it in a series of short, decisive motions, unbuckling it, pulling it out from the loops of his pants and then throwing it down with a hard click onto the white tiles. He got rid of his shoes and socks. Then he pushed down his pants, along with the black underwear he wore underneath, and kicked them away. The scars licked around his narrow waist, one on his left hip wrapping around the top of his thigh, leaving the rest of his legs untouched.

His shoulders hadn't escaped. There was knotted scar tissue along his right one, his right bicep also shiny and twisted with scars.

His jaw was like iron, his stare dark and intense.

He stood in the middle of the white-tiled room, half of him the golden god I remembered, the other half a mass of shiny skin and scar tissue.

It looked as though he'd been embraced by fire.

He didn't look away from me. He didn't try to

hide. The light of the bathroom was merciless and a very deep part of me wanted to go to him and wrap one of those thick, fluffy robes around him, hide him away. And not because the sight of his scars was distasteful to me, but because I could see that they hurt him.

My eyes filled with helpless tears.

His mouth twisted and it wasn't a smile. It was something much harder, almost a sneer.

'I know I'm not pretty for you any more, Vee, but there's nothing to cry about.' The roughness of his voice echoed in the small space, and the change in it suddenly made sense now, as did the bitterness that wound through it. 'And you can probably guess why I didn't tell you who I was.'

'What…?' I stopped, struggling to make my voice work. 'What happened to you?'

He gave a laugh that had nothing to do with amusement. 'A little run-in with a fire.'

This was more than a run-in.

He'd been burned and very, very badly.

'Eli…' My voice sounded small and pathetic, shocked. 'If you're worried about the scars—'

'I'm not worried about the damn scars. It's the complications that come along with them. I make sure my partners are blindfolded so they don't have to see them. So they don't ask any fucking questions about them. So I don't have to go into any long and involved explanations as to what happened and why, and do they hurt, and can I touch them, and how did you survive—?'

He broke off abruptly, biting off the words as if they hurt him. 'Because it's not about them. It's about me and what I want. And what I want is to fuck. So now you know. Now you can guess what happened. And now you understand why it's best if you leave and we never speak of this again.'

I blinked fiercely, staring into those brilliant hazel eyes gone so dark. 'Why?'

He gave a rough laugh. 'Why what? Why do I want you to leave?'

'No, why didn't you tell me who you were the moment I walked into the room?'

His jaw hardened again, a muscle leaping in it.

He should have looked vulnerable standing naked with all those terrible scars on show. But he didn't. He looked like a man who'd literally walked through fire and come out the other side even stronger. Harder too, that much was obvious, and in some ways bigger as well. More muscled.

I couldn't deny it. He had a big, compelling presence. Much more so than the man he'd been years ago. And I couldn't think why. Perhaps it was that harder edge. It was mesmerising.

'Why do you think?' he said eventually. 'Because I decided I wanted you.'

That shivered down my spine in a glorious burst of heat. I leaned against the door frame and looked at him, letting my gaze drift down his body, along those terrible, terrible scars, and further down to where he was still semi-hard. There were no scars there…

The heat inside me twisted and turned, coiling and hot.

He was beautiful there, long and thick and hard, and the way he stood, all scarred and terrible and dark, made him compelling to me in a way I couldn't describe.

I managed to find my voice from somewhere. 'I didn't think you felt that way about me.'

'I didn't think I did, either. Yet my cock seems to think otherwise.'

'Eli…'

'You want to know where these fucking scars come from? I'll tell you. I didn't want to have this conversation, but you took off that goddamned mask and here we are.'

I swallowed, my throat closing. I wanted to apologise yet again, but something inside me wouldn't let me. He was angry and hurt, I got that, and from the looks of those scars he had every reason to be. But I hadn't done anything except take off the blindfold because I wanted to see him.

'You can probably guess why I did,' I said. 'I wanted to see you. I've been thinking about you for so long. Thinking about you, wondering about you…' I let out a breath and went on, because why not? I'd told him everything else. 'Fantasising about you too. And I…wanted to see you. I wanted to look into your eyes, see your face…'

'So you could see why I sound different? Why I act different?'

'No. So I could see *you*.' I wasn't looking at his scars any more, or even at the evidence of his desire for me. I looked into his eyes instead, trying to see the gold and green, the life and warmth that used to live inside him. 'I've missed you so much, Eli.'

His expression became even more forbidding, but I rushed on, heedless.

'It's been so long. And you won't return my calls or my texts or even my damn emails.' I pushed myself away from the door frame, taking a few steps into the bathroom, coming towards him, before I could stop myself. 'I only wanted to make sure you were okay. That I hadn't done anything—'

'You didn't do anything.' He cut me off harshly, a flicker of emerald glinting deep in his eyes. 'I didn't want to see you.'

That hurt. It hurt a lot. It shouldn't, but it did.

'Why?' I sounded bewildered. 'If I didn't do anything…'

'Because I didn't want to talk about this to anyone, least of all you.'

The hurt deepened.

I stared up into his perfect face, ignoring the mass of scar tissue that was the rest of his body. The dichotomy of it would have intrigued me at a different time, but I wasn't thinking about that now. I could only see him—the man I'd loved for so long, I couldn't remember what it was like *not* to love him.

Could only see the anger and bitterness in his eyes, the hard steel where before there had been laughter and easy-going smiles.

Not all the time, though. You know that, right?

Yeah, maybe I did. The smiles I'd got later hadn't been so easy and they hadn't lasted as long. They'd started to look…forced.

'Why not me?'

'You'd want to know what happened. You'd want me to talk about it. You'd want to know every fucking thing, and you wouldn't take no for an answer because you never, ever fucking do.' The harshness of his voice felt like sandpaper, abrading my skin, the low growl in it making me shiver the way it had done when I'd first walked into the room. A good shiver. 'And I didn't want to talk about it. I still don't. And I don't want you looking at me the way you're doing now, like your precious family heirloom just got shattered.'

'I… I'm not.'

'Aren't you? Aren't you looking at me right now, thinking of me the way I was? Thinking about how different I am now? About how ruined I am—?'

'No.' This time it was my turn to interrupt him, my own anger starting to stir in response to his, because he was certainly angry. I could see it in the flicker of green in his eyes and in the tension that rolled off him. 'You really want to know what I'm thinking? I'm thinking about how much that must have hurt. How much agony you must have been in. And how strong you must have been to recover.'

He stared back, searching my face as if he didn't believe me, so tall and so broad and still so powerful even with all those scars. I could feel the heat he gave off; it was as though that fire had crawled inside him and was still burning.

'Full-thickness burns over forty percent of my body,' he said roughly. 'Countless surgeries and skin grafts. Took me nearly two years to recover.'

I had to look away then, had to drop my gaze to the lick of that scar up his throat so he wouldn't see the sadness in my eyes. The sympathy I couldn't quite hide. And, as I knew he wouldn't want it, I lifted my hand and reached out hesitantly, wanting to touch the red, shiny skin of his chest.

He tensed but didn't move away and, as I touched him, I heard his breath hiss out.

Instantly I lifted my fingers. 'I'm sorry. Does it hurt?'

'No. I…don't feel anything.'

I let my fingers descend again, his skin warm to my touch but bumpy and tight. 'Not this?' I stroked along his chest to where there was a join in the scar tissue, obviously the edges between skin grafts. It had created a kind of patchwork effect.

'No.' The roughness in his voice became more pronounced, a note in it sounding like regret. 'There was nerve damage.'

I lifted my gaze and found him looking down at

me, his eyes full of angry emerald fire. The light from above him had turned the tips of his short hair to gold and had done the same thing to his eyelashes, outlining the planes and angles of his face. His features were still so beautiful and yet…

A ruined heirloom. Was that how he saw himself? Ruined? But of course he did. He'd been an athlete. His body and the way it functioned had been his entire career.

It struck me then, forcibly, that this must be why he'd suddenly disappeared at the height of his fame. Rumours had circulated that he'd taken off overseas after his last disastrous game, when he'd been benched for an injury and his team had lost, his glittering future in ruins. But that hadn't been the case, had it? He'd been terribly injured and had spent years recovering.

No wonder he was angry. One lost game, one lost season, was serious, but he might have been able to come back from it. Except after the years this would have taken from his life…no. There would have been no coming back from that.

'There's an art form in Japan,' I said quietly. 'It's called *kintsugi* or *kintsukuroi*. When something is broken, usually a plate or a bowl, they put it back together again with liquid gold.' I gently touched the seams of the scars, following the joins. 'It takes something shattered and turns it into something unique. It creates a work of art. The scars become features, creating beauty.'

He'd stilled beneath my hand, his chest rising and falling a little faster than it had before. 'There's nothing beautiful about this.'

'Isn't there, though?' My fingers skimmed over a smooth, shiny piece of scar tissue. 'Isn't there something beautiful about survival? About living?'

Something flickered in his gaze, but I couldn't tell what it was. Then his fingers closed around my wrist and held on. 'If you're going to touch me, touch me where I can feel it.'

My breath caught and he pushed my hand down over his scarred chest and stomach, where I could still feel the steel of his muscles beneath, and down further to where he wasn't scarred. Where his skin was smooth as velvet and very hot, and where he was as hard as an iron bar.

His hand was over mine, closing my fingers around his cock, applying pressure.

I looked up into his face. 'Can you feel that?'

And there it was, a flicker of gold.

'Yes,' he growled. 'Question is, what are you going to do about it?'

CHAPTER SIXTEEN

Elias

HER FINGERS WERE cool around my aching dick, but the look in those deep-midnight eyes was anything but. The same look she'd given me back when she was sixteen and she unwrapped the present I'd given her, shy yet hopeful, and a little hungry.

Or, no. The expression in her eyes now was more adult than that, the hunger more pronounced, making it clear that the presence of my ruined torso didn't bother her.

I might have thought she was faking it if she hadn't traced all those scars with her fingers, a look of concentration on her pointed face. Hadn't talked about broken bowls repaired with gold becoming works of art, their scars making them unique.

I didn't want that to matter quite as much as it did now, when I'd made peace with my scars long ago.

Have you, though?

I ignored that thought, just as I'd ignored how her eyes had filled with tears after I'd taken off my shirt, along with shock and sympathy and pain. And part of me regretted that. Regretted that I'd caused her yet more hurt.

But there was nothing to be done about it. Better that she should know the truth, that it wasn't only about not wanting to answer questions or talk. That there was something real behind all of this. I owed her that much.

I didn't know why she was still here, though. Why she'd come into the bathroom instead of backing away. Why she'd touched me and talked to me about scars made of gold instead of turning round and leaving. I wasn't the handsome, patient, successful friend any more. Her big brother surrogate. I was scarred and surly and I didn't give a fuck, and yet still she was here. Still she'd touched me, when no other woman had ever done so, not after I'd come out of hospital.

And now she had her fingers around my cock, and my heart was in my throat, and if she walked away now, I didn't know what I'd do.

Back then she'd been the only one who'd seemed to care about the person I was beneath the football star. The only one who'd ever asked me what it was that *I* wanted from my life. Not what my dad, my mom, my coach or my fans wanted. I remember being surprised at the question, because I hadn't even known. I'd never been given the chance to find out.

Not that any of that mattered right now. Not with

her fingers around my aching cock, ink-blue eyes finally looking up into mine, lit with heat and hunger.

And she was looking at me. Not Eli Hart, football superstar. Not even Elias Hart, CEO of Howard and Hart, one of the US's fastest-rising security and defence companies. She was looking at *me*, the man I was beneath those two personas.

And who is that?

But I didn't want to think about that, not when her hand was around me, and the hunger for her to which I'd been trying not to pay any attention had me riveted.

She smelled good, of sex and sweetness, and I was done talking. And if she was touching me then it seemed as if she was done talking as well.

'What do you want me to do?' Her gaze fell to my mouth and stayed there. 'I'll do anything you want, just tell me.'

Who could resist a husky, desperate offer like that? Not me. She'd seen how damaged I was, and yet she was still here, so what the hell?

I squeezed her hand around my dick, letting her get the feel of me. 'You think you can handle that?'

Her lashes, long and thick and black, framed those pretty, pretty eyes. 'Yes. Let me.'

'What would you do if I said no?' A tease and a test.

The necklace I'd given her glittered in the light as she swallowed. 'I don't know. Probably cry.'

Her mouth quirked but I knew that she was only

half joking; and the fact that she was desperate for me only made my cock ache all the more.

It was wrong to keep going, to take more from her when I knew her crush on me hadn't abated. When tonight was all I had to give her. But I was a selfish, selfish man and, if she wanted me, who was I to argue?

'You want to suck me, little girl?' I asked, my voice rasping.

She gave a jerky nod, her breath catching, obviously turned on by the thought.

'Good.' I grabbed a towel from the nearby rail and handed it to her. 'Then it's time to get comfortable. Put this on the floor and kneel.' The white tiles wouldn't be easy to kneel on and I didn't want her distracted.

She did as she was told, letting go of my cock as she arranged the towel and then knelt on it. 'I haven't done this before,' she said, as if I wasn't already aware of just how inexperienced she was. 'So you might have to tell me what to do.' She gave me a naughty glance from underneath her lashes. 'I'm assuming you won't have a problem with that.'

Sexy, sexy Vee.

I liked her being flirty. It made me want to flirt in return. But I was so fucking rusty, I didn't think I'd be much fun.

'You'd assume correctly.' I gestured. 'Take your dress off.'

She didn't hesitate, pulling the fabric up and off,

then tossing it onto the floor, leaving her kneeling in front of me, naked and gorgeous. Her blue gaze had darkened, her red lips parting in anticipation as I stepped up to her. She stared at me as if she was starving and I was something delicious to eat.

'Give me your hand.' I held out mine and she reached for it without hesitation.

Her long, slender fingers were cool, the dark blue nail polish gleaming like liquid midnight in the light of the bathroom. Slowly I drew her hand to my cock. 'Feel free to explore,' I murmured. 'Use your hand, and you can use your mouth too. I'll tell you if there's something I'm not enjoying.'

'You promise?' She was breathing very fast and I could see the flash of anxiety in her eyes. 'I want this to be good for you, Eli.'

I couldn't imagine why she'd want that after the way I'd treated her, but hell, I wasn't going to argue. I didn't understand why she'd think it wouldn't be good for me, either. Then again, if she'd never done this before, then maybe it wasn't such a surprise. After all, it wasn't as if she'd had lots of people in her life telling her she was doing a good job.

'Relax,' I said softly. 'Basically you can't do this wrong, okay? Anything you do is going to be good for me.'

Something in her gaze shifted, the anxiety bleeding away. 'Okay.'

'Good. Now get to it. I'm having bad thoughts

about that mouth of yours, but I want you to have a chance to play first.'

She flushed, then dropped her gaze to my dick. Then she began to explore.

I usually didn't allow a woman to touch me this way. Sometimes I got them to suck me off, but it was only that—a blow job, nothing fancy. I didn't let them run soft fingers up my shaft and then over the sensitive head. I didn't allow them to stroke me, to tease me, to close their hand around me and squeeze.

Her touch was gentle and light, and it was maddening. I watched her face as she did so, her eyes wide. Every so often she'd glance up at me, and I let her see what she was doing to me. She blushed every time, that flush going down her neck and across her chest, yet she didn't look away. She kept staring at me the way she used to. As if I was someone she liked very much and liked being with. Someone who gave her joy. She obviously got a lot of pleasure out of what she was doing to me, and she didn't hide it.

I got off on that as much as the feel of her fingers on my skin. In fact, it was surprising how much her pleasure got me off too, and how my pleasure fed into hers. A connection of sorts that I didn't get with a woman in a blindfold. That I hadn't got with the women from my football days, either, if I was honest.

Because for her to find pleasure in getting me off, it had to matter. *She* had to matter. And Vesta did. She always had.

I murmured things to her, softly at first, and then

my voice got deeper, rougher, as she drove me insane with those light, exploratory touches. Pleasure
curved like lightning down my spine as she leaned
in and began to use her mouth, her tongue hesitant
at first, then gaining in confidence as she touched it
to the head of my cock.

'Yes,' I growled emphatically. 'Fuck yes.'

Obviously taking on board the encouragement,
she gripped me tighter as she began to explore down
my shaft, licking and squeezing, making me grit my
teeth as the pleasure sunk deeper. My hands were
in fists and I wanted to let her explore a bit more,
get comfortable with me, but she tested my control.

I reached for her, sliding my fingers into her short,
silky hair, gripping tight. She made a little sound,
but it wasn't one of protest, more of relief. As if she
wanted me to take control. Good, because I did.

'Open up,' I ordered and she did. And then I was
guiding my cock into her mouth and she was closing her lips around me.

Hot and wet. Slick. Fucking heaven.

She relaxed against me, one hand gripping the
base of my dick, her hair brushing my abdomen. I
couldn't feel it, but I could see it, just as I could see
her pretty mouth around my cock. So fucking erotic.

'Look at me,' I commanded.

Her lashes lifted, her gaze meeting mine, wide
and dark, glazed with desire. Pretty Vee, all flushed
and hot, with her mouth full of my cock.

I guided her head on me, showed her what I

wanted her to do, and she did it, sucking me deep. The pressure was fucking amazing. The pleasure was indescribable. I thrust deeper into her mouth, going faster, and she moaned, her grip on me tightening. Then she put her other hand on my thigh, gripping me there to keep her balance.

It was a beautiful sight to watch her suck me, to watch my cock move in and out of her mouth, to see her beautiful naked body, her round breasts bouncing with every thrust of my hips.

Vee on her knees, worshipping me...

It was getting too much but I didn't want to stop. I couldn't.

'I'm going to come in your mouth,' I said, and it wasn't a request.

She only gripped me tighter, so I let myself go, thrusting into her mouth until the pleasure pulled tight then crested, a current electrifying me. I groaned, my fingers twisted in her hair as the climax hit, and I felt her lips tighten around my cock, her throat moving as she swallowed me down.

So fucking hot.

I couldn't move after that, my eyes closed as my heartbeat slowly normalised, short, sharp electric shocks still moving through me. Her hands slid down my thighs and then around me, and I could feel the warmth of her body against my legs. I had some sensation on my lower abdomen, and could feel the silkiness of her hair and the soft brush of her lips as she kissed me. She leaned against me, holding me as if it was me holding her upright and not the other way round.

The simple affection implicit in her hold made my chest tighten. It had been a long time since I'd had any physical comfort, because I didn't allow it. And I'd told myself that I didn't need it, that I was fine with my weekly Friday night sessions with the women I hired.

But Vee's arms around me, holding me, the warmth of her against me… It seemed I was wrong. Maybe I did need it after all.

The thought was uncomfortable for reasons I couldn't quite articulate so I moved, gently untangling my fingers from her hair and pulling away from her.

She looked up at me, a crease between her brows. 'Was that okay?'

I held her gaze. 'It was more than okay. You wanted to blow my goddamned mind? Well, you blew that as thoroughly as my cock.'

Pink tinged her cheeks and she gave me the most self-satisfied smile. 'Well, excellent.'

I reached down and picked her up, loving how she instantly put her arms around my neck, as if we'd been doing this together for years and not just one night.

'So, what now?' she asked, looking up at me.

'Now?' I flashed her the ghost of my old smile. 'Now it's your turn.'

CHAPTER SEVENTEEN

Vesta

HE CARRIED ME into the bedroom of the suite and set me down on the bed before going out to the lounge and coming back seconds later with a fistful of silver packets. More condoms.

I watched him stride to the bed, still powerful and sleek despite the scars. And if there was a slight stiffness to his movements then it was only that, slight. He didn't quite move with the grace of old, but he wasn't far off.

The intentness in his gaze was back as he put the packets on the nightstand and then joined me on the bed. Gold glittered in his eyes and his cock was hard again.

I could still taste him in my mouth, salty and musky, and the ache between my legs was acute. It had been quite the experience, sucking him off, to kneel at his feet with him looking down at me, tall, powerful and so very beautiful.

And he was beautiful. He wasn't the golden man

he'd been years ago, but then I wasn't the kid I'd once been, either. He'd been a golden man, and his attention had rocked that kid's world, but then he'd left the kid behind. And I'd stopped being a kid. I'd stopped looking to other people for my validation and I'd gone and found it myself.

I didn't need a golden man any more. I needed someone else.

Do you really need him, though? That's the question.

I'd never questioned my adolescent crush. Never questioned the love that had grown out of it, either. Never asked myself why I kept holding on to a man who'd spent the last nearly ten years ignoring me. I wasn't lonely. I had friends. But…they didn't know about me and my struggles. They didn't know about my family. They only saw tattoos and piercings and a spiky and prickly woman. A woman who didn't care what others thought of her. Then again, that was only what I let them see…

Eli got onto the mattress and with an easy movement flipped me over onto my stomach. I lay there face-down on the sheets, my heartbeat thumping, not knowing what to expect, but clearly there was more and, God, I so wanted more.

His hand settled on the back of my neck, warm and heavy, a reassurance.

I relaxed, every muscle going lax as he ran his hand down my spine in a long, slow, stroking motion. I sighed. 'That feels so good.'

He made a soft, rasping sound, his hand moving down over my butt and squeezing gently. 'I know I don't have a right to ask this, but…what have you been doing for the past few years?'

My heart gave a leap, stupid thing that it was. I was pleased that he'd wanted to know about me— even though a little voice in the back of my head kept telling me that, if he'd truly wanted to know, he would have read those emails I'd sent him, or called me at least. And that I should be angry with him for how he'd dismissed me. That I should demand answers for his behaviour, even though the answers might hurt.

But I didn't want to destroy the mood, so I decided to ignore the little voice.

'Dad wanted me to go to college but, as you can imagine, I decided not to,' I said. 'I went to a community art college instead.'

'Good plan.' His hand began another long stroke. 'You were always fantastic with that kind of stuff. What happened after that?'

I noted that he didn't ask what Dad thought of it. But he probably didn't need to ask. Dad had given up on me by then. He'd barely even looked up from his newspaper when I told him that was what I wanted to do.

'I got into tattoo design.' I arched under his hand, loving the warmth of it. 'And I opened my own tattoo parlour. I'm hoping to open a second one in LA, probably in the next six months if I can get the capital together.'

'That sounds amazing.' There was a pause and then he said, 'Did you do these?' His fingers touched my hip where a petal curled around it.

I didn't hide my shiver. 'Yeah. I designed it.'

'It's beautiful, Vee. Really beautiful.' He traced the outline of the petal with his finger. 'If you need finance, though, you don't need to do shit like this. You know that, right? Traj can help out or I can—'

'No,' I interrupted, a whisper of annoyance interrupting the warmth and pleasure I was getting from his touch. 'I want to do this myself. I don't want to be beholden to my damn family.'

Eli's hand on me paused. 'Yeah, I can understand that.' It resumed stroking me. 'Things didn't get any better?'

I knew what he was talking about. My family and what happened after he'd vanished from my life.

He abandoned you, that's what happened.

My throat closed. 'They were fine,' I forced out. 'Same old same old.'

Again his hand paused, big and warm in the small of my back. His thumb caressed me in a slow back-and-forth. 'What did they do?'

I shut my eyes, my face pressed into the pillow. 'They didn't do anything. They'd have to care in order to do something and they didn't care. Dad basically ignored me and so did Mom. They came to my college graduation, I'll give them that, but that was it. I left as soon as I could.'

Eli said nothing, that thumb still stroking me, and there was a long silence.

'When I was about fourteen, I twisted my knee during a game,' he said at last. 'Dad kept pushing me to keep playing. He said I couldn't afford to take time out, and that if I wanted to have a career I needed to suck it up and get on with it. That was the mantra he kept feeding me, the same thing every time I mentioned having a break or taking some time off— that everything was riding on me. That he and Mom had worked so hard for me and now it was my turn to work for them, get them their chance of a better life, be their ticket out of the project. So I ignored the injury, ignored the pressure, sucked it up and kept playing. But it never really came right.

'That last year at college it flared up again, but I kept on ignoring it because I had to impress the scouts. And then that last game…it gave out and I was benched for the season.' His voice got very rough. 'Dad was…so fucking angry with me. After all those arguments about me taking some time off, he'd thought I'd done it on purpose. I'd killed their dreams, he told me. I'd ruined their chance for something better. They'd worked so hard and I'd screwed up and so it was all for nothing. It was my fault.'

I said nothing, listening to him.

'I was angry too, feeling guilty as shit for fucking up their chances, so I went to their place to apologise.

But then Dad started ranting, so I went to a bar to get drunk instead. Then I realised I'd left my wallet back at his and Mom's house, and when I went back to get it I found the house was alight. Dad had fallen asleep drunk on the couch and his cigarette had ignited a newspaper beside it.'

My throat closed up. I knew what was coming next.

'I found Mom in the bedroom and managed to pull her out. And then I went back in to get Dad. The house was shitty, and it burned so fast, and while I was trying to get Dad out part of the ceiling collapsed on top of me. I don't have any memory of what happened after that, but somehow I managed to get us both out. The docs said it was a miracle I survived, but that I had youth and fitness on my side.'

There was a pause, his hand on my skin so warm. 'There were so many surgeries. So many skin grafts. I had a couple of infections. I was in hospital a long time. Mom visited me, but Dad didn't. He wouldn't come. The house wasn't insured and they lost everything.'

'Oh.' The word was more breath than sound, an exhalation of shock and grief and sympathy. He'd never talked about his parents much, and I only knew that his mom cleaned our house and was quiet, and his dad coached him a lot with his games. I thought there may have been some pressure from them, but I'd had no idea of the extent of it.

'Your dad paid the hospital bills for me otherwise

I'd have been screwed, because it was obvious I'd never play again.'

I swallowed, trying to think of what to say, because words didn't seem enough to cover the extent of his loss. I could only think of questions.

'Why didn't you tell anyone about it?' I asked eventually.

'You mean, why didn't I tell you?'

'Me. Anyone. Everyone thought you'd gone off—'

'I know what everyone thought. And I didn't say because I didn't want anyone to know. The medical staff all thought I was a fucking hero, that I saved my dad's life, but they didn't know I was the reason he'd nearly died in the first place. Besides, no one wants that kind of end to a great story. Local boy almost makes good, only to fail in the end and nearly die in hospital.'

'But—'

'I failed them, Vee. And I know I failed them, because Dad didn't even come to visit me. Even though I'm successful in business—even though I got him and Mom out of their shitty neighbourhood, bought them a house and a car, made sure they were comfortable—he still won't talk to me about it. Doesn't matter that I nearly died saving both of them. As far as he's concerned, I got myself benched on purpose. I ruined their lives because I didn't want to play any more.' He paused. 'He said he thinks I'm selfish. And he's right. That's exactly what I am.'

My heart squeezed so tight. I wanted to turn over,

see his face, touch him and tell him that I'd never see him as selfish. That he'd been nothing but generous to me, giving me his time and attention, his patience and reassurance, even when he hadn't had to.

But his hand pressed down on me, keeping me where I was and pinning me to the bed.

'So I decided to embrace it. I decided that I was done with living my life for other people. I had to live it for me.' His voice had dropped even deeper, a subsonic rumble I felt in my chest. 'So I put that life behind me. Everyone. Everything. The only person I kept was Traj, because he was facing the same sort of physical shit that I was. And we decided together that we wouldn't let our limitations stop us. That we'd have everything we were supposed to have before it had all turned to crap. We'd make it happen.'

'So you did,' I said thickly into the pillow.

'Yeah, we did. And I'm sorry I shut you out. I'm sorry I didn't tell you what was going on. But, when I said I was done with that life, I meant it. I was done. I didn't want to explain and I didn't want to justify it. I didn't want anyone else's expectations to get in the way of what I wanted. It was easier to cut that part of my life out completely. And, yes, it was selfish. But that's what I am, Vee. I'm a selfish asshole.'

I could feel the prickle of tears behind my lids, the stupid sorry-for-myself part of me aching at the thought of how easy that had been for him. To just… cut me out. Like I hadn't mattered. Like I'd *never* mattered. And how he'd lumped me in with everyone else who'd demanded things of him...

Except I'd never demanded things of him. I hadn't been just another in a long line of people who'd expected him to change their lives... Or had I?

Of course you did. You're just like all the rest.

My poor, wrung-out heart squeezed again as a flood of old memories filled my head.

Because of course I'd been just like the rest. The day of my sixteenth birthday, with all the people Mom had invited. People I didn't want. But she'd insisted—because how else would I be accepted and cool? And she'd roped in Eli, and they'd all come because of him.

Then, when he'd arrived, everyone had been watching as he'd come to me first, smiling at me. Giving me a hug. Tall and handsome and golden, his smile lighting up the room. Everyone had been so jealous. All eyes had been on me and, as Eli had taken me in his arms, I'd been given a taste of what it felt to be him. To be the centre of attention. To have everyone wishing they were me.

I was only human. Deep in my heart, despite the armour I'd started to develop even back then, I'd wanted that acceptance. That buzz of popularity. I'd wanted to be the one everyone looked at, that everyone wanted. And that day, for the first time, I'd wanted Eli to stay—and not for the warm glow of his presence, but because for a couple of hours he'd made me the most popular girl in school.

Maybe I was just like all the rest. I could tell myself that, no, it was just him that I'd fallen for. But maybe it wasn't. Maybe it was the lustre of his fame that had been the biggest drawcard.

Shame curled through me.

He'd known all along that I was just the same as the others. No wonder he'd cut me out of his life.

I shifted, shrugging off his hand, making for the edge of the bed, needing some space away from him. But his arms suddenly came down on either side of my shoulders, the heat of his big, hard body at my back.

'What's wrong?' he growled.

'Nothing.' I swallowed. 'Need to pee.'

'Bullshit.' One hand came underneath me and he flipped me over onto my back with astonishing ease. His hazel eyes burned into mine, amber and green. He was so different, no longer golden. No longer the carefree, easy-going man with hundreds of women in his bed.

He was darker, more dangerous, somehow. More intense. As if the brush with death had left its mark, smudged and sooty fingerprints on a golden statue.

I liked it. I liked it so much better.

'Tell me what the matter is, Vee.'

CHAPTER EIGHTEEN

Elias

SHE STARED BACK at me, that stubborn look on her face again, the spark of challenge. All pointy angles and sharp prickles.

She hadn't liked what I'd said, and no wonder. The unvarnished truth was always bitter to hear. I probably shouldn't have told her in the first place and I didn't know why I had. I'd always sworn I wasn't going to justify or explain my choices to anyone ever again.

But here I was, doing both for her. Because of the way she'd talked about what she'd been doing the past few years. Her dropping out of high school and going to art college, her business, the slight edge to her voice as she told me she didn't want to be beholden to her family.

That edge had sounded more like pain than anger when she'd said, 'They didn't do anything.'

They'd given up on her, hadn't they? They'd fucking paid my hospital bills—mine, someone who wasn't even related to them—yet they'd basically cut their own daughter loose. And all because she didn't meet their rigid, narrow standards of success.

Of course I'd had to tell her my secrets. It seemed only fair.

After you basically cut her loose too? Yeah, fair seems relative.

The thought ate at me, guilt sitting in my gut like a stone. I'd told myself that I was selfish, that I'd embraced it, that I didn't care about her feelings. Told myself that she likely wouldn't care, either.

But she did and, deep down, I'd always known that. Underneath the prickly armour she wore now, she was still that sensitive, caring girl whose tender heart had been kicked around and bruised by the parents who'd never accepted her for who she was.

And now, here was I, doing the same thing.

The guilt became glass, cutting into me. I wanted to tell her I was sorry again, that I'd never meant to hurt her, but that was a lie. I had meant to hurt her. I'd meant to drive her away. Except she hadn't gone.

She turned her head to the side, her lashes veiling her gaze, silent for a moment.

'You were right not to tell me,' she said at last, huskily. 'You were tired of people's expectations of you and I… I was just one more.'

And now here she was, trying to excuse my own shitty behaviour…

Christ. This was what I hadn't wanted—guilt, pain and regret. Emotions colouring everything, making everything complicated. I'd wanted it to be simple. But it was too late for simple now. We'd both complicated things immeasurably and I wasn't sure it would ever be simple again.

'No, you weren't,' I said gruffly. 'You weren't—'

'I was.' Her lashes rose and she looked up at me, blue eyes so dark they looked black. 'My sixteenth birthday and you turned up. Everyone was there for you, not me, and I knew that. And I didn't care. Because, for a couple of hours, I got to feel popular. I got to feel accepted. I got to feel what it was like to be you.' The look on her face was challenging, as if daring me to say something. 'It wasn't you I was grateful for then, Eli. I was grateful for what you represented. And for what you gave to me.'

I stared at her. 'What? And you felt guilty for that?'

'Shouldn't I? Aren't I like all the rest? Wanting you for what you could give them, not for who you were?'

'No,' I said fiercely, because she wasn't like all the rest. She never had been. 'You know what I thought that day? I thought, fucking finally, I can really do something for you. That was the only time I was ever actually glad I was famous. That all I needed to do to make you happy was smile and pay you attention.' I took a breath, the realisation flooding through me. 'I didn't have to play my best, pay attention to my diet, train every goddamned day. All I had to do was smile at you. It was the easiest thing in the whole world.

And I was glad they were all looking at you, wondering what it was about you that caught my attention. I wanted them to. I wanted them to see what I saw.'

She was very still beneath me, warm and pale in the dim light, her skin breathing candy floss and musk. Her eyes had gone the same liquid midnight as her nail polish and she was staring at me as though I was that man again. Her superhero.

'And what did you see, Eli?' she asked.

I shouldn't say it. It would be a mistake. But I couldn't stay quiet.

'I saw a lovely, special person. Caring and interesting. Who smiled at me like a sunrise every time she saw me. Who asked me questions no one else ever did, and who was interested in the answer. Who taught me about tenacity and being stubborn. She was all heart, that girl.' I lifted a hand and brushed a lock of hair from her cheek before I could stop myself. 'She was precious.'

Her throat moved as she swallowed, her eyes nothing but black, the look in them oddly…almost devastated. As if I was telling her something painful instead of reassuring.

'Precious, huh? So precious you cut me out of your life for nine years.'

Ah, fuck.

Little Vee, with her heart on her sleeve…

'I'm sorry,' I said again, and this time it came out harsher than it had before. 'I thought you had your own life. I didn't think it would matter.'

'Of course it mattered.' She blinked hard, something glittering in the corner of her eye. 'You were the only one who ever saw me, Eli. The only one who ever even liked me. The only one who didn't tell me what I was doing wrong, only what I was doing right.' Her voice had got thicker. 'You were the only one who ever made me feel special and you think I wouldn't even notice you disappearing for nearly a whole decade?'

You fucking asshole.

Anger boiled inside me, but not at her. At the lies I'd told myself so I could feel better about what I was doing. So I hadn't had her coming into the hospital and looking down at me with those beautiful midnight-blue eyes and see pity there.

Yeah, I'd been afraid. Afraid of what she would think of me. Afraid of what she would say. Afraid of what I'd see in her gaze. That she'd realise just what kind of man I was—a man who'd squandered the gifts he'd been given for his own selfish reasons.

'I didn't want you to see me like that,' I said, the deeper truth tumbling out before I could stop it. 'I didn't want you to see me lying in a fucking hospital bed, just one hideous weeping wound. Unable to do anything. I couldn't walk, couldn't do one single fucking thing for myself. I…couldn't bear it. I thought…' I stopped, my heart pumping in my chest, every muscle in my body stiff.

She didn't say a word, just stared straight up at me, waiting.

I couldn't ignore the truth. I fucking owed her.

'I thought you'd never look at me the same way again.' My voice sounded like the bottom of a dry river bed, nothing but dust and gravel. 'That you'd find out the truth about what happened and you'd know that I wasn't…a hero.'

She blinked at me. 'A hero?'

It sounded ridiculous. It sounded like some stupid, fucking childish delusion. And yet…when things had got bad, when the pressure had felt overwhelming, when it had felt as if everyone in the entire world wanted me to be the NFL's next big thing, it was Vee's simple pleasure in my company that had kept me going. Vee, for whom I didn't have to be anyone but myself.

'The way you used to look at me,' I forced out. 'Like I was Superman or something. And then later, when you were older, you looked at me like I was your friend. I didn't have to be anyone with you. I didn't have to do anything. I could just be…me and you would look at me the same way.' I stopped, bizarrely feeling the way I had back in hospital when the bandages from the latest skin graft had come off and my skin had felt every molecule of air on it. I'd become aware of how fragile the human body was. How fragile I was…

I couldn't look at her. That gaze of hers was worse than a debridement sloughing off old skin and scar tissue, leaving me exposed. Leaving me vulnerable.

There was a touch on my cheek, the warmth of

her hand against my skin exerting some pressure, so I had to turn my head to look at her.

The expression in her eyes was piercing and full of something I didn't understand. 'You never had to be anyone with me but yourself, Eli. I never cared about what you could do on the football field. The only thing I cared about was how you smiled at me. How you encouraged me. How you listened when everyone else ignored me. You were the brightest thing in my life and, yes, you *were* my hero. Why would some scars ever change that?'

My chest was so tight I could barely breathe. I didn't want sit there looking into her lovely face, into those beautiful eyes, seeing her soul laid bare for me. I wanted to tell her to protect that soul of hers. That if she wasn't careful life would burn it as it had burned mine, leaving it covered in scar tissue, unable to feel a thing.

But I didn't.

'Why wouldn't it change that?' I asked instead. 'It did for my parents. When all you are to them is the failure of their hopes for a better future, not even their son who nearly fucking died—' I broke off, aware that my voice had risen, that the anger inside me was getting hotter, bubbling and burning like lava inside a volcano. Anger that I'd never put behind me the way I thought I had.

'They were wrong.' There was now fire in Vesta's eyes too. A vivid blue flame. And I could hear the fierce ring of it in her voice. 'And you didn't fail them—'

'Didn't I, though?' I interrupted. 'I should have had my knee looked at. I should have had the team's doctor make sure it was okay, since it was an important game. But I didn't. I told myself it would be fine, that it had held up fine the past few years, so why not now? But deep down I knew it wouldn't be fine. And I still did nothing.'

I took a breath, everything in me tight. 'I didn't want to play any more, Vee. I didn't want to be Dad's hope for a better future. I didn't want to be his ticket out of poverty.' I could feel the tension in my shoulders. Feel it crawl all over me. 'You asked me once, when you were a kid, what I wanted to be when I grew up and I couldn't think. All I ever knew was football. But the day my knee gave out I sat on the bench and all I felt was relief. Because what I wanted, what I *really* fucking wanted, was just a life of my own.'

CHAPTER NINETEEN

Vesta

THE GREEN IN his eyes blazed hot, anger written all over his perfect features. No, not just mere anger. It was rage. And I could understand it. The life he'd had, the promise of a future, had all led to a hospital bed, agony and scars covering forty percent of his body.

It wouldn't have happened if he'd been left to follow his own path. If he hadn't been forced to carry other people's dreams. Not his. He'd never been allowed to have any, had he?

If he'd been given time to decide his own future, what would that have looked like? What could he have been?

My heart hurt for him. For the pain he'd gone through and what he was still going through. And I was angry too, at what had been taken from him, and all because he'd chosen to save his father from a burning house. A father who'd then abandoned him.

It wasn't fair. It wasn't right. It was what had happened to me, and it was lonely.

It made you feel shitty, and worthless, and for him, battling terrible injuries, to then be abandoned...

No wonder he was so angry.

My own anger at him, at the way he'd cut me loose, was still there, but it seemed petty compared to what had happened to him. And all because he'd been afraid of what I would think of him...

A tear slipped down my cheek.

'You should have had that,' I whispered. 'You should have had that life of your own.'

His eyes glittered. 'Yeah, well, I didn't. And perhaps it was karma. For being a selfish asshole.'

'You're not selfish.' I slid my hand along the side of his jaw, up into the short strands of his hair. It was thick and soft, and I gripped on tight. 'You weren't given a choice, and that's not right.'

'They worked hard for me, Mom and Dad. To get me where I was. They sacrificed a lot.'

'Who are you trying to convince? Me or yourself?'

A muscle leapt in the side of his perfect jaw. 'I don't know. It doesn't seem fair to get angry with them when all they wanted was a way out.'

'You weren't a way out, Eli. You were their son.'

He said nothing for a long minute, staring down at me, the green glitter in his eyes sharp. His beautiful face was so grim, as if he hadn't done much smiling in the past few years. As though he didn't even know how.

'And you were my hero,' I went on, wanting to take his anger away, see him smile. 'I remember once when I was quite young, and you were playing computer games with Traj, I went and had a look inside your school bag to see if you had a superhero costume in there.'

Something faded and shifted in his eyes, and there was a silence.

'No way,' he said eventually.

'Yes way. I was very disappointed when I couldn't find one. I thought you probably wore it under your clothes.'

'I wasn't any kind of hero, Vee.'

'You were to me. You were my friend, Eli Hart. And that's pretty much the same thing.'

He still didn't smile, but his expression had changed, moving from anger to something else, something intent and hot. A fierce look sent fire licking all over my skin.

And abruptly I was sick of talking, so I pulled him down, his beautiful mouth on mine. But I didn't want it fast and desperate, I wanted it slow and sweet. I wanted to show him what he meant to me, so this time it was me who showed him what I wanted. I touched his lips with my tongue, getting him to open for me, and then began to explore, hot and slick. Got to savour the flavour of him, rich and delicious, like the truffles he'd fed me just before.

He went still, letting me kiss him. Letting me nip at his lower lip and bite. Letting me kiss him deeper, harder, dragging a growl from the back of his throat.

I'd been angry with him for so long, but I wasn't

angry now. How could I be angry with him when he was so obviously angry at himself?

I put my hands on his broad shoulders and I pushed hard, breaking the kiss so I could shove him onto his back. He let me—because there was no way I was strong enough to have pushed him if he hadn't wanted to be pushed—then I straddled him, my thighs spread over his narrow hips, the hard ridge of his cock nudging the soft, sensitive skin of my pussy.

He reached for me, but I grabbed his wrists and pushed them back up on the pillow on either side of his head. 'No touching,' I ordered, watching his face to see if he'd allow this too.

That hard mouth quirked and satisfaction filled me at getting an almost-smile from him. 'If you don't want me touching, you'd better get working,' he said.

For an answer, I covered his mouth with mine, holding his wrists down on the pillow and leaning forward so my weight increased the pressure. Then I kissed him deeper, harder, more demanding.

I could feel him tense, and I broke the kiss again, but only so I could kiss his jaw and the strong column of his neck, paying extra attention to the lick of the burn, using my tongue to trace the edges of it. And then down further, over the patchwork of scar tissue across his chest. He wouldn't be able to feel it, but he could certainly see my mouth on his skin, kissing him. Adoring him.

He nearly died. You nearly lost him.

I put my hand on his hips, holding on to him as if he might slip away, trailing kisses all over him, closing my eyes against the threat of tears.

But he hadn't died. And he was here with me. Vital and warm and alive. And just for tonight everything was allowed, surely?

Will one night be enough?

Of course it wouldn't be. But it was all I had right now, so I'd take it.

I kissed right down his body to the hard and proud length of his cock, and I kissed along that too, worshipping him.

He growled a low, deep rumble and, before I could do anything more, he shifted beneath me and suddenly I found myself on my back with him above me, our positions reversed.

'Hey,' I said breathlessly. 'You promised no touching.'

'I didn't promise. And rules are made to be broken.'

He bent and took my mouth the way I'd taken his, feverish, hot and slick.

I arched up beneath him, wrapping my legs around his hips, his cock sliding against my bare sex, hitting my clit and sending showers of sparks cascading through me.

He rocked against me, teasing us both, making me pant against his mouth as the sparks became flames licking up inside me.

Then, just when it became too much, he pulled

away, reaching for one of the condom packets on the nightstand. He ripped it open, sheathed himself in seconds flat, then came back over me. He reached for my hand and guided it down between us, wrapping my fingers around his cock, and I knew what he wanted me to do without him saying a thing.

I lifted my hips and fitted him against me, then I guided him inside.

There was no pain this time and only a little sensitive soreness. But I was so wet I barely felt it. He slid in as if he'd been made for me, fitting me so very perfectly, and then he paused, his chest rising and falling fast and hard.

He looked down at me and I met his gaze, the amber in his eyes glowing. Staring at me the way I used to stare at him, as if I was the best thing in his life.

My heart contracted even as my sex tightened around his cock, gripping him, holding him to me. I lifted my hands to him but he shifted again, turning us both once more until he was on his back with me straddling him again. His hands were heavy on my hips, holding me down on him.

'Show me, Vee,' he murmured.

He didn't explain, but I didn't need him to. I showed him what was in my heart.

I began to move on him, rising and falling, his hands guiding me in a rhythm that was at first strange, then interesting and then thrilling. I put my hands on his chest and stroked him, glorying in the scars, the rough with the smooth, and the hard muscle beneath it. In the heat of him. Loving how tight his jaw went and how his gaze was glued to mine, as if he couldn't look away.

I took his hands and guided them to my breasts and he stroked me, his thumbs circling my aching nipples, providing the most incredible counterpoint to the sensations that were building between my legs.

It was so good. The pleasure made me shake.

I put my palms on his chest and leaned on it, moving faster, wanting more friction, rocking my hips and I could hear his breath catch as the movement gave him more pleasure too.

I loved the sound. Loved that I could do that to him—make this god of a man catch his breath due to the pleasure I was giving him.

I loved him. I always would.

But this isn't for ever.

I shoved the thought away, refusing to let it ruin this moment, going faster and faster, chasing the climax that hovered just out of reach. His eyes burning into mine were a deep gold now, his expression so fierce. Hungry. Making me feel like a goddess.

Then he slipped one hand between my legs, finding my clit, giving me the extra sensation I needed, and the climax hit me like a wave, lifting me up so high I swore I could have touched the sky.

I cried out his name, my whole body rigid, a lightning rod for pleasure. I ground down through my body and into his, and I heard him growl.

His hands on my hips tightened and, as I rode through the last few pulses of pleasure, he turned me again so that I lay beneath him. And then he thrust hard, fast, as he found his own pleasure.

He groaned out my name, his hands sliding beneath me, gathering me close to his chest. Then he turned his face into my neck, his breathing harsh and wild, his big body shuddering with the effects of the climax.

I put my arms around him and I held him, my heart full and aching, tears behind my lids.

I love you, I whispered. *I love you so much.*

But only in my head.

CHAPTER TWENTY

Elias

I TURNED ON my side, gathering her close, holding her against me. She adjusted herself slightly, snuggling against me as if that was her rightful place.

The intensity of the orgasm that had gripped me was still pulsing hard in my head, pleasure making me shudder.

She was so warm. She felt so good.

She loves you.

I closed my eyes in the darkness, keeping her close, listening to her breathing begin to slow, become regular. Her body relaxed, as if finally letting go of something, and I knew she'd fallen asleep.

I was pretty sure she hadn't meant me to hear what she'd whispered as the climax had hit. Perhaps she'd thought I wouldn't notice, being too occupied with my own intense orgasm. But of course I'd noticed. I noticed everything about her.

She loved me.

It wasn't a shock. She'd as good as admitted it earlier, but I hadn't thought about it. Deliberately hadn't thought about it. Because complicated was exactly what I didn't want and her feelings for me were the ultimate complication.

That was why I had sex with strangers. Why I paid for it. Why I left my money on the night-stand and walked away. There were no feelings with strangers. No complications.

But, also, not as much pleasure.

I didn't want that thought. I didn't want the words she'd whispered to me, either, but they echoed in my head. And there was a part of me that wanted to let her go and walk away, walk straight out of that fuck-ing door. Never see her again.

But I couldn't bear the thought. She didn't deserve it and I wasn't that much of a fucking coward. I cared about her. That was the issue. And no amount of tell-ing myself that I didn't give a shit made the slightest bit of difference to what was in my heart.

I cared about her feelings, and what she thought, and what happened to her.

It was a goddamned mess.

I wasn't going to sleep so I waited a time, enjoy-ing the feeling of her in my arms, and then I gently eased away from her, getting out of bed and moving out into the living area.

I wasn't sure what I was doing. My body was moving on autopilot, reflexively putting the plates from our snack onto the hotel trolley, along with the half-drunk wine. The blindfold lay on the floor near the couch.

Picking it up, I turned it over in my hands, the fabric soft against my fingertips.

I'd already booked in another meeting with a Strangers employee, same time next week. And this blindfold would be for her.

Except…

Discomfort twisted in my gut, and it took me a little while to realise that the discomfort was reluctance. That I wasn't happy with the thought of another woman putting it on. Another woman sitting in that chair. Another woman following my orders and loving everything I did to her…

No, it wasn't just reluctance. The thought left me cold. Absolutely fucking cold.

You don't want another woman.

I found myself looking towards the bedroom, where Vesta was all curled up, naked and beautiful and so heartbreakingly desirable I could feel myself getting hard yet again just thinking about her.

No, of course I didn't want another woman. I wanted her.

I wanted her to be here next Friday. And maybe the Friday after that too, and maybe for the next month of Fridays. Just her. Only her. I wouldn't even have bothered to second-guess myself if it hadn't been for those soft words whispered to me before she'd fallen asleep in my arms.

I love you.

This wasn't just another Friday for her. It wasn't just a night of great sex. It was her fantasy—I was her fantasy. She'd saved herself for me. She loved me, but she wasn't going to demand anything of me. I knew that already. Knew that when tomorrow came, and I said goodbye to her, she wouldn't protest. She'd turn away and walk out of that door because she wouldn't want to put any expectations on me, not like my parents had.

But that just seemed...wrong.

Vesta had been denied the things she'd wanted all her goddamned life, by her parents and to some extent Traj. But being denied had never stopped her from fighting for her dreams. From going out there and getting them for herself. That college degree and her business, for example. She was a fighter—that was true.

But why should she have to fight for this when I could simply give it to her?

I could tell her that I wanted more, that one night wasn't enough. That maybe we should try another night, or maybe more. Maybe we should go out on a date or two. Or maybe even three. See how it went.

Would that make her happy?

You know what she really wants.

I turned away from the bedroom abruptly, striding to the bathroom. I flicked on the shower and, not bothering to wait for it to heat, stepped under the water.

It was cold, icy on the parts of my skin that still had sensation, but I didn't shiver.

Love. That was what she wanted. That was all Vesta had ever wanted.

But love was demanding. It was pressure. It was injuring yourself and not saying a thing because you didn't want to disappoint your parents. It was playing on that same knee for years, ignoring the pain because things had gone too far now, and two people's entire future rested on you and your ability to play some goddamned game well.

It was going into a burning building and rescuing someone, and then being left to agony in a hospital bed, because even though you'd saved their life they still felt you'd failed them in some way.

Yeah, love was a burn that never healed, no matter how many times you grafted new skin over it, and I wasn't doing that again. Never fucking ever.

So, no. I couldn't give her that.

But I could give her great sex and company. I could give her some smiles. I could make her laugh. I could…help her.

That would be enough, surely?

It won't be. You know that.

But I shoved the thought away as I headed back to the bedroom, getting into bed with her again and gathering her close, pressing my face to the back of her neck. Inhaling the scent of musk and candy floss and Vee.

It would be enough.

It would have to be.

CHAPTER TWENTY-ONE

Vesta

I WOKE TO the smell of pancakes and bacon and really good coffee.

For a minute I lay there, trying to reorient myself, my brain still cloudy from one of the best sleeps I'd ever had, the night before slowly coming back to me.

A blindfold. A chair. Pleasure. Losing my virginity...

Eli.

Warmth filled me in a wave, wrapping me up in its arms and holding me tight.

I'd spent the night with the man I'd loved since I was sixteen. I'd lost my virginity to him the way I'd always wanted. And it had been so good. It had been amazing.

But a night is all you'll ever have, and now it's over.

The wave of warmth receded, leaving me high and dry, and suddenly cold.

Of course it was over. He didn't feel the same way about me as I felt about him, and I was certain of it. And I couldn't ask him for more. I couldn't pin all my hopes on him the way his parents had done. Couldn't force him to be what I wanted him to be. I had to let him be himself…and he was hurt.

It didn't matter. I'd known going in that we'd only ever have one night, so I couldn't be sad about it now. Still, I wasn't sure I wanted to sit there eating break-fast with him, watching the minutes tick by as our time together slowly ran out. That felt as if it would be a lesson in torture to me.

Slowly, I got out of bed. I visited the bathroom, had a quick shower, then pulled on my dress. It was creased from spending a night on the bathroom floor, but there was nothing to be done about that.

My sandals were in the bedroom, so I put them on, taking my time. But I was only drawing out the inevitable, and I knew it. And soon there was no more dressing to be done, leaving me with nothing to do but walk out into the living area of the suite.

The little dining table had been set with a white tablecloth, the morning light gleaming off silver cutlery and glinting off crystal glasses, sliding over beautiful white plates. A spray of pink roses sat in a silver vase. There was food on the table too—fluffy pancakes and crispy bacon and maple syrup and pas-tries. Orange juice and coffee.

And Eli.

He sat there at the table dressed in his black suit, the black shirt he wore underneath open at the neck. The light fell over him, turning his short hair and the tips of his lashes bright gold, reflecting the same hints of gold deep in his eyes. His mouth curved as he saw me, a ghost of that easy, slow-burning smile that used to make my heart leap.

Still had the same effect, judging from the tightness in my chest.

'Hungry?' he asked. 'Thought you might like some food.'

It was beautiful, the set table and the roses—my favourite flowers—the kind of food I liked. And the man I wanted, more than I'd ever wanted anything in my entire life, was sitting there waiting to enjoy breakfast with me.

And for a moment I let myself imagine having this every morning. Having him every morning for the rest of our lives. I'd sit down with him and we'd eat and talk. Or maybe we wouldn't talk. We'd simply eat and read the paper together in companionable silence. And then maybe we'd go back to bed again, lose some hours in each other's arms…

I wanted it. I wanted it so badly, it was pain.

But I knew it wasn't going to happen and suddenly the idea of sitting here with him, pretending that it would, was more than I could bear.

I shook my head, tearing my gaze from his as I scanned the room for my purse. 'Love to, but I gotta run. There's a few things I need to do this morning.'

'Surely you can stay for breakfast?'

I went over to the chair I'd sat in the night before,

very carefully not looking at him, spotting my purse beside it. 'No, sorry. Really, I have to go.'

I didn't hear him move, but when I straightened up and turned he was right in front of me, his expression intent. 'Vesta,' he said.

My throat closed. 'What?'

'What's wrong?'

'Nothing. I just have to run—'

'I don't want you to go.'

My heart shuddered to a stop. 'I…'

'I want to sit down and have breakfast with you. And I want to discuss maybe having this night again.' Gold gleamed suddenly in the depths of his eyes. 'Or maybe having a number of nights. Perhaps we could even go on a date, or a few dates. See what happens.'

This night again. And maybe more than once. A date or two… See what happens…

I swallowed. I'd expected a goodbye…not this. 'You really want more?'

'Yes.' He took a step forward, coming closer. 'It was good, Vee. Better than anything I've ever had, and that's saying something. And I want it again. I want you again.'

Oh, I could see it. Another night with him—a date, even. Us together for however long that might be.

But it's not what you want.

It was more than I'd expected. More than I'd ever thought I'd have from him. But… I looked up at him, into his perfect face, the white lick of the scar marring the golden skin of his throat.

One night. One morning. A few dates, more nights… No, it wouldn't be enough.

I didn't want another night with him, or even more nights, or more dates. I didn't want to 'see how it went.' I already knew how it went. I'd been living it for the last nine years, spending my soul on wishes, prayers and hope that he'd feel for me what I felt for him. Yet, despite all those wishes and prayers, all that hope, getting nothing back.

It was what I'd been doing even before that too. Trying so hard to please my parents, surviving on the scraps of attention they gave me and hoping for more, yet never getting it.

Well, I was tired of it. Tired of trying so hard just to be worthy of someone's notice. Tired of desperately holding on to someone who clearly wasn't interested. I didn't want to go back to that. I didn't want to be sending message after message into a black hole of silence. Calling someone who never answered and who never called back. Giving my heart over and over again to a man who didn't want it.

I wanted nothing less than love because, Jesus Christ, after so long, didn't I deserve it?

My heart felt sore, my throat tight.

'No,' I said, forcing the words out. 'No, I don't think that's a good idea.'

A muscle leapt in his jaw. 'Why not?'

I had only the truth to give him.

'I don't want another night. I don't want a date. I don't want to see how it goes.' I held his gaze, letting him see what was in mine. 'I've spent a long time being unloved and unnoticed. Having people not really give a shit about me or what I do. And for a long time I told myself that I didn't care, that it didn't matter, because I didn't need anyone.'

I took a step forward so I was close to him. 'But I do need someone. I need you, Eli Hart. I'm in love with you. I've been in love with you for years. I don't want to put anything on you, but you should know that. And I'm not refusing because my feelings have changed.' I took a little breath. 'I'm refusing because *I've* changed. I don't want to settle any more, Eli. I don't want to settle for less. I've been settling all my life and I'm not doing it any more.'

He'd gone very still, tension in every line of him. 'So, what do you want?'

'You really have to ask me?' I searched his beautiful face. 'What I've always wanted. You. But not for a night and not for a couple of dates. I don't want to have you but not really have you. I want your heart and, if you can't give it to me, then I understand. I'm not going to force you.' I swallowed, straightening. 'But I'm not going to settle for less than that.'

'Vesta…' My name was a hoarse scrape of sound. 'I can't. What you're asking… I can't give.'

It wasn't a surprise. He'd barely thought of me in years, so why would one night of great sex change his mind? Yet, even though I'd expected it, the pain bit deep.

'Of course you can't,' I said. 'You forgot I existed

for nine years, after all. But I never forgot, Eli. And I never stopped loving you. And…it's time for me to move on.' My heart had grown spines, stabbing into me, hurting, but I was used to the pain and I hardened myself against it. 'This night was all about laying the ghost of you, and I have. I'll remember it for ever, Eli. But…'

I took a breath. 'I'm tired of silence. I'm tired of half-measures. I'm tired of trying so fucking hard for people who don't give a shit. And I'm tired of loving you and getting nothing back. I don't want to live on whatever scraps of attention you choose to give me—not any more.' I looked into his eyes. 'Nine years, Eli. Nine years you ignored me. And now all you have to offer me is a few dates? A few nights? A "see how it goes"?'

His expression was taut, the emerald-green of his anger flickering in his eyes. 'You think I don't feel like the biggest asshole in the world about that? That I don't regret every second? Fuck, Vesta, if I could change anything in the last ten years it would be that. But I can't. Just like I can't give you what you want, either.'

I couldn't stop myself then, stepping right up to him, all the anger, all the pain, rising up and spilling out. 'Can't or won't, Eli? Which is it?'

The tension rolled off him like thunder. There was fury in his eyes and a kind of self-loathing too. Last night I'd backed away from any confrontation, not wanting to add to the burden he was already carrying, and not wanting to destroy the mood. But now the mood was in pieces and I had nothing left to lose.

He wasn't the only one who was angry.

So I didn't back down this time. I stared at him and I did not move.

'You really want to know?' he said finally in his ruined voice. 'It's *won't*. I don't want to love you. I don't want to love anyone. I loved my parents. I would have done anything for them, and I did. But the weight of it was just too fucking heavy. And I'm not doing that again, carrying someone else's hopes and dreams. I'm done.' His eyes blazed. 'I told you I was a selfish asshole. You should have listened to me.'

The pain was bright flames across my skin, but I ignored them.

He was right. I should have listened.

'Good thing I'm listening now,' I said hoarsely. 'But just remember something, Eli Hart. The past is part of you, whether you like it or not. It made you. And you can't cut it away just because you don't like it or because it hurts. Pretending to be selfish, pretending you don't care, won't help. Because you're not selfish, and you do care, and that's the real problem, isn't it? It's not that your skin is scarred and you can't feel a thing. It's because your heart isn't and you can't deal with the pain.'

He went white. 'Pain? You don't know the first fucking thing about pain.'

I just looked at him, struggling to hold the tears

back. 'Just because you can't see my scars, doesn't mean I don't have them. And at least I'm willing to acknowledge that they're there.'

The look he gave me was furious and I thought he was going to say something. But at the last minute he turned away from me, striding back to the table and standing there, giving me his back. Making it obvious he wanted me to leave.

My throat felt sore. I could feel the tears prick at the backs of my eyes and I knew I had a choice. I could cave, do what I'd been doing for nine years and go after him. Tell him I was sorry, that of course I wanted another night or a date. That, yes, we could see how it went. Or I could believe that I was worth more than that and that he was too. That we were both worth the love we'd never had from anyone else, that love that we could give each other. And I could walk away. Hold out.

But I was done with caving. With pursuing. With apologising.

I wanted his love and nothing less.

So I turned, and I went to the door, and I pulled it open.

And he didn't try to stop me. And he didn't call my name.

And, when it shut behind me, there was only silence.

CHAPTER TWENTY-TWO

Elias

ANGER SMOULDERED INSIDE ME, but I let her go. What other choice did I have? All those things she'd said, about not wanting to settle and not wanting half-measures…they were all true. And she shouldn't have to settle. She'd done that all her life, as she'd said, and she deserved more.

She deserved more than I could give her.

What you won't *give her.*

I ignored that and went back to the table as the door shut behind her, thinking I might as well eat, but the appetite I'd had when I'd woken up that morning was gone. I'd pictured her sitting opposite me, talking about what we might do the following Friday. Or even earlier than that. A date tomorrow night, perhaps. Somewhere nice, where I could spoil her, and we could catch up on the past couple of years…

My chest hurt, a pulsing kind of ache.

That wasn't going to happen now. There would be no leisurely breakfast and maybe some more time in bed. And there would be no date. There would be no sweet, candy-floss scent. No stars on warm skin to trace with my fingers. No eyes of liquid midnight watching me as pleasure unfurled across her beautiful face, looking at me as if she'd never seen anything as beautiful.

Me, the ruined hulk of the man I'd once been. A man full of selfishness and anger, who'd had the success he'd always dreamed of and yet it felt like nothing in this moment. Felt empty and meaningless.

A man built of nothing but scar tissue, lacking sensitivity and feeling, with a heart so scarred nothing could get through.

It was better that she walk away from a man like that. A man who'd treated her like dirt. Better that she give up and that she didn't fight. There was nothing here worth fighting for, after all.

That all sounded good—the same things I'd been telling myself for years now without feeling a thing. So I shouldn't have felt anything now.

But my chest still hurt, with a pain that went deeper than my scars. That felt as if it scoured my soul.

I found myself standing at the window, watching the sidewalk outside, watching a small figure in a blue dress go down the steps.

She was walking away. Walking away from me.

You fucking coward. She's loved you for years and that's all you've got to give her? Breakfast and the offer of a couple of dates? Another night?

The pain in my chest deepened, along with a sense of loss I had no idea what to do with. It shouldn't hurt like this. It shouldn't bother me. I'd told her I was selfish, and I was. I'd embraced it. Become it.

So why did I feel as if I'd made a mistake? As if I'd somehow stumbled back into the blaze that had nearly killed me and was burning me all over again?

Pain was there for a reason. It was the body's way of telling you something was wrong. Some pain was good, some pain was useful and had a purpose...

I couldn't figure out the purpose of the agony in my chest now. What did it matter that there would only be me and an endless succession of strangers in a hotel room from now on? Why did that feel like the bleakest thing I'd ever imagined?

You know why. Why would you ever want that again, when you could have her?

But I couldn't have her. I didn't want her. I didn't want to love her. I didn't want love, period.

I didn't want to sacrifice myself for someone again, carry someone's expectations again. Fail someone again. Because that was what love was. Sacrifice and pressure and failure and pain.

How could she ask me to put myself through that again? Go back into the fire again?

Did you ever really come out of it?

My breath caught, freezing in my lungs.

I thought I'd put what had happened behind me, that I'd moved on. I'd cut my past from me like dead tissue from a wound, and I thought I'd healed.

The past is part of you, whether you like it or not. It made you. And you can't cut it away just because you don't like it or because it hurts...

I tried to push away what she'd told me, but it sat there in my head, repeating itself. I'd tried hard to put the past behind me, but it was true—I could never escape it entirely. Not when it was literally burned into my skin.

I'd thought that cutting away the bad pieces of that life would help healthy skin to grow, but...

Sure. Choosing to be a selfish asshole, and also to pay for sex because you can't stand intimacy, is healthy.

Realisation hit me.

She'd said it wasn't the fact that my body was scarred that was the problem. It was that my heart wasn't. And she was right. I was covered in scar tissue, all the nerve-endings damaged or dead. But... my heart didn't have that scar tissue. It still felt. And it was still burned, bleeding and raw. Full of anger at what had happened to me. At how let down I'd been by my parents. At how abandoned and worthless I felt. How helpless. Choosing selfishness in that moment, choosing not to care, had felt like a power move and so I'd embraced it completely.

But...I'd never left behind those feelings, had I?

...You're not selfish, and you do care, and that's the real problem, isn't it? It's not that your skin is scarred and you can't feel a thing. It's because your heart isn't and you can't deal with the pain...

I stared out of the window at nothing, my chest on fire.

She was so sharp. She saw right through me. Because what if selfishness was just a facade? A veneer? A skin graft over a wound? And what if she was right? What if it wasn't selfishness that drove me at all, but fear? Fear of abandonment, of being worthless, of being helpless. Of pain.

It came over me then like a wave. A backdraft in a blaze. I hadn't healed. I hadn't moved on. I was still stuck there in that hospital bed, fighting those goddamned feelings and trying to cut away the part of me that hurt the most.

Like my heart. That had been burned, yet it had never scarred over, was still raw and in pain. And it hurt because, no matter what I told myself, I still cared.

I cared about her.

It's more than caring and you know it.

Outside, Vee walked determinedly along the sidewalk, lifting her hand to her face a couple of times. Brushing away tears…?

The pain in my heart felt like knives. Felt like the truth I hadn't wanted to acknowledge. She'd meant a lot to me—she'd always meant a lot to me. But there was a reason I'd cut her out of my life, and it wasn't to do with putting the past behind me, being selfish or her deserving more.

It was because, if I'd let her get close, I wouldn't have been able to hold out against the feeling that pushed at me, demanding acknowledgement.

At sixteen, I'd loved her as a brother, a protective kind of love. But deep down, right down deep inside, a part of me had always known what she would become, that she would bloom like a rose and shine like a star. And that the love I had for her had the potential to change, to become more adult, more complex.

That was why I'd ignored her. That was why I'd cut her from my life. Why I hadn't let her get close.

Because, if I had, I'd have fallen for her completely and irrevocably.

And I had. And all it had taken was one night.

One night to see the incredible woman she'd become. Brave and strong and tenacious. Blooming like a rose, shining like a star.

One night to show me the lie I was living. The lie I couldn't keep telling myself was true any more. That I didn't need her. That I didn't care.

But I did care and, not only that, the worst had happened: I'd fallen in love with her just as I'd been afraid I would. And, just as I'd dreaded, it was agony and it cut me to pieces.

Yet pain had a purpose. It was a warning that something was wrong, and right now the pain in my heart was telling me that something was critical.

I shouldn't have sent her away. Which meant the only thing to do was to get her back again.

I'd turned from the window before I was even conscious of it, striding to the door and then going through it. I walked fast through the hotel, and then down the stairs outside, and then I began to run, moving through the crowds as I'd once moved down the football field heading for the touchdown.

People turned to look at me but I didn't care. My focus was only her, getting closer now. And then she was right in front of me.

'Vee,' I said hoarsely. 'Vee, wait.'

She shook her head and then slowed, coming to a stop and turning around. Her face was pink and streaked with tears. I could see them in the light. Her eyes were black, and in that second there was no other choice for me. No other decision to make. She was hurt. She was in pain.

And I loved her.

I loved her so much.

'What do you—?' she began.

But I didn't let her finish. I reached for her and pulled her into my arms.

'Hey,' she said breathlessly, trying to push at me, but I didn't let her go.

'You want to know the real reason I cut you out of my life?' I asked hoarsely, staring down into her beautiful blue eyes. 'It's because, if I'd have let you get close, I would have fallen for you. I would have loved you, Vesta. And you were right—it wasn't about selfishness. It was about me being afraid of that. Afraid of the pain, of not feeling good enough, of failing people. Afraid that you wouldn't see me the same way, that you wouldn't…want me.'

She blinked, her eyes filling with tears. 'No. I told

you. Why would you think some scars would ever change the way I feel about you?'

Of course they wouldn't. How could I have doubted her? Nine years she'd held on to me, nine years without a response, yet she hadn't wavered. Not once.

'Because I'm a fucking idiot.' My voice was even rougher than normal. 'And because I was afraid. You were right, though. I can't put the past behind me. I can't cut it away. It's part of me. Like you're part of me.' I held her tighter, drawing her close. 'I don't want to let you go, Vee. And I don't want a night. I don't want a date. And fuck seeing how it goes. I know how it goes.' Keeping one arm around her, I lifted one hand and pushed my fingers into her hair, easing her head back. 'It goes like this.'

And I bent and took her mouth in a hungry, desperate kiss that went on and on until we both had to come up for air.

Then she pressed her forehead to mine, breathing fast, the long streaks of tears on her cheeks. 'So what does that mean, Eli? Tell me. And be honest— because I can't stand too much more of this.'

My heart ached, the pain raw, but this time I didn't run from it. I embraced it, made it mine. She had scars too—as she'd so eloquently told me—and it was time I helped heal hers as she had started to heal mine.

So I released her and stepped back. Then I dropped to my knees on the sidewalk in front of her, not giving a shit about the crowds as I looked up into her lovely face.

'You wanted my heart, Vee. So it's yours. It always was. It's selfish and guilty and filled with regret, but it loves you so much. And it's willing to do whatever it takes to make you happy.'

She was still crying a little, but the smile she gave me was radiant. 'You don't have to do anything, ace.' She took a step closer to me, then reached down and cupped my face in her hands. 'You just have to hold me and never let me go.'

There was only one answer to that.

I got to my feet and swept her into my arms, turning back to the hotel.

She relaxed against my shoulder, her fingers resting lightly in the hollow of my throat where the scars were. 'So, what happens now?'

'What happens now is breakfast,' I said. 'And then I'm taking you to buy a ring.'

'Wait, what?'

I glanced down at her safe in my arms, right against my heart where she belonged. And I smiled. 'I'm going to marry you, Vesta Howard-Smith.'

Her eyes glittered a deep, endless blue, full of the love that had always been part of her and that I'd just been too blind to notice. 'Are you, now?'

'Yes. Any objections?'

'Hmm…' she said, snuggling against me. 'Are there waffles for breakfast?'

'Absolutely.'

'In that case…' She smiled again, the special one she saved just for me. The one I'd missed for so long and never known it. The one that healed something broken inside me.

'No. No objection whatsoever.'

EPILOGUE

Vesta

WE SPENT THE weekend in that hotel room and we didn't leave it. Catching up on our lives. Catching up on ourselves. I'd never been so happy in my entire life.

And he bought me a ring. And a month later I still had no objections.

We married the next month and invited our families and, despite the issues we'd had with them, they all came. It was beautiful. It was the happiest day of my life.

I opened my second tattoo parlour in LA and, after a famous rock star was spotted with one of my designs inked on his chest, my client list went through the roof.

The best part, though, was after hours, when everyone had gone and I had my own personal rock star laid out on my chair, watching me with his intense, glowing stare of gold and green as I inked my design into his skin.

Turning his scars into art. Into something unique and beautiful.

A story of courage and strength.

And, most of all, of love.

* * * * *

BOUND TO YOU

JC HARROWAY

MILLS & BOON

To Julia, romance legend, inspirational woman
and brainstormer extraordinaire.

CHAPTER ONE

Monroe

THE ONLY VIEW better than a Tokyo sunset from Hudson Black's office on the thirty-second floor of Bold Tower is a view of the man himself, with his shirtsleeves rolled up, his tie loosened and a dark shadow forming on his square jaw. My years of experience at ignoring what a fine specimen of virility my business partner is come in extremely handy as I keep my eyes glued to my laptop screen.

'So we concur, subject to Sterling's approval,' I say of the third partner in our global equities company… who's also my ex-husband. 'The Tanako investment looks the most promising, although I'm very keen for the interview with Kunosu Tech tomorrow.'

Today was our first face-to-face strategy meeting, with one of the three founders absent, the first time in a long time that Hudson and I have been alone together. This fact isn't lost on me, if the delicious thrill of illicit anticipation coiling in my belly is any indication. The atmosphere of the entire room is charged, as if I'm aware of him in a whole raft of enthralling new ways I'm required to overlook.

'I wouldn't say we concur one hundred per cent, Dove.'

He always addresses me by my last name, something I pretend annoys me, but that I secretly adore. It's the way his deep, sexy voice caresses the word, combined with the fact that he's never called me anything else.

It's his thing. *Our* thing.

'Do we ever see completely eye to eye?' Hudson's grin is a playful reminder of our usual debates, which can be…heated. That's what happens when you partner three highly competitive personalities together in one company. Complete agreement becomes a rare luxury we reserve for our seven-figure investments, the kind we've discussed today.

Still, I respect the hell out of both my partners. Hudson in particular is obscenely driven, and successful to the point of truly offensive wealth. All thanks to his lowly beginnings, of which he rarely speaks.

'Our successful partnership is built on our ambitious natures,' I volley. Today the boardroom banter, and that frisson I experience around him, seems more volatile. Supercharged. Almost like that of strangers who find each other attractive sharing a first smile.

'Where's the fun in constant harmony?' I close my laptop and sit back in the comfortable leather chair at his glass-and-chrome conference table. 'All three of us are addicted to the friction, I suspect.'

'I agree. A touch of friction is much better than constant harmony.' The sexy twitch of his lips sets off an internal shudder in me. Is it my imagination, or is his deep voice laced with flirtation today? His stare lingers for a heartbeat longer than normal.

I laugh, breathless. I'm no longer sure if we're discussing business but go with it all the same. Harmony *is* overrated. 'Spark-inducing' better describes my relationship with Hudson—both professionally and during our one-time foray into wild, screaming orgasm sex.

Remembering that night from three years ago, I allow my stare properly to traverse his physique. In the six months since I last saw him in the flesh, his lean, toned body seems to have buffed up a little more. Perhaps he's spending a lot of time working out...

My nipples tingle against my bra at the memories of that single time. How, shortly after my divorce from Sterling had been finalised, Hudson had one night effortlessly pinned me to the wall and made me forget my failure and grief.

I kick off my heels under the table and stretch my legs, which are still protesting the long flight from London, where I head up the UK division of BLD Global Ventures, or Bold, as we affectionately call it. 'It's just as well that we're such good friends.

We'll work out any differences of opinion, as we always do.'

We've stayed friends and partners by acting as if our sexy encounter had never happened. I try not to think too hard about our complex little trio, but I suspect we were both conscious of protecting our relationship with Sterling.

My relationship with my ex is convoluted after our amicable divorce. Our marriage was short—both of us realised almost instantly that we'd rushed into it. I was desperately seeking the happy-ever-after my siblings had, and Sterling seemed intent on proving something to his overcritical stepfather. We were equally to blame, so we shelved our disillusionment and hurt. We valued the growing business we'd started after university, and we'd just entered into a lucrative partnership with Hudson. We couldn't allow the divorce to ruin all that. Now it helps that we live on separate continents.

Hudson pushes his chair away from the table and swivels to face me. 'Sterling and I can always rely on you to keep us in check.' He rests his chin in his hand and shoots me a rare look of indulgence. Perhaps he too is enjoying the different dynamic in Sterling's absence.

Interesting…

'I'm glad to hear you acknowledge that you can't spell Bold without *D*.' I grin, delight warming my blood. Sparring with Hudson has never felt this sexually charged.

The sound of his throaty chuckle skitters down my spine, setting off a series of delicious shivers. Clearly I've sorely neglected my sex life of late. But working with two driven, self-assured men requires constant impetus. Hudson in particular will settle for nothing less than global domination. One of the reasons he's pushing to expand Bold farther into Europe and Asia.

'It's the B in BLD that's most important.' He flicks off the screen we've used for our meeting, as if he's won the argument, and then heads to the bar. 'Drink?'

I nod, relaxing now business is done for the day. 'Scotch, please.'

He pours generous measures from a crystal decanter into two glasses and grins. On any other man, his arrogance would be repellent. But playful Hudson, a sight rarely seen, could charm a nun out of her knickers. And he more than compensates for his God-given confidence with his wit, his razor-sharp intelligence and his ruthlessly insightful business mind.

Despite that, I can't allow him to think he's bested me with the naming order. 'Keep believing that if you like.'

He quirks an eyebrow, his expression irresistibly roguish. 'Everyone knows the first initial takes precedence. That's why Sterling fought so hard for the spot and got stuck in the middle.' Sterling's surname, Lombard, accounts for the *L* in BLD.

We laugh, more sparks bouncing between us. Spirited exchanges are how we've managed our attraction all these years since we first met, when I was engaged to Sterling. Neither of us would risk our highly successful multinational company for something as clichéd as meaningless sex.

I join him at the comfortable seating area, which faces his corner office views of Tokyo. The sky has lost its pink and orange hues of earlier and turned drab shades of grey, which dampen the vista of the Imperial Palace gardens thirty-two floors below and the glow of Tokyo Tower.

'Well, as your equal partner, I heartily contest that.' I take the tumbler he offers, my fingers unintentionally brushing his.

Our eyes meet. I watch him over the rim of my glass, excitement fizzing in my veins. I'm taking a gamble by flirting back. Or maybe I started it. I take a sip of the top-shelf liquor, allowing its potency to deliver a delicious thrill.

'Of course you do,' he says.

I love that he knows me so well. I'm the youngest of five siblings. The baby. I'm used to fighting battles, wrestling my share of attention and clamouring to be heard over the hubbub. I've never allowed coming last in the birth order, or in the company initials, to define or hinder me.

We settle side by side on his sumptuous sofa. I hold his eye contact in challenge, enjoying the playful direction our trivial argument has taken. 'Don't you agree that it's the climax that's the best part?'

Hudson brings out my competitive side like no one else, perhaps because in business he himself is so cut-throat. So audacious. So relentless. In truth, neither Sterling nor I are as resolute as Hudson, who's made venture capitalism—risky money-making that makes the world's top financiers quail—a contact sport. But then neither of us has experienced the uncertainty of Hudson's early life growing up in the foster system. His drivers are understandable. And his success is an aphrodisiac. Not that he needs to wield one. Not with that sculpted face and virile body that I can confirm he knows how to use.

And tonight, for some reason, I'm struggling to ignore the potent combination.

Tiny flecks of gold shimmer in his irises. 'In the right situation, I'd have to agree with you about the climax, Dove. I'll concede this one point.' He raises his glass. 'Cheers.'

I smile, awash with happy hormones. 'To Tokyo—there's nothing better than a day of good business and good company in one of my favourite cities in the world.'

Well, perhaps one thing… But we can't go there again. We're colleagues. Friends.

With his unrestrained smile, Hudson relaxes back into the sofa, his glass resting on his flat stomach. It's a captivating sight. I'm so used to seeing him in control, being inspiring, authoritative. I watch him with renewed fascination, as if noticing him for the first time. His broad chest strains against the fabric of his shirt, his muscular arm bulging where he rests, one hand behind his head, his long, powerful legs stretched out.

He settles his stare on me, and that sexual heat we seem to be generating fires my endorphins. This is dangerous.

'It's a shame Sterling couldn't make it,' Hudson says. 'I had plans to take you both to a new saké bar this week.' He rubs at the sexy five o'clock shadow on his strong jaw.

I'm momentarily distracted by the disarray of his usually tamed dark hair. My fingers itch as if my hands were once more responsible. But the reminder that Sterling should be here douses the perilous direction of my thoughts. I nod, genuinely sorry that he was detained by his cousin's funeral. A few times a year the three of us meet face-to-face to reconnect, brainstorm and plan long-term strategies for Bold, rotating Tokyo, London and New York, where Sterling lives.

'We'll catch up in London next week instead,' I say, referring to the impromptu meet-up we've brought forward. 'Besides, I can't make it tonight.' I smooth a wrinkle from my skirt, ignoring the irrational sinking feeling in my stomach. 'I have a date.'

I shouldn't feel uncomfortable admitting this to him, but I do. It's as if my body missed the memo that I'm not supposed to find Hudson Black sexy.

That I'm supposed to forget that one time and how it ruined me for mediocre sex. That I shouldn't be flirting with him just because we're alone. I swallow another sip of Scotch to chase off the errant feelings I don't wish to analyse.

Hudson's cognac-brown eyes trace my face thoughtfully. 'I wasn't thinking of tonight. I have a date too.'

Misplaced disappointment pricks my skin. Silly, because my head is telling me that Hudson and I have been there, done that. That our pretty fierce attraction—there from the day we met—is contained. But he's always been my type. Only after Sterling and I divorced did any thoughts that weren't strictly professional enter my consciousness.

I loved Sterling. I still do; we just didn't work out.

The night Hudson and I crossed the line three years ago I was feeling lonely and disheartened after the divorce. Sterling had just announced he was leaving the London office, where we all worked at the time, and moving back to New York where he grew up. We'd been a little shell-shocked. Once Sterling left, Hudson and I lingered for a drink. Neither of us took a single sip. But it felt good to get it over with and put our chemistry behind us, although sex that good had been far from a chore.

'Oh, look at the sky over the bay.' I change the subject. I don't want to think about Hudson sleeping with some lucky woman tonight. 'That looks ominous.'

A large mass of white cirrus clouds obliterates the horizon over Tokyo Bay. The sunset has turned even darker, gloomy and foreboding.

I shiver and curl my feet under me on the sofa.

'There's a storm due tonight,' he says. 'Typhoon Kano. It's not predicted to reach land, though.' He stretches his arm along the back of the sofa, distracting me from the change in the weather with his spicy male scent. 'What time is your date?'

'Dinner at eight.' I agreed to it because I didn't want to be alone if Hudson had 'plans,' and by that I mean some fortunate goddess in his bed. 'Yours?'

'Nine.' He doesn't elaborate but checks his watch.

A smile twitches my lips. 'So just a sex date, then.' I'm provoking him. Hudson doesn't do relationships.

He shrugs, releasing a sexy smile tinged with boyish charm. A hint of what a heartbreaker he must have been as a teen. 'You know me.'

Yes, I do. Hudson's famous commitment avoidance. At thirty-six he's king of the casual hook-up. Three years ago, I guess that allowed me to take the leap and recklessly sleep with him behind my ex's back. That and the fact Bold was branching out, with Hudson moving to Tokyo. I knew it was safe. That it would just be one time. That we'd move on, business as usual, no harm done.

He didn't disappoint me.

'What about you? Is your date marriage material?' There's a hint of hesitation to his question.

I'm vocal about my dreams for the future. Both he and Sterling know I haven't given up on finding love again. One day I want it all. Like my parents had. Like my older siblings have. Like I naively thought I had with Sterling. I want it for real this time.

No more failures.

I shrug, looking away from his searching stare. 'It's a blind date—a friend's brother who runs his own business, travels a lot and happened to be in Tokyo this week.' My heart really isn't in it tonight. The idea of meeting a stranger who, on paper, I have lots in common with, leaves me feeling weirdly hollow.

I finish my drink and stand, emotions swirling through me like the electrical currents brewing outside. 'I'm just going to use your facilities. Shall we send out for some food? I'm not certain what time zone my body is in, but eight o'clock seems a long way off.'

'I'll organise something. Another drink?'

I nod and he heads to the fully equipped kitchen in the corner of his office. I say 'office,' but his working environment—this penthouse—is more of a second home. He spends so much time here. I know from a previous tour that, besides a full-sized bathroom complete with whirlpool bath and double shower, there's also a king-sized bedroom and a gym behind the various doors.

I make use of the bathroom and wash my hands. I'm not sure I can be bothered to go back to my hotel and change for my date, especially now the weather has turned. A look in the mirror confirms that my gold silk blouse and russet skirt are satisfactory. Reflected me looks good. I carry the self-satisfied aura of a successful professional woman. At thirty, I have plenty of time to find lasting love and marriage and make my own family. When you're the last born to a big family, everything feels like a competition driven by sibling rivalry. Out of the five of us, I'm the only divorcee. The only one without children.

My biggest regret is that my mother died thinking all of us were happy and settled with life partners. And then, a few months after she passed, my marriage collapsed. I let her down.

I shake off my fit of melancholy. I just wish she were still here… I'll make her proud one day.

I slide my fingers through my hair, teasing the mass into a sexy tousle, unsure if it's for my date or for Hudson. But my body knows. My pulse kicks up with the excitement I can't muster for a man I've never met. My cheeks are flushed with arousal and a pulse flutters between my legs. Hudson's company does that to me. For some reason that I can only attribute to his excellent Scotch, and even better easy-on-the-eye company, I slip open the top button of my blouse, revealing just a hint of lace-bordered cleavage.

It's just teasing, but I live by the rule of 'go hard or go home.'

When I return to the office Hudson has produced

a platter of tiny bite-sized sushi rolls from some-where, refreshed our drinks and dimmed the lighting to a more intimate level, which makes the darkening sky and wild weather outside more ominous.

I shiver. 'Oh, wow—the weather's changing quickly.' I watch the many city lights of Tokyo's business district, shimmering and distorted by the torrential rain now lashing the windows. Then I glance back at Hudson.

'Yes. The wind has unexpectedly altered direction. Typhoon Kano is now headed directly towards Tokyo.' He's switched the wall-mounted TV to a news broadcast.

We watch the report, although my Japanese is virtually non-existent. His radiant body heat and his command of the language provide comfort against my growing uncertainty—I've never experienced a typhoon before.

'Should I worry? Are we safe?' Hudson's office feels like a warm and cosy modern fortress at the top of a skyscraper. I inch closer, catching the clean linen smell of his shirt.

'Japan is hit by several typhoons a year—more typically in the summer, though.' He shoots me a reassuring smile and mutes the TV.

'So you put this one on especially for me? You shouldn't have.' I smile but a relieved sigh escapes— I wouldn't want to be alone in my hotel room right now.

'I secretly hoped to trap you here.' His laughter

settles the butterflies in my stomach. I trust him. 'Don't worry, Dove. We're perfectly safe here.'

He winks and my pulse trips with desire. We might be safe from the elements, but his proximity, the new awareness of him, makes me feel reckless.

We retake our places on the sofa. Only now his every move seems to brush against my sensitised skin. He's removed his tie, revealing a tantalising glimpse of dark hair as his shirt pulls across his well-defined chest. I have a violent urge to snuggle into him. To press my face to his neck and see if he smells as good close-up...

Instead I select a mini sushi, dip it in the Japanese mayonnaise and pop it in my mouth. My stomach groans in appreciation at the delicious flavours and textures. The silence as we eat should be comfortable. It always has been in the past. Only tonight there's a looming sense of anticipation heightened by the impending storm. It's as if I'm a human barometer and he's a low-pressure system, pulling me in.

Right, blame the atmospheric conditions for your reaction to him...

My appetite dwindles as we watch the storm and watch each other. I should distract myself with business small-talk about tomorrow's schedule or the Japanese Business Awards dinner at which Hudson has been invited to speak.

But there's only one distraction I want.

Hudson's phone emits a bleep. 'Excuse me.' He pulls it from his pocket and reads the screen.

I sip my drink and watch his angular face, the dark swoop of his eyelashes, his sexy mouth. What am I doing?

'Looks like my date has cancelled.' He tosses the phone aside and returns the full beam of his attention to me.

'What a shame.' Fingers of delight skitter down my spine. 'It does look pretty wild.'

As wild as I feel. Am I seriously contemplating crossing the very well-demarcated line between us?

'It does—the situation is changing rapidly.' He leans over me to reach for the remote control to unmute the TV for an update.

Somehow it feels as if he's sitting closer. I hold myself still, and licks of anticipation mixed with fear heat my skin.

Hudson translates the news report—strong winds, flooding, damage expected. My heart thuds. Fear of the impending typhoon, or fear of missing what now feels like the golden opportunity Mother Nature has presented?

Something major is happening out there in the dark.

We look back at each other at the exact same moment. My breath stutters. Something major is happening between us too.

'I think you should stay here tonight, Dove.' A small frown pinches his brows together. 'It's currently classified as a yellow warning, but they predict it will soon get to red. You don't want to be blown off your feet and soaked through to the skin.'

The dangerous power of the elements is mirrored in the tumultuous veering of my resolve. The universe has delivered the ultimate temptation. I want him.

I cling to our banter, playfully rolling my eyes. 'The lengths some people will go to avoid being alone.' I hold my breath to correctly interpret his suggestive stillness and the lust in his stare.

'I'm used to being alone.' His pupils dilate. 'But if I had to be trapped by a storm I'd want it to be with you.'

I swallow hard, putting up a feeble last fight. 'My hotel's not that far away… But perhaps you're right. I'll text my date to cancel.' Even if the tension building between us goes nowhere, I'd rather be with him than on a blind date.

'Good, that's settled.' With a satisfied smile, he switches off the TV and retrieves something from a concealed closet near the door: a fine, cashmere throw. He shakes it out and drapes it over my lap.

'I noticed you shiver,' he says, pressing another remote so the contemporary fireplace built into the wall flickers to life. The heat and intensity of his stare could get a woman into trouble unless, like me, she knows what's behind that sinful expression—the promise of a good time.

'They're shivers of anticipation.' And delight. 'Storms make me nervous.' I retrieve my almost empty tumbler from the table, ridiculously touched that he thought of my comfort but a little disappointed I'll have no excuse to snuggle and steal his body heat.

'No need to be nervous. We could make some progress on tomorrow's schedule to take your mind off it.'

'I have a better plan.' I hold the glass up between us so the liquid catches the glinting gold reflection from the fire. 'How much Scotch do you have left?' I take a slow sip and lick my lips.

'Enough. But how else will we pass the time if not with business?' He's onto me and my thinly veiled seduction. He shifts, his body inching closer.

I have so many sexual suggestions, I almost choke on my next sip of Scotch. But we're trapped here for the night. There's no rush, unlike the last time we played with this fire.

'Do you have a pack of cards?'

'Of course.' He opens a drawer in a low coffee table and retrieves a brand-new pack.

A thrill shudders through me as I exhale. 'What better way to ride out a storm?' I open the pack and shuffle. 'Poker work for you, Black?'

'I can think of more entertaining games,' he replies with that trademark confidence and challenge sparking in his stare. 'But bring it on.'

Oh, I intend to.

CHAPTER TWO

Hudson

I'M DEFINITELY ON board for whatever game she's playing. She's so damned sexy, she smells fantastic and she's been shooting me signals ever since we finished our meeting. That feels like aeons ago, so thinly stretched is my restraint.

Her teeth sink into her bottom lip as she shuffles the cards. I shouldn't notice those telling gestures. Just as I shouldn't be sneaking surreptitious glances at her cleavage through the open vee of her blouse. But she went into the bathroom earlier with two buttons undone and came out with three open.

I'm only flesh and blood.

The memory of the last time we crossed the line is as fresh as if it happened yesterday. Our chemistry is pretty incendiary. I had to ignore it when we first met, when she and Sterling—a ballsy, engaged business duo—approached me to form a partnership that would go on to become Bold.

Monroe and I are similar. We're both combative

and we both hate to lose, which is why in our game of Texas Hold 'Em I'm fifty yen down, according to my diminishing pile of paper clips—a substitute for poker chips.

'You are so bad at bluffing, so don't even bother this time,' I say as she deals the cards and I examine my hand.

'Am I? Or are you just bad at guessing what's on a woman's mind…?' She peers up from her cards, her eyes fringed with long lashes.

I grin; we both know I do all right with the ladies. But, damn, she's laying on the innuendo pretty thick. I'm starting to think my halo and knighthood must be in the mail, because I bloody deserve them for my stellar display of self-control. Yet the night is young. The weather is wild. We're going nowhere.

I glance at her long shapely legs, which are clad in sheer black stockings. The idea of a long night alone with her sends a kick of lust to my groin. We'd be stupid not to take this to the next level. We've exhausted our supplies of both conversation and Scotch. I'm done losing my hard-earned cash. And we know we're good together. Last time we rushed it. I never got to explore her phenomenal body the way I wanted. This time would be different.

I take a cursory glance at my cards, so distracted by the thought of seducing my business partner that I don't need to fake indifference for the hand I've been dealt. Edginess creeps over me. If Sterling had made the trip I wouldn't even consider it, just like we've avoided a repeat for the past three years. Lying to Sterling through omission leaves a nasty taste in my mouth. He's a friend. One of very few, and perhaps my closest.

But risk is what makes this so damned irresistible. All three of us live for that adrenaline rush—the thrill of spotting a good investment and watching our instincts come to fruition. Just because I haven't touched Monroe since that one time doesn't mean I haven't thought about it—like, every time I see her. Don't I betray Sterling in thought whenever Monroe and I meet?

I place my bet and watch as she reveals her hand—four of a kind—her eyes alight with triumph. I toss down my straight in disgust. 'You win, Dove. I'm done.'

Her playful chuckle twists my gut with hunger. 'Oh, don't be a sore loser.' She scoops the paper clips into a pile and returns the cards to the box. 'I won't even hold you to the bets.'

I've often wondered if she's the female version of me. Sterling used to call her 'the terrier'—she's relentless, and works almost as hard as I do.

But not quite, because unlike me she comes from a large, loving family. She has dreams and aspirations outside of work and lacks the demons snapping at her heels.

'You know me. I hate to lose at anything.' My voice is thick with tension and anticipation. We're alone with our unavoidable attraction while the storm rages outside. What am I doing? There are multiple reasons to avoid Monroe's brand of temptation, the most crucial being our invaluable business.

My life is a true rags-to-riches tale. I've been hungry, scared and alone. I've wondered where I'd be sleeping and how long my current set of foster parents would tolerate an angry kid no one else wanted.

Now, thanks to Bold, my life is the complete opposite. I control everything. I have everything I need. Money and success have removed every scrap of uncertainty from my life. There's no way I'd allow sex to jeopardise that. Bold is my life. My security blanket. In another ten years I can retire early and maintain my lifestyle until I die without ever needing to worry again.

'What shall we play now?' Monroe flicks her hair over one shoulder and the neck of her blouse gapes open, flashing a tantalising glimpse of cream lace.

I ignore her question—there's only one game I want to play with Monroe.

Under normal circumstances I could walk away and go for a run until I'm too exhausted to want her. Somehow knowing there's no escape makes me crave her more.

But Monroe and Sterling are the only real allies I've ever had. Losing my partners could mean losing Bold. The idea of that is enough to keep me up at night. Certainly enough to have controlled the ferocious chemistry between Monroe and me these past three years.

In that second, my phone emits a blaring alert. We both jump, laughing as I silence my device and dismiss the civil defence warning that confirms what we already know—we're stuck here for the night.

'I'll relinquish my bed if you're tired. It's very comfortable.' The alert has shunted my pulse sky-high, but the idea of her naked body between my sheets, leaving behind her warmth and her scent, keeps it at such a punishing rate.

'I'm not remotely sleepy.' She shrugs. 'Jet lag.' Her eyes spark with sultry heat and she shifts, bringing her into closer proximity.

My muscles tighten. I'm aware of every breath she takes. Every movement of her body. Every swoop of her long eyelashes as she blinks. But am I really willing to go there? It could be a great night to rival the last time, or a damaging liability for everything in my life that I value…

'Besides, where would you sleep?' she asks.

I wrap my hand around my glass, my mind awash with the hypnotic motion of her lush lips, the sexy sound of her voice and the subtext of the unspoken. 'I'll probably work. Or the sofa's reasonably comfortable.' Of course, having her in the next room will add a new dimension to the torture. Why am I resisting? We managed to move on without any fallout the first time. Why would this be any different?

She nods, her seductive stare carrying her signature boldness. 'Or we could share…'

So we're definitely going there.

An inferno starts somewhere under my ribs. 'Is that wise?' I want to rip out my own cautious tongue.

She wets her parted lips. 'Don't you ever think about it?'

I tilt my head, flashing her a *don't be stupid* look. 'Memorable sex is hard to ignore.'

We agreed to forget it out of respect for each other, respect for our business and respect for Sterling, who deserves better than a shitty friend like me. I sip my Scotch, hoping the burn will erase the recrimination. I should never have touched Monroe in the first place, or at least should have come clean about it. But there was no point risking our professional relationship over one rushed fuck against a wall.

'Yes.' She nods in agreement.

Lust clamours to be heard in the space between our bodies.

'And I'm sure without Typhoon Kano our nights would have involved less clothes and more orgasms.'

She's right. My 'date' was a hook-up. Fresh desire knifes through me. I want to act, not talk. Monroe tilts her head and the silk of her hair falls across my hand, which rests on the back of the sofa. I rub a lock between my fingers, wanting to bring it to my face and inhale its scent.

'So…what do you want to do about it?' I ask as my temperature soars. It's just sex. One more time. Same rules apply.

She reaches for my glass, slowly takes it from my hand and finishes the last swallow. 'I think we'd be foolish not to take advantage of the storm and the one bed.' She places the glass on the table and touches her index finger to one of my shirt buttons, leaving it there to linger.

The air grows stifling with pheromones. I sit stock-still. Waiting. Weighing the pros and cons. But this couldn't be more risk-free. We work, physically and professionally. We're too similar to allow sex to disrupt the good thing we have. Fuck, I just want her, and can't come up with a single convincing reason why I shouldn't have her.

Monroe extends her hand to my shoulder as if stroking away an imaginary crease from my shirt. Her touch is considered but bold. Exactly the way I know she makes her business decisions. It's a serious turn-on.

Even as my fingers twitch to reach for her, habit forces me to hesitate. I don't want to cock-block myself, but we stopped after one time for a reason. I rarely sleep with a woman more than once. Monroe knows what a dead end I am dating-wise, and she's always wanted more than I offer.

'Stop overthinking it.' She slides closer, her fingernails tracing a pattern through my shirt until my skin feels as if it's been lashed by the needles of rain.

She dips her face close and runs her lips along my jaw. I suck in a breath; I'm not made of stone. Still I hold off, the pressure building. The tip of her tongue touches the skin below my ear and I close my eyes, enjoying the sensation, the anticipation, the way I've learned to enjoy all of life's good things. And Monroe, like top-class liquor or luxury cars, is something to be savoured slowly.

The fight in me dwindles. Tomorrow a new day will dawn. The storm will have washed away today. We can go on as if it never happened.

'Dove…' A warning or encouragement? I pull her onto my lap so she's straddling me. Her skirt bunches up her spread thighs, revealing the tops of lacy black stockings. I fist the fabric of her skirt at her hips and search her aroused stare while my heart thuds in time with the waves of rain smacking the glass.

'Come on, Black, it's just one more night,' she whispers seductively. 'A wild and stormy night. I'll even let you be on top.' She bites her bottom lip, subtly thrusts her breasts in my direction a fraction more and I give up any remaining shred of opposition.

I don't need convincing to re-explore our chemistry in this opportunity delivered by the weather gods.

'You don't have to seduce me, sweetheart. I'm all in.' I'm rock-hard, struggling to think beyond the demands of my dick.

Her eyes sparkle with challenge. 'Good. But just remember whose excellent idea this was.' Her fingers glide through my hair at my nape and I drop my head back, looking up at her.

I want to argue the point. To declare that a part of me hasn't stopped thinking about her this way since the last time. But I'm strung too taut with lust.

Now I've committed, my pulse flies with panic—

we've already wasted two hours playing stupid poker. How much time do we have until dawn and can I legitimately keep her awake all night?

'Oh, fuck it.' I crush her to my chest and taste her mouth. A mouth which, in my brutally honest moments, I've fantasised about a million times.

She whimpers. Laughs. Groans.

Her lips are soft and plump, her kiss just as I remember. Her arms lock around my shoulders and she shunts her hips forward to the ominous sound of ripping fabric. But Monroe doesn't seem to care about her skirt, only about kissing me back with equal desperation.

Her fingers tangle in my hair, tugging. Her tongue meets mine thrust for thrust. I buck my hips up from the sofa, seeking fiery, hot friction between her legs.

She pulls away, panting. Her eyes are ablaze with arousal that I realise has been simmering there since we platonically embraced this morning.

'Please tell me you have a condom.' She pops the top buttons of my shirt and presses her mouth to my neck and chest while her delectable arse wriggles on my thighs.

I drag my wallet from my pocket and locate the foil square before sense deserts me. 'There's no rush.' I want to drag out every second of our stolen time. But we're only here because of chance and circumstance—if the wind changes again, she might leave.

'There's a rush in me.' She kisses me and takes

the condom. 'I've been thinking about this since we closed our laptops.'

Her confession—knowing she wanted this even before the storm changed her plans for the evening—ratchets up my own urgency. I unbutton her blouse to reveal a creamy lace bra covering the perfect breasts I remember. Her nipples are hard peaks, poking through the fabric as if demanding their share of attention. And I'm only too happy to oblige. I wrap my arm around her waist and drag her close, covering one dusky nipple with my mouth.

'Hudson!' she cries out. Every gyrating movement of her hips on my lap massages my aching cock. Bliss and torment. But unlike last time, when we were fast and frantic, I want more tonight. I want her naked. I want to see and taste every inch.

I suck her nipple through the lace and then pull the bra down so her breasts are exposed for me. My thumbs trace the distended peaks, the darker areolas puckering in response to my touch.

I lance her with my stare, every bit of me burning hot. 'Don't think I didn't notice the way you returned from the bathroom with a button undone.' I pinch both nipples in unison, rolling them between my fingers and thumbs to let her know I was onto her flirty game from the start.

She gasps, throwing her head back and pushing her breasts into my palms.

'You wanted this to happen, didn't you?' I drop my

mouth, first to one breast and then the other, sucking and lapping, forcing little mewls from her throat.

She nods, fumbling with my belt as I treat her sensitive breasts to some more oral torture. 'Yes. You know I always get what I want.' Her challenge reminds me why we work so well together in business. Why I know I won't regret this indulgence. Because, aside from each other in this moment, we want different things.

'As do I.' I abandon her breasts and take my belt from her frantic fingers, unbuckling it with speed to release my trapped erection. I allow my eyes to roam, satisfaction ramping up my heart rate. Her skirt is around her waist. Her thighs are spread wide to reveal lacy panties which match the bra. I slide my hands to the tops of her stockings and caress her bare thighs while she palms my cock.

Our stares lock. An erotic challenge.

A thought occurs through the lust fog filling my brain. Why not apply our competitive personalities to tonight? To pleasure? A game of seduction… We've been playing it all evening.

Wanting to win, I glide my thumb over the damp crotch of her panties, stroking her softness. 'Let's make this interesting—you wanted to play and I've already lost once tonight.'

She gasps as I brush over her swollen clit and then she shudders, disrupting her determined tugs on my cock.

'Whoever comes first must chair tomorrow's

eight a.m. meeting.' With a grin, I hand her the condom she's abandoned on the sofa next to us and then shift the lace aside, exposing her folds to my stare.

She drops her head back on a long sigh of surrender as I continue to caress her.

'You like the idea. You're wet for me.' I use my thumbs to part her and then slide two fingers inside her. Her hips undulate in time with my plunging.

'And you're hard for me,' she replies. Her concentration with the condom is no doubt shaken by the way I'm working her higher and higher. With a groan of frustration, or perhaps triumph, she rolls the condom onto my length at last and then braces her hands on my shoulders.

'Besides, that's not a fair challenge, because I *want* to lose.' She rocks her hips, greedily taking what she needs.

She hates coming in last. But I guess with orgasms it's a bit different. 'I'd never leave you hanging, Dove, but be my guest,' I say, cupping her breast with my free hand and toying the nipple erect. 'I have no doubt you'll get your own back, even if you do lose this round.'

'Oh, I will.' She gasps as we pleasure each other. Face to face, our defiant stares lock as we see who can get who off first. Everything with Monroe is a competition. And that's fine by me, because I'm going to win. More than once. Over and over all night long, before the storm finally breaks and we have to pretend tonight never happened.

I look down to where my hand works between her thighs, my fingers swallowed in her tight channel and my thumb working her swollen clit. It's one erotic sight. Her hand is around my cock, her long nails brightly polished, her delicate fingers gripping me so good in just the right spot. I can't help the feral growl that rumbles in my throat.

As if we reach the point of no return together, we jolt into action. I snatch my hand from her pussy and grip her hips, shunting her forward. She braces her hand on my shoulder and kneels over me, directing my cock back towards her entrance. And then she sinks, impaling herself, and I push up into her, sweat breaking across my brow at how good she feels and looks and smells.

I bite my tongue to hold in a groan. I claimed to be the better bluffer—I can't reveal how close she has me.

Our panting breaths mingle as we move together, creating our own storm with frantic thrusts, clenched fingers and the wildness of our locked stares. Arousal streaks across her face. Her dark, glossy hair is a messy tumble around her shoulders. He nipples are thrust into my face, suspended by the cups of her bra.

I bury my face between her breasts and groan out her name as her walls clamp around me. She grips my head and cries out, and the first flutters of her orgasm squeeze me so tight I see stars behind my closed eyes.

I buck up into her and she drops her head back.

Her broken cry is a long, ecstatic wail of release that seems to suck in all of the tension from the room like a vacuum.

'Oh, my... I needed that.' She presses kisses to my face and then plunges her tongue inside my mouth before I can crow my triumph at having won.

'You're welcome. I know how you hate to come last.'

She laughs, but then quickly turns serious, tearing off her bra and blouse and dumping them on the floor. 'Yes, I do, but I can come again.'

She tugs my shirt open, renewed resolve slashed across her beautiful face, and slides her hands all over my chest, brushing my nipples with her fingernails.

I grip her hips as she rides me, her pelvis rocking and her breasts bouncing. I grip tighter, aware that if her skirt weren't there as a protective barrier I might bruise her, so desperate is my need to direct her to exactly where I want her. Because I feel as if she's hunting me down, chasing my orgasm as ruthlessly as she sought her own. Our out-of-control need seems to match the tempest outside.

Monroe wraps her arms around my shoulders and kisses me as I thrust up into her again and again.

She grips the back of the sofa.

'Hudson... I'm coming again!' she cries, her face buried in the crook of my neck.

I let go, exploding inside her, filling the condom in hot jets.

Winning never felt so good.

CHAPTER THREE

Monroe

THE QUALITY OF the tenuous dawn light tells me the storm outside has passed. The fantasy exceeded my expectations, but today is a new day. My stomach sinks, emptiness creeping in. I watch Hudson sleep for a few indulgent minutes, my pulse a confused riot.

His long, sooty lashes form dark crescents on his cheeks, giving him an air of boyish innocence at complete odds with the ruthless sex god who pleasured me over and over. I kind of knew he'd be a phenomenal lover, even three years ago. But what I couldn't know then, what I've rarely witnessed since, is how playful and relaxed Hudson can be. I saw it last night in how he ran me a bath full of bubbles and then climbed in too. How he sent out for burgers when my stomach growled at two a.m., how he invented a new game called 'lick poker,' the rules of which are still hazy but basically involved his tongue worshipping every inch of me regardless of what cards were dealt.

This new side to him steals my breath.

He spent all night winning his little orgasm game until, spent and exhausted, I conceded the fight, surrendering my body to his whim so he could wring a string of climaxes from me as ruthlessly as he wrangles billion-pound deals.

And now, our one night is over.

Almost.

I want to stave off reality a little longer. Otherwise guilt over Sterling, doubt over the risk we took with Bold and worry for our ongoing relationship will spoil what was a night to remember.

I gently shuffle down the bed, careful not to wake Hudson. He'll be insufferably smug if I allow him to end our night together on the high point that was my last—almost coma-inducing—orgasm. Just because he'd turned our chemistry into a seduction challenge doesn't mean I can't snatch the final victory.

Under the sheets his cock is semi-hard, a sign that he'll soon be awake and that my time to exact revenge is dwindling. I press my lips to his silky crown and suck in the musky, manly scent of him. His penis is a work of art—proud and thick. His body twitches in his sleep and I fly into action, my determination to win ramping up my excitement.

I grip his length and take him into my mouth. My tongue laves his head as he grows steely in my hand. My command over his powerful body floods me with triumph.

His hand finds my head, his fingers curling into

my hair reflexively as he mumbles sleepily and incoherently. I toss the sheet aside and look up. His eyes are still closed as he clings to the last vestiges of sleep. Time to up the ante.

I scrape my nails along his hard thighs and suck harder. His gasp shoots adrenaline through my blood. His eyes fly open, landing squarely on mine before taking a frantic tour of my mouth wrapped around him.

'Dove… Fuck, what are you doing?' His voice is thick with sleep and vulnerability. Awake, Hudson would never allow anyone to see him that way. Pangs of privilege shift in my chest. He's always in control, so to have him at my mercy sends flutters of longing through my core.

I don't want to stop. I simply smile around him and hum low in my throat to let him know I'm enjoying myself and fully intend to see this through to the end.

He's alert now, pushed up on his elbows to take in the view. His hair is deliciously bed-rumpled, his sleepy stare shot through with desire. I cup his balls and his hips jerk off the bed. Oh, he's sensitive. I like knowing his tiny weaknesses, because the Hudson I've known for the past five years rarely displays any chinks in his armour.

His thighs spread wider, his cock jerking in my mouth. I grip his shaft and angle him up so I can take him deeper, an act that draws a long, sexy groan from his throat. But his eyes never leave mine.

This power is addictive. This time *I'm* going to win, and I'll enjoy every minute.

'Dove.' His voice breaks, a husky warning. 'I'll come in your mouth...'

I know from watching him come inside me four times last night that he's close. I answer with my eyes and my determined sucking. I want him undone. At my mercy just as I was at his last night, with his mouth on me, his length inside me and his talented fingers stroking my body into eager submission.

His hips thrust in time with my bobbing head. He can't keep still. Even when I'm on top, taking charge, he needs to dictate the pace. That's Hudson. He's an alpha.

But it's my turn to out-seduce him.

I drag my nails up the ladder of his abs to his ripped chest and over his tight nipples while my mouth works him. He grunts. His abs contract. His hands fist in my hair. Fire burns in his eyes.

My heart rate starts its victory lap as I moan out my encouragement. He tries to stave it off. I see the fight in his stare. But I'm too good, too tenacious, and it's too late for him to win this round. He roars my name and comes in my mouth, his climax making every muscle in his body tense.

I flop down beside him with a huge grin on my face, allowing him a few seconds to catch his breath. 'I win. I think it's only fair if the loser gets breakfast.'

Who knew the delicious little pleasure game he started could be so much fun?

It's almost a shame the sexy challenges must end…

But the shift in weather heralds a new day. We had our night. Now it's time to return to being business partners.

A violent hollowness rips through my chest. I hide my disappointment by burying my face against the side of his neck. Great sex coming to an end is regretful. But I'll survive.

He scoops an arm around my waist, hauls me over him and cups my face. I'm pulled down to his kiss, which is as deep and passionate as if he hadn't just come like a freight train.

'That was a fantastic way to wake up.' His sexy voice buzzes against my lips, the tingle transmitted to my nipples.

'You're welcome.' I bite my lip to stop myself from kissing him, hoping to wean myself off quickly and painlessly. 'I couldn't have you thinking you're the only winner around here. It's not healthy for your ego.'

He chuckles. 'Ah…the lengths you'll go to keep up with the pack never ceases to amaze me.'

I drop my chin to my crossed hands, which are on his chest, and laugh. 'I grew up fighting to keep up. Besides, maybe I lead the pack. Did you think of that?'

'When it comes to wake-up head, I'd say you do.' His deep voice rumbles through his chest.

The same urge to snuggle that I had in front of the fire last night roars to life.

To banish the sensation I cannot indulge, I pinch his ribs and roll off him, glancing at the clock on the bedside table. 'Want to join me in the shower? We're tight on time.'

Nothing to do with how you're struggling to keep your hands off, or the fifty-nine minutes we have left before usual business resumes.

He nods and we pad there together, sharing a series of goofy grins. An unforgettable night will do that. And that's all it can be.

I flick on the shower and swallow the hot ache in my throat I hadn't expected. Maybe it's just endorphin addiction. All good things must end, especially this. We're business partners. There are three of us in that relationship. We can't afford to allow sex to disrupt the good thing we've built together.

And yet it already feels complicated. I don't want to hurt Sterling and I know Hudson doesn't either. But in the cold light of day this deception feels somehow seedier. It negates the years of hard work, compromise and communication Sterling and I put in to keep Bold together after our divorce.

No. It was just one storm-bound night. Temporary madness never to be repeated or confessed.

I glance at Hudson, his glorious body wet and his hair slicked back. Does he too have regrets?

I shiver, helpless to resist him when he reaches for me and drags me under the spray, crushing me against his solid body. Even his cock is impressively hard again. His desperation to squeeze the last min-

utes of pleasure from our time together is perhaps
as fierce as mine. He backs me up against the glass
and kisses me until I'm gasping and light-headed.

Who knew Hudson could be the whole package?
Attentive and caring as well as a first-class lover.
His commitment avoidance is the only downside.

Shit, I need to pull myself together. I don't need
dangerous thoughts like that in my head. I know how
hard it is to find *the one*. I've been searching for my
Prince Charming ever since Mum first read me Cin-
derella. I've already had my fingers burnt in love.

I gently shove him away and reach for his luxury
body wash, which smells heavenly and is clearly the
source of his usual yummy scent. I douse myself,
noting the brand so I can purchase some when I'm
back in London—a reminder of this insanely hot
night. I tip some over his chest and we massage the
suds over each other's bodies in slow, sensual swipes
that feel more like foreplay than washing.

But there's no time. I can't chair a meeting flushed
with arousal and wearing last night's clothes.

'I need to pop back to my hotel before the meeting,' I say, my body reacting to his caresses with
disconcerting eagerness. 'I can't meet with Kunosu
Tech wearing my ripped skirt.' I don't mind chairing
the meeting—funding start-up companies is my favourite part of investing. There's just so much drive
and potential.

I clear my tight throat, telling myself how much
I value my business and both of my partners. I need

to stay grounded. That's what I tell my greedy body, which pulses with need for one last dose of Hudson's addictively good touch.

He steps close again, pressing his soap-slicked body to mine and his lips to my neck. 'Don't worry.' His mouth moves over my skin, enticing more ripples through my core. 'I had your suitcase brought over from the hotel.' His fingers latch between my legs and he strums my clit so I forget today's schedule, forget the ticking clock, forget how to breathe.

'You think of everything.' I gasp as he centres that ferocious need between my legs.

He cups my cheek, directing my eyes to his, which are intense with hunger. 'I was thinking of you. All night.'

'Thank you for the suitcase,' I whisper, shocked still by his admission. I tell myself it's only the same consideration I'd show him.

'My pleasure, Dove. Anything I can do to make your trip memorable and comfortable, just ask. Day or night.'

My throat closes, a stinging sensation building behind my eyes. He keeps this side of himself well hidden. Is that because my history with Sterling makes us an established team? When the three of us are together, Hudson often withdraws, leaving Sterling and me alone. Or has his caring side always been there and I've never looked hard enough?

Overcome with a frenzy of confused emotions, I grip his face and bring his mouth back to mine.

'I can't stop touching you.' He nuzzles my neck and palms my aching breast.

'Me neither.' I sigh, my hands roaming his strong back and tight backside. But we'll need to find the strength to stop soon. Sterling will be in London next week for Mum's memorial, which Hudson wouldn't normally attend. He's joining us there for a few days, given Sterling couldn't make Tokyo, so we must appear normal when all three of us are together.

Fresh guilt grips my stomach. With any other man apart from Hudson, my ex-husband would never enter my mind after a one-night stand. But our past, our secret little triangle, complicates things.

I drop my head to Hudson's chest and hold him tighter. Sterling can't know about this. I can't hurt either of them like that, because I'm certain there'd be a devastating fallout. Things could never be the same again. I might lose them both.

'We have about fifty minutes until our meeting.' I'm not sure which of us I'm reminding.

He pulls back and looks at me as if this hasn't occurred to him. As if he's forgotten last night was stolen time. My heart thumps with urgency. There's a big part of me that wants to do it again and again. The fire between us is in no way extinguished. Can we pretend that we don't burn? Pretend that we haven't explored every inch of each other's bodies? Pretend to work alongside one another with only professional and platonic thoughts?

'Well, in that case…' Hudson drops to his knees

and guides one thigh over his shoulder. His mouth covers me, his stare blazing with that ruthlessness he applies to every challenge.

I surrender one last time.

Shingo and Yumi Kunosu, the brother-and-sister team at the head of a Tokyo-based tech company, impress me the minute they enter Hudson's office. As they pitch their business to us through an interpreter on Hudson's staff, I listen with admiration at what they've achieved alone, which has earned them a chance to share their ideas for expansion with Bold. The company develops technology algorithms directed at machine learning, language processing and deep learning. I can never hope to understand those concepts beyond a basic level, but their enthusiasm is contagious.

Only Hudson seems immune.

Kunosu's directors won't be aware, but his usual energy has dropped. Surprising, given this type of company is where his interest lies. It could be a result of how little we slept last night. Perhaps he's just testy because he's struggling to move on, as am I. *Just one more time* has been playing in my head all morning. But I know Hudson well enough to see it's something more.

He glances my way and all traces of warmth— professional or otherwise—are absent.

'We're looking to invest in high-demand products,' he says to Shingo and Yumi. 'What kind of traction has Kunosu Tech had so far in the market and how do you differ from other companies in the field?'

His perfectly reasonable questions are standard, ones the duo would be expecting and no doubt are prepared to answer. Questions I'd ask myself, if Hudson hadn't.

He rolls a pen between his fingers, a tiny tell that speaks to his tension. Prickles of apprehension buzz over my skin. Something's bothering him, even though *he* invited Kunosu here. It's as if I can hear the cogs of Hudson's mind working at about ten percent their usual level. Where's his enthusiasm? His instinct? We've both read the company portfolio— Kunosu is on the rise and we'd be stupid not to play a role in its assent.

We normally find a way to iron out any professional differences of opinion with clear communication. Only we shunned 'professional' last night.

This feels personal.

I half listen to Yumi and Shingo answer, my spirit dampened by my partner's apparent reticence. I adore helping people achieve their dreams. My mother founded her own company when I was a young girl of eight. She'd spent many years raising her large family, so when her own aspirations came to fruition it brought her to life in new ways.

I still recall the celebration dinner we had as a family the day she secured an investor to help get her organic wholefoods business off the ground. The smile on her face as we'd toasted her success is one of my most cherished memories, along with the countless afternoons helping out at her shop after school. Coming from my big family, and Mum giving me my first job, helped me to discover my sense of belonging. It gave me the confidence to fail, knowing I had a safety net under me.

I slide a glance Hudson's way, my mind sparking with the possibility that his hesitancy may be linked to regrets about last night. Because, where this morning in the shower he was the most emotionally open I've ever known, now he's not only the ruthless, calculating businessman I admire, but it also feels like we're no longer a team. He's withdrawn. I'm on my own.

This was the risk involved in crossing that line.

To banish the *I told you so* in my head, I ask my own question, letting my partner see my interest. 'How do you work as a team? Any sibling rivalries that get in the way?'

The air between Hudson and I on the opposite side of the conference table crackles with discordant energy. Vetting Tokyo business is his turf, but he allowed me to sit in on this interview. He even invited me to lead the meeting with his sexy stunt. Why is he letting what happened last night interfere?

Yumi and Shingo smile and make appropriate answers that leave me thinking about my own siblings and the ongoing working relationship I have with my family, given we now collectively run the business our mother loved.

I'm keenly aware of Hudson's stillness, which seems brittle to my highly attuned senses and drags me from my memories. He has no faith in the family unit, and my chest aches for what he's been denied in life.

But this is business.

Kunosu Tech is exactly the sort of company we can take global with the right management and with Bold's connections.

The meeting comes to a close and we say our goodbyes—warm and encouraging on my part and stilted and awkward on my partner's. Hina, Hudson's personal assistant, escorts Yumi, Shingo and the interpreter from the room.

As the door closes behind them, I spin slowly to face Hudson, my stomach knotted with anticipation of a confrontation.

'I like them. A lot.' I return to the conference table and gather their company portfolio together for something to do with my hands. 'What did you think?'

I wish I didn't need to ask.

He retreats behind his desk, unbuttoning his jacket and hanging it over the back of his chair. 'Mmm... I think their turnover projections made no sense. That makes me wonder what they're trying to hide.'

I knew his heart wasn't in it. My energy drains away, my body dragging. 'Seriously... Don't you think you're being a little paranoid? Why would they waste our time like that? We're not naive amateurs. They'd know we'll do due diligence before making a decision to invest. I think we could squeeze them a little on the equity stake too, and the growth potential is obvious.'

He watches me in silence, his expression blank. My ire grows, heat rising like mercury in a thermometer.

I push on with my argument. 'I respected their determined passion. Loved that it's a family business. This is exactly how I want to spend my investment dollar, because with sufficient funding they'll grow as a company and grow together as a family.'

Just like we did after Mum died. We might have lost her guiding light, but we still had a part of her to give us a common cause. I believe my brothers and sisters needed that as much as I did after her sudden death. Continuing her work strengthened us.

Hudson's eyes narrow, razor-sharp. 'You know I'm not sentimental in my business approach. The risks need to be stacked in our favour or there's no point investing, in my opinion.'

I snort. No one could accuse Hudson of sentimentality. But I bristle at his inference. 'I'm not being sentimental. Allowing my emotional intelligence into my decision-making process is what gets me out of bed in the morning, what makes me love my work. I go with my gut. There's nothing wrong with that. And you're usually the person taking the biggest, ballsiest risks.'

I can't help but think he's being more bullish and uncommunicative than usual. What's changed?

'There's nothing wrong with trusting your gut, but I prefer to put my faith in the figures.' His mouth tightens with obstinacy. 'Families argue. Become dysfunctional. Grow estranged. I'm not interested in watching that kind of dynamic sabotage what, as you point out, could otherwise be a highly profitable business venture for Bold.'

I understand his viewpoint, given his childhood. He'd once hinted at the number of foster homes he'd bounced between growing up—Sterling and I had been horrified and frankly a little speechless. But now his hesitance forces me to read between the lines. Would this perfectly standard business discussion, this minor difference of opinion, have mattered as much yesterday? Before we introduced sex into the mix?

I soften my tone in deference to his past experiences. 'Many family-run businesses are hugely successful. Family loyalty can be their strength. This one has the clear and impressive management structure we normally look for.'

From where I'm standing, Hudson is being unreasonably prejudiced. It's as if he's determined to restate his commitment avoidance for absolute clarity and he's using his reluctance to invest in Kunosu to make his point.

I stare him down, my pulse leaping. 'Is there something you're leaving unsaid? Are we just talking about business, or is there some hidden meaning I'm supposed to decipher? I'd rather you just spit it out. You're acting weird.'

He rolls up his shirtsleeves and loosens his tie as he paces towards me with barely leashed purpose.

'Weird?' His face is a cool mask.

'Yes.' I fist my hand on my hip. 'All morning you've been unusually quiet. Hesitant. Withdrawn. Is there something you want to get off your chest? About the sex, perhaps?'

He steps closer. I'm hit with the warmth from his body and his familiar scent. My mind helpfully provides images of him in the shower: on his knees, his mouth between my legs, and then later thrusting into me where I was pressed against the tiles.

'Nope.' His sensual lips emphasise the 'p,' drawing my attention to his mouth and the hundred kisses we shared last night. 'I'm perfectly happy with the sex.'

I look away. 'Good.'

I'm determined not to think about it. As great as it was, look where it's brought us. 'Because for a minute during that meeting it felt as if you were reminding me you're a lone wolf.' I snort. 'I get that, believe me.'

Were we naive to think we could continue as if it had never happened?

'Just because I'm thorough about the numbers

adding up?' Mild irritation narrows his eyes but he smiles. The effect is so Hudson, who does whatever the hell he wants. 'That's just good business. The reason you and Sterling came to me in the first place when you wanted a partner.' His inflexible stare shifts over my face.

He's right. We'd used the trust fund Sterling inherited when he turned twenty-one and my nest egg from the dividends of my shares in Mum's business to make our first few investments. We were young, enthusiastic and smart enough to see the benefits of a partnership with a man making a name for himself.

'I agree, and if that's all this is about then we have no quarrel.' It's usually easy to laugh off his arrogance or calmly fight my own corner. I'm a sole woman in partnership with two big dogs. But, today, his attitude is grating on my nerves. It seems like a front to something deeper.

And, despite what he's just said, the only thing that's changed is the sex. It's as if, having given in to our chemistry last night, he's determined to retreat to a place of comfort and safety, even if it's professional caution.

My stomach pinches with regret. Things are awkward now, muddy and murky. I feel as if I need to check myself before challenging him in business. I wonder if his motives around the investment are purely profit-driven, which normally I wouldn't question.

His decision-making process invariably boils down to maximum growth potential for his equity share. It's what makes him so successful. But sometimes I wonder if he misses the human angle. The potential in people.

'I just don't want us to write off investing in any company that happens to be family run. My family is a good example of how to work together successfully.' I swallow hard, defensive. I'm proud of us. 'Claire and Jeremy run the day-to-day side of things and Elliot, Brie and I are silent shareholders. We all manage to act in the best interests of the company our mother loved. Not everything is about the bottom line.'

I'm not expecting the wobble in my voice. I blame fatigue and the constant ache of missing my mum. She kept our family together, was both a wise and sympathetic shoulder to cry on and our biggest advocate. I tilt up my chin and hold his stare to hide my vulnerabilities from the man I've just shared an intense night with. Am I surprised he won't believe that sometimes the best things come out of relationships between people who share a common goal? I've known him for five years. He's always lived alone. He holidays alone. He's never once accepted an invitation to spend Christmas with Sterling or me.

Acknowledging my part in ruining what was yesterday a perfectly harmonious business partnership, I take a deep breath and back down. 'I think I need some fresh air. We've been cooped up in here for too long.' I tuck my laptop into my bag and offer my most Zen-like smile. 'Let's park this discussion until we can patch in Sterling for his input.'

At the mention of our third partner, the room falls into an uncomfortable silence. I shove my arms into my coat, cursing my timing at mentioning my ex's name. Bringing him up—a reminder that any investment over seven figures into a single company requires unanimous sign-off by all three of us—feels as though I invited him into the bedroom last night.

'Yes.' His tone is brittle. 'Thank goodness there are three of us.' His eyes glitter, as if he's no longer talking about business.

I stare, my body doused in chills. Our trio has never attracted personal tensions before. Sterling will surely put two and two together as soon as he sees Hudson and I together, given that a simple everyday business discussion is awkward as hell.

Should we keep our fling a secret or come clean?

I clear my throat, desperate now to get some air, and some perspective on the implications of our changed dynamics. 'As you say, perhaps Kunosu's financial reports will remove the need for further discussion.' I sling my bag over my shoulder.

'I'll organise my car to take you to the hotel,' he says, retrieving his phone from his pocket.

'Please don't. I want to walk.' I smile, regret driving me to get away from him. Perhaps I'm just tired. Jet-lagged. Stir-crazy.

He looks as if he wants to argue, but only says, 'Are we still on for saké tonight?'

I breathe through the tightness constricting my throat. I want to nod, to declare I'm looking forward to some downtime during my remaining four nights in this fabulously vibrant city. Instead I hold back. Each second I delay pulses through me to the tips of my toes. Can I spend platonic time with him, or have we broken our easy friendship and camaraderie too?

My silence has stretched way beyond comfortable.

'We didn't sleep much.' I button my coat. 'I'm going to have a long soak in the bath. Can I let you know after that?'

No one is more disappointed by my hesitation than me, but I need some time away from him and his uncompromising masculinity to gather my thoughts. To reset my mind to our post-sex reality. To refocus on work and to detangle personal feelings from our professional relationship.

'Sure.' He shrugs. 'I'll be here.' He presses a chaste kiss to my cheek and moves back behind his desk.

On heavy feet, I wheel my small case to the lift, wondering where, in the short time from the shower this morning to now, we went so horribly wrong.

CHAPTER FOUR

Hudson

THE MINUTE SHE enters the bar on the ground floor of her hotel I'm hit with a vibrating wall of energy. It's as if I thought I'd never see her again after our spat. I stand, sling my hands in my pockets, convinced now I need to make things right between us.

She's my partner. I brought personal shit to work. How could I not? We walked straight from an incredible night into the office, trailing our baggage.

Why did I think one night would be enough? Unlike the first time three years ago, when we hardly kissed before rushing to the main event, now I know every inch of Monroe's body—what makes her moan, and how she's even competitive between the sheets. Now I'm supposed to somehow *un*know those things. Scrub them from my brain as if it never happened. No wonder I failed to do that today.

I watch with rising arousal—clearly my dick can't forget either—as she clips across the marble foyer towards me, her heels high, her stunning body encased in a red sheath dress and her eyes alight with passion and determination, as if I'm in her sights.

After our disagreement, it's what I expect of Monroe.

I dug in my heels over the Kunosu Tech investment because I was grappling for control—over the desires unleashed by our night together, over my unexpectedly fierce reaction to her and over the fear my concerns for Bold were justified.

I straighten my shirt cuff, my fingers encountering the cufflink there. It reminds me of the times I had nothing more than the clothes on my back and a few more in a sad little carrier bag. Those days, I had no control over anything—where I lived, where I went to school or even what food I ate. I never want to feel that helpless again. For the first time in years, today when we disagreed in a way we never had before, I had a glimpse of what losing it all could look like.

I'd barely heard half of Shingo and Yumi's pitch because I'd been reliving our night together. I don't normally struggle to concentrate when I'm considering investing my hard-earned cash.

But one night with Monroe could make a man forget his own name.

We meet each other halfway across the expansive foyer, the symbolism appropriate. I kiss her cheek, my head awash with the delicious scent of her, and I immediately remember her naked. I can't seem to stop.

'Dove. You look beautiful.'

'Thank you. I like your shirt. Blue suits you.' Her smile carries its usual warmth, telling me our small professional difference of opinion is surmountable. Monroe is a passionate woman. Driven and tenacious. Especially when it comes to fighting her cause. But, if we're to salvage this week, I either need to stop thinking about her in a sexual way or break my one-night rule and continue our fling until we leave Tokyo for London in three days' time.

'I'm glad you changed your mind about saké.' I slide my hand to the small of her back and ignore the tightening in my groin that touching her provokes. Monroe and I spark white-hot—sustaining a few work-related flesh wounds is a small price to pay for that kind of chemistry.

'I had a nap and awoke feeling energised.' She shoots me a look, confronting the issue head-on. 'I don't want to miss out because we forgot to keep what happened last night out of the office.'

Her view is as valid as mine—our stipulation about unanimous agreement for large investments has stood us in good stead all these years. No need to disrupt our perfect working model over a handful of unforgettable orgasms.

I smile. 'Quite right. Sex is sex. Business is business.'

Nothing is more important than Bold. Making money saved me from a life of feeling as if I didn't matter. I made my first million working day and night for a big firm after university, before branching out on my own. With my first solo investment, I finally felt that I had a purpose in this world. That someone was benefitting from my birth. That I wasn't useless trash to be discarded time and time again.

After my inconsistent start in life I could so easily have taken a wrong path. Instead I took all of my negative feelings and channelled them into the hard work that's brought me to where I am today. I'm good at making money. Money makes a big difference in all areas of life. No one ever said I have too much. And I have plans to expand Bold, as well as my charity, Blackhearts.

'I'll do better to observe the demarcation.' I direct her through the hotel's revolving door to my waiting car and driver.

'No, *I'll* do better.' She climbs into the back seat, smoothing her dress over her long legs.

I join her with a chuckle. 'It's like that, is it? We're going to bring competition into restraining ourselves?'

She shrugs, giving me a playful sidelong glance. 'You're a man of excesses. I'm guessing that you suck at restraint, so I can't lose.'

'A man of excesses?' It's true my life now contrasts wildly with the unpromising boy I was, but the only thing I do to excess is work. Work at making money. Which gives me the ultimate control of my life. I don't have to ask anyone for anything. I wear and eat what I like and live where I choose.

'Don't make this too much of a challenge now, Dove.' Renewed desire shoots though me—she's irresistible. All my shaky good intentions disintegrate. Why not continue our seduction game for a few more days? 'Perhaps I'll just let you think you're winning, the way I let you be on top.'

She laughs and relaxes back against the leather. 'Well, the point is moot anyway. We agreed to only one more night.' Her small sigh tells me she might now regret that as much as me.

I press my lips together and nod slowly, my mind working on a compromise. I've struggled to keep my hands off her since our shower this morning. I don't normally physically escort her through doorways and into cars. She's perfectly capable of walking unaided. But there seems to be no end to the compulsion to touch her in sight.

'Of course, we're our own bosses,' I say, warming to the idea. 'One is just an arbitrary number we plucked from thin air.' A number I now realise was wholly inadequate. I want more.

Her stare sparkles, intense and assessing. 'Well, if you think about it, all numbers are arbitrary.' I think she's playing along, but then she looks away and my stomach twists with something akin to dread. Perhaps she's done.

'Did you…reschedule your missed date?' something makes me ask. The pulse in my neck throbs loud and fast.

She raises her chin defiantly. 'Not yet. Ben asked to meet tomorrow instead.'

Acid burns my throat. 'Ben?'

She nods. 'Ben Haslam—do you know him?'

I know everyone who's anyone that does business in Tokyo. 'He's in commercial property development, right?'

'Yes, that's him.'

'And you've never met him before?' I'm struck by a second flare of jealousy in twenty-four hours. The first was when she mentioned Sterling in the office earlier—I felt a searing, primal wrenching in my chest I've never experienced before.

'No.' She looks at me curiously.

'You won't get along.' I've never been more emphatic. Ben is a serious guy, bordering on dull. He'll stifle the life out of her. But, unlike me, he could probably offer her the full package—a relationship, marriage, the happy family.

Monroe stiffens beside me and I realise my mistake. She's like a bull at a red flag. The surest way to make her do something is to tell her she shouldn't.

'I'll be the judge of that.' She watches me intently as the car grows stifling with caged energy.

'Of course.' My voice is tight. I want to drag her mouth to mine and remind her how good we are together. How explosive is our chemistry. How many orgasms she had at my hands. How she could have more if she forgot about Ben and I forgot my one-night limit.

'So, let me tell you about this saké place.' As bright flashes of Tokyo pass by the car's windows, I talk about Gansue, one of the city's newest, hippest saké bars. I spout some facts about saké, trying to act normally while my mind trawls everything I know about Monroe's blind date. I should butt out and allow her the chance to click with another man. Not that she needs my permission. Instead, I plan ways I can selfishly nudge him out of the running.

It's not a long drive and we're there before I succumb to the urge to scrap the evening entirely and persuade Monroe to come back to my place. But, much as I'd like to, I can't imprison her naked and in a state of orgasm-induced coma. That doesn't mean I won't play dirty in my role as host. She embraced the seduction game. If we keep it going, she'll have no need for any other downtime but with me.

Inside the tiny, dimly lit bar we sit at the counter, which runs along the narrow open kitchen so we can watch the chefs prepare our food. The atmosphere is relaxed. A wall of colourful saké bottles and one-of-a-kind pottery saké cups warms the clean tones of the interior décor. I thought of Monroe as soon as I saw them—she has her own collection of pretty bone china teacups at home.

'The locals call saké *nihonshu*,' I say, gesturing to the various brands lined up behind the bar. 'There are as many different varieties and unique flavours as there are wines or beers.' I've become something of an enthusiastic convert to the Japanese national drink. Yet, now, the idea that Monroe might keep her date with Ben fucking Haslam leaves my throat too dry to swallow a single drop.

'I love it here.' She flashes me her radiant smile. 'Good call.'

Gansue's intimate and eclectic atmosphere brims with authentic Japanese elegance, and I can tell from the appreciation gleaming in Monroe's eyes that she's enchanted.

Something shifts in my chest—the warmth of intimacy. I felt it this morning when we shared a moment in the shower. I know this woman. Aside from being long-term business partners and temporary lovers, we're also friends. I respect her place in my life. I enjoy her company, her warmth and her big heart. Putting that enchanted look on her face could become addictive.

I observe the uniqueness and delicate beauty of her features, marvelling at how different her familiar face looks through the lens of a lover. She's piled her dark, silky mass of hair on top of her head in a relaxed up-do. It exposes her neck, and I'm reminded of how she moaned and clawed at my back when I kissed her there last night. I want to kiss her there now and test her resolve.

Can she move on and ignore the kind of sex that all other encounters are measured against? I knew from last time that we'd be great together but being trapped in a cocoon of intimacy by the storm seemed to heighten every touch, as if we could hear the countdown ticking. We barely slept. I couldn't seem to get enough of her. And now, even if I could walk away, I don't want to just yet.

I slowly lift my hand to brush an escaped tendril of hair from her cheek. Her eyes widen with surprise.

'Hudson…' Her voice is hesitant, almost a plea.

I drop my hand, gathering my scattered wits. We stare, the connection that bound us together in insatiable need last night still there.

'I've been thinking.' She touches my leg under the bar, looking up at me with seductive eyes. 'In terms of the arbitrary numbers you mentioned earlier, don't you think *five* has a nice, clear ring to it?' She trails her fingers along my thigh. For the first time since we stopped kissing and touching and started work this morning, I breathe easily.

I grin, elation tugging at my cheeks. Five is the number of nights she's in town.

'I'd have to unequivocally agree with you there, Dove. Five is a perfect number for a game of seduction.' Making it competitive keeps it light and playful. And with a set end-date there's no risk of emotions sneaking in. We've got this.

I lean close and enjoy her small shudder when I exhale on her neck. 'Wanna get out of here? If I had my way, we'd have never left your hotel.'

Her throaty laugh makes my cock twitch. Excitement flares in her eyes. 'I want dinner and saké.'

My smile widens. 'I guess we should eat, as we'll be burning up so many calories.' I can tell from her shallow breathing and the pulse fluttering in her neck that she's thinking about the four remaining nights every bit as much as I am.

We order food I'm no longer hungry for, and are quickly served warm saké in an ornate pottery bottle with matching cups. Monroe moans at the first delicious sip.

'Good?'

She nods, her eyes half closed in delight. 'So good.' She licks her lips and I look away to block out the memories of that mouth wrapped around my cock this morning.

Guilt slams into me; I'd planned to bring both Monroe *and* Sterling here. Instead I fucked my friend's ex-wife all night long. I respect the hell out of Sterling and he's the only person I know who's as ballsy in business as I am. And yet I have the same plan for tonight. I take a slug of saké to dash the shame robbing my appetite.

The feeling worsens as I recall how he'd come to me for advice after their marriage imploded. It was a tense time for us all, professionally and personally. My role shifted from that of the outsider, one I was used to, to being the one caught in the middle of two people I care about. Both were hurting and grieving and desperate not to cause the other further suffering. All I could offer was an unbiased ear and support in the office. I had no personal wisdom to share, having no experience with what they were going through. Out of self-interest, I advised them to keep the lines of communication open, for the sake of their years of hard work in building a business. And it succeeded.

'You've drifted off. Are you okay?' Monroe strokes my arm and my body clamours to be closer.

'I was remembering the day we all met. How fearlessly you and Sterling propositioned me.' We share a smile. I'd given the keynote address at the European Investment Summit in London when they'd approached me to suggest a partnership.

'Yes.' There's a twinkle in her eye. 'We'd been plotting for weeks. Sterling had read about you in the *Financial Times*. We knew you were speaking, and thought, why not go big and present one of the industry's best with an opportunity he couldn't refuse?'

I'd laughed them off initially. I was doing all right on my own. I couldn't see why I needed a couple of younger hotshots who had ambitions beyond simply working for me. Needing partners had never previously crossed my mind. But they'd been so passionate and driven. They reminded me of me. Once I'd given them a chance to pitch their figures and projections if we joined forces, I was hooked. We'd set a trial period for the newly formed Bold, but six months in none of us had any regrets.

Our food arrives. Deep-fried broad beans, Yakitori, and Takoyaki—delicious octopus balls topped with nori flakes and Japanese mayonnaise.

Monroe picks up her chopsticks and digs in, pop-ping a broad bean into her mouth and sighing with pleasure.

'Just think how dull your life would be if we hadn't convinced you that three is better than one.' Her smile is flirtatious but layered with intuition and compassion.

She couldn't have known at the time what a huge step it was for me to allow anyone into my life. A step I might not have taken if our meeting hadn't occurred during a week I was feeling particularly isolated. On some unfathomable impulse I still can't explain, I'd reached out to the first foster parents I remember, Wendy and Bill, only to discover that Wendy had died years earlier from her long battle with cancer.

'Yeah, well, you just happened to catch me on a bad day.' My smile feels brittle. Learning of Wendy's passing had opened up those childhood wounds, resurfacing a deep loneliness I thought I'd overcome. Rather than take my usual solo stance, I'd been open to taking a risk with two new business partners.

Looking at Monroe now, even after last night's veer into personal territory and this morning's professional wobble, I know the gamble paid off. And this new risk…breaking my rule to have her in my bed for the next four nights…? Let's hope neither of us regrets it down the track.

CHAPTER FIVE

Hudson

'LET'S WALK TO the crossing,' she says after dinner.

It's a beautiful, balmy evening. At this hour the crowded streets are bustling—youngsters in search of night life, commuters heading to the station and tourists enchanted by the big city glow from the overhead neon lights. I've grown used to the crush of bodies around Shibuya's famous intersection—the Shibuya Scramble Crossing—but I took Monroe's hand the minute we left the bar. My mind says keeping her close is a safety thing, but her hand in mine is scarily natural.

I watch her, admiring her wide-eyed excitement for the atmosphere. 'You love it here, don't you?'

She beams. 'Yes. Don't you?'

'I guess.' I've lived in Tokyo for three years and it still doesn't feel like home, but then nowhere does. A man without roots can live anywhere.

'Sterling and I had a whole sightseeing itinerary planned this trip, things we missed out on during previous visits.' She shrugs. 'I guess I can do some of it alone.'

'What kind of things?' I owe her an insider's tour. Every time I visit them in London and New York, they invite me to new places and include me in their social lives.

'I'd love to see some cherry blossom, as I'm here at the right time of year, and Sterling wanted to visit the Sensō-ji Temple, but we can do that next time we're here together. Otherwise I'm happy to just eat and drink and absorb the ambience.'

'You want to see a bunch of trees lose their petals?' I grin, wanting to kiss away her adorable outrage.

'I do. What—too romantic for you, Black?'

My grin widens. 'No comment.'

She laughs and then looks down. 'I need distractions. Mum's memorial is next week.' When she looks at me again, the excitement has faded from her eyes.

I wince. 'Yes, I'm sorry. I know it's a hard time for you.' I squeeze her hand and clamber for something appropriate to say to a woman still grieving her mother's passing. 'Remind me. How long has it been?'

She sways closer until her arm is flush with mine and pastes on a bright smile. 'We lost her just over four years ago. Every year since, my family hosts a memorial at Dad's place in Cambridgeshire, although we try to make it more of a celebration. My sister Claire organises everything, despite having three children. She's the one who still runs Mum's business. It's normally just us and a few friends and Mum's old work colleagues. People whose lives she touched.'

She swallows hard, clearly struggling with deep emotions. She was close to her mother. We don't normally discuss much of our private lives when we meet up, preferring to focus on the work we love, and socialising after hours. But I recall Monroe's devastation when her mother died vividly. I'd felt helpless, and inadequate to help. The same feeling renders me uncomfortable now.

'Will Sterling be at the memorial?' Sterling had been her husband. He'd know exactly what to say if he were here right now. For her sake I hope he'll be there next week, but jealousy writhes inside me nonetheless.

'Yes, he'll be there.' Her searching expression leaves me restless.

In the early days of our partnership, I was inexplicably envious of Monroe and Sterling's relationship—not because I was attracted to Monroe, although I was. Their closeness made me wonder for the first time ever if I might be missing out. Their love, their happiness, at times heightened my loneliness. I was the odd one out, reminded of the years I'd spent as a boy, passed from family to family, home to home, school to school.

Monroe's voice is wistful as she continues. 'We

try to make it a time of laughter and good memories, because there are heaps of those. A lifetime's worth. Mum can't just be remembered by a brass plaque at a chapel of rest.'

I nod, my lips mashed together and a hollow feeling expanding my chest. How do I comfort her now we've spent the night locked together physically? In past years I've sent flowers and a brief email stating I'd be there if she needed me.

She hadn't.

I'd even gone to the funeral, tried to support a grieving Monroe. But she had Sterling and her large family to offer comfort. She hadn't needed a man who, having never known his own parents, couldn't fully understand what she was going through. The closest I've come to that was discovering that Wendy had died, and I'd managed that unsettled time with my usual coping mechanism: work.

'She was a special lady,' I say, stroking the back of her hand with my thumb. I met Cathy Dove once or twice around the time of Monroe and Sterling's wedding, shortly after we founded Bold. I recall a lovely, warm, nurturing woman, always quick to laugh. The busy and noisy Dove household had regularly seen people dropping in for one of Cathy's famous scones or lethal gin and tonics…

I'd felt out of my depth there.

'You look like her,' I say in lieu of anything remotely consoling about the imminent memorial.

Sterling once confessed he didn't think Monroe

would ever get over Cathy's death. He even attrib-
uted her part in their marriage failure to Cathy's un-
timely passing, saying she'd pushed him away and he
hadn't been able to compensate for what she'd lost.

'Do you think so?'

I turn to face her and nod, drawn to bringing back
her smile. 'You have the same hair colour.' I cup her
cheek, my fingers flexing in the silky strands of hair
at her nape.

Her smile is my reward. 'And the same eyes.'

We keep walking.

'Oh, sorry.' She sniffs. 'I don't know where that
heavy turn in the conversation came from. I must
still be tired.'

'Don't apologise. I hate to see you hurting. It rips
me open.' With my arm around her shoulders, I drag
her close and kiss her forehead. I ache for my playful, sassy Dove.

And now my own unwelcome memories resur-
face, ones I've spent my entire adult life suppress-
ing. Wendy was the only remotely motherly figure
I had before she got sick and I had to leave. I recall
elaborate birthday cakes—a train, a spaceship and a
football. Shiny new shoes at the beginning of every
school year that didn't pinch my toes… And cautious
hugs I was too scared to trust.

My stomach lurches at the guilt that I didn't reach
out to Wendy and Bill until it was too late. I missed
my chance to say thank you.

The crowds in front of us come to a halt at the red lights.

'I forgot that you met Mum at the wedding,' says Monroe. 'She was so happy that day, to see the last of her brood safely hitched.' She turns pensive once more.

I grow impatient with the wait for the trains to stop and the crossing to spring to life. I want to see Monroe smile again, so I rack my brains for something happy. 'Yes, we had a brief chat. I was sitting in a corner and she came up and hugged me.'

Monroe smiles. 'Yes, Mum could always spot the person most in need of a hug.'

I laugh. 'She had something of a priest's or doctor's knack of drawing out confessions, if I remember rightly.' I hadn't bothered with a date for the wedding, so I guess I'd been conspicuously alone. 'I told her how I felt mildly envious of what you and Sterling had together and her eyes lit up.'

Monroe's small frown and perceptive appraisal give me pause. I've never before confessed that personal detail to her or Sterling. It's not their fault I'm happy alone.

'I'm sorry if Sterling and I made you feel…excluded.' She squeezes my fingers. 'We always tried to keep physical contact out of the office and encouraged you to bring a date when we went out together.'

Rather than feel comforted by her closeness, I feel strangely uneasy, forced to re-examine that time. I'd thought I was well used to feeling alone by then, but it had snuck up on me the night of their wedding. Perhaps because in business we were the three musketeers, but personally it was them and me.

I press a brief kiss to her lips. 'I didn't tell you that to make you feel bad. I just wanted to give you a nice memory of Cathy. She claimed to know lots of young women who'd trip over themselves for a date with me.'

Pride gleams in the periphery of Monroe's eyes. 'Yes, that was Mum, always matchmaking. Keen to see everyone happy.'

'I didn't have the heart to set her straight,' I say, 'to tell her mild envy would never turn into a reason to join the married club.'

Monroe stills beside me. 'Why not?'

Earlier today she called me a lone wolf. I'm not sure why I brought this up—I could have left out that part of the story.

'I just can't imagine being that close to someone. Giving another person any sort of control over my contentment.' When you've been powerless, power becomes everything. I shrug. 'I guess I'm too set in my ways.'

Monroe flashes her compassion. 'I understand, although Mum and Dad's advice on marriage—or any partnership, for that matter—was to remember you're part of a team with a common goal.'

Why are we talking about marriage when all I want to do is drag her back to bed?

'It's good advice. But, just for the record, I *was*

happy for you and Sterling. I felt, if anyone could make it work, it was you two.'

She looks at me with curiosity, her eyes still carrying sadness. 'And yet we couldn't make it work. Somewhere along the way we forgot we were a team.'

I don't want to think about Sterling, not when I plan to seduce Monroe into exhaustion over the next few days, but I can't stop myself. 'And yet you kept working as one. I've always been impressed with the way you managed to stay friends and stay professional.'

That degree of dependence is alien to me. Trust is something life has never taught me. Just before my tenth birthday I was moved on from Wendy and Bill. I learned to shut down emotionally. I stopped waiting for my real parents, who I don't remember at all, to miraculously claim me in some sappy, happy ending. I stopped hoping for the perfect foster family to take me in and discover I was the missing piece they needed to be whole. I started looking inward for my strength. Self-reliance became a habit that still serves me well today.

'I think that was the problem,' she says. 'We worked as friends and business partners, but we married for the wrong reasons. I thought I'd found *the one*, and had blinkers on so I could join the couple's club my siblings belonged to. And Sterling had to prove something to his stepfather, I think.'

'Do you still have regrets?' I know she dates. That she's still searching for a lasting relationship.

'I regret the heartache caused. I was naive.' She stares up at me and I tighten my grip on her shoulders. 'I had romantic expectations. I wanted to see perfection, and then I struggled to compromise when I realised that it was an illusion. No relationship is perfect. I put a lot of pressure on us as a couple because I wanted to recreate the sense of belonging I'd felt growing up.'

For some reason her candour and insight make me uncomfortable. Then she shakes off her melancholy, her eyes turning playful once more.

'I haven't given up the search for my Mr Right. When I find him, you and Sterling will need to take over the business while I raise my own brood of children.'

My smile is rubbery. We want very different things from life. Just as I know she wants a husband and family one day, she knows she'll never find that with a man like me.

The crossing lights overhead change to green, snapping me from my daze.

'Is there anything I can do for you…you know… to help with the memorial?' She must know that, despite being atrocious at emotional support, I'd do anything for her and Sterling.

Anything but keep my hands off her, it seems.

She offers me an indulgent smile as we wait for the crowd in front of us to surge forward. She must see how out of my comfort zone I am. 'That's a very thoughtful offer. Right now, I think the most helpful thing would be distraction.'

She purses her lips in the sexy way she does. At least she's no longer thinking about her failed marriage or her mum.

'I'll happily distract you for the next four nights.' I rub a hand over my chin while I pretend to consider some options, but really there's only one way I want to occupy Monroe.

She sounds forlorn when she says, 'As long as you don't have other…plans.'

I lead her into the flow of human traffic as the crossing becomes a moving sea of bodies lit from above by the giant advertising screens. I slip my arm around her waist and lean close. 'I'm happy to make *you* my plans. I happen to know of a competitive little seduction game that's currently at a draw.'

She tilts her head to one side, her lips parted with excitement. 'Well, we can't have that. Someone has to win…'

My head is awash with distraction techniques. In all of them, she's naked. But now we're stuck in the middle of Shibuya Crossing.

'We could do a few tourist things. I can take some time off and show you the sights. I'd like to see the Cherry Blossom Festival too.'

'Is that the best you can do, Black? I don't want to brag, but if we were in London I'd show you a *really* good time.' She flicks me the look that kept me awake hour after hour last night—pure sin and temptation. Sleep was irrelevant, given the way we'd scorched the sheets.

I pull her to a halt in the centre of the crossing. I sweep her into my arms and kiss her the way I've wanted to since we entered my office this morning, freshly showered and newly wary of each other.

She returns my enthusiasm, wrapping her arms around my neck and sighing against my lips. Relief shudders through me. People swarm around us, parting like a river around a rock.

I pull back, determined to make this trip to Tokyo her best yet. 'I guarantee total mind-blowing distraction for the rest of your stay.'

Heat and playfulness and challenge gleam in the green-gold pools of her eyes. It's as if we're the only two people on the planet.

'That's a pretty tall order. Are you up to a mission of that undertaking?' She stands on tiptoes and rubs her lips against mine provocatively.

A chuckle rumbles through my chest as we step back into the flow of human traffic. 'The seduction challenge is back on. I'm happy to continue my winning streak if you're happy to take a thrashing, Dove.'

'Always such a high achiever.' She laughs, the throaty sound and her glittering stare tugging my mouth into a grin while arousal and satisfaction pound through my blood. 'Challenge accepted.'

CHAPTER SIX

Monroe

THE PRESENTER, ONE of Bold's mid-level executives here in Tokyo, has a droning voice, but my inattention at this morning's meeting has absolutely everything to do with my daydreams. Of Hudson spending the night at my hotel—our second night of more orgasms than hours of sleep. Hudson waking me up with a kiss. Hudson ordering a large pot of English Breakfast Tea from room service because he knows that I can happily forgo breakfast but cannot start the day without my favourite beverage.

A girl could get used to this...

The man himself, overachiever extraordinaire when it comes to pleasuring me out of my mind, sits across the room near the front. How can I be expected to focus on industry trends and the fund management reports of our top performing portfolio companies with such an absorbing distraction so near?

I observe him in almost fanatical detail, noting

the dashing sprinkling of salt-and-pepper grey at his temples, the way his handsome face is fixed with concentration and the cut of the charcoal suit I helped him select this morning from the collection he keeps in a closet at his office.

My pulse thumps behind my breastbone as I recall the tortured look on his face when he confessed how he'd felt envious of my relationship with Sterling. Oh, he was quick enough to remind me that marriage still wasn't for him, but I'd seen past that to a glimpse of his vulnerable places.

Reading between the lines, interpreting what he didn't say, I reasoned at times he must have felt excluded and lonely when the three of us were together and Sterling and I were a couple. And yet he's always seemed so content to be single. So comfortable with his own company.

What if that's all a front designed to protect himself? And why is that notion so…intriguing?

We're discussing the final item on the agenda when Hina slips inside the room. She creeps around the edge of the large conference table and hands me a couriered package. I take the bulky brown envelope and absently slide my fingers under the seal while Hudson fires questions at the associate presenting his analysis of the latest business models and forecasts for the Asian division of Bold.

From across the room I catch Hudson's eye. My insides flip; my body's Pavlovian response is to expect pleasure when he looks at me that way. On the surface he seems work-focussed, his usual sharp-minded and thorough self. But there's a gleam in his eye, a layer of heat that makes me shiver and recall his mouth between my legs at the crack of dawn.

I slide my hand inside the envelope, expecting a sheaf of documents or a company prospectus. Instead my fingers encircle a firm, phallic-shaped object that can only be a sex toy.

I freeze with my hand still inside the envelope. My eyes slam back to Hudson's as my temperature soars. His associate is still talking to the room, spouting facts and figures he no doubt hopes will enamour him to the boss. But, from the small twisted smile on Hudson's sinful mouth, his mind is elsewhere—on the contents of my envelope, to be precise.

He raises an eyebrow in defiance.

Oh, yes, he's responsible for this delivery. He's trying to win the seduction challenge with dirty tactics. How am I supposed to concentrate on work with his thoughtful gift in my hand?

I mouth *Bastard* at him, shivering with delight when he grins. He wanted me to open it during this meeting. To derail me or make me wild with need for him. I want to laugh. To kiss him until he's too horny to be smug. Instead I narrow my eyes, wrapping my hand around the toy as I formulate a plan to raise the stakes.

The meeting wraps with Hudson's 'Thanks, team—keep up the stellar work.' I shove the package into my oversized handbag and stand, my belly fluttering with anticipation.

The room clears, leaving Hudson and I alone.

We face each other across the glass-topped table. Sparks zap between us. His plan worked. Faced with only a quick lunch and an afternoon of meetings, I'm tempted to drag him into his office, lock the door and try out his gift.

'You shouldn't have…' My voice is hushed. The door to the outer offices is wide open.

'Ah, I disagree.' He pushes his hands inside his pockets and rolls back his shoulders so his chest puffs out.

I want to press my face there so I can feel the thud of his heart and inhale the delicious scent of his freshly laundered shirt.

'Some gifts are purely selfish.' His wicked mouth quirks up.

We stare, suspended in a sensual stalemate for a few agonising seconds. Then he caves first, heading for the door and escorting me from the conference room towards the lifts. I check my disappointment that we're not locking ourselves away in his bedroom with a *do not disturb* sign on the door.

As we bypass Hina, she holds out my coat.

I take it and glance up at him, trickles of warmth and excitement settling in my stomach. 'Where are we going?' Secretive Hudson is irresistible.

He winks, slipping his hand to my back. 'I'm taking you to see the cherry blossoms—it's a beautiful spring day.'

I gape, part-delighted, part-disappointed. I really wanted to break open the toy.

'Come on, Dove, it's too lovely to be cooped up inside.'

'It's…very thoughtful of you but we have…meetings.' And a gift to unwrap. The fight in me is half-hearted and born of an addiction to his touch. His jubilant and playful mood is contagious. I really do want to see the cherry trees in bloom.

'Nothing that won't keep.' He waggles his eyebrows, as if he's talking about a sexy rendezvous, not our afternoon of business.

We enter Hudson's private lift. Recognition zips between his body and mine, despite the perfectly respectable and professional distance we maintain for the benefit of his employees.

The minute the lift doors close, it's a different matter. We reach for each other in frantic unison. Need drags a gasp from my throat as we kiss. Hudson presses me against the wall so the handrail digs into my back. But I don't care. I hike up my skirt and he shoves one thick thigh between my legs, the fine wool of his trousers scraping the bare skin at the tops of my thighs above my stockings. I grind against him, desperate for the friction.

His kisses are wild, his fingers strumming my nipple through my blouse and bra. It's not enough.

I want more. I want him to stop this lift and finish what he started with his provocative delivery.

He tears his mouth from mine as the lift slows. 'Fuck, you drive me to distraction.'

'That's what I was going to say.' I grip the lapels of his suit and bring his mouth back to mine. 'I'd rather have you than a toy, but I can't wait to torture you for your sneaky attempt to win this round.'

He chuckles, leaning over to press a code into the panel on the wall, which stops the doors from opening.

His eyes darken, his stare fierce and hot. 'Hold that thought, Dove.' He's hard against me, his hips jerking. 'Fuck, that meeting was interminably long. I couldn't concentrate. I wanted to clear the room and do this and then splay you over the conference table.'

'What would you have done?' I pant, torturing myself, but also him, for denying me whatever fantasy is in his head.

He groans. 'Everything. Every single future meeting I have in there, that's all I'm going to think about. Me eating you out and then fucking you…'

'Sounds good to me.' I trail kisses up his neck and over his ear. 'We should have thought of it the night of the storm when we had the place to ourselves. But let's park that idea until everyone else has gone home.'

He pulls back, breathless. 'You have a dirty and devious mind.' The look he shoots me is layered with the heat and determination that precedes him issuing some sexual order, like *Come for me* or *Touch yourself* or *Suck me harder*.

'But I agree. No more wasted opportunities.' He grins, pressing his erection between my legs, and then drags his lips along my neck to my earlobe. 'Still want to see the cherry blossom…?'

'No…' My eyes roll back as he finds exactly the spot that makes my whole body tingle. Fingers of desire dance down my spine. It's hard to think about anything coherent with his hands roaming. I'm so tempted to abandon sightseeing, even though it's only been hours since we fell into an exhausted sleep in my hotel. But his reminder last night of his stance on relationships keeps me grounded. Hudson is Hudson. Even though we're having heaps of great sex, I need to remember what *I* want. No more rushing in or seeing things that aren't there.

Plus, I really do want to see the Cherry Blossom Festival.

'Wait. Yes, I do want to go, although it pains me to say it.' I shove at him so I can see his face which is harsh with arousal. 'We could always come back later tonight and do the conference table thing…'

He rests his forehead against mine, catching his breath. 'If you say so, Miss Goody Two Shoes.' But there's humour in his eyes.

I laugh, besotted with his playful side. 'This does feel kind of naughty—obviously the heavy petting in the lift. But also cancelling meetings. It's as if we're bunking school or something?'

He brushes my hair from my cheek. 'I bet you were far too sensible to have bunked off school.' He eases back, pushes my skirt down and adjusts his erection.

I feign outrage and then divulge the truth. 'No, you're right. But in my defence I had older brothers and sisters always watching me.' I finger-comb my hair and reapply my lipstick. 'It was like having four extra parents. I could never get away with anything.'

He buttons his jacket and straightens his tie while I re-tuck my blouse.

'Ready?' he says, a rueful grin on his face.

I nod, pasting on a bland expression so I don't look like a woman who's been dry-humped against a wall. By the time the lift doors open at the ground floor foyer of Bold Tower, we're once more two presentable business executives.

Inside the car Hudson reaches for my hand and shoots me a look brimming with playful reproof. 'Just think, Dove—you could be coming by now if you weren't such a goody-goody.'

I shudder, trying to calm my runaway heartbeat. Because the way he's started holding my hand, the way he comforted me last night over Mum's memorial, is all starting to feel as if we're dating. My chest grows tight with confused longing. He offered solace even though he clearly felt out of his depth. I wanted to hold him right there in the busy street until we both chased off our anguish. But I held back. We're *not* dating. It's just sex.

I shake my head and grin with exasperation. The seduction game he started helps me stay grounded in reality. 'Why is everything about winning with you?'

'Because I'm good at it.' His smile-and-wink combo is incorrigible. He seems younger. Happier. A woman could so easily fall for him. I wonder how many have over the years.

'So you mean to tell me that *you* skipped school?' It's hard to imagine him ever having been blasé when it comes to his goals. The Hudson I know is driven to the point where he's made professional success and money-making an art form. He's famously quoted as saying, 'You can't ever make enough money.' I've always assumed it's his security blanket, because he's not remotely flashy.

His confident grin falters a fraction. If I wasn't so attuned to him, I might have missed it. 'Of course. Unlike you, I had no one to grass me up. Surely I've told you about my misspent youth?'

The energy in the car buzzes like static. My pulse thuds, each beat more powerful. 'No, you haven't, but I'm listening.'

I'm risking the sexy, playful mood with my bout of curiosity, but there are two Hudson Blacks. The one I've known for five years, but don't really know, and the one who is currently my lover. Beyond the fact that he's funny and thoughtful and crazy-hot, this second version is something of an enigma.

I stay silent, waiting for any insight into the real Hudson, the one he protects with his competitive drive, tireless work ethic and famous commitment avoidance.

His sigh rings with defeat. He slips his hand from mine and spears it through his hair. 'I went to a total of seven schools before I was sixteen.' His eyes crinkle with a sad inevitable smile. 'Some were worse than others. Some I actually liked.'

His irises turn almost black, haunted with vulnerability. I want to hold him but resist. This is the real reason he doesn't date. He lived with the certainty that at any minute he'd be moved on. It's no wonder he fears rejection. There's no way he'd allow himself to grow attached to anyone after the abandonment of that first family. And that had spilled over into all of his relationships. Fear of failure is a hard taskmaster. After my divorce, I know.

'Were you bullied?' I want to comfort him. Instead I sit perfectly still, waiting for the pieces that complete the Hudson puzzle.

'Not really, but I was always *that* kid—the loner, the outsider, the foster kid.' He shrugs. 'Some days it was easier to just skive off, even though I was smart enough to realise that an education was the only way to drag myself up from the reject pile.'

'You were not in the reject pile.' My throat burns for the boy he must have been. Alone. Scared. Feeling unloved. 'Where would you go when you skipped school?'

He laughs then, his gorgeous mouth twisted into a wry smile. 'The library. I saw enough kids in the system who coped in other ways—drugs, self-harm. I wanted something different, although I could so easily have taken that route.'

I ache for the young Hudson who felt safer physically and emotionally withdrawn. Who learned somehow to strive to control his environment.

I rest my head on his shoulder, inadequacy shredding me up inside. 'I'm sorry you had that experience. I respect you even more now for what you've achieved.'

His smile is once more confident. 'Money makes money. It gives you control. Once I saw that, I was hooked. I had some great opportunities early on with Foster McVeigh,' he says, referring to the global investment bank he joined after university.

He presses his mouth to my forehead. 'You have the real gift, Dove—people skills.'

'Do I?' I frown. 'Some days the huge chunk of me missing after Mum's death makes me feel defective.' When she was alive, I felt invincible.

I lift my head from his shoulder and kiss him. The more he opens up, showing me glimpses of the things that have shaped him, the more I'm drawn to him. I can't help myself.

'Did you ever know your parents?' The question hurts my throat, but I want to understand him better beyond his astute sense for high-risk, high-return investments. I want to be there for him the way he is for me.

His body stiffens, his jaw tense. 'My father was

never on the scene. I was two when my mother could no longer cope and handed me over to the state. I don't resent her. In fact, I'm glad. She was an addict. She died of an overdose when I was six, apparently. At least I had a better life than the one she'd have provided.'

'I'm sorry.' It's not enough. Not what I want to say. But I'm wary of crossing a line with him and invading his personal pain. He'd hate that.

'You're kind of killing the mood here, Dove.' He grips my face and slides his mouth over mine, teasing my lips apart to the exploration of his tongue. I cling to his arms and surrender to his distraction technique, even though I want to blow off the festival and go somewhere quiet so we can talk and talk and talk...

I pull myself together with a deep inhale. Talking isn't on the approved list of distractions. And that's good. I can't become swept along in Hudson's heartache or misinterpret his rare emotional confidence.

He glances out of the window. 'We're here. Let's go marvel at some cherry blossom.'

I smile, but inside I'm a mess of contradictions.

His driver, Takao, parks up in Nakameguro, a trendy residential area not far from the financial district. Hudson jumps out and strides round to my side to hold open my door.

'Such a gentleman. You really want to win at all costs, don't you?' I aim for the playful vibe that seems to be our sweet spot, but it's hard to keep things light and superficial.

He winks, taking my hand and dragging me towards the mingling crowds.

My heart is no longer in it. I crave connection with the man he's showing me in minute glimpses. I long to understand the inner Hudson as well as I know his body. But I also know my tendency to see perfection, to rush in too soon and too eagerly. Next time I fall, I'll do so slowly with my eyes wide open. Because I've lived through one major relationship failure. I can't do it again.

As we walk in silence, I observe his profile, my mind racing.

I've been blessed with people who love me. Sometimes too many people, each of them with an opinion on how I should live my life. What sort of a person would I have been if I were totally alone, like Hudson? Would I have had his incredible strength of character, his conviction in his abilities and his unrelenting drive? It's easy to have dreams and goals when you have security and acceptance in which to grow.

But what if that growth was against the tide? What if you were overcoming life's obstacles alone and from a starting point of nothing? Avoiding the greatest risk of all—exposing his heart—is understandable.

The more I learn about Hudson, the more I question what I know and feel for him.

'What?' he asks, sensing my pensive mood.

I shake my head, forming my features into a neutral expression. 'Nothing. I'm just wondering… Were you close…? With any of your families?'

I need to know he had someone who cared. Some sort of parental figures. I was close to my parents, my mother especially.

His eyes are the colour of cognac—dark with emotion he's powerless to conceal. My chest aches. I can't stop seeing a younger Hudson, abandoned and alone. Let down by the world and vulnerable. Was teenaged Hudson angry? Emotionally withdrawn in preparation for being moved on from his latest 'home'? Did he have a girlfriend he'd been forced to leave behind? Friends?

With a small sigh of defeat, he throws his arm around my shoulders and guides me through the milling crowds. 'I have fond memories of my first family, Wendy and Bill. I was with them from the age of two until ten.' He speaks carefully, as if he's trying to keep a lid on his emotions.

I swallow hard, fighting the sting behind my eyes. 'I'm glad you had that but also sorry it didn't last.'

He shakes his head. 'Don't be sorry. It was a long time ago.' His sad smile all but tears out my heart.

I know the pain of losing a mother figure. It crushes me still, shaping my decisions, goals and dreams. I wouldn't change a day of my own busy, noisy childhood. My annoying siblings could be my worst enemies one minute and my absolute heroes the next. I even had my parents to myself for a while, in particular my mother, given the age gap between me and my older brothers and sisters.

'Besides, I'm not that hostile, scruffy little kid anymore.' He flashes a playful grin. 'I have everything I need and more. Look at me—I'm my own boss. If I want to take the afternoon off to be with a beautiful woman, there's no one to stop me.'

I laugh, my head woolly. At first glance he does have it all, but I wonder if there are gaping holes in his life. With balance, would he smile and laugh more often, as I've witnessed him do these past few days? Would he push himself and Bold so hard for world domination if he had someone to go home to?

When he changes the subject, I let it go. My heart is heavy while he talks about the annual Cherry Blossom Festival, which happens for a few weeks in late March and early April, when every Sakura tree in the city blooms almost overnight. I want to be caught up in the buoyant atmosphere, the magic of Mother Nature, but understanding him is making me question parts of myself I'd thought were set in stone.

We walk beside the flowering-cherry-tree-lined canal. The laden boughs arch over the river and form a canopy of pale pink candyfloss. Petals, delicate pink snowflakes, fall on us like confetti. It's magical and stunning, an oasis of natural beauty in the middle of an urban jungle, and I'm speechless at his thoughtfulness in bringing me here.

It's only when I catch Hudson staring at me with

an indulgent smile on his face that I realise I've been silent for a while—staring in wonder but also lost in my thoughts.

'Thanks for this—it's so pretty.'

His smile is wide.

I flush and bump shoulders with him. 'You live here. You get to see it every year.'

He shrugs. 'This is my first visit to the festival. I'm normally too busy to bother.'

He takes out his phone and tugs me under his arm, positioning us in a photo that's backdropped by clouds of blossom and the shocking pink lanterns that hang from the trees.

I smile for the selfie, choked with a well of emotion. 'Well, in that case, I'm glad we could see it together.'

I kiss him briefly, holding a part of myself back. I can't push Hudson Black into the mould of my perfect man. I'm looking for real, not fairy-tale fantasy. What we're doing this week has nothing to do with feelings. We're just messing around for another fifty-one hours and nineteen minutes.

He picks a blossom petal from my hair. 'Are you hungry? Let's get some food.'

I want to be hungry. The narrow side-streets teem with cafés, bars and eateries, and rows of outdoor stalls sell festival-themed food. *Hanami dango*, the iconic pink, green and white sweet dumplings; exquisitely crafted sushi, which look too pretty to eat; and delicious *karaage* chicken. There are even stalls of frothy pink champagne in tall flutes, decorated with strawberries.

I purchase two glasses of the champagne from a nearby stall. 'To skiving off. I wish I'd tried it years ago.'

Hudson grins and clinks his plastic flute to mine. 'I'll make a rebel out of you yet. Come on. I have a surprise.' He leads me to a spot near the river where people are seated under the trees on picnic rugs.

'I arranged a picnic,' he says, collecting a basket and blanket from a woman dressed in a beautiful silk kimono decorated with a blossom pattern.

'*Arigatō gozaimashita.*' Hudson thanks her and we find a spot to spread out the rug at the water's edge.

'I don't know what to say…' My voice wobbles. 'This is so perfect. Thank you. Are you trying to win the "most romantic gesture" award as well as the "sexy seduction" trophy…?'

I take a seat, my heart fluttering. I could so easily be swept along. I was brought up to believe I could have it all without compromise. My mum and my two older sisters juggled family and a career as well as finding deep romantic love. I won't be short-changed from my birthright just because it didn't work out with Sterling, and I won't make the same mistake twice. I learned a lot from my brief marriage, mainly about myself. Next time I fall, I'll take my time and make sure it's right for me.

'No.' His stare flares with heat but he laughs good-naturedly. 'It's a Japanese tradition. They call it *hanami*, which means "flower viewing." It's a spring celebration that dates back centuries.'

I look around. Yes, there are tourists here, but it's obvious this festival is a big part of Japanese culture.

Hudson pops the cork on a chilled bottle of pink champagne and tops up our glasses while I enthusiastically unpack the delicious-looking food and try not to overinterpret what this means. Long term, I want more than great sexual chemistry with a wonderful man. I want a lover who shares my dreams and aspirations, not just my professional ambitions. I want my own large family—boisterous birthday parties and Christmases and any other excuse to get together.

My family isn't perfect, but Mum and Dad taught us the importance of staying together. We turn to each other when times are tough and celebrate each other's successes. I want to continue the family traditions and make my own in the future. To keep Mum alive in any way I can.

'This trip is going to be disastrous for my waistline,' I say, desperately trying to return to our easy vibe.

'I'm happy to provide hourly workouts if required,' he responds with an inviting gleam in his eye.

'Now, there's a training regime I could get with.' I celebrate the return of our banter, marvelling at the canopy of blossom overhead.

'Mum would have loved this,' I tell him with a

sigh. 'When I was at uni, before I met Sterling, we travelled together every opportunity we had—mainly around Europe. I was single, Dad was still working, and my brothers and sisters were busy with their lives and their children, so girls' weekends became our thing. She never voiced regrets about having a big family and starting young, but she encouraged all of us to spread our wings and fly.'

'Perhaps she saw herself in you.' He strokes the back of my hand. 'She'd be proud of you, you know.'

'I hope so. I think she died content that all of her grown-up children were happy and settled.'

'She'd understand. About the divorce. You're not the only couple in the world to grow apart. And at least you gave it a shot.'

'I know. I just wish I could tell her that I'm still okay. That I haven't given up on my dreams just because my life took a fork in the road.' Losing Mum six months into the marriage had amplified my feelings of failure over the divorce. I missed her hugs and advice and her ability to listen when I needed it most.

'She knows. You do everything with passion and enthusiasm, Dove. Your personal life won't be any different.'

I gape, slightly taken aback that he sees me so well. That he's bothered to notice.

'I so desperately wanted the marriage to work, and so did Sterling. It seemed the harder we tried, the further apart we grew.' I run my fingers through the petals littering the grass, ashamed of how I misjudged the relationship so badly, and sad that I hurt a wonderful man. 'I was just too focussed on the end point to appreciate the journey, I guess.'

We need to get away from all this personal stuff.

'What about your personal life?' I ask with a wink. 'Do you have a date for the Business Awards dinner tomorrow? Because I'm not playing gooseberry! If we're taking dates, you'll have to find me some dishy businessman friend. Or should I invite Ben Haslam…?'

His eyes become flinty with determination. 'I'm taking *you*. No need for any businessman besides this one, especially not Haslam.'

I press my lips together, concealing my smile of delight. 'You don't like Ben?'

'I like *you*, Dove. You need a date while you're here—you have one.' He stabs his thumb at the centre of his chest. The heat I've grown used to around him consumes me, sliding over my skin like liquid arousal.

'Okay, then. If you're going to be all needy about it, I'll tag along with you.' I hide my full-body shudder of pleasure and heap my plate with delicious delicacies from the picnic to stop myself from barrelling him to the grass in front of all the families.

I look up when I notice he's grown still. He's frowning, his expression hesitant. I've never seen him wear that look before.

'Would you like to…tag along with me this afternoon…to my place?'

I swallow, my heart banging at my breastbone. On the surface his invitation reflects our pretty constant need to get each other naked. But scratch the surface and it's monumental.

My previous trips to Tokyo with Sterling were business-heavy. We managed to squeeze in one or two tourist things, but we've never been invited to Hudson's home. He's a lavish and generous host, always, but he protects his inner sanctum like he protects his vulnerabilities.

Rampant curiosity and longing sweeps through me. I tell myself I can't get carried away by our deepening connection. I only hope I can control the urge.

'I'd love to come to your place.'

CHAPTER SEVEN

Hudson

MONROE'S EYES ARE wide with appreciation as she moves around my living space, making her way to the floor-to-ceiling windows to look out at my view. I remove my jacket and tie and try to pretend that I'm comfortable having her in my penthouse apartment, just as I pretended to be comfortable talking about my past.

In truth, no woman has ever been here before.

'It's a beautiful neighbourhood. I like your view,' she says about the landscaped gardens below and the distant vista of Tokyo's skyline.

'Thank you. To be honest, I don't spend that much time here. The office is so convenient and comfortable.' And often full of people.

Yeah, sometimes the echo from these walls is too harsh.

A reminder that I'm alone. Perhaps that's why I invited Monroe. Her gentle prying, her own revelations about her mum… It opened up not only our contrasts, but also wounds I'd rather not pick at.

Having her in Tokyo this week without Sterling has been an epiphany. I never realised how much his presence prevents me from getting to know her on a deeper level—not through any possessiveness on his part, but because he already knows these things about her.

It's a double-edged sword. The more time we spend together, the more I enjoy her company. But it emphasises my usual solitary existence. Is that the reason I recounted my childhood?

I try to block out those years. The memories bring inadequacy, as if I'm only good enough to be abandoned. Rubbish to be thrown away time after time. Even when the financial evidence, my string of assets and my net worth says otherwise, remembering my past makes me question my value.

That's why I avoid relationships. Because the closeness they bring carries expectations of emotional intimacy. Sharing and confiding. I don't want to be ripped open for all my fears to spill out in an ugly mess.

'Would you like a drink? I have more of that pink champagne if you're interested.' I focus on the simmering arousal I feel when Monroe is close. I need to concentrate on the physical aspects of our relationship. God knows, they're absorbing enough.

I can keep the rest at bay for a few more days. Then, with this fling over, I'll return to normal.

Focus on things I can control—my simple one-night stands and work. Without this unsettling feeling rumbling away inside me like a volcano.

'Yes please.' She takes off her coat and wanders around in her stockinged feet, appraising the sparse, clean and open space. I cast my eyes around, viewing its lack of homeliness as if through her eyes. Her house in London is warm and inviting. Filled with eclectic furniture, from sleekly modern to antiques she's inherited from her grandparents. Chic, soft furnishings and colourful rugs.

And personal touches are scattered everywhere—family photos of her hordes of nieces and nephews; neat rows of Mason jars lining the kitchen shelves filled with the dry goods and whole grains she likes to cook with; and the tiny yoga studio she's created in the conservatory, where the morning sun streams in to bathe an array of healthy houseplants.

My place couldn't be more different. Low, minimalistic wooden furniture, bamboo flooring and lots of natural light. The only clutter comes from a stunning bonsai tree I was gifted by a business associate when I first arrived, as well as two photo frames.

'I know—it's far from homely. But I'm the only person who spends time here.' I bought the Azabu apartment three years ago. The hillside residential area favoured by international executives and diplomats has a cosmopolitan, village vibe. A kind of suburban oasis in the heart of the city. The building boasts a highly useful bilingual concierge and my apartment has a private rooftop garden with stunning views of Tokyo.

She looks over her shoulder and regards me with that curiosity I'm beginning to dread. 'I thought it would be a bit more…lavish, I guess.'

'Like a gold-plated toilet seat and walls full of Pollack originals?' I grin, peeling the foil from the bottle of champagne.

She laughs. 'No, I guess that's not you.'

'I'm rarely here. You know me, Dove. I live to work.'

'Don't you ever get lonely?' Her back is to me, her voice carrying a faraway wistfulness that pokes at me harder than if she'd hurled the words like an accusation. Because it tells me she too feels lonely sometimes, despite her big family. She wants more than this life of financial wealth and work. She wants a lasting relationship, motherhood, things she deserves and will excel at.

The pop of the cork snaps the tense atmosphere. 'Not really.' I lie easily, because I've told myself the same untruth a thousand times. The need for other people brings out feelings of rejection. I try to keep that shit locked away.

Monroe looks slightly dejected, but she recovers quickly. 'Who are these gorgeous scamps?' She holds up one of the framed photos of a group of boys between the ages of nine and fifteen. The other photo is of a younger Sterling, me and Monroe, wearing huge matching, self-congratulatory grins on the day BLD Global Ventures joined the three-comma club.

'Those are Blackhearts,' I say, placing two glasses of chilled champagne on the table and fighting the strange disquiet that's been riding me since we left the office. Talking about the charity I started for foster children won't improve my mood. But, now I've brought her here on some strange impulse, I'll have to face the consequences.

'Blackhearts.' She frowns in concentration. 'Your charity?'

I nod, loosening my cuffs and rolling up my shirt-sleeves, trying not to see my own face amongst the smiling boys in the picture. 'Yes. Those are some local boys.'

I take a slug of champagne, restless now she's looking at me with new interest, as if I'm a previously undiscovered beetle she can catch and observe at her leisure.

I stare hard, letting her see the urgency building in me. 'Why don't I give you a tour of the house?' My voice is strangled with need. 'Starting with my bedroom.' I want to get her naked. To have her look at me with passion verging on desperation, not with curiosity and compassion. I want to banish her inquisitive mood with pleasure until we both forget that I'm anything other than supremely content and absolutely winning at life.

At least she's no longer looking at me with pity, the way she did when I talked about my foster homes.

She places the photo back on the shelf. 'You don't want me to be nosy. I understand. We have shared a lot today.'

She takes a shuddering breath and swipes her tongue across her lower lip, as if remembering why we came here.

'But the bedroom... Isn't that a little...conventional for a man on a mission to out-seduce his partner? Especially when I have a brand-new gift to break in.' She reaches for her glass and takes a slow, sensual sip, her eyes locked on mine over the rim.

Relieved to be off the hook, I step closer and trace my fingertip over the notch at the base of her throat. Her breathing kicks up, the heat of her skin burning my fingertip.

'It's a big apartment.' I circle her nipple through her blouse, smiling at her tiny gasp. 'But, if you'd rather start elsewhere, how about the hot tub? On the roof...'

Excitement flares in her eyes, her skin warming with a peachy flush. 'Sounds good, except I don't have a bikini.' She looks down, watching the path of my finger disappear into the vee of her cleavage where I loosen the top button of her blouse.

'That works for me.' Feeling more like my old self, I deposit our glasses, wrap my arm around her waist and drag her flush with my body. This is what we need. No more talking. Just sex.

I drag her mouth up to mine and taste strawberries, all decadent and classy. She moans, curls her fingers into my hair and angles my head under her kiss.

Controlling this insatiable need that erupts every time I touch her makes me feel alive and invincible. The only other thing that comes close to this is seeing an investment strike gold. Knowing that without me a company wouldn't reach its full potential. That I've made a difference to someone.

Monroe pulls back and slowly starts to unbutton my shirt.

I'm hard against her stomach, desperate to slake all of my pent-up doubts in physical release. I grip her hips, pressing her where I want her while she tugs my shirt free of my trousers. My thoughts turn possessive, for all of her pleasure. 'You won't need the vibrator.'

Her eyes flick to mine, bright with lust.

I undo another blouse button, the torture of unwrapping my prize—her—ramping up my desire. 'You said you prefer me, anyway.'

'I did. I *do*.' She shudders against me, dropping her mouth to my neck in nipping kisses that make me growl.

I quickly peel the blouse from her shoulders and drop it on the floor while she tackles my fly. I want to linger over her delicious breasts, but I also want her naked. Where Monroe is concerned, my wants are multiplying exponentially.

I haul her close and unzip her skirt. She steps

out of the garment and shoves down my trousers and boxers.

With a pinch of my fingers at her bra clasp and the glide of lace over hips, I win the race to render each other naked.

We stand panting, face to face. Her eyes are glazed with arousal. I press a kiss to one of her shoulders, sucking in the scent of her skin.

'Do you feel seduced yet?' I comb my fingers through her hair so it falls down her back and across her breasts in the glossy waves that I love, watching with satisfaction at how her nipples harden for my attention.

'Yes. You're too good at this game.'

I bask in her praise, grateful for the reminder that it may be intense, but our connection is still temporary.

I stoop to retrieve a condom from my trouser pocket and take her hand. On the way to the roof, I grab a couple of robes from the hall closet. I wrap Monroe in one, slipping my hand around her waist and tugging her close for a kiss. 'It's a shame to cover such an exquisite sight, but if I don't we won't make it to the hot tub.'

'I don't care.' She shrugs, mischief gleaming in her eyes. 'Right here is fine.' She looks down at the bare wood floor.

I release her with reluctance and don my own robe. 'Come on, Dove. Don't be so conventional. I'm trying to win here… I want you to come overlooking my view of Tokyo.'

She laughs and collects our glasses while I carry the ice bucket containing the rest of the bottle and we head to the roof.

As we emerge onto the terrace, she gasps. The views are impressive. The previous owner had strung a million solar-powered bulbs across the space so even at dusk, before the city puts on its own spectacular illuminations from a million windows and streetlights, it's pretty magical up here.

'Is this really all you've got to impress the ladies?' she asks, sounding breathless.

I place the ice bucket down at the edge of the pool and switch on the bubbles and underwater lights. 'I don't bring women here. Only you.' I step close, tug her robe open and let it fall to the floor, enjoying her shock as she looks up at me.

'I'm a woman,' she whispers.

'I can see that.' I rub my lips over hers, the ache in my balls demanding I speed this up. But I want to savour her. To forget the countdown, the diminishing time we have left. 'But you're also my friend and business partner, so you're special.' And precious. And therefore risky.

Arousal blooms under her skin, releasing a wave of her body heat, which carries her delicious scent.

'Does that mean we'll have to discuss business?' She bites her lip and looks at me from under her lashes as she undoes the belt of my robe and presses her naked body to mine.

'You can talk any kind of dirty you like while I make you come, Dove.' I take her hand as she steps down into the sunken hot tub and lowers herself under the water. I remove my own robe and join her, tugging her close.

'So overconfident.' She sits astride me and parts her lips over mine. Our tongues meet, dancing a routine that's become second nature. Her naked skin and her soft curves slide against my hard edges. I feel her sigh and taste longing in her kiss. Pressure builds in my chest as if I'm running a marathon. I want to plunge inside her and chase away the memories that I was ever anything other than the man I am now—in control, self-reliant, secure.

But Monroe, whether I'm inside her or not, makes me think. Makes me question and compare, as if with her I could have more than this. More than just money in the bank and every creature comfort at my disposal.

Lifelong security is all I've ever craved.

She pulls back, her eyes glazed in that way I love. 'You sure know how to fight to win.' She strokes my cheek and jaw with one fingertip. 'How will I ever top this grand seduction you've had going all day?'

I grip her backside and shunt her closer to where I need her. Her hips undulate and her breasts break the bubbling surface.

'You always rise to a challenge. You'll think of

something.' I cup her breasts, raising them up to my lips. I take one into my mouth and then the other, laving at her hard nipples, because it makes her squirm. Makes her greedy and demanding and wild for me.

'You're right, I will.'

She kneels up astride me on the seat, tips my head back against the edge of the pool and covers my mouth with hers. Then she pulls back and stares down at me. 'Why don't you invite me to stay the night so I can level the playing field?'

I didn't plan on her leaving. We've spent the past two nights doing nothing but fucking, and I want to gorge myself until we leave Tokyo for London in one of the company jets.

'What's in it for me?' I ask, my cock flexing at the idea of having her at arm's reach all night, even when my brain tries to retreat. No woman has ever slept in my bed downstairs.

She smiles her 'cat that got the cream' smile. 'You'll have to wait and see. Where's the condom? I can't take any more seduction—I want you now.'

'Thank fuck.' I reach behind me to snag my robe from the chair and retrieve the condom from the pocket.

She shuffles off my lap and I quickly sheath myself and then drag her to me once more. This fire consuming us has been building all day. Knowing we have only three more nights to indulge this fling ramps the urgency skyward until she's all I think about. From first thing in the morning to when I finally succumb to exhaustion at night and every minute in between.

What kind of magic is that?

Dangerous, that's what kind.

She guides me to her entrance and then sinks onto me with a low moan, her head thrown back and her breasts thrust in my direction. I cup them and direct one nipple towards my mouth, feeling the grip of her internal muscles tighten as I tongue the bud erect.

She rocks above me, her arms braced on my shoulders and her eyes locked to mine, riding me with the Tokyo skyline as her view. I forget that we're playing a game. Forget that having her here is a first. Forget the hours we have left and simply lose myself to the pounding waves of desire.

I thrust up into her, pressing my fingers to her clit and watching arousal darken her eyes and turn her areolas dusky.

'H-Hudson.' She stutters my name between gasps and contracts around me as she comes, giving herself entirely over to the pleasure. It's an addictive sight. As I crush her in my arms and chase my own release, there's a tiny piece of me that acknowledges the vision of Monroe's pleasure is a privilege I wish I could keep for ever.

CHAPTER EIGHT

Monroe

IT'S FULLY DARK OUTSIDE, but neither of us has yet surrendered to sleep. It's as if we're both counting the hours. Both driven to insanity with the need to keep touching each other. Every kiss, every cry, every climax brings us closer to the end. I briefly close my gritty eyes; I can't bear to think about that.

Hudson's heartbeat under my cheek, where I'm sprawled across his chest in a sexually satisfied heap, helps to soothe the panicked feeling bubbling away in me.

'Tell me about the photo of the Blackhearts boys,' I mumble, my voice thick and sleepy. I'm not ready to close my eyes on another day. And what a day it's been...

He tenses. He doesn't need to say it—to him Blackhearts is deeply personal. He rarely mentions his charity work, which he started years ago when he lived in London. My desire to know intensifies.

The photo taking pride of place on the shelf all but tore out my heart.

His deep voice is sleepy too. 'The need for the mentoring programme for kids in the foster system has grown. Now we operate in twenty-three countries. But I'm always looking to expand.'

'Of course you are.' I lift my head and press my lips to his in a slow, languid kiss that says everything I want to voice. 'It's something close to your heart, isn't it?' Now I know more about his past, I understand how important it is to him.

I wonder if he discusses it with Sterling. They often hit the gym together when we're in the same country. What do they talk about when I'm not there?

He shrugs as if to say, 'of course.' And he's right. Why didn't I notice when I was just a business partner and, I like to think, a friend? I'm still those things, I hope. But becoming lovers has thrown a spanner into our well-oiled machine, and I'm not sure I want to stick in my hand to retrieve it.

His fingers idly trace a line up the centre of my back. 'Yeah. I want as many youngsters as possible to have access to counselling as well as fun outings and experiences. A safe place where they can just be normal kids is important.'

'Yes, it is.' I want to ask if *he* had those things, but something holds me back—perhaps the nauseating instinct that he didn't.

My patience is rewarded when he continues.

'Some children have great foster families but others need contact and consistent support outside of their foster homes. It's vital for them to make social connections with other kids. When I was fourteen my social worker put me forward for an outward-bound youth group. I think that stopped me from veering off the rails.'

I swallow hard. My heart bleeds for the boy he was and for the man trying to make a difference for other kids. 'I didn't realise you took such an active role.'

'I don't, really. My job is to donate large chunks of cash, invite very well-connected businessmen and women to the fundraisers, and occasionally put my face to the marketing campaigns.'

He's also emotionally invested, even if he doesn't want to admit it. 'So where was the photo taken? It looked like you were enjoying yourself.'

'Yeah. There's a branch here in Tokyo. I joined them for a soccer game and picnic at a nearby park. I got roped into playing goalie.' He chuckles, a lovely, rich sound that vibrates through his chest and makes me yearn to make him laugh every day.

'They kicked my butt.' His smile is full of warmth, his eyes faraway, as if he's remembering the day fondly. 'My Japanese isn't brilliant, but I think I took a ribbing for being the oldest and slowest on the team.'

I bury my face against the side of his neck and try to breathe evenly, but it's becoming increasingly difficult in his presence. Today has been magical in many ways. I'm humbled that he invited me to his home. I've discovered so much about him that I didn't know. It's made me wonder what it would be like if this fling had no time limit. What if Hudson wanted more than our few nights? Surely, if he can open his heart to Blackhearts, he can one day open it to the possibility of a lasting relationship?

But could I rely on my instincts and explore a relationship with *him*? Someone with dreams opposite to mine.

My head pounds with arguments for and against. It's crazy. Hudson lives in Tokyo and I'm in London. There's Sterling to consider—he'd surely feel betrayed by the idea of us and the fact that we've messed around behind his back on more than one occasion. Not to mention the biggest obstacle—me. I love my career, but I've always wanted more—a family. It's as if it's in my DNA.

'Do you like living here?' I slide my fingers into his thick hair, which is inky-black in the darkness.

'Yes. But I can run Bold from anywhere.'

He has no ties. I try and fail to imagine what that's like. To me, family is my security, but for Hudson security is success and wealth. Except there's also Blackhearts. He's not the emotional island he probably tells himself he is.

We stare, our hearts thudding against each other, as if both conscious of what we're leaving unsaid.

'What?' he asks, rolling us onto our sides so we're face to face.

'Nothing.' I pull back from probing what-ifs. 'You're just full of surprises, that's all—romantic, philanthropic, good with kids.'

He shakes his head but his smile is relaxed. 'I'm also a single, workaholic loner. Besides, all three of us are involved in charity work—that was one of our goals for Bold from the outset.'

I nod and entangle my legs with his under the sheet. 'Just because you're often alone doesn't make you a loner. I've seen you with your team here. They respect you. They know they can challenge you. You empower them. That's a sign of a natural leader.'

'Is that right...?' He's distracted, his erection surging against my thigh.

'Also, it's a total aphrodisiac imagining you kicking a ball around a park with a bunch of kids.' I rock my hips against him, sighing with pleasure and triumph when he rolls on top of me and nudges my thighs open with his knees.

Smoky desire fills his eyes. 'Is it?' He brushes his mouth over mine. 'You have very strange ideas about what constitutes sexy.' He lays kisses along my jaw and down my neck to my collarbone.

'Mmm-hmm,' I moan, because he's moved to my breast, his mouth and tongue working my nipple into a frenzy of sensation. 'You're right. I am weird. I find commitment sexy. I think dads are sexy. But at the moment there's nothing sexier than *you*. Just you.'

He takes a moment to stare, as if he's puzzled by my admission, time enough for me to remember I want more than this. He grabs a condom, sheathes himself quickly, and pushes inside me once more. But, as I lose my mind to our physical connection, I wonder how I'm ever going to survive without it.

It's so early that the outer offices where the assistants and associates sit in open-plan cubicles are deserted. My reflection bounces from the many windows and glass partitions turned mirror-like by the still-dark sky outside. I look like a woman with winning on her mind—careful make-up and red lips, tousled hair styled into glossy waves and bright eyes. My breath catches with illicit excitement for my mission.

When I woke this morning, alone in Hudson's expansive and comfortable bed, urgency gripped me until I vibrated with a sense of panic. We have two more days to outdo each other in our sexy little game of seduction. Two more nights before we fly to London and meet up with Sterling. Forty-eight hours to indulge this fling, which has completely taken me by surprise.

Hudson's complexities are forcing me to examine my own drivers.

Before I left his bed this morning I logged onto Blackhearts's website and made a large anonymous donation. Then I spent a frustrating half-hour trawling the website for more clues about the man I can't push from my mind, even for five minutes.

My throat aches anew for young Hudson. For all the children out there who believe that no one cares. It's hard for me to comprehend—most of my life I've felt as if I've had multiple caretakers. My parents *and* my older siblings. It was a blessing and, for a teen-aged Monroe, at times felt like a curse. But it shaped me, allowed me to discover who I was in safety.

Hudson had no one.

Instead of growing bitter and angry, turning to drugs or crime as a coping mechanism, he's devoted his adult life to financial security and helping others succeed. I know him better than ever now. Relationships mean risk. He's protecting himself from further abandonment.

But the tortured and caring and romantic Hudson—he could make me lose sight of everything I've always wanted.

Shoving away my confused emotions, I roll my shoulders back and head for his office. My seduction plan helps to keep my wildly budding feelings in perspective. This affair began with a competition—that's where I need to stay focussed.

Outside his door I drag in a breath. I hear his fingers clicking away at his keyboard. He must have been here for hours, perhaps half the night. Did I chase him out of his home by staying over? He's not used to having his space invaded. Now I know the depth of the demons chasing him, it's easy to understand why he pushes himself as he does professionally. Why he spends so many hours here at his office.

Why Bold is perhaps the only marker of success he can trust and control. I don't blame him.

Powerlessness sticks my feet to the carpet. Helping him overcome his past to see that he's more than just an outstanding businessman seems as colossal as the skyscraper we're in.

Except I do have power. I feel it every time we're intimate. And if that's the only way I can reach him, the only way to give him something, anything that shows him he has people in his life who care, then I'll take it. I want him to know that opening himself to me emotionally, something that must have felt like a trip to the dentist's chair for him, isn't life-threatening.

And you're also reminding yourself that you're still just fooling around, that you will return to normal, that you too are safe.

I cinch the belt of my trench coat, as if tightening my resolve. I push open the door, my heart banging against my ribs. At first he's too focussed on the screen to notice me standing in his doorway. Then some sixth sense must alert him to my presence, or perhaps it's my audible sigh at the sight of him. He's wearing a black T-shirt and well-worn, soft-looking jeans. There's a sexy shadow on his jaw and his hair is untamed. He looks as if he's just crawled out of my bed and is as sexy as he looks in his bespoke business suits.

He notices me. Heat and something close to longing chases away his surprised expression. My heart clenches painfully.

'What are you doing here so early?' He pushes back from his desk and makes to stand.

'Don't move.' I hold up my hand. 'Stay right there.' I try to make my voice sound like a sexy purr, but I want him so desperately, I'm scared of giving myself away.

He obeys, a curious glint in his narrowed eyes as he takes in my outfit. Swallowing hard, I close the door behind me, turn the lock and drop my bag on the floor. My legs wobble as I sashay closer, anticipation and frenetic energy coursing through my nervous system.

I can do this. I'm here to seduce him. Nothing else matters for now.

'We have unfinished business.' I stop before him, noticing the way his thighs are spread and his arousal already bulges at the front of his jeans. That I do that to him bolsters my resolve.

'We do? I thought we were up to speed.' Confusion dims the lust glimmering in his stare. He's doubting his instincts, which are spot-on: I'm not here on Bold business. I cut him some slack—he hasn't slept much for three days and it's before dawn.

I finger the knot in the coat's belt, slowly sliding the fabric free. 'You left me alone in your bed.'

My disappointment had been an ache only pacified by a snoop around his apartment for more clues about the real Hudson. Apart from discovering his well-loved home gym and a stuffed bookcase of crime thrillers, my search left me far from gratified.

'I wanted to catch up on a few things I postponed yesterday afternoon.' His voice is tight with desire.

My trusty trench coat is working its magic.

The reminder of our wonderful day beneath the cherry blossom, our chats and watching the sun setting from the hot tub floods me with chills of doubt. But I can't give in to any weakness where he's concerned. I know what I want long term, and Hudson doesn't even come close.

But he could...

Instead of indulging any more flights of fancy, I focus on my big reveal. I abandon the loosened belt and slide my hands up my torso to the top button of the coat, which sits just above my cleavage. My nipples tingle against my bra, begging to be set free, begging for his mouth. The heat building behind his dark eyes like an inferno drags me back to the reason we work as lovers.

Our chemistry has always been undeniable. That doesn't mean we'd work in a relationship. I can't risk making another mistake.

I drop my voice to a smoky whisper, embracing my seductress role. 'You can't show a woman a good time the way you did yesterday and then expect her not to want to share breakfast...'

I reach out and trace a finger across his parted lips, smiling at the gusts of excited breath he can't control.

'You don't eat breakfast, Dove. And I don't usually do mornings after.' He spreads his thighs. His erection must be pretty uncomfortable trapped behind the denim. But I want to prolong the anticipation until he can't take any more.

I ignore his reminder of how we differ in our approach to dating and pop the first two buttons, my pulse pounding between my legs when his gaze drops to the parting fabric and my cleavage.

'That's right, I don't. I'm impressed you remembered. That's because I always take my workout in the morning.' I pop another button and catch the sound of his rough inhale. I look down and see that my new black mesh bra is on display. His eyes linger there, his pupils flaring as he stares.

'So you see…it's payback time. You took me home and let me sleep over… Seems to me the least you could do is provide morning sex.' I battle the renewed urge to read too much into his gesture, as I did last night. I *am* different from the women he normally sleeps with, but only because I'm also a business partner.

His glittering eyes narrow, shocking desire through my body like lightning. I'm playing with fire. But challenging Hudson has become an addiction I have no desire to shake.

'Did you walk here from the hotel like that?' His voice is rough and urgent, and he blatantly adjusts his cock behind his fly.

I continue undoing the coat's buttons. 'Takao took me back and waited for me to change.' And every move I made on the way here reminded me of my seductive plan. By the time I made it into his personal lift, which bypasses all the floors below us, I was soaking wet.

'Fuck.' He makes a fist and then releases it. 'Takao would have a heart attack if he knew what you're wearing.'

I finish undoing the coat and push the two sides open, bracing my hands on my hips so he sees the full effect. 'What...? This old thing?' The matching panties are sheer and leave nothing to the imagination, and of course I'm wearing my signature lace hold-up stockings and my favourite high heels.

'I thought you'd like it.' I want him to know the lengths I went to for his seduction. To understand that he was the first thing on my mind when I opened my eyes.

His stare moves over every inch of my body, sending powerful shudders through me to my core. Then his gaze flicks to the door and outer office beyond.

'People will be arriving in a little while.' His hands grip the arms of the chair, as if he's dying to touch me. And I want his hands all over my body, a feeling more addictive than our game of sexual one-upmanship.

I shrug off the coat so it falls to the crook of my elbows and stand between his spread thighs. I brace my hands next to his on the chair-arms and lean in close to whisper in his ear and to flash him a clear and uninterrupted view of my breasts.

'So what are you waiting for...?'

My heartbeat deafens me for a handful of tense seconds.

'I have no idea.' He scoops one arm around my waist and tumbles me into his lap as if he's performed the smooth move a hundred times.

Sitting across his steely thighs and crushed to his hard chest, I'm breathless, desperate for him to snap and kiss me. Instead, I press my index finger to his soft lips and trace their fullness. 'Remember, this was *my* idea.'

And then I can't toy with him any more because he cups my face, hooking his fingers around the back of my neck, and brings my mouth crashing to his in a rush of lips and tongues and the collision of teeth.

Our kiss is frantic. As if we hadn't spent most of last night in each other's arms, rolling around in his massive bed until the sheets were a tangle.

He pulls away first. 'You are a raunchy sex goddess.'

My laughter dies in my throat as he traces one nipple and dusky areola through the mesh of my bra.

I tease him back, stroking my fingers along the length of his erection, which surges against his fly. 'Well, I couldn't have you outdoing me.' I pop the button on his jeans and feel the wet patch on his underwear where he's leaked for me.

'Now you're just making this competition thing way too exciting, Dove. My mind is working overtime…' His fingers slide over my stomach and down, down, down until he grazes my mound. 'Are you wet? Did you get yourself all worked up concocting this plan, walking in here wearing nothing under-neath this coat but this tiny excuse for underwear?'

He slides his fingers along the soaked crotch of my panties and my head drops back as I release a groan. 'Yes… Yes, I did.'

'I can see that.' He strokes my strip of hair and swipes my clit. 'Where the fuck did you get this outfit?'

'Like it, do you?' I pant as he strokes my lips through the underwear, his touch increasingly de-manding.

He emits a low growl. 'That's an understatement.'

'I bought it thinking of you. This city really is open day and night. I found a store that delivers within the hour.' I thrust my hips in his direction and tug his mouth back to mine. While I enjoy his kisses, my hands are free to roam under his T-shirt. His skin is warm and smooth, the muscular slabs a sure-fire sign that he spends a lot of time in that home gym I found.

I release the remaining buttons of his fly and then remove the two items I have stashed in the coat pocket—a condom and the vibrator. I shove them at him and tug at his shirt. 'Hurry… The clock is tick-ing.' As much as I want to kiss every inch of him, the work day will soon begin with the arrival of his staff, and we'll miss our opportunity.

His eyes widen at the sight of the vibrator which we never got round to using last night. He places it on the desk and shifts his hips so I can yank his jeans and boxers down. I free his erection and cover him, and then he springs into action.

In one brisk move he stands and deposits me on the desk in front of him. I shrug off the coat and toss it to the floor as he removes his T-shirt and shoves his jeans down. His cock juts out from between his strong thighs, his abs contracting.

My mouth waters. 'You are the hottest thing I've ever seen. I want to suck you.' I'm addicted to his salty taste. To the guttural roar he makes as he comes in my mouth. To the helpless vulnerability in his eyes for a few seconds afterwards.

'I was just thinking the same thing.'

He pulls down the cup of my bra, exposing one breast before covering the nipple with his mouth. I cry out at his mind-blowing ministrations, releasing the mewling sounds I can't contain.

I lean back on my hands, uncaring of his open laptop behind me or the pile of documents that crinkle under my butt. The sight of this urbane, zealous businessman losing control and splaying me over the desk from which he runs our multi-billion-dollar company makes me pulse with need.

His fingers slide the crotch of my underwear aside and then push inside me, plunging in time with his suckling on my nipple.

He abandons my breast to look down at the sight of his pumping fingers. I widen my thighs and gasp as he scissors the two inside me wider and rubs at my clit with his thumb.

With his free hand he picks up the vibrator. 'Turn it on.'

I obey and then watch with mounting desperation as he brings the buzzing tip to my exposed, wet nipple. The first touch makes me gasp, the sensation so confronting I want to move away. But before I can he shifts the toy to the other side and pinpoints the other nipple through the mesh of my bra.

'You're right, Dove. This was a genius idea.' He slides his mouth over mine, catching my moans, his eyes wide open to watch my every reaction to his torture.

'Hudson... I need you inside me.'

He turns off the vibrator and tosses it to the floor. Then he grips my arse cheeks and shunts me to the edge of his desk. I cling to his shoulders as he grips his cock and notches it at my entrance, sinking onto me with a ragged sigh as if he's waited far too long.

The feeling echoes in me.

His face contorts with pleasure, his eyes ablaze with lust and vulnerability. 'What are you doing to me...?' He grips my hips, his fingers digging into my flesh, and then he thrusts long and deep and hard.

'Only what you're doing to me,' I say, resting back on my hands. I lock my arms, desperate to counter the onslaught of his hips, both for maximum friction and because of the same bloody-minded competitive streak that shapes our every interaction.

Because I know he likes my hair—I caught him sniffing it last night in bed—I loosen my messy bun and shake free the long waves until they're splayed over my shoulders. His eyes flash fire at the sight.

Greedy for more, I wrap my thighs around his hips, crossing my ankles in the small of his back. I'm burning up and only he can quench the flames.

Beads of sweat break out at his hairline. His eyes lock with mine, sending jolts of pleasure through me, and something else. A deeper connection than was there last night. Now it's more defined, its edges sharper and brighter. Does he feel it too? Perhaps he does, because he momentarily scrunches his eyes shut, as if overwhelmed.

I cup his face and press my mouth to his as my orgasm starts. I'm his in that moment—any seduction plan or life plan smashed and tattered by the force of my feelings. I cry out against his lips. Triumph washes over me, strengthening the final spasms of my climax as he opens his eyes once more, roars my name and shudders against me in release.

We stay locked together for what seems like an age. Hudson's head grows heavy on my shoulder. My butt aches against the hard desk. But I don't want to move in case something seismic happens. The moment, the silence, feels that portentous.

Eventually he shifts, and when he lifts his head he's composed, back in control, and my stomach plummets.

'Well, that was a great way to start the working day.' He kisses me, pulls out, and then removes the condom, wrapping it in a tissue from the box on his debauched desk. Then he glances at the locked door, tension around his eyes.

Feeling dismissed, I right my underwear and bra, goosebumps breaking out over my skin.

'Any time,' I say with a smile that feels rictus-like. Because that's a lie. It can't be any time. His reminder of where we are and that his employees will soon arrive robs every shred of good feeling from my body. He's reinstating the boundaries. And he's right. But for a moment there I felt an emotional closeness I know he reciprocated. Something more than sex.

Trust. Communication. Togetherness.

Yet I'm dismissed.

'Mind if I jump in your shower? I brought a change of clothes.' My voice sounds normal but I can't wait to cover up, as he's doing, shrugging into his T-shirt and buttoning his fly.

I won't hide, though. No matter how vulnerable it makes me. I brazen it out, standing tall in my sexy outfit and heels, as if to say, *look what you could have every day, if only you were interested.*

But that's only half the truth. I want more than great sex, and we both know it, presumably the reason he's struggling to look me in the eye as he straightens the papers on his desk.

'Of course. Take as long as you like. I was going to suggest we split up today. I'm happy to handle the meeting with the lawyers if you want to catch up with Sterling and get him up to speed on Kunosu Tech.'

I scoop some fallen documents from the floor and

place them carefully on the desk, my stomach tight with the pain of rejection.

'That sounds like a plan.'

'If I'm not back in time,' he says, 'I'll send Takao to take you shopping for tonight.'

We're attending the Tokyo Business Awards dinner, at which he's been invited to give the after-dinner speech.

I don my trench coat, which now feels about as sexy as a bin liner, and retrieve my bag from near the door. When I turn and head for the bathroom, he's back to his usual self, apart from having hair mussed from my fingers and a cagey expression.

'I'll catch you later, then.' I present my cheek for his kiss, as I have a thousand times before over the years, only this time his perfunctory peck leaves me frozen to the core.

'Give my best to Sterling.' His eyes are devoid of warmth, even though he's pasted on a smile. But it's the reminder I needed.

This *is* meaningless sex. In three days, we'll all be together. Neither of us wants to hurt Sterling. There's no sense in confessing a casual fling. Hudson and I will need to try way harder than we're currently achieving in order to pretend that nothing has changed between us.

Right now, we're fooling no one, least of all ourselves.

CHAPTER NINE

Hudson

THE TOKYO CITY view on the fifty-second floor of Mori Tower showcases Tokyo at night to its best advantage—a sea of colourful lights laid out like a carpet of stars, with the glowing Tokyo Tower in the foreground. The Business Awards dinner is in full swing. Our delicious main course has been cleared away and the dancing has begun before speeches and dessert.

I wish I could leave and drag Monroe with me.

'Mr Oshima lives near Mount Fuji,' I say, introducing her to a long-time business associate who runs a manufacturing company here in Tokyo. 'His home is beautiful, and he has three charming little girls who cheat at paper, scissors, rock.'

Monroe laughs with delight and engages Mr Oshima in a three-way conversation with the interpreter I hired to make her feel comfortable tonight. My mind drifts once more to this morning, when she'd stormed into my office looking like a goddess of temptation. I've spent the whole day reeling. And fuming at the way I shut down after, effectively dismissing her.

I paste on a bland smile, pretending to partake in the conversation, but inside I'm cursing my stupidity. I should never have taken her home. Waking up with her in my bed, her scent on my pillow and her clothes on my chair... It all but knocked me on my arse. This is what it would feel like to have someone permanent in my life. Her toothbrush next to mine, her brand of tea in my cupboard and a million other ways of sharing a life. Even opening up about Blackhearts seemed to shift something in me—a new closeness I wasn't expecting.

For the first time ever, *what if?* crept past my guard.

I fled to work before dawn to escape the crush of possibility. Only she's everywhere I look—my office, my car, my home. I struggled to breathe this morning after her trench coat stunt, not because I'd come harder than a baseball bat to the back of the head, but because I never wanted to move. She gripped my face and stared into my eyes and seemed to give me more of herself than I'd ever ask for. Violent urges to close the office and ignore work for the rest of the day overtook me. I wanted to take Monroe back home and lock out the rest of the world. Cancel our flight to London and slake this need over and over again until I was back to normal.

But what if normal has gone for ever? What if I can never stop craving her?

Watching her smile as she asks Mr Oshima about his family, I'm compelled to make amends for my dismissive behaviour. I ache to touch her. Hold her. I wake in the night hard for her. I reach for her in my sleep. I look for her around the office. She's in my blood and I'm so fucked.

The conversation comes to a natural end, and Mr Oshima bids us goodnight and moves away. I speak to the translator, suggesting she take a break.

'Dance with me,' I say to Monroe.

'I'd love to.' She looks up at me with trust and acceptance I don't deserve. It makes me more restless.

We move to the dance floor, my hand unapologetically on the small of her back, because I can't *not* touch her. She's wearing a full-length black dress that hugs her beautiful body like a second skin. I tug her into my arms, holding her at an appropriate distance for a business colleague, even though I want to crush her close until my heart stops its wild, erratic thudding.

Monroe is more than a colleague. She always has been. But what the hell does that mean for the future us? I'll have to stop thinking about her, stop touching her, stop wanting her.

'I'm sorry if I was…abrupt this morning in the office.' I grip her tighter, needing her body against mine to stop the riot of frustration inside. 'To be honest, you took me by complete surprise with the whole trench coat thing.'

My cock stirs in my trousers just thinking about the vision of her splayed on my desk. 'I won't ever forget that sexy little stunt, Dove.'

In fact, I'll never be able to work again without remembering. My fingers flex between her shoulder blades, itching to touch her bare skin.

Her eyes spark playfully. 'Me neither. It was fun payback.'

She's saying all the right things to reassure me that we're still on track. That there's no risk of feelings creeping into this casual fling. But if anything that makes me more unsettled. It makes no sense.

'Are you nervous?' she asks. 'About your speech?'

I shake my head. 'No. I'm not thinking about that at all. I'm actually wondering if you're wearing underwear under this dress.' It's easier to admit the constant desire than risk showing too much of the panicked, confused mess inside me. Monroe has her mother's knack of seeing beneath my layers.

A small crafty smile touches her full lips. She slides her hand slowly from my shoulder to rest over my breast pocket. Over my thudding heart.

'Now, what makes you think I'd be commando under here?' Her eyelashes bat and she swipes the tip of her tongue over her top lip so my hard-on presses against her stomach. Shit, I'm due onstage in fifteen minutes.

I glance at her hand, at her fingers gliding back

and forth over my silk handkerchief in my tux pocket. That's when I notice the handkerchief isn't its usual white colour. It's silvery grey. I catch sight of some lace in the depths of the pocket.

When I look up, she's all mock-innocence. It's sexy as hell.

'What is it?' she asks, her voice breathy.

'Did you stuff your underwear in my pocket?' I grow harder. We'll never make it off this dance floor. I'll have to fake a medical emergency to avoid my speech. Then I remember that I came here straight from the office. They gave me a room in which to change. I can exact revenge…

'Now, why would I do that when you'll be standing on the stage in front of Tokyo's business elite? Do you think I want you to be thinking about me or something…?' She leans closer. 'It's not as if I'll be wet watching you, waiting for you to finish and take me home…'

I groan in my head and grip her tighter. 'Oh, well played, Dove. Trouble is… I'm going to make you pay, sooner than you think.'

'Just like I made you pay for the phallic package I opened in the conference room?'

I nod. 'Just like that.'

'I can't wait.' She stares up at me, her beautiful smile tugging at something in my chest. Every beat of my heart demands I say something more meaningful than sex talk and innuendo. But what is there to say? I can't promise her anything more than this.

She's seen every corner of my life now. She knows about my past. Bold is my future. With me, this is as good as it gets.

I change the subject, wishing I could change my thoughts as easily.

'I arranged for a tea ceremony at the Sensō-ji Temple tomorrow.'

'Thank you. That's a lovely thing to do on my last day in Japan.'

'But it won't be your last visit. You'll be back next year.' Tension seizes my muscles. How will we manage seeing each other in person but no longer being lovers? Will the desire fade even remotely?

I wish…

'Besides, you may love Japan, but you'd never consider living anywhere but London.' What prompted me to say that? Why am I fishing? Of course she'd never live away from her close-knit family.

She presses her lips together, her eyes darting sheepishly as if she's thinking the same thing. When she looks back up, she's grown pensive.

'Sterling once asked me to move to New York, before we met you. Before we married. Just for a few years. I wouldn't even consider it back then.'

'You didn't want to move so far from your relatives.' My voice is flat with assertion. She wouldn't even move for the man she loved.

'No. And I'm glad I didn't.' She looks up, imploring me to understand. 'I couldn't have known, but my mother didn't really have that long to live. I'd have never forgiven myself if I hadn't been there.'

'Of course.' I nod, a strange weight settling in my gut. Why does it matter to me that she'd never live anywhere but London?

I scramble for another change of subject.

'I wondered if you'd like to visit Blackhearts on the way home from the Sensō-ji Temple tomorrow. There's a teen disco happening.' My voice feels alien, my heartbeat throbbing in my ears. Until just now I hadn't even decided if I planned to attend myself.

'I'd love to.' She looks up at me with that intuition and perceptiveness that makes me feel exposed. 'I never realised how important they are to you...'

I try not to stiffen, my hairs rising with discomfort. 'Why would you?'

'Because we're...friends.' Her expression says *isn't it obvious?* 'Friends are supposed to know each other well. Be there for the other person unconditionally.' She looks away and, when her eyes return to mine, they're ablaze with emotion. 'I'm sorry if there were times that I wasn't there for you. I meant to be. You've always supported me.'

I presume she's talking about the divorce, or perhaps the flowers I send every year for Cathy. I frown, a trapped feeling settling in my gut. How have we arrived here when only minutes ago we were discussing her underwear in my pocket? This shit doesn't come up when you're an emotional island. Yet, as alien as it is for me to open up, I've also enjoyed getting to know Monroe better, one on one.

'You haven't let me down, Dove. I've just never needed you in the same way.'

Her tiny gasp makes me feel as if I've struck her. I rush to qualify. 'I don't mean it as an insult. I just haven't got any family like you do.'

She still looks hurt. 'Sterling and I are your family. Even though we live on different continents, we're not going anywhere.'

I cringe at her reassurance. 'I'm not an easy friend to have. I've spent most of my life completely self-sufficient.'

I want her to know the way I am isn't personal. It's survival.

'Mr Oshima seems to value your friendship. He told me how you've managed to tend that bonsai tree he gave you, the one at your apartment. I think you're just selective with who you trust emotionally. Most people are.'

I nod because she's right—I only really trust myself. 'It's something I'm wary of with Blackhearts. I try not to get too attached to any of the kids or allow them to get close to me—their circumstances change often. Some get adopted, some move to a foster home in a different area... That's why I lurk in the background.'

Compassion shines in her eyes. 'Well, in that case, perhaps I won't come. I don't want to confuse anyone. But I really appreciate you asking me.'

We dance on in silence until she speaks again. 'I too have an invitation. Would you come to Mum's memorial?'

My feet shuffle to a stop, the flight mechanism ransacking my nervous system. 'But that's private. A family thing.' I always stick out like a sore thumb at those kinds of gatherings.

She frowns and hurt flashes over her features. 'It's a party. It's not sad or anything. If the weather's nice we hold it in the garden. Lots of food and drink and music. The grandkids running around and jumping in the pool...'

At my continued hesitation, she trails off.

Then she lifts her chin. 'Sterling will be there.'

The reminder of the other man who's been in her life smacks me in the head. But, unlike him, I'm a grown man who needs convincing to go to a party to remember Cathy.

'That's different. He used to be part of the family. You were married to him.' Why am I talking about another man while her underwear is in my pocket and I ache to bury myself inside her?

'So? You're part of my family too. I'm not having you sitting alone in a hotel somewhere while we socialise. I want you there.' Her tone softens. 'Just... think about it. Please.'

My hesitance feels like a fight for life, but of course I'm overreacting. Still, I can't give her any reassurance when I feel so strung out. 'Okay, I will.

I'd better go. It's almost time for my speech. Do you want me to escort you back to our table?'

She steps away from me and shakes her head. 'I'll be fine, thank you.' She squeezes my arm. 'Good luck.'

Before she walks away, I snag her hand and lean in to whisper, 'Meet me backstage after. Payback time.'

I walk away, mildly gratified I could put excitement back into her eyes, even though our conversation has left me more dismantled than ever. I'm not Sterling. I'm no good at the kind of emotional commitment it takes to form a relationship. I'll let her down and she'll see the gaping differences between us even more clearly.

My memorised speech is brief. After an introduction in my stilted Japanese, I switch to English, knowing the event organisers have pre-translated my talk and are projecting it on screens to the audience. I'm not given to sentiment, so as I talk about my humble beginnings, hinting at my unorthodox start in life and the luck and drive of my early success, I focus on the thought of Monroe's underwear in my pocket. It works as she intended and in ways she couldn't have guessed—a distraction from the chill of my childhood memories and how they still shape my relationships today.

The silk and lace burn a hole in my pocket. I glance out at the crowd. Speaking at the prestigious awards ceremony is an indication of how far I've come. Of the power I now wield over my own destiny, and that of others through Bold.

And yet tonight I feel jaded.

It's Monroe—what she brings out in me.

After London, we'll go back to seeing each other a couple of times a year. Will my work be enough of a consolation? It hits me then, so I stumble over my words. Embarking on our affair has changed things, perhaps for ever.

But it's not too late to redress the boundaries. That's what I need to chase off the feeling I'm going around in circles. I shove Monroe from my mind and shift closer to the microphone to deliver my closing points.

'People often ask me for my business philosophy. It's simple. Distilled into three key principles. One, work as if you are the only person you can rely on.'

I find Monroe's eyes in the audience, the predictable desire shooting along my every nerve. Her words bombard my brain. *You're part of my family too.*

I'm not. Not really. And I can't get lured into her seductive web. I can't need her or anyone else. I know how that weakness ends—with me alone again.

I swallow hard with resolve and continue. 'Two, apply integrity to all of your business dealings and with everyone you meet—you never know when they'll be your greatest professional ally.'

Sterling and I are your family... We're not going anywhere.

An easy promise to make. But, if Sterling knew about us, he'd understandably feel betrayed and hurt. Who knows how he'd react? Possessive heat roars through my blood. If the positions were reversed, if Monroe had once been mine, I'd struggle to stay civil and carry on as if nothing happened.

Focussing on my final point reminds me where my priorities must lie. Where they've always been. 'And, lastly, accept that you can never be too successful.'

I smile, accepting my round of applause, and stride from the stage. Monroe burrowing under my skin is an itch I need to fight. The panties in my pocket help, a clear reminder of our seduction match and how currently she's in the lead.

But I can change that.

Monroe is waiting for me backstage. After a smile and a few words of thanks for my hosts, I grip her elbow and guide her away from the ballroom, leading her to the room set aside for me to change. I need to get her alone, to remind us both how good the sex is so we forget about everything else—our connection, how spending time together makes me crave the unattainable and how I might never feel normal again.

'You were great,' she says, her voice breathy as she keeps pace with me in her heels. 'I'm always impressed by your Japanese.' Her mouth is saying things that shouldn't cause offence, but her body language is prickly. I've offended her somehow. But I can make it right. I know what her body needs to sing. I'll distract her with pleasure. Distract us both, because right now my desperation for mindless oblivion seems to have outstripped hers.

I key in the lock code and push inside the room.

'Tell me how I've managed to upset you.' I take the scrap of lacy underwear from my pocket, remove my tux jacket and tie, and toss them onto the chair. 'But tell me quickly.'

She stops near the door, arousal staining her throat and cheeks, her nipples peaking through the fabric of her dress and her breath coming in excited pants, even as her eyes spark with defiance.

'I'm not upset. Just surprised that you managed to talk about your business success without once mentioning your long-term partners.'

I fist the panties and curse under my breath. It wasn't intentional.

'Forgive me, Dove. An oversight, I assure you. I'm used to thinking and talking about myself. The organisers wanted me to keep it short and focussed on my guiding business ethos. I didn't want to speak for you and Sterling.' I lock eyes with her. 'I'm fully aware of how you've enriched my life these past five years. Bold is what it is because we're a team.'

'Are we?' She's still battling disappointment. Not the emotion I want. 'Your speech made me wonder how you truly see us. Perhaps we're disposable to you, superfluous to your requirements. As if you could cut us loose and work a bit harder—eighteen hours a day instead of fourteen—and achieve the same things alone.'

I take a step in her direction, as drawn to her as ever. 'If you were disposable, I wouldn't have spent my entire speech thinking about you sitting in the audience without these.' I dangle the lace from one finger as I prowl close. I catch the scent of her from the fabric and need rumbles in my groin. 'How could I ever forget you, Dove?'

I wish it were that simple. I wish I could scrub her from my mind and move on as if this week never happened.

'Be honest.' I crowd her personal space, every cell screaming to drag her close and slake all of this pent-up turmoil. 'Do you feel neglected professionally or personally? Because I want to make it up to you.'

She takes a step back until she's flush against the door, her stare hooded and her lips parted, almost in invitation.

I rein in my most urgent needs. 'I want you. Now.' I wanted her the minute she fastened her trench coat this morning. Her stunning eyes carry the same hurt I saw then. 'Are you too disappointed with me to let me touch you?'

Silence buffets us, the air pulsing. She shakes her head, her pupils flaring.

I stifle my growl of triumph. 'Then show me what I want to see.' I raise one eyebrow and wait, the underwear still dangling from my finger. This is where my focus needs to remain. On this crushing desire. Not the past or the future. Just now.

With agonising slowness, she bunches the silky fabric of her dress in her fists and raises the hem. Her legs, covered in her trademark black stockings, are revealed to me inch by glorious inch. Shapely calves, slender thighs, the tantalising lace tops of the stockings.

And then her nakedness.

I drag my eyes away from the gorgeous view. 'You play a very dirty game to win.'

'So do you.' She pants, her lip trembling.

'That's why we're so good together.' I cover her hands with mine, gripping the dress so it doesn't fall. I press my body to hers and she tilts her chin, straining for my kiss.

It takes everything I am to withhold my mouth. But I want her forgiveness. I want her in no doubt of what she's come to mean to me—the most important person in my life.

'Seducing you, fucking you, has nothing to do with Bold, understand?' I kiss her, rubbing my lips over hers, my tongue surging inside. Then I slide my mouth to her neck and feel her shudder under me when I locate the correct sensitive spot. 'Bold is the three of us. A team—I *never* want that to change.'

I'd be nothing without Bold.

She thrusts her hips forward and I take pity on her, grinding my hard cock between her legs. She's wet. I can feel her through my clothes. I hoist the dress higher until it reaches her waist. 'Hold it here.'

I kiss her once more. Her head falls back against the door. Then I drop to my knees and spread her thighs open. I don't want to drag my eyes away from the sight of her pink and wet for me, but I look up as I trace my finger over her strip of hair to her clit. 'You torture me. Night and day. There's no reprieve.'

It's agony and bliss.

She gasps, her face streaked with pleasure, her breaths quick. 'Hudson… Don't tease me.'

I push my finger inside her. 'Why not? You drive me crazy… You're too good at our game. A little revenge is well-deserved, don't you think?'

I pump my finger in and out, watching it disappear and reappear covered in her wetness. 'Tell me I drive you insane.'

She drops her head forward so she too can watch. 'You do… I ache for you.'

I look up, yearning stealing my breath. 'Tell me we'll handle this chemistry somehow. That we'll never let it disrupt the company we both care about so much.' I add my thumb, pressing it to her clit. Her word is vital. I need it almost as much as I need her.

She nods, her eyes desperate. 'Yes… I promise.'

When I have what I want, I deliver her reward and mine. I cover her swollen clit with my mouth and push a second finger inside her. She bucks against me, writhing and gasping. I know she wants to grab my face, to tangle her fingers in my hair, but if she lets go of the dress she'll lose her view.

I watch pleasure turn her from a sophisticated professional to a wild and demanding woman. A kick of satisfaction ramps up, my own desire past boiling point. We might have strayed towards personal emotions, but we're still both focussed on this uncontainable compulsion.

Bunching the dress in one hand, Monroe grips the back of my neck with the other and holds me close—not that I'm going anywhere. She rides my mouth, one, two, three grinds of her hips, and then she shatters, coming with her eyes locked to mine and her core squeezing my fingers.

I stand, flip her round to face the door and tear into my fly. I cover myself with a condom and grab her hips, dragging her back so I can bury myself in her from behind.

I thrust into her, channelling all the out of control emotions this woman makes me feel. 'You're the only woman in my life, understand?'

'Yes!' she cries, almost accusingly.

'I don't want that to change. I don't want *anything* to change.' I pound harder and she meets me, her arms braced against the door.

My fingers dig into her hip and I slip my other hand between her thighs, rubbing her clit so that, when I come she follows me, the battle lines of this insane connection fully reinstated.

CHAPTER TEN

Hudson

DIFFERENT CONTINENT. DIFFERENT time zone. Same all-consuming need.

As I watch them talk in Monroe's favourite Covent Garden restaurant, envy slices through me like a rusty blade. Monroe and Sterling are like an old married couple, but then they *were* a married couple. They know things about each other I will never know. They've seen the best and the worst of each other. Shared ecstatic highs and desperate lows. They've made vows and chased dreams, the idea of which is enough to threaten the return of what I've just eaten.

I curl my fingers into a fist under the table and smile as if I have lockjaw, tuning back into the conversation, which for the last five minutes hasn't required any input from me.

Because you're the outsider. By choice.

Sterling glances my way sheepishly. 'I'm sorry,' he says, clapping me on the shoulder to invite me back into their bubble of intimacy. There's tension around his green eyes and his sandy hair is in mild disarray. Perhaps he's jet-lagged. Perhaps he has his own shit to deal with. They've been discussing his cousin who died, preventing him from joining us in Tokyo. Of course, Monroe knows all of his family. She was once *part* of his family, as he was hers.

And family connection is something I'll never understand.

'I'm monopolising our Monroe.' He takes a sip of wine and raises his eyebrows, waiting for me to dive back into a three-way conversation.

His words churn my stomach as if he's kicked me in the balls. Because she's been *our* Monroe. He's loved her and I can't stop craving her, even now when our arbitrary five nights have elapsed. When it's supposed to be over.

Reality couldn't be more different. She's constantly in my head. Physical need for her throbs beneath my skin. The thought of never touching her again makes those lonely, scared boyhood years and the endless powerlessness seem…inconsequential.

No, a bond like the one Monroe and Sterling share would make anyone feel lonely. Who stays friends and business partners with their ex?

I can't think of a thing to say that won't show how I feel, so I stay silent.

'Tell me about Tokyo,' Sterling says. 'I hope you showed Monroe a good time and didn't just make her work twenty-four-seven.' He smiles, glancing between us, me beside him and Monroe across the table from us.

Bitterness sours my throat. Why didn't I sit next to her when we arrived at the restaurant? Guilt, probably. Some twisted notion that *he* has prior claim. In answer to his question, part of me wants to come clean and let Sterling know exactly what went down in Tokyo. A courtesy—it happened, it meant nothing, it's over. Would he be more hurt that we went there or that we kept our affair a secret?

But telling him gives our fling too much weight, or trivialises it. It's complicated. The only way I can cling to my belief that I'm happy to always be the odd one out—because one day both Sterling and Monroe will meet someone who for them is a game-changer—is to play down what Monroe means to me. Pretend I respect her, but don't care about her like that and can easily walk away. But I *do* care. I cared before I laid a finger on her.

I avoid looking at her now, certain she's evading me too. I'm too scared I'll do something stupid like wait until she needs the bathroom, follow her and drag her into the alley at the back of the restaurant so I can show her that I have something to offer. As much as any other man. That I have all she'll ever need for the rest of her life.

Only I don't. It's a lie. I don't want a relationship, a wife or a family. My jealousy towards Sterling makes no sense.

I just don't want to give her up yet.

As if she's waited long enough for me to fill the awkward silence, Monroe speaks up in a rush.

'It was beautiful at this time of year. Cherry blossom everywhere. And, on my last day, Hudson took me to the Sensō-ji Temple that we planned to visit.'

A green haze filters my vision. If Sterling had made the trip to Tokyo as planned, my sightseeing services wouldn't have been required. Nor would she have needed me for distraction or emotional support.

Sterling peers at her with mock-disbelief. 'He gave you time away from business to sightsee?'

'Yes, he did.' Monroe laughs but her face flushes. She covers her telling reaction with a big slurp of wine.

We've done little but fuck for the past seventy hours. We even fucked in the car on the way to said temple—a shrine dedicated to Kannon, the Buddhist goddess of compassion. For most of the twelve-hour flight to London we couldn't keep our hands off each other. We reasoned being airborne, crossing time zones, created a grey area, stretching out the last twenty-four hours so that technically it didn't count as an additional night.

But it's not enough.

'So, thoughts on the Kunosu Tech investment,' I say, trying to drag my mind away from Monroe and appear normal. Otherwise Sterling will be able to tell something is up. The last thing I want is a scene. I'm selfish. If he learns about us and feels upset, there's less of a chance Monroe will let me touch her again.

My mind is so focussed on making that happen, I can barely think straight or contribute to this evening's conversation.

'Oh, no, no, no.' Sterling flags our waiter and requests another bottle of Burgundy. 'No business talk tonight.'

He's in a strange mood himself—overly upbeat, as if it's an act. I want to pry but my head is so fucked it would be the ultimate act of hypocrisy.

'Now you see what I've been dealing with without you in Tokyo,' teases Monroe with a playful wink in my direction. 'Also, I need you to help me persuade Hudson to come to the party at Comberton tomorrow.'

My stomach sinks. No matter how hard I wriggle, I can't extricate myself from the invitation to Cathy's memorial. Not now Monroe's enlisting Sterling's help. And it won't be that bad. It's just that family shit always makes me feel…irrelevant. I'm selfish enough to want to avoid that at all costs.

Still, it's not worth upsetting Monroe over.

Sterling's expression turns serious and full of compassion for Monroe. 'I'll bring him to Comberton.' Then he faces me. 'I'll pick you up at eleven.'

I bristle at being discussed like an errant child. But I nod, my eyes on Monroe. 'I wouldn't miss it, Dove.' Shit my voice couldn't be more telling.

Silent communication passes between us. Her eyes say, *I see you, I know you*, and maybe even, *I want you*. But in reality she doesn't. She wants more than me. She still wants all of the things she did a week ago. We're just both hooked on the physical connection.

I shudder and clear my throat. Perhaps she thinks she can change me. That I'll miraculously wake up one day and want to be her knight in shining armour.

'Thank you,' she says, looking between Sterling and me, her eyes shiny.

I look away first because I'm emotionally moribund. I don't know what I'd do if she cried. Sterling knows her better. He'll know how to console her tomorrow, just as he did four years ago when Cathy died.

The rest of the meal passes in a similar vein. Them laughing at shared jokes, chatting about common acquaintances, and trying to include me, when I prefer to count the minutes until I can get Monroe alone.

As we leave the restaurant and head outside for our cabs, I physically wedge myself between them.

'I'll see Monroe home.' I keep my gaze averted from their expressions. I don't give a fuck what it looks like. I open the rear door of the front taxi and turn to Sterling. 'There's no point both of us going. Why don't you head back to the hotel? You said you had a few calls to make.'

He nods amiably but his stare is assessing. It makes my stomach twist. I'm a shitty, deceitful friend. I say I don't want to hurt him, but I can't seem to quell my need for Monroe. I want to come clean, but I don't want anything to change.

Before he heads to the second cab idling behind, he kisses her cheek and grips her shoulders warmly. 'See you tomorrow. Let me know if we can bring anything.'

She hugs him hard, lingering for a few seconds. My stomach lurches so violently, I have to look away. I've watched them embrace a thousand times over the years. I've even watched them kiss, back when they were in love. Now I want to rip them apart and punch Sterling in the face when it's me who's the snake.

It makes no sense, beyond some Neanderthal urge to beat off the competition, and he deserves better.

Monroe and I don't speak a word in the cab. The space between us on the back seat crackles with tension, as if we're both fighting the urge to touch. My mind races for some clever quip or outlandish seduction scenario but I'm too strung out for anything beyond basic instincts. And every one of those drivers demands I hold her, kiss her, push my way inside her until the ferocious internal instability I'm battling fades. Until I'm a different man, the only man she needs.

She's silent too. Does she feel as out of control as me? Has she too realised what a mistake we made by starting this?

At her house, I pay the cab driver and walk her to the door, my hand tingling on the small of her back. I feel her tremble. She's there with me. On the edge. Desperate. Doomed.

There's no stopping this.

She swings the door inward and I follow her inside without hesitation. If she doesn't want me, she'll kick me out.

The click of the lock has barely echoed off the walls before she spins and launches herself at me. I drag her into my arms and press her up against the wall.

'I can't stop wanting you.' I pant, ripping at her coat and heeling off my shoes. 'Tell me to stop. Kick me out.' My words are as jumbled as the mess in my brain. Every sentence is punctuated with my tongue in her mouth and my teeth tugging at her soft lips. 'Make me leave.'

'No, I want you too.' She shoves my jacket from my shoulders and tears open my shirt, buttons scattering on her hardwood floors. 'Hurry…'

We find bare skin at the same moment, her moan as violent as my growl of triumph. I hoist her dress above her head and flick her bra open with one hand, tossing the garments away with impatience. They're keeping me from her. From the scent and texture of her naked skin. From her perfect breasts and the haven between her legs. I'm wild enough for her to crush anything that stands in my way, including my own sense of self-preservation.

'Hudson!' she cries as I slide her panties aside and palm her soaking core.

'You've wanted me too, haven't you? All night.' I toss my shirt and loosen my belt, walking her back towards the stairs.

'Yes, yes…every minute.' She sits on the stairs and tugs me to my knees in front of her. I lean her back, kissing her closed eyes, her cheeks and her neck while I rub her swollen greedy clit. I move lower, sucking her nipple into my mouth. She grips my hair, directing me first to one side and then the other, demanding, desperate and, like me, beyond the stage of denial that in any way we've got a handle on this ferocious want for each other.

It's as if we've never touched before. Our first time. Only better, because I'm fully addicted to her, certain the next hit will surpass all previous ones combined.

I scrape my teeth across her distended nipple and plunge my fingers inside her, my cock surging at her cries of unabashed pleasure.

It's not enough. I want her ecstasy. I want her climax. Her orgasmic exhaustion. I want her too pleasure-drunk to remember any man of her past or to crave anyone in her future, selfish bastard that I am.

I rip my mouth from her breast and ignore her aggrieved cry. With my hands under her arms, I hoist her up to the stair above and shove her thighs open wide.

'I need to taste you.'

'Yes.' She grips my face, urging me close as I drag her underwear off.

There's no time to admire the view of her glistening wet for me or splayed open, waiting. I bury my face between her legs and lick her from her seam to her clit, a guttural groan of encouragement ripping from my throat when she cries out and fists my hair.

I toss one thigh over my shoulder. 'Yes, give me everything you've got. Tell me what you need.' I dive back in, covering her folds with my mouth, sucking and laving at her flesh until she's a panting, delirious mess. Begging. Writhing. Chanting my name with a hoarse voice.

But she's magnificent. Debauched, she's even more beautiful, and I know in that moment I'll never get enough of Monroe Dove. I'll die craving her.

Before that thought can send me into a panic, she grips the back of my head with one hand and holds on to the bannister with the other as she rides my face, her eyes locked on mine.

'Suck me,' she says, her demand snatched from her throat by her broken cry.

I focus on her clit, spreading her open with two fingers, plunging them inside her tight channel. In that moment she's mine. I want to roar a victory yell. But there's no time. Monroe comes on my mouth, her hips jerking, her head craned back on the stair behind and her fingers fisted in my hair as she's racked by the powerful spasms.

I sit back on my haunches and tear open my fly, releasing my aching cock and appeasing it with a few lazy tugs. Monroe drags me between her legs and my hips slot there so perfectly, she could've been made for me and I for her.

I brace my hands on the stair on either side of her waist while I kiss her, and my foggy brain recalls how my wallet and my means of protection are somewhere near the front door in my jacket pocket.

Monroe fists my cock and slides the tip through her drenched folds, crying out as she rubs me over her sensitive clit. She wraps her legs around my hips and encircles my shoulders. 'Hurry. Forget the condom. I'm safe if you are.'

She's panting, on the edge, her mouth swollen and her eyes glazed. Her hair is a sexy mess that I fist in my fingers. I mash my mouth to hers and pour everything that I am into kissing her. It's an erotic duelling of tongues and teeth and lips. It's a sensual sharing of parts of our souls, but it's not enough. It will never be enough.

With our stares locked, I push into her in a single, steady thrust that makes us groan together. I wince and close my eyes as intense pleasure—the likes of which I've never known—overwhelms me, body and mind.

'It's too good,' she says, resting back on her elbows. I grip her hips and plunge inside her time and time again. Telling myself this time will be the last. It can't be beaten and it will be sufficient for me to walk away.

I capture one breast with my mouth and lave at the bud, my cock squeezed by her internal muscles.

'Hudson...' My name is a plea on her lips. 'Don't stop...'

I scoop one arm around her hips, still thrusting for all I'm worth, and rub my thumb over her clit. She detonates around me, squeezing me so tight my vision blacks and I follow her, coming so hard in violent spasms that I don't know where she ends and I begin.

But I know one thing: every word I've just told myself is a lie.

CHAPTER ELEVEN

Monroe

HE PUSHES INSIDE me from behind and I moan, tangling my fingers with his where his arm is banded around my waist. I'm sore. I'm certain he must be too. He's been hard for hours. I've lost count of the number of times we've come. It's as if it's our last night of human existence—we're both utterly exhausted but aware that every second counts. There is no containing this degree of pleasure. This desperate compulsion. It's all-consuming torment.

I reach behind me and tangle my fingers in his hair, directing his lips back to the tender spot on my neck where I'm certain I must have a love bite, because he's kissed and sucked that place so much in the past few hours. But I don't care. I want his marks on my body, the sign of his relentless possession, which fortunately shows no sign of abating.

Dangerous, dangerous wants...

Hudson cups my breast, his thumb rubbing over my nipple as he thrusts into me from behind. Doubt dampens my pleasure, allowing memories of the awkwardness at dinner earlier to rush in. Was Hudson jealous? I knew the minute he walked into the restaurant that it isn't over for him, just as it isn't for me. Did Sterling notice the lost look in Hudson's eyes when he let his guard slip? Could he interpret my nervous chatter? Any minute I expected me or Hudson to blurt out our secret over dessert.

Guilt bombards the flood of desire taking me hostage. I don't want to hurt either of them. Or Bold.

During dinner I had a blinding moment of clarity. For Hudson to become the man I need, he'd not only have to risk his personal fears—of being abandoned, of never being loved, of not mattering to a single soul on this Earth—he'd also need to risk Bold. Both of us would. Because there's no denying there would be fallout if we confessed to Sterling—a fallout that could be both enormous and destructive.

Could he do that? Could *I*?

What am I doing?

Hudson abandons my nipple and slides his hand down my stomach to my swollen clit. I gasp, my muscles fluttering around him in the first stirrings of another orgasm.

'Please…' I don't know why I'm begging. To come? Because I can't? Or am I begging for this night never to end?

With the ruthlessness I expect from him, Hudson doubles his efforts, his thrusts deepening, his fingers strumming more rapidly until I crack open for him, my climax tearing through me on an inevitable wail of pleasure.

He buries his face against my neck and pumps his own release into me, crushing me in his grip.

'We need to stop,' I murmur as my breathing settles and my heart ceases its exhausted pounding. I open my eyes and see that the digital clock on my bedside table reads four-twenty a.m.

'I need to get up in two hours to travel to Comberton.' Even as I speak I'm still grinding my hips and gripping his buttocks, holding him inside me, because I don't want him to pull out. Ever.

My heart clenches. Getting up, showering, dressing and continuing with life as normal will force me to acknowledge that something has changed for me, something monumental. I'm not ready to face that. Not today. Mum's day.

But everything *has* changed. Otherwise we would have stuck to our five nights and ended this back in Tokyo. I think back to last night, to that first frantic time on the stairs. We didn't speak in the car, didn't even argue that we shouldn't do this or rationalise one more night. It's as if our passion is a forest fire, and the blaze has quickly spread out of control, so the only sane solution is to burn.

If there was anything left to say, now would be the moment to voice uncertainty or a change of heart. But we're both silent. Today will be difficult for both of us, but for very different reasons: for me because family is everything, and for Hudson because he doesn't know how to be anything other than alone. He's been emotionally withdrawn most of his life. Except he's let me in, whether he realises it or not.

How can I expect more from such a man? And yet how can I not, for my own needs? Am I ready to abandon my own hopes of 'for ever' for a chance that he might, one day, decide he wants a relationship after all? Even then we live on different continents, the ultimate in long distance.

It's impossible.

He softens and slips from my body. His arms tighten around my waist. His fingers squeeze mine. His soft sigh kisses my shoulder. Wordlessly, he rolls away and stumbles to the bathroom.

Shivers break out over my skin. I clamber from the bed and put on my robe, cranking up the thermostat to try to warm myself. But there's ice in my veins. I've let in a man who can't give me what I need. To build a relationship with a family and a home and a life together in every way. He's never been in love the way I need to be loved.

When Hudson emerges from the bathroom, he's fully dressed and achingly beautiful in that broken way. I want to hold him, to reassure him that I don't expect anything of him, today or ever. And it's partly true. But that also means I can't risk my heart to any greater degree where he's concerned. Or I *will* want more. I'll want it all, and I'm terrified to test him for fear he'll let me down.

For fear that I'll fail again.

'I'd better head back to the hotel.' He scrubs a hand through his haphazard hair. 'Sterling will expect to see me at breakfast.'

I nod, folding my arms across my chest and gripping my biceps to stop myself from shivering. This day is always sad, always hard for me, no matter how much we dress up Mum's memorial as a party. She's still gone. I still miss her all the time. I want more than anything for Hudson to hold me, to stroke my hair and shower with me. To drive me to my childhood home and hold my hand all day, just to let me know he's there.

But he can't, and I can't ask him for any of that. If I force it, I might see just how misguided I've allowed myself to be once more.

'Yes, good plan. I'll see you later.' Mum, my family, is the only thing I can think of right now.

He presses a kiss to my forehead, lingering for a heartbeat too long, as if he has more to say. But then he's gone and I'm alone with only my own strength for company. It's enough, but I wish with all of my aching heart it could be different.

The family home Mum loved is in Comberton, a quintessential English village six miles from Cambridge. Dad maintains the expansive lawns and pretty herbaceous borders, which are bursting with spring colour, as a tribute to her. The weather has come out to celebrate Mum too. The sun warms my face as I watch my nieces and nephews play football on the lawn, fighting to score by kicking the ball be-tween two battered cricket wickets Dad has pushed into the grass to act as goal posts.

Hudson, dressed in a casual shirt and dark chinos, and so sexy I could weep, is deep in conversation with my older brother Elliot. Only the slight tired-ness around his eyes provides any clue as to how he spent the night.

Every time one of the younger kids mis-kicks the ball, either Elliot or Hudson breaks off their conver-sation and retrieves it from the bushes, tossing it back into play with endless patience. I expect that from my brother. After all, three of the children playing belong to him.

But Hudson...

Our eyes collide for the umpteenth time, a violent connection passing between us across the garden. I take a shaky sip of Pimm's, which does nothing to settle the rage of emotion inside me. Emotion he's drawing to the surface as effortlessly as he makes my heart pound.

This is bad.

'He's good with the kids,' my sister Brie, seven years my senior, says.

I hadn't even noticed she'd come to sit next to me, so engrossed am I in the man I seem to need like oxygen. I shield my eyes from the sun and squint at the game taking place.

'Who...Elliot? I should hope so.' My deliberate misunderstanding fools no one. Brie shoots me an

'I'm onto you' look. There's no point trying to pull the wool over any of my siblings' eyes. They know me too well.

'Yes, he is,' I admit on a sigh, recalling the wide smiles of the Blackhearts' boys from Hudson's photo in Tokyo. 'Shame he doesn't want any, though… He'd make a great dad.' My throat grows tight. I gulp some of my ice-cold drink to fight off the choking feeling.

I'm seriously falling for Hudson Black. It's the only explanation for the terrible, wonderful way I feel.

'How do you know he doesn't want any?' My sister interrupts my flight of panic. 'It's something most men don't even think about until they meet *the one*, or get married.' Brie looks and sounds so much like Mum sometimes, it's hard to talk to her. I can imagine Mum sharing the same wisdom over a vast glass of wine or bottomless cup of tea.

'Well, that's just it—Hudson doesn't want to get married. I've never known him to have a relationship, even. He's a committed lone wolf.' I knew that from the start and I stupidly allowed feelings to develop.

And now what? Do I pretend as if everything is normal, as I promised I would back in Tokyo? Do I tell him how I feel, freak him out? Should I ask Sterling's advice and risk hurting him too?

This was exactly the kind of mess I'd hoped to avoid.

'Perhaps you're *the one*.' Brie makes air quotes.

'You could be the woman to make him change his mind.'

I glare at my sister, fear and longing warring for control of my pulse.

'Oh, come on, sis.' Brie nudges my arm. 'You're looking at him the way you used to drool over my Barbie playhouse when you were four.'

'Well, you should have let me play with it, then. Perhaps I'd be more inclined to confide in you now if you had.' I turn away from her in a huff and then snigger at my ridiculous lifelong grudge over my sister's doll collection. I've never been able to hold on to resentment for long where my siblings are concerned. They've rescued me more than they've dragged me down or disappointed me. And it seems they're still at it, as Brie's gentle intervention proves.

She regards me with compassion, the way only a sister can.

I collapse in defeat. 'You're right. We have been fooling around. But we haven't told Sterling,' I hiss, my eyes darting around the garden in search of my ex. I don't want him to overhear us. I'm not sure I want him to find out at all. Hudson's leaving soon. Life will go back to normal. Why rock the boat and cause unnecessary pain?

Because a part of you hopes that Hudson will tell Sterling he wants to keep seeing you...

No. That's a fantasy I can't indulge.

'Have you fallen for him?' asks Brie.

I sigh, abandoning my drink altogether and gripping my hands in my lap. 'I think I could.' My eyes burn. I can't look at Brie, and I'm grateful for my sunglasses. 'But it's pointless. We want different things.'

'Are you sure about that? He can't seem to keep his eyes off you. Claire's noticed too,' she says, referring to our eldest sister. 'You won't be able to hide it from Sterling for much longer if he carries on like that.'

I sigh, understandably exhausted, both physically and mentally. 'The thing is, I've always wanted to be like Mum and Dad, like you lot. You know—a husband, a family, the whole package.' I glance up at my parents' beautiful Tudor cottage with the thatched roof and remember endless summers, when us kids built forts and dens by stringing blankets between the trees to play house or castles…

'But…?'

I roll my eyes in defeat. 'But, when I think of Hudson, I think I could be happy just the two of us. Living together, here, in Tokyo, anywhere. The white dress and the rush for a family seems…less important, somehow.'

'And that bothers you?'

'Not really. Just surprises me. It's not that I'd be willing to give up my dreams for him. It's more that my dreams seem to have shifted. I don't know what to do.'

'Well, love will do that to you,' says Brie.

My head whips to the side and my jaw drops. 'I'm

not in love with him. I just…care.' Blood whooshes through my head.

'Aren't you? Pretty close, I'd say.' Brie's toddler, Ami, runs into her arms at that moment, distracting us both. They share a brief hug and some conversation about snails before Ami rushes off again in her bare feet.

Panic fills every cell of my body. I can't be in love with Hudson. It's ridiculous. Utterly ridiculous.

'The thing is,' continues Brie, her tone full of sympathy, 'when you find the one, you work all that other stuff out with them, together. Kids, where you're going to live, who gets to empty the dishwasher. Mum and Dad didn't always agree. He wanted another child after you and she didn't. At one stage his job wanted to relocate him to the States and they planned to pack us all up and move before it fell through.'

I gasp. 'Really? I didn't know that.'

My sister nods. 'My point is that life often turns out different from how we expect, but love and respect are the keys to compromise, and that's really all it takes for any relationship to work. Look at you and Sterling—it didn't work out, but you still love each other. Still respect each other enough to stay friends and work together. How many couples achieve that?'

I nod because she's right. I'd been in search of perfection when I married Sterling. I put so much pressure on us. I was inflexible and he had his own hang-ups to contend with. We only really started communicating and compromising well once we agreed to split but decided to keep the business partnership intact.

I stare at Brie, my head spinning. What if she's right? What if I have fallen in love with Hudson? What will I do? It's destined to be a bigger fail than the last time I was in love. And I vowed that next time I'd get it right.

'Oh-oh,' she says under her breath. 'Incoming.' She looks up and grins at whoever is approaching. I turn, temporarily blinded by the sun, then making out Hudson's tall, broad outline.

'I thought I might head back to London,' he says. 'Sterling suggested I can take his car, if he can grab a lift with you later.'

My blood runs cold. I can't see his eyes behind his dark glasses, but I can tell from the rigid set of his shoulders that he's out of his comfort zone and withdrawing. He's probably been uncomfortable since the moment he arrived.

Brie and I stand.

'Okay,' I agree, hiding my disappointment. I shouldn't have forced him to attend. I hoped he might come home with me tonight, as he's leaving London early the day after tomorrow.

Hudson bids my sister farewell and he and I move through the garden, passing from group to group so he can say his goodbyes.

We crunch across the gravel driveway to the hire

car Sterling drove here—a cute cherry-red Porsche convertible.

'Nice car,' I say. Sterling loves cars.

Hudson nods and fiddles with the keys.

It's like we're strangers, not two lovers who didn't sleep the night before because of our incendiary desire for each other. I scrape my foot through an uneven gravel patch, searching for something to say that won't convey my feelings.

But desire isn't love. As far as I know, Hudson's never been in love. Do I want to risk my own dreams and happiness and security to be his test case, even if he wants a relationship with me beyond sex? Can I fail again? Break the promise I made to myself in memory of Mum?

I look up. He's standing close, but he too is at a loss for words.

I take pity on him, because it's not his fault that he's out of his depth emotionally, or that he can't love me back. 'Thanks for coming. It means a lot to me that you were here. I know it's not your kind of thing.'

He grips my elbow and presses a kiss to my forehead, his lips lingering for a few fraught seconds.

When he pulls back I almost blurt out my feelings. Beg him to stay. Convince him that we have something worth taking a risk on.

But the words that emerge tell me I too am scared to break what we've built these past five years. 'Drive carefully—don't fall asleep at the wheel.'

'You too.'

It's our only acknowledgement of our lapse last night. There's no secret communication this time. No promise that tonight there'll be another lapse.

My chest feels hollow as he jumps in the car and drives away. I watch the road for a whole minute and then return to my family, my realisation iron-cast.

Brie's right: I do love him.

CHAPTER TWELVE

Hudson

THE KNOCK AT the door jacks my heart rate sky-high. Please let it be Monroe. I push my wet hair back from my face and pull the door inwards.

Air rushes from my chest on an excited exhale.

'Hi. I just wanted to check on you.' She's wearing her dress from the party as if she's come straight here. I hold open the door and she strides inside the hotel suite and drops her bag on the chair.

'Did you bring Sterling back with you?' I ask, because I want to reach for her, but also need a reason to stop myself.

'Yes.' Her eyes roam over my naked torso and my cock responds under the towel wrapped around my waist. The greedy fucker can't help but react to her.

'Did you tell him…? About us?' Acid burns my throat, jealous that they might have shared confidences after I left. But I need to know if he's likely to punch me at breakfast tomorrow.

She shoots me a look full of hurt and accusation. 'No, why would I do that? What is there to tell?'

She's right. There's nothing, except this endless, almost incapacitating craving. But it can't be endless. I'm leaving in thirty-five hours. I'm fine. Great. I just allowed the sex to go a bit too far and I'm addicted. Time to start weaning myself off.

Right...

Before I lose my mind, I drag her close and kiss her the way I've wanted to all the long day. Only she can stop this tornado of need in me. And I'm running out of time. I can't help selfishly gorging myself until I have to give her up for good. Soon.

Not yet.

Monroe tugs at the towel on my hips and it drops to the floor. She palms my cock, encircling my length and running her hand up and down in a way that makes me boil with heat.

'I want you.' Her stare is alive with sincerity and passion and bravery. She's so open and fearless. She brings me to my knees, time and time again.

I tug down the zip at the back of her dress and strip it overhead so she's naked but for her lacy white bra and panties. I spear my fingers into her luxuriant hair and angle her head so I can trail kisses along her neck and collar bone. I want to kiss every inch of her, to imprint her on my brain like an indelible brand, something I can carry with me for ever. Something no one can take away.

I flick open the bra and spin her to the bed, removing the garment that is only in my way. She lies back, her hand gripping mine to tug me down with her, but I resist. I want to look at her, to commit every inch of her perfect body to memory—the freckles dotted on her shoulders, the exquisite hourglass curve of her waist and hips, and her long shapely legs and dainty feet.

'Hudson,' she says, her colour high on her cheeks. I feel her desperation. It pounds through me too. But I want so many things all at once, and I'm terrified to miss out. I want more hours in the day. To delay the inevitable and just exist like this with her.

'I want to look at you. To kiss you everywhere. Call it old-fashioned seduction, if you want.' I smile, trying to inject this moment with the playfulness we enjoyed in Tokyo, but it doesn't work. Her eyes stay intense and searching, and my smile feels rubbery.

I wrap my fingers around her foot and raise her leg, pressing my lips to her ankle and then kissing a path along her calf. She gasps. Shudders.

'Ticklish…' She sighs as I kiss the back of her knee and drag my tongue up her thigh.

'Put your hands over your head,' I murmur against her sweet-scented skin.

She does what I ask, her stunning hazel eyes half hidden behind her heavy lashes. With her arms overhead, her beautiful breasts are thrust up, her nipples erect and begging for my touch.

I kneel over her, entwine my fingers with hers and then press our joined hands into the bed, pinning her in place. I lower my mouth to her breast, flicking one nipple with my tongue and blowing a stream of air over her puckered flesh. She writhes under me, her thighs parting and her hips jerking.

'Do you ache for me as much as I ache for you, my beautiful Dove?'

'Yes…so badly.'

I take her breast into my mouth, sucking hard. Then I alternate, treating the other side to the same attention until she gasps and begs.

'Don't move your arms.' I trail my lips over her stomach and position myself between her thighs so I can lavish her pussy with the same adoration. I grip her thighs, holding her open, and then I cup her arse and lift her hips from the bed, bringing her up to my mouth.

My cock weeps. My balls are desperate for release, but I never want to stop. If I delay her climax, I can keep her here for ever, hovering on the edge.

'Please, please…' She moves rhythmically against my face, a fine sheen of perspiration blooming over her chest. I abandon her clit and run my tongue along the length of her torso, tasting more of her salty sweetness. I push my tongue into her mouth, swallowing her cries as I glide inside her in one smooth thrust.

She moans long and low in her throat and wraps her legs around my hips so I sink closer.

'Hudson… I'm so close.' Her mouth is slack with desire, her stunning eyes glazed. I slowly tilt my hips, each gentle thrust deep and disciplined, as if I have all the time in the world.

I *want* all the time in the world.

Her arms are still over her head, one hand gripping the other. I lay kisses over her breasts and her lips and all the places in between.

'You are so perfect. You feel perfect wrapped around me. You taste perfect too.' Words start to spill from me as fire builds along my spine. My hips pick up speed, the race to empty myself in her too powerful to stave off any longer.

'Come with me,' I say, rearing up on my elbows so I can see all of her perfection splayed out beneath me.

'Yes…yes.' She squeezes my fingers, centring me, holding me to the earth.

I watch in wonder as she detonates at my command, clamping around me like a vice, her face shattered in ecstasy. And I spill into her with a feral roar that I know will leave me altered for ever.

It's a long time before either of us speaks, but I feel her questions beat against me like the insistent knocking at a door.

I wrap my arm around her waist from behind and press a kiss to her temple. 'I'm sorry I left the party early.'

Standing in her father's picture-perfect garden, surrounded by her large, loving family, my chest was so tight I couldn't breathe. But it was more than claustrophobia. I felt split open with longing and grief. For what I'd missed out on. For what I'd denied myself. For what might be. And, more than that, I'd wanted to go to Monroe with an intensity that had shocked me to the core. I had to leave before I did something stupid and unforgivable.

'That's okay. I know how hard today was for you.'

I wince. She's comforting me when it was *her* mother's memorial. I'm the worst friend. Even a lover would be able to put their personal stuff aside and be there for her. I push up on one elbow and turn her to face me.

'No—it was a hard day for *you*. I let you down.' I remind myself that I've promised her nothing, but the self-loathing remains, perhaps because I wish things could be different. That *I* could be different. But I can't be her saviour. She has her family and Sterling for that—I saw the evidence today with my own eyes.

'You didn't let me down.'

I press a finger to her lips. 'Let me explain. Remember I told you about Wendy, my first foster mother?' My throat grows scratchy.

Monroe nods.

'I think her and Bill would have kept me longer, perhaps even have adopted me, but Wendy got sick and they had to give me up.'

She blinks rapidly and I plough on. 'I try not to think about Wendy too much, but today kind of reminded me. She was the only real mother figure I had and…well…she died. Years ago.'

She cups my face, shock and pain in her eyes. 'I'm so sorry. Why didn't you tell me?'

I shrug, wanting the memories to disappear. 'I found out just before I met you and Sterling. I'd contacted Bill for the first time since I had to leave them, although I'd almost reached out so many times over the years, but then always chickened out. She had already passed. I'd left it too late.'

My breath feels like ground glass.

Monroe wraps her arms around me. 'You weren't to know.'

'No.' But it proved to me I was beyond repair. A whole person would have contacted them the minute he was able to as an adult free of the system, just to say thanks. Whatever happy memories I had were down to them, and yet it took me a lifetime to show my gratitude and concern.

I'm not whole and Monroe deserves better. She deserves a man to worship her, to sweep her off the market and spend the rest of his life sharing her dreams.

'What about Bill?' she asks in a whisper.

'We've stayed in touch. We're planning a visit next time I'm in London.'

'I'll come with you if you need company,' she says with conviction. 'I'm happy you told me how today made you feel.' New resolve flashes in her eyes. 'I wouldn't want you to go through those feelings alone.' She brushes the hair back from my forehead. 'Plus, you were a huge hit with the kids. Elliot already has some business idea he wants to run by you and Claire practically burst into tears when you gave her the flowers.' She presses her mouth to mine—tender and soft. 'Thank you.'

I clear my throat, battling strong emotions I can't name. 'You have a gorgeous family, Dove. They love you very much. They're proud of you too.'

She nods, her eyes becoming shiny.

Her family hadn't meant to, but the kindness and acceptance they extended me brought out all my ancient insecurities and made me feel like a fraud. An alien who didn't belong. The contrast between Monroe's big, caring family and my solitary existence is massive. We're chalk and cheese. Even if I could overcome the things holding me back from pursuing a relationship, I could never be everything Monroe needs.

'You know,' I say on a whisper, 'I see how it is for you. Your older siblings have paved the way and seem to have so much in common. You want to remember your mum, to be just like her too, but it's okay to be yourself, to be different. It doesn't make you any less.'

She stiffens under me and frowns. 'I know that—you make me sound a bit pathetic. What's your point?'

Good question. Why am I giving her emotional advice? What the hell do I know about complex relationships and family dynamics?

'You are so far from pathetic, Dove. You're smart and funny and ambitious. I don't know what it's like to have a family, but I know about work. And I know you. Are you really willing to give up everything you've worked hard for to keep house and change nappies? I can't see you being satisfied with that.'

I'm crossing a line with her, but I want her to see that she's perfect as she is. That she doesn't need to compare herself to anyone. 'Perhaps you have some unresolved grief over Cathy. It's understandable. You're the youngest. You had less time with her than your brothers and sisters—'

'You're wrong.' She shoves at me, extricating herself from my arms. 'I don't want to give up anything. I want it all—a career, a life and a family. I thought you understood that. And why shouldn't I have it?' Hurt turns the green flecks in her irises to burning gold.

'You *can* have it all. You *should* have it all.' I cup her face, my thumb brushing over her cheek. 'I'm saying this all wrong. I just meant that Cathy would be proud of you just the way you are.'

'I know that.' She swings away and sits on the edge of the bed. I stroke her back, my palms burning to feel all her skin.

'Don't leave.' I press my lips to her shoulder, silently begging. 'What the fuck do I know? Just ignore me.' I rest my forehead against her back and suck in air, sick with the urge to drag her under me and chase away these feelings of inadequacy and confusion, to forget the torment shredding me alive. Why else would I have stepped out of my comfort zone to offer personal advice?

She spins to face me, speaking with those ex-

pressive eyes of hers, which glimmer with her forgiveness. 'You know me better than you think. Your
advice is as valid as anyone's. And perhaps you have
a point—I *am* still grieving. But it's just because my
parents, my family, gave me such a strong sense of
belonging, I feel like I need my own tribe one day.
Does that make sense?'

I nod, thinking of Sterling and her and Bold—my
own place to belong.

'Yes. Yes, it does.' I hold her tight, my panic settling.

'While we're on the subject of grief, I want you
to know something too.'

I brace myself.

'I'll always be here for you, Hudson. Always.'

I want to reject her compassion and insight, which
is much more finely tuned than my own clumsy attempts. It's not the words but what she leaves unsaid
that makes me feel raw and exposed. Because, where
I know I can trust her professionally and as a friend,
I've never trusted anyone beyond that.

The next morning, I glance through the glass wall
of Monroe's office to where she's chatting to her assistant in the open-plan area beyond. She's wearing
a pink silk blouse and tight skirt with heels. She's
relaxed, smiling, animated. I watch her like a man
lost in the desert watches the drip of condensation
on an ice-cold glass of water. And still I'm parched.

She left the hotel some time in the early hours of

this morning. Despite being desperate for sleep, restlessness infected me for the remainder of the night. A vile thought muscled its way into my mind. Soon I'll be back to my old self. The next woman I sleep with will be a one-night stand. The idea should bring me peace. A sense of normality returning to my life.

Instead I want to puke.

No. I'll simply focus on work for a while. Monroe and I have had enough sex to last a lifetime. Although right now it feels as if I'll never be satiated.

Sterling shifts beside me, scrolling through his phone. We're here for our final meeting. I'm leaving before dawn tomorrow—and making a quick business stop in Singapore before heading home to Tokyo. Only it no longer feels like home. It never did.

Before Monroe, I never needed a home. But she's made me question everything about my life. She's stormed through my world and forced me to examine my sad existence. Now there's no way back to where I was before Typhoon Kano struck.

I pace to the bar in Monroe's office and pour myself a glass of water. 'Can I get you a drink?'

'No thanks,' Sterling says, his voice tense. The clatter of his phone as it hits the glass table draws my attention. 'So are you going to tell me what the fuck is going on, or do you want me to ask Monroe?' His expression is stony, and I know I'm busted.

Relief washes through me as I stare at the view of Canary Wharf from Monroe's window. I've been a coward to avoid this inevitable conversation. The decent thing to do was to confront it head on. At least I can finally offload some guilt by coming clean.

The skyline blurs before my eyes as panic shunts my blood too fast. This is the train wreck I dreaded. Sterling's anger and betrayal will be justified. It's not the ending I'd have chosen, but at least I can admit that this thing with Monroe is over.

'You're right. Dove and I... We...' I don't have the words to explain what me and Monroe are. No longer just friends. More than fuck buddies. 'Fling' sounds inadequate, and yet it was always temporary.

I make a fist of self-directed frustration. I turn back to my friend and business partner, the mixture of guilt, remorse and failure a foul taste in my mouth. I never wanted to hurt anyone, especially my partners. The closest thing I have to family.

'You're sleeping together, aren't you?' His expression is unreadable but he must be pissed at me. I'd be pissed at him if the positions were reversed. In fact, I'd be fucking furious. The idea of him and Monroe, together intimately, turns my stomach. I look away, seeking composure. I have no right to be possessive over Monroe. I can't give her one tenth of what she had with Sterling. And even that wasn't enough.

You should never have touched her.

'I'm sorry.' My voice comes out rough thanks to the pressure constricting my throat. 'I didn't know how to tell you. I wasn't even sure I should. It wasn't serious.'

His muttered curse echoes across the room. 'So it's over, is that what you're saying?' His hands are gripped in front of him on the table, and he's coiled with tension, as if he could fly into a rage at the slightest provocation.

I shrug. Nod. Squeeze the glass in my hand so hard I fear it might crack. 'Pretty much. I'm leaving tomorrow.'

'Does *she* know it's over? Have you spoken about it, or are you just going to sneak off like a coward and leave her wondering?' His expression turns murderous. He loved her once. He knows me and what I'm capable of. Or incapable of. He knows Monroe and what she wants.

I abandon the glass of water and shove my hands in my pockets. 'Don't go getting all protective, as usual. I never played her. We both knew what we were doing. That it was temporary. She knows me as well as you do, remember.'

I glance at Monroe in the outer office. She's bent over her assistant's shoulder, pointing out something on the computer screen. The way we left things last night was as ambiguous and non-committal as you could get. She dressed, kissed me goodbye and left. I waited all night for the relief that we'd started to wean ourselves off sleeping together. Only, the minute the door closed behind her I wanted to chase after her and drag her back. Never to sleep again if it meant I could stay suspended in the insatiable need I have for her.

'You're right.' I sigh. 'I plan to talk to her today. I think she'll be fine.' We don't need to officially end it because it always had an expiration date. It was never a thing.

It felt like a thing...

'So you're going to go back to being colleagues? Or do you plan to fuck her whenever the three of us meet up, because I'll tell you right now—she deserves better.'

A defeated sigh blasts from me. 'I agree, she does. She knows that too—she's not stupid. She knows I'm a bad bet.'

'Are you sure about that?' His astute stare narrows.

I look closer, see new fatigue around his eyes. Something is off with him too.

'I didn't promise her anything. We still want different things. Monroe wants a big family, marriage…'

'So?'

'So, if you couldn't make her happy, what hope do *I* have? I'm not used to all that. I don't know how to be anything other than alone.'

I pace back to the conference table and brace my palms on the glass top. 'She won't find what she's looking for with me. Anyway, there's more. We messed around once before—after the divorce.'

'You fucking bastard…' He jerks to his feet.

I nod, taking it on the chin. There's a line you should never cross, and a friend's ex is on the other side of that line. 'It was just one time. I haven't laid a finger on her since.'

'Until now,' he spits. 'The one time I'm not there, and you two can't keep your hands off each other.'

He makes it sound as if we planned it. As if we couldn't wait to have him out of the way.

'It wasn't like that. There was a storm… It just happened. But it was my fault.' I should have resisted. Fought harder.

'Bullshit.' He paces the room. 'There's always been something between you two.'

My head whips round to stare at him as if he's sprouted a second head. My 'No!' is like the crack of a whip.

'I'm not saying she didn't love me,' he qualifies. 'She did.'

The reminder shouldn't bother me, but nausea threatens.

'Only Monroe and I are responsible for the breakdown of our marriage.' He shakes his head, demoralised.

'I know. I was there,' I mutter, recalling how conflicted I'd been, wanting to support them both, and then later fighting my attraction to her. Monroe and I *were* an inevitable mistake waiting to happen.

'You don't know everything. I told you how *I* fucked up, but she was to blame too. Yes, she's looking for commitment, but she didn't fully commit to me.'

My pulse ricochets around my chest. 'What do you mean?' I don't want to talk about her like this, behind her back. But, by the same token, I want to know.

'Before we met you, I begged her to consider moving to New York with me, just for a couple of years.

She refused point-blank. Said she could never move away from her family, and I accepted that.'

'Yes, she told me…' An ache settles under my ribs. It's ridiculous to think we could have a future. She lives here and I'm six thousand miles away.

But you don't want a future…

'After her mother died she pushed me away. It was as if I couldn't do anything right. Try as I might, I couldn't compete with the support she had from her family, nor could I compensate for what she lost. I hate feeling like a failure, so I switched off too. We never recovered.'

Nausea burns my chest. If Sterling, who has so much more in common with Monroe than me—who is so much more emotionally available than me—failed, how can I possibly ever be what she needs? If I try, I'll fail too. Only I'll lose more. Sterling will always take Monroe's side. They'll be a team again. They'll both hate me. Bold will implode. I'll lose everything I've worked for my whole adult life. Funding Blackhearts. My emotional peace of mind. My financial safety net.

I could never rebuild it all alone.

Sterling and I fall into uncomfortable silence. Resolve settles over me like an invisible shield. Knowing when to walk away is my stock-in-trade. Some investments just aren't worth the risk.

CHAPTER THIRTEEN

Monroe

RETURNING TO MY office is like entering a walk-in freezer, or perhaps a lion enclosure at feeding time. They're both standing, and there's a caged and prowling energy to my business partners. I only ducked out of the room for a few minutes, but something major has gone down in my absence.

I swallow. I can guess.

I keep my smile glued in place. Sterling has worked it out and Hudson has confirmed our fling. My instincts brace for an attack. Except I'm a grown woman, not a child. I don't have to defend myself to my ex-husband and the man I've been sleeping with.

I bring up the next screen on our meeting agenda, acting as if everything is normal. I've been acting for days.

'Excuse me for that interruption. Shall we conclude with the last agenda item—Hudson's proposal for expansion?'

I wait for them to retake their seats, keeping my

eyes averted. I can't bear to see Hudson's panicked face, telling me he's reached his limit. He looks as though he's already decided we can't work beyond what we've shared this week.

As for Sterling—it's none of his business who I fuck.

'Hudson, do you want to zip through your plan?' Keeping my face a bland mask takes eye-watering effort.

He swallows and launches into his spiel—taking on more corporate investments and fund management for third parties, expanding across Europe and Asia and the rest of the States. We've heard it before. On paper it makes sense. But now that I know the driving force behind Hudson's money-making—to protect the vulnerable parts of himself—I'm determined to take a second look.

'I'm concerned that we'll be spreading ourselves too thin,' says Sterling, voicing one of my own arguments against radical expansion. 'It will mean a lot more travel for each of us and less work-life balance.'

I wince internally, because Hudson has very little of that. He's an island. He doesn't need other people, as he proved yesterday when he left Mum's memorial instead of confiding in me about Wendy.

'Not necessarily.' Hudson clenches his jaw. 'We start a mentoring program—bring in the best newcomers. Start them off small and make them prove themselves. Dove?' He turns to me, his beautiful eyes so familiar I see every emotion displayed there.

I look away.

'My preference at this point is to focus new business on start-ups and continue to manage and grow our existing funds. Personally, I'm as busy as I want to be.'

I meet his stare, resolved. There's more to life than making money, at least for me, and it seems for Sterling.

The ensuing debate is fraught with an unthinkable disharmony.

Then Sterling's phone emits a tone, snapping the tension. He checks the screen.

'I don't think we're making progress. Can we revisit this discussion at our next video meeting?' He stands, tucks his phone into his pocket. 'Something has come up that I need to sort out.'

'Of course. Nothing serious, I hope?' I accept his kiss to my cheek, frowning at the strain pulling at his expression.

'No. Just New York business.'

We're all on our feet now, our easy camaraderie a distant memory.

'I'll see you tomorrow at brunch,' Sterling says, to me only. 'Eleven, the Dorchester. Don't be late.'

He shakes Hudson's hand. They wish each other safe flights, but there's no warmth in their farewell. It cracks my heart in two.

And then he's gone, his long legs carrying him across the outer office to the lifts with purpose.

With dread sitting in my stomach like a rock, I face Hudson.

'What happened while I was out of the room?'

He rubs his hand over his face. 'He figured it out. About us.'

'I thought as much.' I wince; I don't mean to sound accusatory, but I already sense Hudson's withdrawal. 'How did he take it?' I've seen him more upset. Something else is going on with Sterling— he's been distracted this visit.

Hudson's shuttered expression speaks for itself.

'He warned me off, of course. He knows us both. He knows that you need more than I'll ever be able to offer.' He can't look at me.

'What I need is for *me* to decide.' Pressure builds at my temples. I can't avoid this any longer. I've been holding myself back for days. Making myself small to accommodate Hudson's feelings. His fear. I've tried to move at his pace. But last night, in his arms, I felt worshiped, adored, loved. Even after he'd clumsily tried to warn me off or sound me out, I'd come so close to telling him how I feel that I had to leave to stop the words breaking free.

'What do *you* need?' I ask, seeing the answer written on his handsome face, that glutton-for-punishment part of me needing confirmation.

His sad smile slashes me deep. 'Outside of Bold, I don't *need* anything, Dove. I told you that.'

I press my lips together and nod. There's no malice in his stare or his tone, only heartbreaking inevitability, as if we were destined to arrive here.

Only I'm not just going to lie down and take a beating. I'm going to fight my corner, as I always do.

I fill my lungs and inch closer. 'The thing is, I've fallen in love with you.' My voice breaks but I plough on. I need to say this. He needs to hear it. 'So you don't have to need *me*, but I'd like you to want me.'

His face falls in shock. 'No... Don't say that.'

I breathe through the first sting of rejection. I expect a fight. But he knows I'm tenacious.

'I want us to have a relationship. I know you're not in the same place yet, that you didn't want anything to change, but it has.' I know he feels it too. 'I just want some reassurance that you want more than to say goodbye. That perhaps one day you could want more. With me.'

I touch his arm, reassuring him that the horror in his eyes is unwarranted. 'You don't need to promise me marriage—it's not the game changer I thought it was. I just want you in my life, and I think you want the same.'

His face contorts with anguish. 'Monroe...' His tone is laced with warning, his use of my first name a red flag. I should heed it, but I've never been able to accept that something is out of my reach.

'I'm tired of denying it, Hudson. Of holding back because you're not ready to hear it. But what if you're never ready? I've got nothing to lose.'

His stare hardens and I wither inside.

'Why are you doing this?' He scrapes a hand over

his face in frustration. 'We have *everything* to lose, don't you see? We had a good time. Don't—'

'What? Ruin it?' I interrupt. 'That's what you were going to say, isn't it?'

He looks down, his eyes almost black. 'No… Yes… I don't know.' He's cornered, fighting for his life, and I love him enough to relent.

'Sterling is never going to accept what we did.' He stuffs his hands in his pockets. 'It's driven a wedge between us already, and that wedge will split Bold apart. We'll lose it all.'

His words bombard me like arrows. He only cares about money. About professional success. About Bold.

'I told him it was over,' he says.

Shock jolts through me. I search his handsome face. How can the man I've known for five years, the man I've shared this past week with, end this without even telling *me* first? How can *he* be the place where I belong?

'So all you care about is how my love threatens the business?' Ice trickles through my veins, because I see his excuses for the lies they are. He's not worried about Sterling, who would have to come around to the idea of a relationship between us, just as Hudson had to deal with our divorce. He's running scared.

'I never promised you anything.' It's a whisper, almost as if he's ashamed to hear his own words. 'I've always been alone. I'm happy with that.'

'Oh, I know. But guess what? I want more anyway.' I fist my hands on my hips.

'You had more with Sterling, but you couldn't make it work. You wouldn't move, even for him. Wouldn't live away from your family. So how exactly would *we* work when you live here and I live in Tokyo?'

'I don't know. I hadn't thought through all the logistics—'

He interrupts. 'I can't compensate for your big family any more than Sterling could. What makes you think I could offer more than he did? I'm fucked, Monroe. I always will be. You're searching for this Holy Grail of relationships—the one…perfection. But you're looking in the wrong place if you think I'm what you need.'

He grips my upper arms, his wild stare clashing with mine. 'What do you see when you look at me, when you imagine yourself to love me?'

He doesn't wait for my answer.

'You see an ideal, something I'm not. I'm flawed and broken. What makes you think a man with my past can make you happy and give you everything you want—commitment, children?'

I break free of his hold. 'I'll tell you what I see. You're a fraud. I always thought that you were the boldest of us, but you only take calculated risks. You only take risks that aren't emotional… Because you're scared, Hudson. Scared to let yourself be vulnerable. Scared to feel and to care. Scared that everything you think you have will be snatched away from you. But what do you *really* have? What have you truly ever risked, apart from your money? Nothing.'

'I'm perfectly happy with my life.' He looks like a man being led to a firing squad.

'Good for you. But there's more to life than work and amassing a fortune you'll never spend. You think your achievements keep you in control, make you worthy. But you're already worthy—of love. Don't you see that?'

He shakes his head, dismissing the truth.

'You think you're alone. That no one cares. But Mr Oshima cares. Sterling cares. *I* care.' My voice breaks, just short of a sob. 'It's your strength I love. Your determination. Your passion. You showed me all of those things this week. They're in you. They *are* you.'

'Stop, Monroe.' His mouth mashes into a grim line.

I can't. Not until he believes me. 'You argue that you can't do emotional intimacy, but you can. I feel it so deeply when we're together, I can barely breathe.' I press my hand to my chest and fight the rising panic. 'You can fool yourself you have everything you need, fill your life with work. But it will never be enough if you're using it as a way to stay emotionally detached.'

I've gone too far, but there's no point holding back. I've survived losing love once, and I'll survive it again. I won't compromise my dreams or desires, not even for him.

His face, his entire body, might as well be carved from stone.

'You don't have to love *me*, but until you open your heart and take the risk—that it could fail and it will hurt, but it won't kill you—you'll never be content.'

My eyes burn. I push on, uncaring of how much damage we've created. 'I may want things that seem unrealistic to you, like true love and a family. But I won't compromise. Unlike you, I'm prepared to put everything on the line, to take those emotional gambles, because I know the payoff has the potential to be everything I want.'

I deflate at the futility of my dreams with Hudson. He's right. He is too damaged to be what I need. He has no desire to change. He told me that in Tokyo.

'It's okay.' I offer a wobbly smile. 'I wanted more with you, but I misjudged things.' I swallow hard. This isn't how I envisioned us ending.

His grief, pain and confusion tell me we're in different leagues emotionally. I'm expecting too much from him.

'There's one more thing you need to hear. I love you enough to go back to just being your friend if that's all you want. You can push me away, but I'll *never* abandon you.'

Hudson

The drone of the plane's engines should lull me to sleep, considering how little of that vital commodity I've had these past seven days, but I don't think even a general anaesthetic could knock me out. Every inch of my body aches. Every time I close my eyes I see Monroe's exquisite face, pale and slashed with pain. Pain I caused. Because I can't love her back.

No. She wasn't demanding love. She knows me. Perhaps better than I know myself. And the thing is I *do* love her. I always have. As a close friend. A respected colleague. A person.

Even perhaps with a romantic love.

I rub my hand over my face, my breathing shallow and tight with panic. It's not admitting the emotion I find terrifying, it's trusting it. What do I know about love? What do I have to offer? I've never wanted the trappings she has, but that's not what she asked for. All she wanted was more. For me to be open to a relationship.

I blink, fatigue making my eyes gritty. I glance around the luxurious cabin of my private jet—pristine and empty, just like my penthouse, which is all that awaits me in Tokyo. Is Monroe right? Am I a suit addicted to the office so that he doesn't have to feel the gaping inadequacies of his life? Is that truly all I want?

I'll never abandon you.

Her final declaration loops through my head, every pass bringing recrimination and self-loathing. I feel the words, the sentiment and truth behind them wash over me. Haven't I always felt her acceptance?

Hers and Sterling's? It's what allowed me to let them into my life in the first place.

This past week, Monroe has shown me that with her I'm safe. She laid herself open to me, even at the end when she saw how huge the chasm is between her own feelings and mine. She continued to offer her friendship, even after I rejected her love. She wants me to heal even if I can't be whole for her.

And I offered nothing in return.

My hand hovers over my phone—she's just a call away. Every cell in my body wants her to be happy and fulfilled. To have all of her dreams come true. I want to see her smile and laugh every day, the way she does when she's around her family.

I think of her a year from now—if Bold as it is currently survives the fallout of my thoughtlessness. Will she visit Tokyo again? Will she be in a relationship? Will her eyes sparkle the way I've watched them do a thousand times this week, only for another man?

I grit my teeth and swallow hard. Jealousy is no reason to hold on to something as precious and unique as Monroe.

My phone rings. It's Sterling. I calculate the time in London. We're a few hours from Singapore, which means he and Monroe will have just finished their planned brunch after my early departure. What if she's not okay?

I snatch up the phone and accept the call, my pulse a riot. 'Hello.'

Sterling sighs down the line. 'I don't know whether to tell you what I'm about to tell you, or just hunt you down and kick your ass.'

I make a fist. 'Is she…okay?' I hate it that I don't know. That I have to ask him. That *I'm* the reason she might not be.

'She's fine. She's the strongest, gutsiest woman either of us knows. That's why we're in business with her. It's also why I'm ringing to urge you not to throw away the only chance you'll have.'

My throat is tight. Just thinking how much I've hurt Monroe makes me want to thump something.

'Look, man,' he continues, 'neither of us knows what you've been through, growing up the way you did. But do you really want to be alone simply because you're shit-scared? Is that a good enough reason to lose her? You'll never find another woman like her. I know. I lost her too. But I live with that because I was partly to blame.'

I close my eyes, picturing the two of them together—an intimate *tête-à-tête* where he comforted her and advised her, the way I did when their marriage disintegrated.

'You know she's right about you—she's always right.' He chuckles, but I don't have the stomach to join him. 'That's why we concede to her more often than not.'

I suck in a breath. 'What did she tell you?' I'm too scared to ask if she's done with Bold and, more importantly, done with me.

'She said she loved you enough to question the importance of marriage. She said she knew a relationship would be hard for you, but she told me how you've been putting yourself out there emotionally, with her and with Blackhearts, and it gave her hope. She said she expected too much from you. So now you have to ask yourself one question. If you could only wake up one more day, would you want to wake up alone or by her side?'

I concentrate hard, allowing the emotions I usually push away to flow through me as I contemplate his scenario. The end of the world, a zombie apocalypse, me struck down with some terminal disease...

I recall the dawn breaking after Typhoon Kano on that first morning. Think of all the dawns I've witnessed this week—a week of hardly any sleep. Monroe was beside me for most of them. Would I even want one last day alive without her...?

'Fuck...' I whisper under my breath, because the answer is so straightforward. I don't want tomorrow without her, or the next day, or the day after that.

Sterling's snort reminds me that he's still listening. 'I'll never say *I told you so,*' he says. 'Just make this right.'

'What do I do? How do I change?' My voice whines with desperate panic.

'Don't ask me, man, I have my own shit going on. Besides, for some crazy reason, Monroe seems to love you just the way you are. That's a good place to start.'

We disconnect and I fire off an email to Hina, instructing her to cancel all of my meetings for the next week. Then I head to the cockpit to speak with the captain. He'll have an hour to refuel and lodge a new flight plan.

We're going back to London.

CHAPTER FOURTEEN

Monroe

MY MORNING RUN from my home in Kensington Place takes me through Kensington Gardens, past the palace and the Albert Memorial, and along the edge of the Serpentine, the lake that separates the gardens from Hyde Park. It's a route that never fails to uplift me because, as much as I want to be in the zone, I also love this part of London. The park is alive come rain or shine. The criss-crossing paths cater to dog walkers and mums with pushchairs. The lake teems with ducks and swans and their fluffy offspring, and swathes of cheerful daffodils shelter under the trees.

With my lungs burning and my muscles lax from the exertion, but feeling in no way uplifted—a tall order for the park today—I finish my run and head for my favourite coffee shop. I buy a large latte and an almond croissant I have no appetite for. But purchasing my favourite treat gives me hope that one day I'll be hungry again. One day, hopefully soon, this crushing pain will fade and I'll forget that I love Hudson Black.

Only I can't forget him. I have to talk to him and Sterling tomorrow in a video call. How will I survive seeing his face, his beautiful cognac-brown eyes concealing his pain? Because I know it's there. It's so deeply buried he may never overcome it totally. But it's not my place to offer comfort, to hold him and love him until its grip lessens. He doesn't want that from me. He wants nothing but our professional relationship.

And I can do that. I won't let my misplaced feelings jeopardise Bold. I kept it together after Sterling, and I can do the same with Hudson.

I just wanted more…

I round the corner of my street and check my phone for the time. I have thirty minutes to shower before I head to the office after a largely sleepless night. I tug off my ear buds and bound up the steps to my front door, where I almost collide with the man on the top step.

Hudson.

He's wearing the same suit he wore on his last day in London, his tie stuffed in his breast pocket and his top two shirt buttons undone. He looks as though he slept on a park bench.

I'm so confused I just stand and stare, gaping and dizzy.

'I thought you'd left for Singapore.' I brush my hair back from my face, wishing I wasn't carrying a bag of pastry and a hot takeaway coffee and could tighten my ponytail. I'm hot and sweaty and probably an attractive colour of lobster-red. But who cares? He doesn't want me. I need to find a way to move on.

'I did leave,' he says. 'Then I came back.'

Hope soars in my chest, squeezing out air. Why? What does it mean? But then I remind myself it's humanly impossible he feels anything he didn't feel forty-eight hours ago. He's still the same man I begged to allow me into his life on the vague chance that he would, one day, reciprocate my feelings.

'I see.' I nod and step past him to my front door. I realise my mistake instantly, because I'm so close I can breathe in his scent and see the fatigue around his gorgeous eyes, which are bleak.

I shove the key into the lock, balancing my bag and coffee in one hand.

'You look beautiful.' The catch in his voice slices through my heart. 'It's so good to see you.'

Agony pulses along every nerve. 'Don't,' I snap.

I don't want his platitudes or compliments. I want what he can't give me. I won't compromise, no matter how tempting. I shove at my front door and step inside, turning on the threshold to face him.

'I'm late for work. I'm going to have a shower.' I pull the door half closed behind me, filling the space with my body as a barrier. The last time he came through this door, I barely made two paces before I succumbed to my need for him. Allowing him inside now would be like ripping off my body armour, my last line of physical defence.

Correctly reading my reluctance, he steps back. 'Can I see you after work? Please… I want to apologise.'

He's so devastatingly handsome, even in slept-in clothes. I want to cry and cave and drag him inside and forget about work and my pride and the heartbreaking things he said. Most of all I want to forget that he threw my love back in my face.

But the memories are alive in the jagged tears in my heart, throbbing with every beat.

'I'll check my schedule when I get to the office and let you know a convenient time.' This is what he wanted. What he begged me to promise him. That Bold would be safe. That nothing would change in his life. I don't want his apology, but he's my business partner. Even if I wanted to, I can't ignore him or never see him again. And that amplifies my pain. There's no escape.

He nods and backs down the steps towards the pavement.

'Hudson,' I call before I shut the door. 'Get some sleep.'

Behind my closed front door my heart gallops and my hand on the knob burns to fling it open and chase him down the street.

I abandon my coffee, then shower and dress in a trance. I make it to work only three minutes late for my meeting. The day passes in a blur. It's as though

I've been drugged. Everything is fuzzy and distant, as if I'm existing under water. Three times I pick up my phone to message him a meeting time and place. Three times I chicken out. I have nothing more to say, and I'm not ready to hear his justifications and explanations.

I'm lost in thought as my driver drops me outside my home later that night. But, when I climb from the back of the car and bid him goodnight, Hudson is exactly where he stood this morning. He's changed into jeans and a T-shirt but he still looks broken and haunted.

I feel as if we've been apart for weeks, not hours.

'I know you don't want to see me, and that's fine,' he says. 'I just don't want the sun to set on another day where I've let you down.'

I'm too tired to fight it, so this time, I invite him in. Fighting tears, I toss my coat and bag aside and head for the kitchen at the back of the house on my wobbly legs. My wine fridge is well-stocked. I retrieve an ice-cold bottle of Sauvignon Blanc and pour two generous glasses, not bothering to ask him what he wants. I carry our glasses out through the conservatory to the garden like a robot. The crackle of electricity buzzing over my skin tells me he's following.

I leave his glass on the table and sit on a garden chair. I take a hefty swallow, looking out at the pretty garden I created to remind me of the one Mum had nurtured and tended at Comberton.

'I couldn't face you, to be honest,' I say. My stomach tumbles until nausea forces me to abandon my wine. 'I knew we'd have to see each other again. Despite what you said, I care about Bold, and have every intention of getting things back to professional—I just hoped I'd have a few days to adjust.'

Hudson shifts in my peripheral vision.

'The things I said were unforgivable.' His voice is rough with emotion. 'I didn't mean them.'

I look up and his eyes latch to mine in the dusk.

'It's no excuse but I was reeling from your declaration.' He steps closer, his face taut with pain. 'No one's ever said it before.'

I frown, my heart in my throat. 'Said what?'

There's so much anguish in his eyes I want to go to him more than I can stand. I dig my nails into the arms of the chair.

He looks to the garden where the roses bloom before tall sentry-like delphiniums. 'That they love me. Not that I remember, anyway.'

My hand flies to my mouth. Tears sting the backs of my eyes. I can't believe that's true, but it must be. He was two when his mother gave him up. Maybe Wendy hadn't said it. And he's never allowed anyone close enough to get attached.

My pulse thunders in my head. Would I have said those momentous words if I'd known? Oh, I'd still have felt it, but I might have chosen my moment more carefully rather than just blurting it out and expecting him to know what to do with my overwhelming confession.

'I'm sorry.' I swallow back the burn in my throat and fight the urge to go to him. 'I wouldn't have said it if I'd known.'

He steps towards me then, his face twisted with agony as he drops to his knee in front of me. 'It's a wonderful thing to hear. Don't regret it.' His voice cracks. 'Tell me, how do I change?'

My heart breaks open, disintegrating into a million pieces. I don't want him to change. I don't want him to hurt. I just want him to want me in return.

'Don't.' I reach out, cup his cheek and feel the day's worth of stubble under my fingertips. 'You don't need to change.'

He places his hand over mine and holds it to his face. 'But I want things. You've made me want things I have no idea how to want. I can't stop. I can't leave you.'

I hold my breath, my head swimming. 'What things?' It's all too much, but this has been a desperate whirlwind from the start.

'You.'

A tear falls then. It's exactly what I want to hear. Only, how can I trust it? I know he means it—he's not a liar. But, where back in my office two days ago it all seemed so easy, us being together now seems insurmountable.

Still, my own feelings compel me to help him. 'It's like going on a roller coaster—you embrace the fear and do it anyway. You know the high is coming and, if you survive, it will be worth every horrific second because you've let love in.'

He presses a kiss to the centre of my palm. 'Sounds terrifying. Tell me more.'

I shrug, my resolve wobbling. I love him so much that I fear my strength, my conviction, won't be enough. Not for the two of us.

'You've opened your heart before. When you let Sterling and me into your world. When you reached out to Wendy and Bill. When you founded Blackhearts. Every time you moved on to a new home, a new school, as a boy, you found the strength. You didn't give up, you survived, you flourished.'

He grips both of my hands, his earnest expression slaying me. 'Is it too late? Because I want more with you like I've never wanted anything else in my life—not Bold or my billions or even my next breath.'

I shake my head, my vision blurring. 'No. It's not too late.' My pulse beats in the tips of my fingers. Can he feel it?

'Sterling asked me a question,' he whispers, his thumbs rubbing back and forth over my wrists. 'He said if I only had one more day to live, would I want to wake up alone, or with you.' He looks up and my heart stops altogether. 'I'd choose you. Only, I want to wake up with you every day from now on.'

I cup his cheeks and lean forward, pressing my mouth to his. I collapse into his hard chest. His arms band around me and almost squeeze the air from my lungs.

I pull back, happy tears spilling free. 'You don't have to promise me anything. I want us to be real. I need to live in the moment, not jump several steps ahead, as I've done in the past. I still want a family, but I know I don't need it to feel whole.'

He nods and stands, tugging me to my feet. He squeezes both of my hands, his stare so full of everything I want to see that I sway on my feet.

'I promise you I want to be with you, every day.' He cups my face in his warm hands. 'I want to go sightseeing with you, and have picnics in the park, and dance with you while your underwear is in my pocket.'

I laugh. Cry. Kiss him.

'I'll stay in London,' he says.

'I'll move to Tokyo,' I blurt, laughing as he pulls me in for another kiss.

I tug him inside and lead him down the hall. When we reach the bottom of the stairs, he scoops me up in his arms and carries me up to the bedroom.

We strip and touch and kiss and sigh. Hudson lays me down on the bed and traces his mouth over every inch of my body, as if re-learning every contour, every sensitive place. Desperate for him, I drag his mouth to mine, but he pulls back.

'I do love you, Dove.' His eyes burn.

I shake my head, too choked to speak. I don't want him to say it until he means it absolutely.

He presses his fingers to my lips, then drops soft kisses all over my face as he talks. 'I've always been half in love with you all these years. I just didn't want to label it. And this week… How could I not fall completely? You're the better part of me. *You* make me whole. You make me want things, all of the things.'

Tears seep into my hair at my temples and he kisses those too. 'I've got a long way to go, a lot of relationship stuff to learn—but don't for one minute think I don't love you as much as you said you love me.' He presses my fingertips to his mouth, kissing each one.

I shudder, sigh, surrender to the feelings that need no labels. They're just there.

'Just remember who said it first.' I laugh and drag his mouth back down to my kiss.

And then he loves me with his body.

EPILOGUE

Five years later
Hudson

'RUB HARDER…' SHE SAYS. 'Oh, yes! That's the spot.'

'You are still as demanding as ever, my love,' I say, pressing my thumbs into her instep as part of my famous foot massage she can't live without. 'Why wear the heels if they torture your feet so badly?'

She turns on the hot tap and tops up the bath water. 'They make me feel sexy. After two babies, I need all the help I can get in that department.' She offers me her other foot over the edge of the bath and relaxes back into the bubbles. 'Did you wrap everything?'

I nod, extending the massage to the back of her calf, working the tightness from the muscles. 'Yes, but I had to wait for them to go to sleep first. And Brie dropped round the birthday cake.'

'Can everyone make it? The twins adore all of their cousins and I promised they'd come.'

'It's all under control,' I reply, sliding my hand behind her knee. 'Even Bill will be there. Relax.'

She smiles an indulgent smile because she knows how far I've come with her love to guide me. Bill has become the father I never had and grandfather to our twins. 'Relax…? I'm trying.'

My beautiful wife does look a little tired. We don't travel like we used to since we moved our offices from Tokyo and London to our home office in the Cambridgeshire countryside. And because of the twins we take it in turns when we do need to go overseas.

This trip was Monroe's turn.

'I missed you,' I say, watching her breasts break the surface and marvelling at how I became such a lucky bastard.

She moans and opens her eyes, glancing at the black square of the window, which is being pelted by winter rain.

'I missed you too. Time to show you just how much, I think…' She rises from the water like a sea nymph, rivulets of suds gliding down her gorgeous body. She steps out of the bath and hands me a fluffy white towel.

'Can you dry my back, please, darling?' Her voice is a seductive purr I know so well.

Communication, compromise and our ongoing seduction game is how we keep our marriage strong.

I glide the towel over her skin, kissing every place I dry. 'Are you trying to seduce me, Mrs Black?'

'Yes.' She turns to face me, and I follow the same routine with the towel and the kissing across her front until I'm hard against my fly and she's panting, her nipples erect.

'There's a storm coming,' she says. 'Remember how we rode out Typhoon Kano?' She grabs my hand and we head for the bedroom.

'How could I forget?' I strip so I too am naked. Our hands roam each other's bodies, teasing and caressing.

'Want to hunker down again, Black? Same rules apply…' Her hazel eyes are alight with love. How was I ever stupid enough to deny myself such a gift?

'Sounds like a plan, but no poker this time.' I take her nipple in my mouth and she gasps, dragging me onto the bed. We're tangled together under the covers, kissing and stroking and laughing, because our love makes us both happy.

I entwine my fingers with hers and push inside her, kissing up her moan of delight. 'First one to come, Dove, gets up with the twins,' I say, knowing my wife won't let me get away with anything.

She laughs. 'No way, Black. I've missed them too. I'm doing the breakfast routine tomorrow.'

'How about we do it together?' I love my family. I hate missing out. 'It's their birthday.' I move inside her so she starts clawing at my back.

She nods, her eyes shiny with emotion. 'Good idea. Sleep is overrated anyway.'

'Yes, it is,' I agree, silencing her with another kiss.

We spend the rest of the long, stormy night proving that, with love, everyone is a winner.

* * * * *

COMING SOON!

We really hope you enjoyed reading this book.
If you're looking for more romance, be sure to
head to the shops when new books are
available on

Thursday 18th February

To see which titles are coming soon, please visit
millsandboon.co.uk/nextmonth

LET'S TALK
Romance

For exclusive extracts, competitions
and special offers, find us online:

- facebook.com/millsandboon
- @MillsandBoon
- @MillsandBoonUK

Get in touch on 01413 063232

MILLS & BOON

THE HEART OF ROMANCE

A ROMANCE FOR EVERY KIND OF READER

MODERN
Prepare to be swept off your feet by sophisticated, sexy and seductive heroes, in some of the world's most glamourous and romantic locations, where power and passion collide.
8 stories per month.

HISTORICAL
Escape with historical heroes from time gone by. Whether you passion is for wicked Regency Rakes, muscled Vikings or rugge Highlanders, awaken the romance of the past.
6 stories per month.

MEDICAL
Set your pulse racing with dedicated, delectable doctors in the high-pressure world of medicine, where emotions run high an passion, comfort and love are the best medicine.
6 stories per month.

True Love
Celebrate true love with tender stories of heartfelt romance, fr the rush of falling in love to the joy a new baby can bring, and focus on the emotional heart of a relationship.
8 stories per month.

Desire
Indulge in secrets and scandal, intense drama and plenty of si hot action with powerful and passionate heroes who have it all wealth, status, good looks…everything but the right woman.
6 stories per month.

HEROES
Experience all the excitement of a gripping thriller, with an int romance at its heart. Resourceful, true-to-life women and stro fearless men face danger and desire - a killer combination!
8 stories per month.

DARE
Sensual love stories featuring smart, sassy heroines you'd want best friend, and compelling intense heroes who are worthy of
4 stories per month.

To see which titles are coming soon, please visit

millsandboon.co.uk/nextmonth